PRAISE FOR JULIE ORTOLON AND:

DEAR CUPID

"What a wonderful story! It is filled with clever wit and funny scenes . . . Recommended." — *Huntress Book Reviews*

"An absolute delight! Ms. Ortolon has created wonderful relationships among all the characters, thrown in some very spicy romance, and blends it all together with her fantastic humor. *Dear Cupid* is another winner for this talented author."

— *Reader to Reader Reviews*

DRIVE ME WILD

"A wonderful debut novel." — *Romantic Times*

"A smart and funny story that I found very enjoyable to read."

— *Rendezvous*

"Julie Ortolon's debut contemporary for Dell, *Drive Me Wild*, will drive readers to ecstasy in this superb romance about a handsome TV anchor, who returns to his Texas hometown for a 'Dating Game' fundraiser and ends up winning a wild ride to finding true love when he chooses his childhood best friend. Ms. Ortolon is a gem of a new author and readers will certainly want to watch for her future books!"

— Patricia Rouse, *Romantic Times* columnist

"*Drive Me Wild* is a fun and completely captivating story from this bright new author. Ms. Ortolon has given us believable characters with a wonderful range of personalities . . . Many of the scenes really sizzle! I thoroughly enjoyed *Drive Me Wild* and recommend you not miss this first offering from a promising new author."

— *Romance Communications* (romcom.com)

More . . .

Falling for You

Julie Ortolon

St. Martin's Paperbacks

FALLING FOR YOU

ISBN: 0-312-97872-3

Printed in the United States of America

St. Martin's Paperbacks edition / April 2002

St. Martin's Paperbacks are published by St. Martin's Press, 175 Fifth Avenue, New York, NY 10010.

10 9 8 7 6 5 4 3 2 1

To David, Eileen, and Annette,

for teaching me firsthand about love between siblings

SPECIAL THANKS TO

Susan Arnold for answering all my questions about the exciting world of banking. Any mistakes are entirely my own. And to all the bed-and-breakfast owners who have welcomed me into their inns with such gracious hospitality. I'm sure the extra inches I gained while writing this book had nothing to do with their fabulous cooking.

CHAPTER I

The sun was shining off Galveston Bay, the wind held the warmth of spring, and Rory was happy. But then Rory was always happy when she was headed for Pearl Island.

She grabbed the awning support as the pontoon tour boat hit another wave. The white shirt of her uniform fluttered against her chest as she brought the microphone to her mouth. "In a moment, folks, we'll come to the most exciting part of your Galveston Bay boat tour, the haunted house on Pearl Island."

Interest showed on the passengers' faces as they glanced toward shore. In truth, a mere hundred yards separated Pearl Island from the main island of Galveston and a private causeway spanned even that small gap. But, in other ways, the island was a world unto itself, filled with intrigue, romance, and rumors of ghosts.

As the boat pounded through the waves toward the cove, Rory loosened her knees to keep her balance. A long corkscrew curl of golden-red hair whipped across her face. She released her hold on the awning to fight the waist-length mass and pitched sideways into the boat's owner.

"Hang on there, darling," Captain Bob said as she braced herself against his muscular shoulder. His shirt matched hers in style, with navy blue epaulets and gold buttons, but the rolled-up sleeves stretched taut around his massive biceps. "I know I'm irresistible, but not in front of the passengers, please." He nodded toward the rows of cushioned seats that held a mishmash of tourists with the usual cameras, souvenir T-shirts, and sunburns.

"I'll try to contain myself," Rory teased back.

"Just don't try too hard, beautiful." His teeth flashed white against stubble-darkened cheeks as he tugged on the bill of his captain's cap.

Outboard motor exhaust rolled over them as they swung into the protective cove and Captain Bob pulled back on the throttle. Shielded from the wind by the island, the boat settled into a gentle rocking motion as they began a slow circle.

Rory glanced toward the mansion. Pink granite walls rose above a stand of palm trees in majestic defiance to the acts of God and man and even time that had battered it for a hundred and fifty years. Along the edge of the steep, gabled roof—barely visible from such a distance—winged gargoyles snarled down at all who dared to approach.

Bringing the mike back to her mouth, Rory began the story that gave her goose bumps even though she'd told it a hundred times. "Of the historic sights in Galveston, this house has one of the more colorful pasts. It was built by the notorious Henri LeRoche, a 'businessman' from New Orleans who moved to Galveston in the mid-1800s—some say to escape prosecution for his questionable shipping activities. The house was a wedding present for his bride, Marguerite, an opera singer known as 'the Pearl of New Orleans.' "

With the microphone in hand, Rory walked down the center of the aisle toward the bow. "Because of her scandalous past, Marguerite was never quite accepted by Galveston's budding society. And the fairy-tale marriage she expected turned into a nightmare when Henri became brutally possessive. After years of being a virtual prisoner in her own house, Marguerite met and fell in love with one of Henri's sea captains, the dashing young Jack Kingsley, who was a blockade runner during the Civil War."

Rory turned to face her audience, enjoying her role as storyteller. "Henri found out she had a lover and went insane with jealousy. He locked Marguerite and their daughter upstairs, swearing she'd never leave the house alive.

"Afraid for her life, Marguerite sent a message to Captain Kingsley, begging him to rescue her." Rory lowered her voice for dramatic effect. "On the night he came for her on the pretext of delivering a shipment of arms to Henri, he sailed his ship into this very cove. Marguerite and her daughter escaped from her room with the aid of a servant. But Henri stopped her on the grand staircase. The two fought, and she fell down the stairs to her death.

"Enraged with grief, Henri rushed to the balcony, there, off the third floor, and fired a cannon." Rory shielded her eyes against the sun as she pictured the scene. In her mind, she conjured a stormy night filled with violence, passion, and death. She could see Henri LeRoche on the balcony, hurling curses at his rival as he lit the fuse.

"The cannonball struck the wooden vessel broadside, igniting the cargo of gunpowder. The *Freedom* sank quickly, taking Captain Kingsley and most of his crew down with her to a watery grave. Only a few were able to swim to shore and tell the story that has become a favorite Galveston legend.

"In fact"—Rory turned back to her audience—"we're passing over the wreckage of the ship now. If you look straight down, you might be able to make out the main mast and crow's nest."

The pontoon boat rocked as the passengers bent over the rail.

"Where's the ship, Mommy?" A little girl leaned way out to peer into the water. "I don't see it."

"Careful, sweetheart," the mother said, holding the girl's waist.

Rory made her way back down the aisle. "Another intriguing aspect of the tale is that Captain Kingsley's grandfather sailed with Galveston's most famous pirate, Jean Laffite. Some believe Jack Kingsley had Laffite's legendary 'missing treasure' on the ship when it went down. As you can imagine, this has made it difficult for the owners of the island to keep scuba divers out of the cove, even though no one has ever found any evidence of a sunken treasure."

"You said the house is haunted?" asked a burly man wearing a hot pink T-shirt and black dress socks.

Rory nodded. "Many believe the ghost of Marguerite remains in the house waiting for her lover, and that Captain Kingsley haunts these very waters, searching for a way for them to reunite."

"Is the house occupied?" another man asked.

"No, it's been empty for about fifty years. Although it is still owned by descendants of Henri LeRoche, through his nephew," Rory explained with a slight edge to her voice, "not his daughter by Marguerite—the *rightful* heirs."

"Careful, Rory, your jealousy is showing," Captain Bob teased her, for he knew her family descended directly from Marguerite Bouchard's daughter and had an ongoing grudge against the LeRoches.

"Not my jealousy," she told him. "My sense of injustice."

"Is that one of them there?" the young mother asked.

"Hmm?" Rory looked toward shore. As the pontoon moved past a line of palm trees, she saw a man standing on the overgrown lawn, just outside the chain-link fence that protected the house from vandals. He appeared to be hammering a sign into the ground. Surprised to see anyone on the island, she grabbed the binoculars from the wheel pulpit and held them to her eyes. The man had his back to her, but he was too blond and slender to be John LeRoche, the current owner of Pearl Island. Her gaze moved to the words on the sign, and the air left her lungs: Bank Foreclosure—Property for Sale.

"Oh, my God," she breathed and felt the hair on her arms stand on end. "Bobby, pull closer to the pier."

"What for?" he asked.

"Just pull closer, will ya?"

"You're not going to get out or anything, are you?"

She lowered the binoculars as conviction swelled within her. "Yes, actually I believe I am."

"No way, Rory. That's private property. And we're on a schedule."

"Fine. I'll swim." She kicked off her deck shoes and prepared to strip down to the swimming suit she always wore beneath her tour guide uniform.

"You would, too, wouldn't you?" He shook his head as she tugged the shirt from the waist of her shorts. "All right, all right, I'll let you get out. But what are we supposed to tell them?" He nodded toward the tourists.

Putting her shoes back on, she raised the mike to her mouth. "If you folks will sit tight for just one minute, we're going to pull up to the pier so you can get a good look at the house."

Bobby snorted but eased the boat alongside the dock. Grabbing a mooring line, Rory jumped out and secured the boat before she took off at a jog. The pier gave way to sandy beach, then a rutted path that led up toward the house. As she approached from behind, the man continued to swing the hammer, each stroke moving the shoulders beneath a white dress shirt.

"Spineless wimps!" he cursed. "Get me to do their dirty work, will they?" Bam! The hammer came down on the stake, driving it into the sandy soil. "Cowards!" Bam, bam! "Make me look like a traitor. What do they care?" Bam, bam, bam!

"Excuse me," she said from behind him.

With a start, the man whirled around, dropping the hammer on his foot as the wind sent the sign flying against his back. He yelped, ducking his head and clutching his shin.

"Oh, I'm sorry!" She rushed to push the sign off him. "Are you okay?"

"I'm fine! Splendid! *Argh!*" he shouted as he toppled backward to land on his backside at her feet.

Rory struggled not to laugh as she stared down at the man. Behind wire-rimmed glasses, he had a boyishly handsome face. His blond hair was cut short on the sides, but long enough on top to fall across his forehead. He straightened his glasses as he stared at her long bare legs, then his gaze traveled upward past her blue shorts and white shirt to her face and the unruly hair that whipped about her on the wind. "Aurora? Aurora St. Claire? Is that you?"

"Do I know you?" she asked as she gathered her hair in one hand to get it out of her eyes. He did seem slightly familiar. Although no one but her teachers back in school and her aunt Viv called her Aurora.

For a moment, he just gaped up at her, then he swallowed hard as if to clear his throat. "I'm Chance," he said as he scrambled to his feet, dusting dirt from his trousers. "I went to school with your brother."

"Chance?" She thought for a moment, then remembered. "Oh, yes! Short for 'Chancellor,' as in 'Oliver Chancellor,' right?" She blinked in amazement when he straightened, for he topped her own height of nearly six feet by several inches. "Wow, you grew."

"Yeah, into my big clumsy feet," he grumbled.

Not only had he grown taller, he'd filled out—well, a little bit. From what she remembered, he'd been a gangly kid none of the girls would even have noticed except that his family was one of the wealthiest in Galveston.

She was surprised he remembered her, though, since prominent families like the Chancellors didn't exactly run in the same circles as the disreputable and outrageous descendants of Marguerite Bouchard, many of whom had inherited Marguerite's passion for the stage.

"What are you doing here?" he asked.

"I saw you putting up the sign—Oh! The sign!" She

turned and lifted it so she could read it. "Foreclosure! Is this for real?" She scanned the sign for details, but the words jumbled together in her excitement.

"Unfortunately, yes." He took the sign from her and thrust it back into the soft ground that refused to hold it upright.

"The bank is foreclosing on a loan to John LeRoche?" she asked in disbelief.

"Do you think I'd drive all the way out here to put up a sign if we weren't?" Bam! Bam!

"But when? How? Why?"

"The same reason we foreclose on anyone who doesn't pay their loan back."

"Oh, my god," she whispered, trying to take it all in. The house that should have belonged to her family was actually for sale. "How much will it go for?"

"Depends on how much the bank is offered." He shrugged.

"I want to buy it."

"What?" He glanced at her. "Are you kidding?"

"No, I'm serious. In fact"—she took a breath to calm her racing heart—"I've never been more serious in my life."

"Aurora." He frowned. "I don't mean to be nosy but, well, what I mean is . . . can you qualify for a home loan of this size?"

"Qualify?" She blinked at him. "I don't know. But I have good credit." Actually, she had no credit, but she figured no credit was better than bad credit.

He shook his head. "I'm afraid, for a mortgage loan this big, you're going to need more than good credit. You'll need proof of income, collateral, or a co-signer. Trust me on this, I grew up in banking."

"That's right!" She snapped her fingers. "Your father *owns* the bank."

"My father *used* to own the bank. Now it belongs to an

East Coast banking chain, like every other bank in this country."

"Rory!" Captain Bob's voice floated up from the pier, barely audible over the wind. "Hurry it up, will ya!"

"Hang on!" she shouted, then turned back to Chance. "What about a business loan? Could I qualify for one of those?"

"It depends. Do you have a business?"

"Well, no." She squirmed. "Not yet."

"How about a business plan?"

"Of course I have a plan." She looked through the chain-link fence as images from a lifetime of daydreams superimposed themselves over the neglected structure. She saw the mansion fully restored, the storm shutters thrown open so the windows gleamed in the sunlight, people lounging in chairs on the veranda, colorful flowers spilling from the flower beds. Oh, yes, she had a plan. A plan so near to her heart, she'd never dared to speak of it aloud. "I plan to succeed," she said at last. "That's what I plan to do."

He chuckled. "I'm afraid planning to 'succeed' isn't a business plan. It's a goal—and a good one—but if you want someone to loan you money, you need an in-depth, written plan with demographics, cost analysis, projected growth and income."

Panic welled at the thought of putting her dream down on paper for other people to scrutinize, but she let the sight of the house give her courage. "If I get one of those, a business plan, your father's bank will loan me the money?"

"I didn't say that." He gave her an odd smile, partly amused, partly intrigued.

"Rory!" Bobby shouted from the boat. "Move your tail! We have a schedule to keep here."

"I'm coming!" She gave Chance a pleading look. "I gotta go. I'll come see you tomorrow. At the bank." She grabbed his hand and gave it a good businesslike handshake. "We'll talk more then." Her voice floated behind her as she jogged down the path. "Oh, I can't wait to get home and tell Adrian and Allison. They're just gonna flip!"

"But—" Chance held out a hand as she dashed to the pier on long tanned legs, the wind plastering the white shirt to her tall, curvy body. He felt as if a whirlwind had just knocked him over as he watched her climb into the boat beside the muscle-bound driver. With a cheerful smile, she waved at him while the boat pulled away from the dock.

Chance returned the wave numbly as he willed his pulse to slow. Aurora St. Claire. Heaven help him and all mortal men, but didn't the woman have a clue what that body, that face, and all that flame-bright hair could do to a man!

He shook his head hoping to clear it. It didn't work. There was no shaking off the effect of Aurora. Once she bowled a guy over, he was down for life. Chance should know. He'd been in lust with the girl since he was a boy. Only, he wasn't a boy any longer. And God have mercy, she definitely wasn't a mere girl.

The ringing of the phone clipped to his belt brought him slowly out of his haze. "Yes, Chance speaking."

"Oliver, where are you?" His father's deep voice pricked a hole in Chance's euphoria. "I expected you back at the bank an hour ago."

"I know, I'm sorry, sir." He glanced uneasily at the sign, wondering if his father had seen the paperwork on the foreclosure yet. Since his father sounded more curious than angry, he guessed not. "Brian had an . . . um . . . errand he wanted me to do."

"Since when does the vice president of operations run errands for the loan department?" his father asked.

Since the bank was taken over by a bunch of out-of-town wimps who don't have the guts to get between you and the new owners back East, Chance thought bitterly. Although he couldn't blame Brian Jeffries, the senior vice president of loans, for asking him to put up the For Sale sign. If anyone else did it, Chance's father would fire the person on the spot for embarrassing the LeRoche family in so public a manner.

"Never mind," his father sighed. "I was about to leave for the day and wanted to remind you about Paige's welcome-home dinner tonight."

"No need to remind me. I'm looking forward to it." Chance smiled, thinking of Paige Baxter, the girl he intended to marry. Now that she had graduated from college and returned to the island, they could finally start dating in a more official manner. When summer was over, he'd ask her to marry him, they'd have a respectable engagement of six months or so, and marry next spring. He imagined his mother and Mrs. Baxter were already planning the wedding.

"We'll expect you at the house by six-thirty, then?" his father said.

"Yes, sir. I'll be there." Hanging up, Chance felt his smile fade as the tension of the day settled back over his shoulders. He glanced at the cove and saw the tour boat had disappeared. Odd how the wind seemed calmer now. While Aurora had been there, the air had been charged with electricity as if lightning were about to strike.

He picked up his hammer and returned to pounding the sign into the ground. In the back of his mind he wondered if Aurora was serious about coming to see him at the bank. A smile tugged at his lips. Now wouldn't that be a sight— Aurora St. Claire sweeping through the bank in a swirl of energy and light? He could almost see the portraits of the bank's founders crashing to the marble floor of the lobby in her wake.

CHAPTER 2

"Adrian! Alli!" Rory shouted as she burst into the small house in the historic district where she lived with her brother and sister. She'd run all the way from Pier Nineteen hoping to catch both of them at home. Glancing at her watch, she saw it was five-thirty. Perfect. Her sister would be home from her job at the antiques shop and her brother had mentioned that morning that he'd be going in late today for his shift as assistant chef at Chez Laffite.

Sadie, her sister's sable and white Sheltie, trotted in from the back of the house, swishing her sassy tail with glee.

"Hey, there, girl, where is everyone?" Rory asked as she obeyed Sadie's demand for an ear scratch.

Sadie offered a happy bark that was no help at all. The front parlor was empty, except for the usual clutter. Old daguerreotypes vied for space on the walls with framed playbills, hand-tatted doilies graced the arms of their great-grandmother's red velvet sofa, newspapers and novels sat in piles everywhere. The living room and front bedroom had once been the entire cottage, but more rooms had been added over the years.

With Sadie at her heels, Rory maneuvered past the piano stool through the dining room and bounded into the kitchen at the back of the house. "There you are!"

"Rory!" Allison turned from the counter with a start, a mixing bowl in hand. Soft black curls framed Allison's delicate face and blue eyes. While Aurora had inherited their father's height and their mother's bright hair, Allison had the bones and coloring that spoke of their French lineage. "Must you always make a grand entrance? Can't you simply arrive home quietly, like a normal person?"

"Of course not. I'm a Bouchard," Rory said, claiming the maiden name of their famous ancestor. "Ooo, is that a chocolate cake you're making?" She snitched a sample with her finger, barely escaping a swat from the handle of the wooden spoon.

"I hear Rory's home." Her brother entered the kitchen in her wake. He occupied the front bedroom since their aunt, "the Incomparable Vivian," was starring in a long-running production of *Hello, Dolly!* on Broadway. The three of them had moved in with Aunt Viv after their parents died in a car wreck while touring with a theater troupe when Rory was a toddler.

"I trust you have dinner under control," Adrian said as he came forward to sniff the steam rising from a pot on the stove. Wearing a white chef's jacket, he looked wickedly handsome with his black ponytail and gold earring. Wrinkling his nose, he pinched a bay leaf from the bundles of herbs hanging overhead and tossed it into the pot.

"Go away, Adrian." Allison bumped him aside with her hip as she continued to stir her cake batter. "That's my leftover gumbo you're messing with."

"And I'll say what I said on Saturday. It needs more filé."

"It does not," Allison protested.

"Guys!" Rory interrupted before they launched into a full-blown argument about cooking filled with French passion and offended egos. "You'll never guess what I found out today."

"What's that?" Adrian said as he reached over Allison's head toward the spice rack.

"I'm warning you, Adrian." Allison clutched her wooden spoon like a sword. "Stay away from my gumbo.

Unless you want to go back to doing all the cooking around here."

"No, no, you're doing a fine job," he hastened to say, even as he added a pinch of spice to the pot.

"Would y'all listen?" Rory pleaded. "This is really big news. The old mansion on Pearl Island is for sale!"

Adrian and Allison both went still. In concert, they turned to face her.

"You're joking, right?" her brother said.

"No, I'm serious. There was a For Sale sign posted and everything."

"Well," Allison said, "there's obviously been some sort of mistake. We all know the LeRoche family would never sell the house, even though they moved out of it years ago. As long as Marguerite's spirit is trapped inside, they'll keep it. 'The Pearl' is their good-luck charm. Whether that's true or not, whether there's even a ghost or not, is beside the point. All that matters is that the LeRoches believe it."

"Maybe it is true," Adrian said. "I mean, you have to admit, they've certainly led charmed lives when it comes to making money."

Allison shrugged. "Too bad their personal lives aren't as successful." While the LeRoche family no longer lived in Galveston year round, they maintained a beach house and were a favorite topic of gossip—not just locally but in newspapers and tabloids nationwide.

"I, for one, would pick happy over rich any day," Allison said.

"Well, there is that," Adrian agreed.

"Wait a second." Rory waved a hand to get their attention. "I didn't say John LeRoche was selling the house voluntarily. The First Bank of Galveston foreclosed on the property," she said. Even though the bank had changed its name to Liberty Union National Bank when it changed owners, all the locals still called it by its original name. "John LeRoche has already lost Pearl Island."

"The First Bank of Galveston foreclosed on John LeRoche?" Adrian's laugh rumbled forth. "Yeah, right, sis. Now I know you're pulling our leg. Nice try, though."

"No, I'm telling y'all, it's true. Don't you see? This is our big chance."

"Big chance for what?" Her brother gave the pot of rice an experimental jiggle.

Looking from her brother's bored face to her sister's worried one, she realized she'd gotten ahead of herself. "If y'all would come sit down for just a minute." She took the mixing bowl away from Allison and put it on the chopping block that sat in the middle of the room beneath an assortment of hanging pots.

"Rory!" Allison protested, holding her hand under the spoon to catch any drips.

"Just for a minute." She took the spoon and put it in the bowl. "This is important. Really."

Her brother checked his watch to see how much time he had before he needed to leave for work. With a shrug, he joined them at the breakfast table. The open windows that overlooked the small backyard let in the salty smell of Galveston Bay.

Once they were seated, Rory took a deep breath and wondered where to begin. The dreams that crowded her mind had been there so long, she feared they'd come spilling out in a jumbled mess the second she started speaking.

"Okay." She exhaled. "I have an idea. Actually, it's something I've thought about forever, but I never mentioned it because it didn't seem possible. Then I saw that sign today and I knew this was *it*—our big chance!"

"Our big chance for what, Rory?" Allison sighed.

Rory placed her hands palms-down on the table. "What would y'all think about opening a bed-and-breakfast?"

They both stared at her. Even Sadie cocked her head to the side.

"On Pearl Island?" her brother asked at last.

"Yes." Rory sucked in air and felt as if she would float

right off the ground. "What could be more perfect, since the place should rightfully have been ours anyway? But that's beside the point. With its history and setting, people would come from all over to stay there. We could even offer scuba diving in the cove so guests could go down and see the old shipwreck. Adrian"—she reached out and took his hand—"you could be in charge of the cooking. And Allison"—she took her sister's hand—"with your knowledge of antiques and flare for decorating, you could handle the remodeling. Maybe even open your own gift shop in the parlor."

"But Rory," Allison said, "who would run the inn?"

"I would." Rory saw doubt enter their eyes and sat back. "All right, I'll admit I'm not the most business-minded person, but we could hire a bookkeeper to help out with that and I'd handle the guests." The skeptical looks grew deeper. "Come on, you have to admit you'd love to own your own business. Adrian, you wouldn't have to put up with the head chef's egomaniacal tantrums anymore. You could cook what you wanted, be the king of your own kitchen. And Alli, aren't you tired of getting paid slave wages while making the owners of the Strand Emporium rich?"

Adrian and Allison looked at each other, then back at her. "There's just one problem with your plan," Adrian said. "We'd have to buy the place and restore it, which will likely cost a fortune, not to mention the other expenses involved in starting a business. I'm not sure we have that kind of money."

"We have the money from Mom and Dad's life insurance," Rory pointed out.

"Which might cover the purchase price," Adrian said, "if we manage to get the property at a steal, but it won't come close to covering the rest."

"Then we'll take out a business loan," Rory offered. "I already talked to Oliver Chancellor about it today."

"Oliver Chancellor?" Allison's eyes widened. "Of the

banking Chancellors? You talked to a banker about this?"

"He was on Pearl Island, putting up the foreclosure sign," Rory explained. "That's how I found out about it."

"And he agreed to give you a loan, just like that?" Adrian snapped his fingers.

"No, of course not," she said. "But I bet he'll help us apply for one."

Adrian smirked. "Of course he will."

"What's that supposed to mean?" Rory straightened.

He gestured toward her wild hair, tall body, and long legs exposed by her shorts. "Any male between puberty and senility generally agrees to give you anything."

"It's not like that." Rory rolled her eyes. "Oliver Chancellor isn't interested in me." *Good grief,* she thought. They were so far apart socially, they might as well come from different planets.

Adrian gave her a pointed look. "You think just because he's a scrawny geek he's not interested in girls?"

"He's not scrawny." She frowned at her brother.

"But he is a geek," Adrian pointed out.

"Well, yeah," she admitted as she pictured Chance standing before her in his button-down dress shirt and wire-rimmed glasses. "I guess. But in a cute sort of way."

"Oh, Rory," Allison sighed. "Don't do this to the poor guy. I remember him from school. He always seemed so nice."

"Do what to him?" Rory asked.

"Break his heart," Allison said. "Like you do all the boys."

"I do not." Rory snorted. Why did Adrian and Allison always accuse her of leading men around as if they were love-sick puppies? True, men in general tended to be nice to her, but that was because she was a friendly person, not because of how she looked. Sure, she was attractive— she'd have to be an idiot not to know *that*—but she didn't come close to Allison's fragile beauty. With a wave of her hand, she brushed the nonsense aside. "Do you think we could get back to the real subject here, which is the fact that Pearl Island is for sale? *If* we're interested."

Her brother shook his head. "Rory, I realize you are the original sunshine girl, but this idea is a bit far-fetched, even for you. No banker in his right mind is going to loan us the kind of money it would take to buy an entire island so we can open a bed-and-breakfast."

"Well, it never hurts to ask," Rory said.

"Rory." Allison gave her fingers a squeeze. "It's not that simple."

"How do we know—if we don't even try?"

Adrian cocked a brow at Allison. "She's right, you know."

"Adrian!" Allison scolded. "Don't encourage her."

"I'm just saying she's right. We don't know if we can or can't do anything unless we look into it."

"Then we'll do it?" Rory brightened. "Together?"

"We didn't say that." Allison frowned at both of them.

"But you won't get mad if I go down to the bank tomorrow and talk to Chance about it."

"Do we have a choice?" Allison asked.

"Of course you do," Rory insisted. "If you don't want this dream, then what's the use of me pursuing it? I don't want to push you into anything. This is something we do together, for ourselves, or not at all. So, what do you say?"

Allison looked to their brother. "I guess it wouldn't hurt to look into it."

"Are you kidding?" A devilish smile broke over Adrian's face. "I'd kill to be in charge of my own kitchen. But Rory, I'm warning you not to get your hopes up. This is a one-in-a-million shot we're talking about here."

"I know," she said. "But one in a million is better than nothing."

He hesitated a moment before nodding. "All right." Rising, he ruffled her hair. "You go for it, sis. In the meantime, I'm off to work."

"Thanks, Adrian," she called to him as he left the kitchen. Squeezing her sister's hand, she added, "Something good is going to come of this. I can just feel it!"

Her sister looked less than convinced.

Chance welcomed the strong breeze as he stepped out onto his parents' back deck. Worries over the LeRoche foreclosure had kept him on edge all evening, in spite of the good food and familiar company. He took a deep breath, willing his shoulders to relax.

An occasional light or sound of laughter came from the decks of neighboring houses along the golf course. Moonlight silvered the country club grounds, and in the distance the pulse of the gulf beat against miles of sandy beaches.

"Oh, I have missed this," Paige sighed as she joined him at the rail. "There's no place in the world that feels quite like Galveston. It's as if the very air holds magic."

A burst of night wind carried the scent of rain, and somewhere far out over the gulf, lightning flickered.

"Magic?" He leaned a hip against the rail to study her. She had the quiet, cultured sort of looks he found comfortable, with her pale blond hair pulled back into a neat ponytail. The diamond studs that sparkled at her ears complemented her silvery blue slip of a dress. Her dainty body had always made him feel masculine, even back in the days when he was a scrawny adolescent. Although now that he towered over her a full foot, he idly wondered how well they'd fit together in bed.

He pushed the image aside, feeling somewhat guilty for trying to picture the act of sex with Paige. For as long as he'd known her, Paige Baxter had possessed a pristine quality that discouraged base thoughts in her presence. He supposed, if they were going to be married, he needed to get over that.

The sliding glass door opened, and Chance turned as their parents joined them.

"Ellen, your dinner was superb as always," Marcy Baxter said to his mother as the ladies made their way to the grouping of outdoor furniture amid the potted palms. The striped awning that shaded the deck during the day had been retracted so they could enjoy the stars. "I don't suppose I could get the recipe for that praline flan?"

"I'm afraid even I can't get it," his mother laughed as she settled onto a cushioned settee. The long Oriental silk top she wore with wide-legged pants shimmered softly as she made herself comfortable. Even staring the age of sixty in the face, with threads of silver weaving through her brown hair, Ellen Chancellor was a handsome woman. "I made the dinner but Carmen made dessert and you know she never shares her recipes with anyone."

"Well, you should make her give it to you," Marcy said as she perched on a chair, tucking her short skirt about her legs. "She does work for you, after all."

While Ellen accepted the advancing years with grace, her lifelong friend was fighting them every step of the way with dyed blond hair to hide the gray and the latest trends from Neiman Marcus.

"How about a cigar?" Chance's father, Norman, asked Harry Baxter as the men headed for the outdoor bar beneath an overhang at the other end of the deck.

"I'd love one," the land developer answered in his deep, booming voice. His short, powerful body provided a sharp contrast to Norman Chancellor's tall, masculine grace.

"Harry," Marcy warned her husband with a pointed look. "You know what the doctor said about your blood pressure."

"Bah, one cigar every now and then isn't going to kill me." Harry selected a fat Cuban from the box Norman presented. Chance caught his father's look of longing as Harry puffed the cigar to life. Since his heart attack two years ago, Norman had to settle for smoking by proxy.

"So"—Harry leaned back in the high-legged bar chair allowing his full stomach to relax—"what's this rumor I hear about your bank foreclosing on Pearl Island?"

The tension snapped back into Chance's shoulders.

"Hmm, what's that?" Norm asked, distracted by a plume of aromatic smoke.

Chance closed his eyes as he waited for Harry to answer. He'd hoped he could tell his father about the foreclosure personally—and in private.

"One of the real estate agents I work with was out boating today," Harry said. "Told me he saw a foreclosure sign in front of the house on Pearl Island."

A heartbeat of silence followed in which Chance could almost hear the thoughts spinning through his father's mind. The confidentiality of a bank customer was sacred to Norman Chancellor. He would never publicly humiliate anyone by putting up a foreclosure sign. But then, Norman Chancellor didn't own the bank anymore. While the new owners had kept him on as bank president, they operated behind his back all too often, expecting Norman and his old-fashioned ways to be little more than window dressing to keep the Old Money accounts happy.

"Foreclosure? That's nonsense." Norm flashed a look in Chance's direction, a look that demanded an explanation. Helpless, Chance gave his head an infinitesimal shake, letting his father know they'd talk about it later. Norm forced a laugh as he turned back to Harry. "The LeRoches have been depositors at the First Bank of Galveston since my ancestors founded the bank. I don't care if it is the Liberty Union now, or if the LeRoches only vacation in Galveston these days, we still consider them locals. What's the point of doing business with a local bank, if you aren't extended a bit of leeway now and then?"

"Well, if anyone needs a bit of leeway right now, it would be John LeRoche," Harry said. "From what I hear, his first wife took him to the cleaners, and that young model he's taken up with is spending him out of house and home. Although," Harry added with a booming laugh, "from the looks of her, maybe she's worth it! Did you see the picture of her on the cover of that magazine? What's the name of it?" he asked his wife.

"*Glamour*," Marcy answered, her lips pursed with disapproval over John LeRoche's behavior.

Seeing her expression, Norm cleared his throat. "If you want my opinion, few women are worth losing a fortune over, much less making a fool of yourself in public. As for the foreclosure, it's bound to be a simple mistake." He scrubbed his face with a long-fingered hand. "I'm telling you, Harry, sometimes I wonder about the folks I sold the bank to. It was the best decision from a business standpoint, just the way of the world in banking these days, but those East Coast Yankees don't have a clue how we do business down here in the South. It's as if the term 'gentleman's honor' has no meaning to them."

"I hear you there." Harry puffed on the cigar.

"Chance," his father said, "we'll meet on this tomorrow. But first, find out who put up that damn sign and see that it's taken down."

"I'll talk to Brian in loans about it," Chance answered evasively, dreading the inevitable confrontation.

"Norman," Chance's mother scolded lightly. "Can't you men talk about something other than work?"

"You're right." Norm nodded. "Sorry."

"Miss Ellen?" Carmen, the housekeeper, appeared in the doorway to the kitchen. "I have coffee ready if you like."

"Oh, yes, I'd love some. Marcy?" Ellen asked her friend. "You'll have some coffee, won't you?"

"Only if it's decaf," Marcy answered.

"Chance? Paige?" his mother called. "What can Carmen get for you?"

"Nothing, I'm fine," Chance answered, suddenly eager to escape the entire evening. "Paige, do you want anything?"

"Actually"—she hesitated—"I think I'd prefer a walk."

Her face tipped up to his, and he saw perfect understanding in her eyes. It was this knack she had for reading him that had drawn him to her from the first. For as long as he could remember, Paige had always been there, at her parents' house just up the street, ready to listen to his problems. "Would you like to go with me?"

"Yes, I would." He smiled and moved his arm so she could link her hands about his elbow.

"Paige, dear, don't forget your sweater," Marcy Baxter said. "It feels like that storm is moving in."

"Yes, ma'am." With a barely audible sigh, Paige ducked back inside and returned with a lightweight cardigan.

Chance took the sweater and draped it over Paige's shoulders before they descended the wooden steps and headed for the golf-cart path. With the neighborhood located on the west end of the island, where the ground barely rose above sea level, all the houses were elevated. Garages and storage rooms filled in the ground level with the living areas above. The houses on the gulf side of the street backed up to the golf course. Houses on the bay side, like the Baxters', were set on a series of canals with boat docks in back.

The moment they passed a row of oleanders that shielded them from their parents, Paige pulled the sweater from her shoulders and draped it over one arm. Overhead, the wind rustled the palm trees that lined the path.

"I take it all is not well at the bank?" Paige asked quietly.

"You might say that." Chance snorted, wondering where to begin. So much had happened while Paige had been off at college. They'd kept loosely in touch, but only saw each other when she was home. And then she'd spent most of her time with her friends from McConnell High, the private school she'd attended.

Dating would have been easier if she'd gone straight to college after high school, but she'd waited four years. So, while he and most of her friends were at UT, she'd been in Galveston. Then when he'd returned home, she'd left, which had delayed any serious involvement.

That arrangement had suited them both. Though they'd never discussed it openly, they each knew that someday they'd marry. Chance had decided it would be best if they tested other waters while they were still young, rather than spend their *entire* lives together. Since Paige hadn't objected, he assumed she felt the same.

They strolled easily together, with him shortening his long-legged stride. "Do you want to talk about it?" she asked.

About our marriage? he wondered, having lost the thread of the conversation. Then he remembered the bank and laughed at himself. "Actually, my mother's right. I talk about work too much. I'd rather talk about you."

"Oh, really?" Her voice held a touch of pique.

He glanced down at her, but could see little more than the top of her head. "You sound surprised."

"Well, yes, I suppose I am." She tilted her face up, revealing an expression that looked as accepting as it always did. "Since I've been home a week and you haven't made any attempt to see me."

Has she really been home a week? He mentally scrolled down his desk calendar and realized she had. "I was giving you time to get settled."

"Chance." She stopped, so he did the same. "I'm staying in the house where I grew up. How much time do you think I need to get settled?"

"Oh," he said, chagrined. She shook her head at him, and they resumed walking. He tried to think of a conversational gambit, and wondered when talking to Paige had become a task. And an awkward one at that. "So, um, you're going to live with your parents this summer?"

She heaved a sigh. "It's a little hard to get an apartment when you don't have a job. And Daddy would kill me if I touched my trust fund."

He glanced at her in confusion. "But you have a degree

in interior design. Don't you plan to use it?"

"Did you honestly think my father would let me work?
Good heavens, it took me four years simply to convince
him I wanted to go to college and get a degree. Actually
wanting to use that degree seems beyond his ability to
comprehend." She made a sound that came dangerously
close to a snort. "To think, I was actually hoping to go to
work for his architect and design team. But you know how
he is. He expects me to be his pampered darling until I
marry. And then he expects me to be my husband's pampered darling till the day I die."

"And what do you expect?"

She didn't answer. As they passed from shadow into
moonlight, he noticed emotions flickering across her brow.
Before he could read them, they slipped back into shadow.

"Chance?" she asked as they stepped onto a footbridge.
"Why haven't you ever kissed me?"

CHAPTER 3

"What are you talking about?" Chance stared at Paige, stunned. One moment they'd been having a rational conversation. Now he felt as if he'd been hit in the head with a two-by-four. "I've kissed you." He thought for a moment, his mind racing. "The first time I kissed you was during the Connelys' Christmas party when Nerdy Ned ran over and held mistletoe above our heads."

Paige gave him a disgruntled look. "A kiss on the cheek doesn't count."

"Of course it counts. Everyone in the room was watching. I thought my face would catch on fire I was so embarrassed, but I knew if I didn't do it all our friends would call me a coward. Trust me, Paige, anything that traumatic counts."

She just leaned against the bridge rail and shook her head.

"Okay," he persisted, "the first time I took you to a school dance. I distinctly remember kissing you on the lips when I drove you home. We were standing on your parents' front porch, and I kept expecting your dad to open the door and point a shotgun at my chest."

"He wouldn't have done that!" Paige gaped. "Even if he and Mom were watching from the living room window. It still doesn't count, though, because it was a polite, thank-you-for-the-date kiss. Not a *real* kiss."

"And what exactly do you call a *real* kiss?"

She plucked at her sweater rather than look at him. "The year you were a senior and you took Carri Hempstead to your prom, the next day in the locker room before dance class, she called you Clark Kent."

"Clark Kent?" Chance slumped back against the opposite rail, wondering if he'd slipped into the Twilight Zone.

"Hmmm." Paige's eyes twinkled as she looked at him through her lashes. "Carri said you might look mild mannered, but when you kiss, you turn into Superman."

"She said that?"

"She said you could take a girl flying through stars with the way you kiss."

"Really?" His chest expanded with pleasure as he remembered that night with Carri Hempstead in the back seat of his father's Lincoln.

"So"—Paige crossed her arms—"how come you've never kissed me like that?"

Kiss Paige the way I kissed Carri? Images flooded his mind of his hands on Carri's naked breasts, of her fingers tugging at his shirt. Lips locked, tongues entwined. The rush of cool air on his backside when he finally kicked free of his pants. And the glorious heat of Carri Hempstead's eager body taking his virginity. At least one of them had had experience that night. And oh, the wicked things she'd taught him all through the following summer. The carnal feast had ended on friendly terms when he'd left for UT in Austin, and she headed for Texas A&M.

He tired to imagine doing those things with Paige and his mind drew a complete blank. Paige stood waiting, all but tapping a sandal on the wooden bridge.

He looked around, hoping for a graceful way out of this predicament. Only . . . why would he want out of it? Wasn't this the moment he'd been waiting for? He should *want* to kiss Paige. But once he kissed her—kissed her the way a man kisses a woman he wants to take to bed—the courtship would officially begin. It would no longer be a thing in the future. They'd be headed straight down the path of dating, engagement, matrimony, mortgage, children, diapers, IRAs, retirement, and vacations spent on cruise ships.

It all loomed over his head, ready to crash down on him the minute his lips made contact with hers.

"Paige, you know how interested I've always been in you."

She mumbled something that sounded like "You could have fooled me."

"What?"

"Nothing." She smiled sweetly.

"But going from being friends to being . . . something more is awkward."

"Why?"

"I don't know." He gestured outward with his long arms. "It just is. And it's not something we need to rush."

She looked stricken. "Do you really find the idea of kissing me that offensive?"

"No! Of course not. I just don't want to rush you into anything. You've only been back a week. Surely you want to spend time with your friends before I start monopolizing you."

"I see." She hesitated, her brow dimpled. "I guess we aren't as suited for each other as people think, if you find me so repulsive." She turned and started walking back toward his parents' house.

"Paige, wait!" He caught up with her and took hold of her arm. She refused to look at him and he wondered if she were crying. "I'm sorry. I guess I'm just feeling a bit pressured. Aren't you? I mean, all our lives people have talked about what a perfect couple we'd make, and I've always agreed with that. I just didn't want to act on it too fast. I wanted to give you time to grow up first."

Her head whipped around and he saw moonlit tears shimmer in her eyes. "You think I need to grow up?"

"No!" He felt as if he'd just kicked a kitten. "But, well, don't you find it daunting to have something that has al-

ways been off in the future suddenly . . . you know . . .
here?"

"Actually, yes, I do." She dabbed beneath her wet
lashes. "I just thought maybe we should get this one thing
out of the way. You make me nervous, Chance. All week
I've been jumping every time the phone rings, wondering
if it's you, and if you'd want to see me. Want a date. A
real date. Then, this evening I've barely been able to
breathe, wondering if tonight would be the night you'd
finally kiss me. Do you have any idea how many times
I've tried to imagine what it would be like? I don't care
about what happens after. We don't have to start dating
right away. To be honest, I'd like a little time to myself
rather than going straight from college to being tied down.
I just want you to kiss me and get it over with so I can
quit being sick to my stomach. Okay?"

"Okay," he said softly, willing to do anything to stop
her tears.

"Okay?" Her eyes widened.

"Okay." He stepped forward, his heart pounding as he
cupped her jaw. His thumb stroked her wet cheek. Steeling
his nerves, he lowered his mouth to hers.

Her lips were soft and pleasant. But the scent of baby
powder distracted him, made him remember how she'd
looked as a little girl, so tiny and lost and looking to him
to protect her. It was an image to inspire brotherly affection, not great passion. Brushing her lips a second time,
he searched his mind for something more erotic, anything
to get him through this moment. A mental image to turn
him from Clark Kent into Superman.

The memory of Aurora St. Claire flashed to life. He
saw her towering over him, the long bare legs leading to
a body made for pleasure and all that glorious golden-red
hair flying about her. With a groan he deepened the kiss,
molding and tasting the lips beneath his as arousal rushed
through him, tightening his groin.

The instant erection made him jerk back, breaking the

kiss. Paige swayed toward him, off balance. He caught her shoulders to steady her, thankful his hips hadn't been pressed against her. Still, he was mortified that he'd been so violently turned on with thoughts of another woman while kissing the woman he intended to marry.

Aurora was a fantasy in the flesh. Paige was his sensible reality. He needed to remember that.

He struggled to slow his breathing as she blinked up at him.

"How was that?" he asked at last.

A frown flickered briefly across her brow. "It was . . . nice."

"Yes, nice," he echoed, trying not to be disappointed. Maybe he could keep his mind on her while kissing if she'd wear perfume instead of baby powder. He wondered how rude it would be to mention it, and promptly rejected the idea. He'd just have to get used to the scent. At least she'd quit crying, he noticed with relief. "Should we head back to the house?"

"All right," she agreed reluctantly. When they turned to walk along the path, he took her hand in his. Her bones felt small and fragile.

As they neared the house, his mind drifted back to Aurora. He couldn't help but wonder how he would have felt if he'd just kissed her in the moonlight. Somehow he didn't think "nice" would properly describe the experience.

The enthusiasm that had kept Rory up half the night faltered when she reached the Liberty Union National Bank. Stepping through the glass doors framed in polished brass, she tried not to gape at the opulent lobby. Mahogany paneling rose twenty feet to the coffered ceiling. To one side of the entrance, leather sofas bracketed Oriental rugs, and financial magazines lay in regimented order on antique coffee tables.

A low hum of voices drew her attention in the opposite direction, where tellers sat behind a long counter, waiting on customers. Two of the tellers she recognized as classmates from high school, girls who'd gone on to college and now worked at a job she couldn't even fathom. The thought of all those numbers they dealt with so effortlessly made her stomach clench.

Between customers, they bent their heads together and laughed over some bit of gossip, then glanced toward an older woman with mocha skin and jet-black hair smoothed into a French twist. When the older woman looked up, the tellers instantly sobered, like schoolgirls spotting their teacher.

Rory noticed the older woman's desk guarded a hallway lined with closed doors. Chance's office would probably lie behind one of those doors. Never one to let intimidation hold her back for long, she took a deep breath and crossed the lobby. Her rubber-soled deck shoes squeaked on the marble floor, making her cringe. She'd worn her tour guide uniform since she planned to go straight to work afterward. Galveston was a casual community and she'd never felt out of place wearing shorts—until now.

"Excuse me," she said in a subdued voice when she reached the desk. "I'm here to see Oliver Chancellor."

The older woman looked up and took in Rory's attire over the tops of reading glasses. "Is he expecting you?"

"Yes, of course, I'm Rory, I mean—" She took a breath and slowed down. "I'm Aurora St. Claire."

The woman ran a finger down a list of names. "I don't see you. What time was your appointment?"

Rory squirmed. "I didn't exactly make an appointment. But I did tell him I'd be coming in today."

"Regarding?" The woman arched a black brow.

"He'll know," Rory said, hoping he remembered.

"Hmm." The woman's lips compressed. "I'll see if he's available."

"Thank you." Rory offered a smile that seemed to go unnoticed.

As the woman picked up the phone and spoke in a

hushed voice, Rory tucked her hair behind her ears and wondered if she should have pulled it back. People who worked at real jobs always seemed to have a secret set of standards she could never quite grasp. Looking about the lobby, at the framed portraits of men with dark suits and serious expressions, she suddenly felt like a bit of flotsam that had been tossed by a storm onto a manicured lawn.

"Aurora?"

She turned to see Chance striding toward her and her heart skipped a beat in surprise. He looked quite fashionable—and intimidating—in an olive-colored suit. Yet something in his welcoming smile made her nervous stomach relax.

"You came," he said. "I wondered if you would."

"Yes, of course. I said I would, and here I am." She spread her arms to either side.

"So I see." His gaze swept downward, toward her legs, then darted away. "Perhaps you'd, um—" He cleared his throat. "Care to step into my office."

"Certainly." Her enthusiasm returned and tangled with her nerves as she followed him down the hall. She caught her breath when she passed through the door, for the room was every bit as grand as the lobby, but on a smaller scale. "Wow," she said. "What a great office."

"Thanks," he said from behind her.

She turned and saw him smile as he pushed his wire-rimmed glasses higher on his nose. He really was cute, in a scholarly sort of way. Except for his mouth. His mouth wasn't cute at all. It was well defined, full, and . . . sensual. The kind of mouth that put thoughts into a girl's head.

Glancing about, she took in the massive desk, the wet bar set discreetly within the custom-built cabinets, and an oil painting of the beach at sunset. "You must love working here."

"Why do you say that?"

"You know, the office, the bank, everything." Her gesture took in the whole room. "God, it must have been wonderful to grow up knowing you had all this waiting for you. You know"—she laughed and waved her hand—"instead of being like me and wondering what the heck you would do with your life." When he just frowned as if confused, she clasped her hands to keep them still.

"Can I get you anything?" He nodded toward the coffeepot on the bar.

"No, nothing. I'm fine."

"Well, then, have a seat." He gestured toward a pair of chairs that sat on either side of an end table and lamp that gave the room a homey feel. "I assume you're here to talk about Pearl Island?"

"Yes!" Trying to contain her excitement, she took a seat in the closest chair and waited for Chance to sit in the other. "I, we, what I mean is, Adrian, Allison, and I talked about it and they agreed with my idea. Well, actually, they didn't *agree,* but they didn't object to me looking into it."

" 'It' being . . . ?" Chance prompted, smothering a smile.

"What?" She blinked at him. "Oh! Sorry," she laughed. "I got ahead of myself."

He watched, enthralled, as energy sparkled in her blue eyes. How could one person contain so much joy for life?

"We want to turn the house on Pearl Island into a bed-and-breakfast."

With her face distracting him, the words took a second to sink in. But when they did, the enormity of such a project—the complications, cost, possible solutions, potential income—clicked through his mind. "I assume you've looked into the logistics behind something like this?"

"Not yet," she admitted. "I mean, I've thought about it off and on over the years, but more as a dream, not something that could actually come true. Then, when I saw you putting up that sign, I just knew it was meant to be!" She gestured with her hands and hit the lamp on the table between them.

"Oh!" She gasped as they both grabbed the lamp. When it was settled, she folded her hands in her lap. "Sorry."

"It's okay." He chuckled. "At least it wasn't me knocking something over."

His smile faded, though, as he absorbed her lack of business expertise and weighed it against her obvious passion. Passion, he knew, could make the difference between a new business succeeding or failing. But it was an uncertain element, and best left out of the equation.

"Aurora," he said, leaning forward to brace his forearms on his thighs. "You do realize that what you're proposing will be impossible to pull off without a great deal of financial backing and research."

"Yes, of course." Her expression showed the first signs of doubt. "But I figured you could help me out with the money part. As for the research . . ." She glanced away. "I'll think of something."

He cocked his head. "What do you mean, you'll 'think of something'?"

She shrugged. "It's just that I've never been very good at that sort of thing. Researching, I mean. I guess I could get Adrian and Alli to help me some. Maybe."

He watched her shoulders slump. "I don't understand."

"I'm not good at analytical stuff." She leaned forward and a scent, like exotic flowers washed by the rain, drifted to him. Subtly, he breathed it in as she lowered her voice. "You know, reading up on things, filling out paperwork." Her gaze met his and the anxiety he saw in her eyes confused him. "I'm not stupid or anything. I'm just . . . a bit slow . . . at certain things."

"I see," he said, even though he didn't see at all. There didn't seem to be a single thing "slow" about Aurora St. Claire. She'd always struck him as being very bright, from her quick wit to her shining personality. "Unfortunately, research is the first step in forming a business plan. You'll need to do that before you even think of applying for a loan."

"Oh." Her shoulders slumped a bit more and her eyes beseeched him. "I don't suppose you'd know someone who could help me."

The longing he sensed reached right inside him and grabbed hold. Logically, he knew he should discourage her from this wild idea, but logic had nothing to do with the way he felt when he looked into her hopeful blue eyes. "I could probably help you some. Point you in the right direction, at least."

"You could?" Her whole face brightened. "Oh, Chance, that would be great." She laid a hand on his arm and the contact sent a streak of awareness through his system.

"I, um . . ." He struggled to think straight, but every breath filled him with her fragrance. "What I mean is, Ron and Betsy McMillan, who own the Laughing Mermaid Inn, do their banking here. Maybe I could give them a call and ask for advice on where you should start."

"Do you really think they'd help?"

"I don't see why not." His gaze moved to her smile and he wondered if her lips tasted as good as she smelled. "Is there a number where I can reach you?"

"Oh, yes, of course." Leaning back, she fumbled through the mesh bag she carried as a purse. "Do you have something I can write on?"

He rose and retrieved a notepad from his desk, then took a breath to clear his head. "Here." He turned to hand it to her and found that she'd followed him. Taking the pad, she bent over his desk and began to write. He tried not to notice how the shorts rose up to show the backs of her thighs. God, she had great legs.

"Here you go." She straightened and handed him the pad. "That's the mobile number for the tour-boat office. We usually turn it off when we're out on the water but you can leave a message and I'll call you back."

"Sure." He frowned as he remembered the muscle-bound boat driver and wondered if they did more than work together. "Why don't you take my card, so you'll know how to reach me?"

Taking the card he offered, she ran her thumb over the gold print and cream linen paper. "Nice card," she said quietly.

"Thanks. I'll, um"—he swallowed hard as she caressed the raised type that spelled out his name—"be in touch with you as soon as I've talked to Ron and Betsy."

When she glanced up, the space between them seemed to shrink. "I can't thank you enough. You have no idea what this means to me."

"You're welcome," he said, as heat hummed through his veins. "Although maybe you should wait until you've talked to the McMillans to thank me." Needing some space to cool off, he moved to the door to show her out. "You may not like what they have to say. Starting a business is a huge undertaking."

"I know. Whatever they say, though, I appreciate your help."

He opened the door, bumping it against the back of his shoe.

She extended her hand. "And thanks for not laughing at me, even though I know you probably wanted to." She wrinkled her nose, and he noticed she had freckles, a light dusting of them on the bridge of her nose.

"Not at all." He took her hand, intending to shake it, but wound up standing there, simply holding it.

"Well," she said, seeming perfectly comfortable with her hand in his, their bodies almost touching in the confines of the doorway.

"Yes." He admired the lively blue color that danced in her eyes. "Well."

"I guess I should be going." She took a step back, bumped into the doorjamb, and laughed.

"Careful!" He laughed also, and reached toward her head. "Don't hurt yourself."

"I'm fine." A pink blush stained her cheeks. "Just clumsy."

"That's probably my fault. I didn't realize it was contagious."

"If it is, you're in trouble." She wrinkled her nose again, and he had the wild impulse to kiss those fascinating freckles. Or maybe her mouth. Definitely her mouth. Man, it was gorgeous, so ripe and full-lipped. The red color appeared natural, not from cosmetics. In fact, she wasn't wearing any cosmetics. "I really do have to go."

"Okay," he said.

"I guess I'll hear from you later?" She stepped safely into the hall this time.

"As soon as I talk to the McMillans."

"Okay, then." She waved and took a few steps backward before she turned and headed across the lobby. His gaze followed her all the way to the door, mesmerized by the spring in her stride and those long, bare legs.

The moment she disappeared, though, doubt raised its head. He hoped his father wouldn't take offense at his offering to help a descendant of Marguerite Bouchard buy Pearl Island. He knew his father wanted to give John first right to buy the place back, but so far the man had showed no interest in doing so. Rumor had it John LeRoche had fallen into some serious financial difficulties since he'd put the house up as collateral.

Those rumors were almost enough to make Chance wonder if Pearl Island really was a good-luck charm—that is, if he was the type to believe in magic and ghosts.

CHAPTER 4

Rory left the bank and headed on foot for Pier Nineteen. Throughout the historic downtown district, tourists wandered in and out of antiques shops and art galleries, admiring the façades of nineteenth-century buildings. A horse-drawn carriage clopped by, and she smiled at the tour guide who sat sideways pointing out attractions to his passengers.

On Harborside Drive, the buildings changed to newer shops and restaurants built of weathered wood. Flowering baskets hung from replicas of old-fashioned street lamps along brick walkways. She breathed it all in, enjoying the sounds and scents of Galveston, a blend of fried seafood and salt water, the shriek of seagulls and the blast of a tugboat bringing in a barge. Somehow, today, it all seemed brighter, more vivid.

"Hey, there, gorgeous," Captain Bob said when she stepped into the small metal building that served as the tour-boat office. " 'Bout time you got here."

"Sorry I'm late," she offered, still lost in dreams of the future, plans and possibilities. Slipping behind the counter, she tucked her bag away.

"Catching up on your beauty sleep?" He leaned on the opposite arm of the L-shaped counter, crunching on a peppermint with those flashing white teeth of his. "Not that you need it."

"No, I just had an errand to run this morning."

"Hey, you okay?"

"Hmm?" She looked up to see the smile had vanished. "Oh, sorry," she laughed, understanding his concern. Normally, she matched him tease for tease, which was why they got along so well. She never took Bobby or anything he said seriously, while other women trailed after him with their tongues hanging out, making absolute fools of themselves. And heaven forbid he should flex his tanned muscles, or favor some female with one of his wicked grins. Then they melted into cooing puddles at his feet.

Rory, however, had never put much stock in physical appearance. She came from a long line of legendary beauties and her own brother was so good-looking, tourists frequently asked if he was a movie star. But the lesson Marguerite had passed down to her daughter, and all the Bouchard descendants, was that beauty wasn't always a blessing. The true measure of a person was what lay beneath the surface. So while Rory found Bobby charming at times, she'd realized early on how irresponsible he could be about everything but his boat.

When it came to the *Daydreamer,* however, responsibility was his middle name. Moving to the doorway, she admired the pontoon boat tied to the concrete landing. The open area for passengers took up the forward half of the vessel with a cabin and small deck aft. Up top was an observation and sunning deck with a slide to the water. In addition to guided tours, Bobby chartered the boat for private parties.

On the dock, a steady stream of tourists passed by on their way to the nearby shops and restaurants. More than one stopped to look over the boat and pick up a pamphlet for prices and schedules.

"Was it hard to start your own business?" she asked.

"Not really." He stepped past her and scooped up a brass lantern and a polishing cloth. Taking a seat, he set to work; the arms exposed by his rolled-up sleeves bulged and flexed with the task. "What with my old man being a shrimper down in Corpus Christi, I sort of grew up on the water. Never did care much for getting up before dawn, though, to go shrimping—especially after I'd been out partying half the night." He winked.

"That sounds like you," she chided as she leaned against the doorjamb where the sun slanted in to warm her legs.

He shrugged. "Mostly, I just love boats. I guess I've crewed about every kind of rig that floats until I saved up enough to buy one of my own." Pride shone on his face as he looked at his vessel. "The *Daydreamer* may not be the fanciest boat in the harbor, but she's all mine."

Mine. Closing her eyes, Rory tipped her face toward the sun and let the dreams tumble through her mind. Overhead seagulls screeched and the breeze carried the scent of seafood from Chez Laffite.

A mobile phone rang and she heard Bobby rummage through the tools at his side, searching for it. "Captain Bob's Big Bay Boat Tours," he answered. A moment later, his voice changed, became strangely formal. "Aurora St. Claire? Yes, I believe she might be available." Her heart skipped a beat at the sound of her full name. She opened her eyes and found Bobby staring at her with raised eyebrows. "Might I inquire who's calling?"

"Bobby!" She jumped down from the doorway. "Give me that."

"Oliver Chancellor?" Bobby turned to keep the phone out of her reach. "One moment, please." He lowered the phone and managed to cover the mouthpiece before he spoke. "New boyfriend?"

"No, he's not my boyfriend." She glared at him.

"Too bad." Bobby grinned. "He sounds rich."

"Would you give me that phone!" She grabbed it out of his hands, then took a deep breath, composed herself, and brought the phone to her ear. "Chance, hi. I didn't expect to hear from you so soon."

"I just finished talking to Betsy McMillan, and thought you'd want to hear what she had to say." His voice sounded smooth and cultured, and deep enough to be sexy.

"Yes, of course!" She stepped back into the office, hoping for a small amount of privacy.

"Betsy's eager to meet you," Chance said. "Turns out, she and the other bed-and-breakfast owners have an association that meets once a month. She said they'd be happy to help you however they can."

"Really?" Hope soared at his words.

"In fact, the McMillans are hosting the next meeting tomorrow. It's going to be an afternoon tea, four o'clock in their courtyard garden. Betsy asked if you'd like to come."

"An afternoon tea?" Rory placed a hand over her chest, excited at the opportunity to meet an innkeeper, but unnerved at the thought of meeting so many of them at once. And at a tea party. Did she even have anything appropriate to wear?

"Only one catch." Chance sounded hesitant. "Betsy invited me to come, as well, and I wasn't sure what to say. It's late enough in the day I could easily get away from the bank, and she's been inviting me to one thing and another at the inn for years. I'm afraid if I turn her down this time, she'll never forgive me. I don't want to offend one of my accounts, but I don't want to barge in on your time with her, either."

"Actually, I'd love for you to come. Really." She all but pounced on the idea. The thought of Chance being with her somehow made it less intimidating.

"If you're sure you don't mind, I'll call Betsy back and tell her to expect both of us around four."

"Four o'clock?" She bit her lip, wondering how she'd talk Bobby into letting her off work early. Although midweek wasn't that busy since the summer tourist season wouldn't be in full swing for a couple of weeks.

"Is that okay?" he asked.

"Certainly." She closed her eyes, deciding to deal with Bobby later.

"Should we meet there, or would you like for me to pick you up?"

She thought fast. If Chance picked her up, she wouldn't run the risk of arriving first. Nor would she have to juggle with Adrian and Allison for who got what vehicle. Between the three of them, they only had a Jeep, their aunt's luxury sedan—which was big and awkward for her to drive—and Adrian's motorcycle. But then they all worked within walking distance of the cottage, so transportation was rarely a problem. "I'd rather you pick me up, if that's okay."

"I'll be glad to drive. Do you still live in the old Bouchard Cottage?"

"Yes," she answered, not a bit surprised he knew where she lived since the Bouchard Cottage was on the historic walking tour. Anyone who was up on the island's history knew who lived there.

"I'll see you shortly before four, then."

She turned off the phone, feeling dazed. She had an appointment to meet an innkeeper. Several innkeepers. The first step toward making her dream a reality!

"Hot date?" Bobby asked from the doorway.

She turned, laughing. "Yes, in a manner of speaking, I have a very hot date." And she could hardly wait.

On Wednesday, Chance left the bank and drove the few blocks to where Aurora's family had lived since before the Great Storm of Nineteen Hundred. In Galveston, everything fell into two categories: pre-Storm and post-Storm.

On the gulf side—or beach side—of the island, where he lived, nothing had survived the wall of fury that had slammed into the Texas coast, killing more than six thousand people in Galveston alone. While the hurricane had failed to wipe "the New York of the Gulf" from existence, it had left a permanent mark that had literally reshaped the island.

After the storm, a massive concrete retaining wall,

known as the seawall, had been built along the beach, seventeen feet high and stretching for miles. In the years following the wall's completion, massive amounts of dirt had been pumped by pipeline to fill in behind the wall, physically raising the level of the island's east end.

Just as noticeable and lasting a reminder, though, was the boundary that marked where the devastation had ended, a boundary where the pile of broken houses, pier pilings, carriages, and the bodies of the dead had become so great that even one of the worst hurricanes in recorded history could no longer push it inland. Everything on the gulf side of that barrier had been destroyed, while the downtown area and a small circle of neighborhoods around it had survived remarkably intact.

The St. Claires lived within that boundary among treasures from a more romantic age, beautiful Victorian, antebellum, and Greek Revival homes, from small cottages to lavish mansions. Some had been restored, but many had not. Older families lived in homes they'd inherited but could barely afford to maintain next to New Money couples who were renovating houses from the ground up. The gay community mingled with the straight; wealth lived among the middle class; and everywhere tropical flowers offered a colorful contrast to rugged Texas oaks.

That jumble of people and plant life was one of the things he liked best about Old Galveston. There were no geographic lines of distinction, no good neighborhoods or bad neighborhoods, no rich areas or poor areas, no white, Hispanic, or black sections. Everyone lived side by side.

Unfortunately, the invisible lines of social status weren't nearly as vague. The Old Money families might live beside new wealth or old poverty, but they knew who was one of them and who wasn't. In that respect, Galveston was famous for its snobbery.

Chance accepted this with a resigned sigh, a fact of life as old as Galveston itself, as he pulled to a stop before the one-story white house just east of downtown. He could already hear the whispers that would ripple all the way out to the west end of the island when word got out about whose dark blue BMW had been seen parked in front of the Bouchard Cottage.

As he got out of the car, he glanced at the plaque that stood on a pole just inside the white picket fence. There visitors could learn that the charming little cottage with the lovingly tended flower beds had been built in the late 1800s by Henri LeRoche for his daughter, Nicole Bouchard, an actress who had been the toast of New York, London, and Paris.

What the plaque didn't say—but everyone who'd lived in Galveston for more than a generation knew—was that the cottage had not been built as a present from a loving father, but as a place for a brutal man to banish his only child when she shunned his name in favor of her mother's maiden name. Or that Nicole had died in that house, a destitute divorcée.

When it came to the Bouchards, the old families of Galveston would always remember the scandalous deeds as if they'd happened yesterday. Shaking off the thought, he passed through the gate and headed up the brick path to the cool shade of the front porch. Deep green shutters added a touch of charm to the windows.

Through the screen door, he heard the sound of a baseball game battling with the buzz of a vacuum cleaner. The door rattled on its hinges when he knocked. A dog barked and a second later a Sheltie appeared on the other side of the screen with tongue lagging and tail wagging. There was a friendly gleam in the brown eyes, the certain knowledge that Chance had come to see her—or him. Actually, Chance decided, any creature that flirtatious had to be a her.

"Hang on!" a male voice called. As the vacuum cleaner went silent, Chance caught the sound of a bat cracking against a baseball. The excited announcer called the play over the pandemonium of the crowd.

"Go, go, go! Yes!" the man beyond the door shouted. The dog bounded out of sight, barking with glee. "Woohoo! Sadie, did you see that, girl?"

A second later, Adrian St. Claire appeared in the doorway, bending down to scratch the dog's ears with one hand as he opened the screen with the other. "Hey, Chance, long time no see. Come on in."

"Adrian." Chance nodded in greeting as he stepped inside. He remembered Adrian St. Claire from high school, even though they had run in different circles. Adrian had been the most popular guy on campus, someone who excelled in every sport and never lacked for a date. He had been Chance's first lesson in all the things money couldn't buy. It pleased him to realize he no longer begrudged Adrian any of that.

The dog gave a demanding yip, and rose up on her back legs to plant her front paws against Chance's thigh.

"Sadie, get down! You'll have to excuse her." Adrian smirked at the unrepentant dog. "The women in this house spoil her rotten."

"That's okay," Chance chuckled. "Is Aurora ready?"

"Actually, she's not even home yet, but she should be here any minute. Come on in and have a seat." Adrian scooped a pile of newspapers off the sofa and tossed them on the floor. "Bagwell just hit a grand slam, bottom of the eighth. Astros seven, Cubs five, Caminiti's up next."

Instantly sidetracked by the game, Chance took a seat and turned his attention to a TV that had been fitted into an antique armoire. Adrian remained standing, his arms folded over the handle of a vacuum cleaner as they watched.

"Shit!" Adrian said a second later when Caminiti struck out and the station cut to commercial. "Hey, you want a beer or something?" he asked as he unplugged the vacuum and wound the cord around the handle.

"No, I better not," Chance said. "Betsy McMillan may

not appreciate me showing up at her tea party with beer on my breath."

"You're probably right—but it's my night off, and I plan to enjoy it." Adrian disappeared toward the back of the house with the dog trotting after him.

Chance took a moment to glance around the room. The furniture was a hodgepodge of antiques, as if the décor had evolved over many years, rather than being professionally coordinated to re-create a certain era. But what really captured his attention were the sheer number of framed photos covering the walls. Some were candid shots, but most appeared to have been taken to promote live stage productions. There were also numerous playbills and framed props.

Along the mantel, though, were family photos of the St. Claires. He spotted a picture of Aurora as she had looked when he'd first started noticing her. Smiling, alive, beautiful. The first time she'd come to watch Adrian play football, Chance and his friends had spent most of the game trying to figure out who the knockout was sitting with Adrian's aunt. Probably some actress, they'd decided, and way out of their league. They'd been stunned after the game to learn she was Adrian's baby sister and out of their league because she was too young!

That hadn't stopped Chance from watching her as she grew up, and indulging in a few fantasies along the way.

Adrian reappeared with a load of laundry and a beer. "Is the game back on?"

Chance gave a guilty start. "Not yet," he answered as Sadie jumped onto the cushion beside him and made herself comfortable with her head in his lap. After a moment of surprise, he gave her the petting she obviously expected.

"Let me know if she's bugging you," Adrian said as he dumped the laundry onto the marble-top coffee table and took a seat in a Queen Anne chair. Chance's eyes widened when he realized the pile of clothing consisted entirely of women's undergarments: a bright sherbet-colored mound of satin, silk, and lace. As if it were an everyday occurrence, Adrian set his beer on a coaster and started folding and sorting. "Rory says you're going to help us apply for a loan."

Chance snapped his gaze away from the pile of panties and bras. "Actually, I just offered to point her in the right direction for writing a business plan."

"Better you than me," Adrian said, then turned his attention to the TV as the game came back on.

"Does that mean you're against her idea of starting a bed-and-breakfast?" Chance asked, trying not to stare at the bits of silk and lace that had tumbled dangerously close to his left knee. Did Aurora wear that lemon-yellow bra? The image that came to mind had him shifting his weight to hide the slight bulge growing beneath his zipper.

"Not at all. I just hate doing paperwork." Adrian picked up the bra, folded the cups together, and placed it on a stack of floral-print panties. "So what do you think the odds are that we can get the loan?"

"I . . . um, wouldn't know without reviewing the financial statements of all principal parties."

"Well, if Rory manages to pull this off, at least it will solve one problem."

"Problem?"

"Where the three of us will move when Aunt Viv retires from the stage and wants her house back." He gestured about the room with a frilly-edged scrap of peach satin. "It was crowded enough around here when the three of us were kids. I can't imagine four adults living in this cramped place."

"Yes, I seem to remember your aunt is in theater. Broadway, or something. Right?"

"She's starring in *Hello, Dolly!*"

Chance glanced around, looking at everything but the lingerie on the coffee table. His gaze fell on a framed playbill from a high school production of *Guys and Dolls*.

"Hey, I remember that. Didn't you play a lead role or something?"

"Sky Masterson," Adrian confirmed, then gestured toward the TV with a bra covered in bright butterflies. "Oh, man! That was a strike, you moron. Get some glasses." Snorting in disgust, he returned to folding laundry.

Chance studied him, curious. "Everyone always assumed you'd take up acting professionally. Why didn't you?"

"I had two younger sisters to raise," Adrian answered. "Besides, I saw enough of the acting life when my parents were alive—always on the road, sleeping in cheap hotels, eating cold sandwiches backstage. Not exactly glamorous, or the best way to raise kids." He shook his head. "After our parents died and we came to live here, I promised Alli and Rory they'd never have to sleep on hotel floors or eat bologna again."

The sound of a bat crack drew their attention to the TV as a Cubs player charged past first base and headed for second. "Get the ball! Get the ball!" they both shouted, nearly coming to their feet. "Throw it, throw it, throw it!"

"Yes! He's out!" Adrian punched the air and the dog joined the celebration with supportive barks. "Good play, eh, Sadie girl?"

The screen door banged and Aurora bounded in. "I am so sorry I'm late," she panted, out of breath as Sadie jumped up to greet her. Her skin glowed and her hair tumbled about her in its usual mass of curls. "Our last tour ran long, and then Bobby had a million things he wanted me to do before I could leave. And he *knew* I wanted out of there early."

"No problem." Chance came to his feet, checking his watch. "We still have time, and the Laughing Mermaid is just a few blocks away."

"Great, I'll be ready in five minutes." She started to turn, but her gaze fell on the coffee table. "Adrian! What are you doing?"

"Folding laundry." He looked at the garments, obviously seeing nothing wrong.

"You're folding underwear!" She rushed forward, scooping up piles of panties and bras, clutching them to her chest until the stack reached her chin.

"Whaaat?" Adrian said. "I've been folding your underpants since you were in diapers."

"Not in front of company!" Her cheeks turned bright pink. "Oh, and you're getting them all mixed up again. We've told you and told you, the solids are mine, the flowers and butterflies are Alli's."

"Hey! She who complains gets to do double laundry duty."

"You're right. Sorry. Just don't do it in front of people, okay?"

Adrian settled back with his beer. "You think Chance here has never seen women's panties before?"

"Adrian!" she growled, then sighed in defeat and turned to Chance. "Give me five minutes to change."

"Certainly." Chance offered a stilted smile, even more disconcerted seeing the underwear brush the underside of Aurora's chin than he'd been with it lying on the table. "Take your time."

"Thanks." With the dog bounding after her, she disappeared toward the kitchen.

" 'Take your time'?" Adrian raised an eyebrow, looking at Chance as if he were an idiot. "You're already running late, and you tell a woman to take her time changing clothes?"

More uncomfortable by the minute, Chance shrugged and resumed his seat.

"You don't have sisters, do you?" Adrian asked.

"Actually, no."

"I didn't think so." Chuckling, Adrian took another draw off his beer and turned back to the game. "Make yourself at home, man, you could be here a while."

CHAPTER 5

"How late are we running?" Rory asked as Chance opened the passenger door to his BMW.

He glanced at his watch. "Only a few minutes. It'll be okay."

She smoothed the matte-jersey fabric of her dress as he came around the hood and climbed into the driver's seat. Alli had taken her shopping the night before and helped her select the outfit. It was a simple sapphire-blue tank dress that draped to mid-calf. She'd belted it with a tropical-print scarf and fixed her hair in a single, thick braid that hung to her waist. Her sister had assured her the outfit was perfect: not too casual, not too dressy. But as Chance drove the few blocks to the Laughing Mermaid Inn, she wondered if she should have worn heels instead of sandals, and her arms suddenly seemed far too bare with the air conditioner blowing on them.

"How many people do you think will be there?" she asked, trying to sound calm even though the butterflies in her stomach were taking up all her air.

"I'm not sure," he answered easily. "With all the B and Bs in Galveston, I imagine their association has quite a few members." He looked so relaxed, driving one-handed in his white dress shirt and gray slacks. What would it be like to always know what to wear, what to say, how to act?

Chewing her thumbnail, she watched the houses slip by. They crossed Broadway, the main thoroughfare that connected the island by a causeway to the mainland, then turned down a street where every house on the block had been lovingly restored. The "painted ladies" stood shoulder to shoulder showing off their bright faces and fancy, Victorian trim.

Chance pulled to a stop before a three-story house painted buttercup-yellow with Kelly-green accents. A picket fence enclosed a tiny yard bursting with flowers. White wicker chairs waited patiently for guests on the veranda. On the rail of the second-story balcony, a fat orange tabby napped in the sun.

"Oooh." Rory sighed at the sheer beauty of it, while Chance came around to open her door. "Isn't it perfect?" she said as she climbed from the car.

He glanced toward the house. "The McMillans did a good job. The inn was really run-down when they bought it. You ready to go inside?"

Standing on the sidewalk, Rory held a hand to her stomach. "As ready as I'll ever be."

Chance gave her an odd look. "Are you feeling okay?"

"I'm fine. Just nervous."

"Why?" He rocked back as if dumbfounded.

"No reason," she laughed. "I'm always nervous when it comes to meeting people."

"You're kidding, right?"

"I wish I were." She pressed her hand harder to her stomach to still the little electrical currents jumping around inside.

"I don't understand," he said. "You've always seemed so . . . outgoing, and easy around people."

"Outgoing, yes. Easy around people, no. The doctors call it 'social anxiety.' " She rolled her eyes, trying to make light of it, even as bands of tension tightened around her chest. "Kind of a fancy name for getting the jitters, eh?"

She thought about telling him the attacks of anxiety were just a side symptom of another problem, but he was already looking at her as if she were weird. He didn't need to know why the thought of appearing stupid in front of people nearly paralyzed her.

"You know," he said, "if you don't want to do this, you don't have to."

"No, no," she hastened to say. "I want to. Really. And I'll be fine once I get past the first few minutes. Besides, I've never believed in letting a little fear keep me cowering in the corner." He continued to frown at her, and she forced herself to take her hand off her stomach and place it on his arm. "I'm fine, really. And I want to do this."

"All right." He nodded and turned toward the gate.

"Just do me one favor." Her fingers tightened on his arm. "Stick close to me for a little while, okay?"

Though he didn't say a word, he covered her hand with his and gave a little squeeze. Together they went through the gate and up the steps to the veranda. The front door opened an instant after they rang the bell.

"Chance, hi there! Come on in!" The woman, dressed in shorts, T-shirt, and hand-quilted vest, barely came up to their shoulders. She had a kitchen towel over her shoulder, a cookie sheet in one hand, and a youthful face that called the gray hair on her head a liar. "This must be your friend Aurora."

"Yes, ma'am," Chance said as they stepped into an oak-paneled foyer. "Aurora, I'd like you to meet Betsy McMillan. She and her husband, Ron, own the Laughing Mermaid."

"I'm so pleased to meet you." Rory forced a smile past her anxiety. "Thank you for letting me come today."

"We're happy to have you," Betsy said. "Come on out back and meet everyone." They headed down a long hallway. "Just let me put these cookies on a tray," Betsy said as they entered the kitchen. "Chance, can you grab that other plate?"

"Certainly." He lifted a plate of finger sandwiches from

the counter and they headed out a back door into a courtyard garden.

"Hey, everybody," Betsy called. "I want y'all to meet
Aurora St. Claire. She's thinking about opening a bed-and-
breakfast and thought we could give her some advice."

"Don't do it!" called a gentleman who was pouring tea
from a porcelain pot at one of the umbrella tables.

"Oh, Ron, hush!" Betsy waved a hand at the man while
everyone else chuckled. "That's my husband," she told
Rory. "So just ignore him. Now, let's see, introductions."

Before Rory had a chance to take in the whole scene,
the woman was ushering her around the tables, reciting
everyone's names, where they were originally from, the
name of their inn, and how long they'd been in business.
The barrage of information nearly overwhelmed her. Most
of the couples were older and had turned to inn-keeping
after retiring from other careers. Surprisingly, none were
originally from Galveston—until they reached the last table.

"And this is Daphne Calhoun." Betsy introduced a
heavyset woman with an expansive bustline, carrot-colored
hair, and orange lipstick that bled into the creases about
her mouth. From a gold chain hung a pendant with the
letters BOI, standing for "Born On Island."

"St. Claire . . ." the woman mused in the gravelly voice
of a smoker. "Aren't you one of Vivian Young's nieces?"

"Yes, ma'am," Rory answered, feeling a fresh flutter of
nerves. "I'm the youngest."

"I thought so!" The woman laughed and motioned for
Rory to join her and the young man seated at that table.
"Come sit here. Tell me how that gorgeous brother of
yours is doing. He's the spittin' image of your father. Not
that I knew your father personally, but I surely did love
watching him on stage the summer he and your mother
did *Romeo and Juliet* at the Grand Opera House. I'm surprised the women in the audience didn't flood the building
with drool."

"Gorgeous brother?" The young man beside Daphne came to attention. "Where?"

"Calm down, Steven," Daphne said as Rory and Chance took their seats in the shade of the umbrella. "Her brother's straight. Besides, you're attached."

"Well, a guy can still look, can't he?" Steven complained.

"As long as David doesn't catch you." Daphne smiled like a satisfied cat.

"True." Steven glanced at a man with a stocky build and military crew-cut who was talking to Betsy's husband across the courtyard. Turning back to Rory, he held his hand out for a handshake. "Hi, I'm Steven. David and I run a gay-friendly inn."

"As if she couldn't figure that one out on her own." Daphne rolled her eyes.

"Hey, don't knock it till ya try it, sweetheart." Steven blew the older woman a kiss.

"Like I'd give up men." She snorted.

"My sentiments exactly." Steven sighed dramatically.

Rory laughed, and felt her stomach begin to relax. "Well," she said, "I can see I landed at the right table."

"Oh?" Daphne arched an orange brow. "You're gay?"

"No." Rory shook her head. "But I'm always more comfortable with the rebels in the crowd." She glanced sideways at Chance and found him studying her with thoughtful eyes. She was glad to see he wasn't nervous around Steven, as some straight men would be. Well, at least not too nervous.

"Hey, I like you!" Steven plopped his elbow on the table and dropped his chin in his hand. "What kind of advice can Daphne and I give you?"

"Anything!" Rory said. "I'm pretty much starting from scratch."

"*So You Want to Be an Innkeeper*," Daphne said, nibbling on a pastry.

"Oh, yes, more than anything," Rory said.

"No, dear." The older woman patted Rory's arm. "That wasn't a question. It's the title of a book. After you read that, if you're still crazy enough to want to run a bed-and-breakfast, I say go for it. It's not an easy way to make a living, but it's a great way to live."

For the next hour, Daphne and Steven bombarded her with advice on restoration, hotel codes, and names of suppliers. Chance noticed she looked dazed, but the nervousness had faded. In its place he saw a building excitement that refused to crumble beneath the numerous horror stories.

As the food and the tea finally dwindled, the guests began to disperse. Many of the innkeepers stopped by and invited Aurora to come visit their B and Bs and said they hoped to see her at their next meeting.

"Oh, yes, definitely," Aurora promised.

"And next time, bring your brother." Daphne winked as she made her departure.

"I suppose we should be going, too," Aurora told Chance, although she looked reluctant to leave.

"Hang on," Betsy said as she broke away from the few remaining guests. "I thought maybe you'd like a quick tour of the inn."

"I'd love that." Aurora glanced at Chance, her eyes asking if he minded.

"I'm in no hurry," he said, and realized he wasn't. He would gladly spend the rest of the day watching Aurora. Her enthusiasm was so contagious, he felt lighter and more relaxed around her than he'd felt in a long time.

"Well, then, come on." Betsy led the way back inside. "I had a saleswoman check out of the Rose Room this morning. If you don't mind, I'll grab some linens so I can get the room ready for the newlyweds that are checking in this Saturday while we visit."

"I don't mind at all," Aurora said. "In fact, I'll help."

"You don't have to do that." Betsy waved the offer

aside as she stepped into a laundry room off the kitchen and retrieved a stack of linens.

"No, really," Aurora insisted. "It'll give me a taste of what I'm getting myself into."

"It will that." Betsy laughed and handed Aurora a stack of towels.

Chance followed the two women up the oak stairway, smiling as he watched Aurora. She was so immersed in the moment, he thought a hurricane could hit the island and she wouldn't even notice. At the top of the stairs, Betsy pointed out a small sitting room, explaining that she set out coffee and tea each morning so the guests wouldn't have to come downstairs for their first cup.

"Not that we mind if they come down in their bathrobes," Betsy said as they turned down a narrow hallway. "We're very informal here."

A motion detector at the end of the hall turned the lights on automatically. Aurora glanced over her shoulder and smiled at Chance as if to say, "Did you see that? Isn't it neat?"

Her smile sent unexpected warmth rushing through him. As she continued down the hall, his gaze followed the length of her braid to her swaying hips. How could a woman have such a natural, unpretentious way about her, yet fill a man's head with visions of stripping her naked and kissing every luscious curve of her body?

"Here we are," Betsy announced as she opened a door at the end of the hall. Each door sported a wreath of silk flowers and a small, hand-painted sign with the name of the room. "This is the Rose Room. Not our largest, but it's one of my favorites."

"Ooh," Aurora sighed as she stepped inside.

Chance stopped in the doorway at the sight of the bed. Antique headboard. Mattress waist high. Rumpled floral sheets and a pile of pillows trimmed in lace. And there in the middle of it, his mind saw Aurora, the long, nude length of her lying crosswise, her face smiling, eyes laughing, and her hand reaching toward him in invitation.

Arousal swept through him with staggering speed.

"Chance, isn't it wonderful?"

"What?" He snapped his gaze away from the bed. Aurora stood before a bay window where sunlight poured through the sheer white curtains. She turned in a slow circle with the towels clutched to her breast.

Something unfamiliar stirred inside him, something that had nothing to do with desire. She saw her dream so clearly, wanted it so much. He wondered if he had ever felt that way about anything. Or was he like Paige, calmly accepting the role into which he'd been born? To the point of subconsciously choosing his friends based on social status and his job based on family tradition? Had he ever once questioned if his life were what he wanted, rather than simply what was expected?

The room, the bed, Aurora herself, suddenly held a world of temptation. Standing in the doorway, he felt shaken—as if he'd stepped too close to the edge of a cliff. He mentally scrambled back by turning his head away. Still, he could smell the scent of fresh linens, hear the rustle of fabric as Aurora helped Betsy change the bed. All the while, the women kept up a steady stream of conversation.

The ringing of his phone came as a welcome distraction and he unclipped it from his belt. His relief died, though, when his father's voice came through, controlled, chilled, and angry. "Oliver, do you mind if I ask where you are right now?"

The question jarred him, since his father didn't normally pry into his private affairs. "Is there a reason you'd like to know?"

"I take that to mean the rumor I just heard is true. In that case, do you mind if I ask if you've lost your mind?"

Resentment flared at this evidence that the Galveston Grapevine was in fine working order. Didn't people have anything better to do with their time than talk about each other? Feeling Aurora's questioning gaze, he lowered his voice. "Could I call you back? I'm, uh, losing my signal."

"I take that to mean you're with the St. Claire girl," his father guessed. "Very well, I'll be waiting for your call . . . and an explanation."

An explanation? Since when did his father expect an accounting of how he spent his personal time? Although this wasn't personal. It had to do with the bank and the LeRoche foreclosure, which made it his father's business.

After disconnecting, he turned back to the room to find Aurora watching him, her expression puzzled. He offered both women a smile. "If y'all will excuse me, I'll step out in the courtyard. I think I can get a better signal there."

"Certainly." Betsy smiled and waved him away.

Rory watched him go, wondering if something was wrong. She'd felt the shift in his mood like a change in the air. Although whatever had upset him was likely none of her business. She and Chance were merely acquaintances. Yet her thoughts lingered on him as she helped Betsy get the room ready for the newlyweds.

When they finished, she headed downstairs to look for Chance. She stepped out the back door, but the courtyard appeared empty.

"Chance?" she called, half wondering if he'd left her stranded.

"Over here."

Relieved, she followed the sound of his voice around a rose trellis to a secluded area she hadn't noticed before. Tall shrubs shielded a hot tub from the main house and the neighbors, creating a private alcove. She found Chance sitting on the edge of a cedar deck that surrounded the tub.

"Hey, is anything wrong?" she asked.

"No, I was just thinking."

"Oh?" She stepped closer, unable to read his expression, but unhappiness hung about him like a dark cloud. "About what?"

"About your plan to buy Pearl Island." He rose and

stood before her with his hands thrust deep in his trouser pockets. "So"—he cocked his head to the side—"now that you've heard what to expect and had a taste of cleaning rooms, is your heart still set on opening a B and B?"

"Absolutely!" A smile blossomed from deep inside her. "I know it won't be easy, and you probably think I'm crazy, but I really want to do this."

"I see." He studied her a moment. "Aurora, I have to be honest with you. Your chances of succeeding are not good."

"I know." She fidgeted with the scarf about her waist.

"However." He took a deep breath and met her gaze directly. "I want to help you."

"What?" She stared back, not quite sure what he was offering, but sensing it was something big.

"I want to help you write your business plan. Not just point you in the right direction, but help you with the actual plan. It's going to take a great deal of work, but I know the kinds of things the bank will be looking for. If there is a way for you to have your dream, I want to help you succeed."

"Oh, my God," she breathed, pressing her hands to her cheeks. "Are you serious?"

"We'll need to meet pretty regularly, go over hotel codes, get some bids on the renovations, come up with projected costs for furnishings and fixtures. We'll also need to look into promotional options and operating expenses."

She stared at him, afraid she'd do something silly like cry.

"That is"—he hesitated—"if you want my help."

"If I want your help? Are you kidding!" She flung herself against him and hugged his neck. "You're wonderful! Thank you!" With her arms still around him, she pulled back to smile up at him. His expression caught her off guard and made her heart skip a beat. At this close range, he didn't look scholarly, or cute. He just looked very male.

A flare of heat in his eyes made her aware of her body pressed full-length against his. It didn't feel like the thin body of a geek. It felt lean and hard.

She started to step away, but his arms went about her. "Aurora," he groaned an instant before his mouth descended. He stole her breath as his lips brushed hers, stole her thoughts as his hands spread over her back. A second brush had her pulse humming. He didn't take as some men would, just lightly teased, shaping her lips with his until they tingled.

The tingles spread outward, turning to tremors. She moaned and strained into him, needing more. Finally, his mouth settled more firmly and she tasted wet, hot desire. His tongue nudged her lips, and when she opened her mouth, he carried her away on a wave of sensations.

He kissed her again and again, making her greedy, ravenous. Never in her life had desire swelled within her so beautifully, or with such stunning force. She wanted to crawl right out of her skin and into his.

Her arms tightened around his neck and she returned his kiss with rising abandon. Their heads tilted for better angles as she pressed her body more snugly against his. Breast to chest. Hip to hip. His arousal rose strong and hard against her soft belly, and she moaned with a sweet rush of need.

The sound seemed to jar him.

His lips and hands stopped moving.

She opened her eyes and found him staring at her, their mouths still touching. For one heartbeat, neither of them moved. Then he sprang away.

"Aurora, I—I don't know what happened—I mean . . ." He ran his hands through his hair to straighten it. "When I offered to help you, I didn't mean to imply—What I mean to say is, it would be strictly business."

"Yes, of course. I knew that," she responded quickly, too rattled to know what else to say.

"It's not that I'm not attracted to you, I mean, obviously

I am." He pushed his glasses into place. "It's just that I'm almost engaged to someone else. Well, sort of. Never mind, it's difficult to explain."

"You're engaged?" The air left her lungs.

"Not officially," he rushed on. "It's just always been understood that Paige and I would get married. Eventually."

Paige? He was "almost engaged" to someone named Paige? Did he kiss his "sort-of fiancée" the way he'd just kissed her?

"I see," she said, staggered by an unexpected stab of jealousy. She managed a casual wave of her hand. "This doesn't have to be a big deal. I was just carried away, you know, by the moment."

"Same here." He sighed in relief.

"Okay, then." She forced a smile. "It didn't mean anything. Just one of those caught-in-the-moment kind of things."

"Yes. Absolutely. We'll pretend it didn't happen."

She nodded. "If you'd rather not help me, now, I understand."

"No! I want to help you. This doesn't have to affect that. I mean, I can forget it, if you can."

She held her hands palms-up, smiling as if nothing in the world were wrong. As if her heart weren't pounding and her insides weren't quivering. "It's already forgotten."

"Good. Hey, look"—he glanced at his watch—"it's getting late. I should probably take you home."

She nodded, knowing if she had to hold her smile a second longer, her face would crack. "I'll go find my purse."

The minute she rounded the rose trellis, she pressed a hand to her chest and fought to catch her breath. *Holy cow! Forget that kiss ever happened?* She didn't think she could do that if she lived to be a hundred! Good grief, who would have thought Oliver Chancellor would be such a hot kisser?

CHAPTER 6

The five minutes it took to drive Aurora home were some of the most uncomfortable of Chance's life. While she sat twisting the ends of the scarf tied about her waist, he fought the urge to explain. But explain what? That the course of his life was set and she wasn't part of the plan? Yes, he was incredibly attracted to her, but the attraction was impractical. They were totally unsuited for each other.

Aurora was spontaneous, the type of person to follow her heart wherever it led.

He had been trained from birth to follow the rules. Those rules might chafe at times, but he respected structure. People who lived outside the rules lived in chaos. As much as he desired Aurora as a woman, he did not desire the chaos that would come with her.

So why did he feel so compelled to aid her in her mad scheme?

He couldn't begin to understand the need inside him to see her succeed, but neither could he imagine leaving her to flounder on her own. If he didn't help her, he feared she'd fail. She didn't understand the rules—and passion alone would not turn her dream into reality. He should try to talk her out it, but as he pulled to a stop before the Bouchard Cottage, he realized he'd sooner cut out his tongue.

He turned off the engine and quiet descended.

"Thank you," she said, not looking at him. "For intro-

ducing me to Betsy, and for your offer to help, if . . . if
you're sure you still want to do it."

"I said I did, didn't I?" The words came out with more
irritation than he intended. He wasn't irritated with her,
but with the situation, and with himself for making things
uncomfortable between them. How could he have lost control and kissed her like that? His hands tightened on the
leather-covered steering wheel as he remembered the feel
of her in his arms, the way her body fit so perfectly to his.

And her taste . . . like a drink of some sweet nectar that
was instantly addictive.

He'd been right when he'd thought that "nice" wouldn't
adequately describe the experience. He wasn't sure a word
existed that would describe the heat that had rolled through
him, robbing him of all rational thought.

Aurora St. Claire kissed the way she lived, all passion
and no restraint.

He cleared his throat. "If we're going to do a business
plan, we should get started right away. Before someone
else makes an offer on the house."

"Do you think that could happen?" Fear flashed in her
eyes.

"It's possible, but not probable. The place needs too
much renovating. Even if it didn't, I know how hard it is
to sell old mansions like that from my family's experience," he said, referring to the stately old house that had
been in his family until recent years. "When my grandparents died, we ended up donating Chancellor House to
the state just to get out from under the property taxes,
insurance, and upkeep."

"I thought your family did it as a gesture of generosity."

He shrugged. "That and the tax write-off."

"Oh." She nodded, but her brow wrinkled with worry.
He imagined bending forward and kissing her right there
above the nose, where the red-blond brows were trying to
meet. Then lower, on the light smattering of freckles on
the bridge of her nose. Then her lips . . .

"What do we do first?" she asked.

He imagined several things he'd *like* to do, but forced his mind back to business. "Our first step is for you to have a look at the inside. Are the three of you available this weekend?"

"Weekends are hard for us to get off work. Is there any way we could see it during the week?"

"Sure. Just tell me when, and I'll call the real estate agent who listed the property for the bank."

"Tomorrow or Friday would be fine."

"You got it." He started to reach for his door handle, so he could walk her to the front porch.

"No, don't bother," she said. "I can see myself in, and I've already taken up too much of your time."

"No you haven't. It was my pleasure," he said. Although she was right; walking her to the door would seem too much like a date. "Well, then, I'll call you tomorrow, as soon as I have an appointment set up with the agent."

"Thanks again for everything."

With that, she let herself out of the car and headed up the front walk. He waited until the screen door banged close behind her. He had the strongest urge to follow her inside, but had no idea why or what he'd say if he did. Besides, he'd told his father he'd come by so they could finish their discussion in person, rather than arguing over the phone.

Resigned, he started his car and headed for his parents' house. As soon as he left the east end of the island, the land opened up to fields of tall grass and scrub brush. New developments had sprung up over the years, built around inlets for boat access, while horses and cattle still grazed in other areas. To his left, the white-capped waves of the gulf tumbled and crashed to the long stretch of beach.

Turning into his parents' neighborhood, he parked in their circular drive. He found his father upstairs in the game room, playing a solitary game of pool. Even with the sun still high, shadows filled the dark-paneled room.

A stained-glass pool lamp lit the green felt of the tabletop and haloed his father's white hair.

"Grab a stick," his father said without glancing up from the cue ball. "We'll play a game as soon as I finish running the table."

"Take your time."

Balls cracked and scattered as his father made his shot. The three ball bounced off the side, an inch from the pocket. *"Goddammit!"* Norm swore with more force than was warranted. Straightening, he shook his head at Chance. "I can't believe you'd be stupid enough to go on a date in broad daylight now that Paige is home."

"It wasn't a date. I had a business meeting with Aurora St. Claire about a loan application," Chance replied evenly.

"Business meeting, my foot." His father snorted. "I'm not a fool, Oliver, and I'm not so old I don't remember what a pretty face can do to a man."

"And I'm not so young that I'm ruled by my body," Chance shot back before guilt made him blush, since he had been ruled by his body that afternoon. But that was an exception that wouldn't happen again. Quieter, he said, "I'd appreciate a little credit, and privacy, in that department."

His father studied him a moment, then nodded. "Point taken." He leaned forward to line up his next shot. "I'm just concerned about how this will look to the Baxters, now that you and Paige are 'an item,' whatever that means." He straightened with a contemplative frown. "Why do women come up with things like that? Why can't they simply say you kissed the girl the other night? Why do they have to invent phrases like 'an item'? I swear, sometimes I think they talk in code just so we can't understand a thing they're saying."

Chance blinked, surprised that his father knew about the kiss. "What is it with this town?" he demanded in disgust. "Can't a man do anything without the whole island knowing?"

"Not that I'm aware of," Norm said philosophically. "The rest of the country has Barbara Walters. We have Marcy Baxter."

"I can't believe Paige told her mother I kissed her."

"I would imagine Marcy asked. Oh, by the way, the official report is that you're a good kisser. Not fireworks on the Fourth of July great, but good." His father grinned. "Your mother thinks I should talk to you about that. Give you a few pointers."

"I can't believe this."

"I'd get used to it if I were you. Marcy Baxter's a sweet woman, but she'll be a challenge as a mother-in-law."

"Do you think we could wait until I propose to Paige before we start referring to Marcy as my mother-in-law?"

"Just don't drag your feet too long, son, or they'll plan the wedding without you."

With a curse, Chance crossed to the wet bar and retrieved a Coke from the refrigerator. He set it down and braced his hands on the counter. "Dad, I didn't come here to talk about my relationship with Paige. I need to talk to you about the LeRoche foreclosure."

A heartbeat of silence followed. "I already told you, I'm not going to take Brian's decision lying down."

Chance turned to face his father. "John LeRoche was six months behind on his payments. How lenient do you expect the bank inspectors to be?"

"As lenient as it takes. If John LeRoche had no intention, or means, to pay off his loan, that would be one thing. But that's not the case. He's just hit a temporary rough spot. The First Bank of Galveston did not build its reputation as the neighborhood bank people could trust by foreclosing at the first sign of trouble. And on those occasions when we were forced to take action, we certainly never did it in so public a manner!"

"We're not the First Bank of Galveston anymore. And we're not talking about foreclosing on widows and orphans. We're talking about a man whose financial problems are caused by his irresponsible lifestyle!"

Norm braced his hands on the table, bringing his upper body into the glare of the lamp. "We're talking about the fact that the new owners are using John LeRoche as an example. They are sending a blatant message to the people of this community—not about what will happen if they don't pay their loans on time, but that I'm no longer in charge. *That's* what this is about! It's their way of publicly slapping me in the face, *and you know it*!"

His father's harsh breathing filled the silence that followed. "You're right," Chance said calmly, worrying more about his father's weak heart than the bank. This much emotion couldn't be good. "Which is why I'm asking you to let it go. Fighting them on this is only drawing more attention to it. If you let it go, people will forget about it."

His father continued to stare at him.

"Will you at least think about it?" Chance asked.

An eternity passed before Norm pushed himself upright. *"Dammit!"* He looked away, then back. "You're right. When did you get so smart?"

Chance relaxed. "I get it from you." He thought of telling his father about the St. Claires' plans to buy Pearl Island, thought about broaching the subject of retirement again, but decided to let it rest for now. One small victory a day was enough. These last two years, since his father's heart attack and the subsequent selling of the bank, had taken their toll on both of them. He wanted the dad of his youth back, the man who knew everything and would live forever. He didn't want this role reversal, or this growing stubborn streak in his father.

Gesturing toward the pool table, he fell back into familiar territory. "So, if you're finished warming up, how about a real game—if you're up to the challenge?"

"Oh, so the kid thinks he can take on the champ, does he?" His father's eyes lit with glee as he chalked the end of his cue stick, once again the confident leader of men. "Very well, son. Prepare for your humiliation."

CHAPTER 7

Thursday afternoon, Rory could hardly contain her excitement as she sat beside her brother in the back seat of the real estate agent's Explorer. The only thing that kept her from babbling away was Chance's presence.

He sat in the front seat with his elbow propped on the window ledge, his fist resting against his mouth. He hadn't spoken a word since they'd started for Pearl Island. Was he thinking about yesterday and the kiss they'd shared in the garden?

Her stomach fluttered at the memory of his lips on hers, his hands running over her back, their bodies moving together. Heat flared deep in her belly. She shifted in her seat and forced her mind back to the conversation.

"Someone told me you can't have a gift shop in a bed-and-breakfast," Allison said. "Does anyone know if there really is a restriction against it?"

"There is one within the city limits," the real estate agent answered. The woman, who had the remarkable name of Summer Love, dressed and acted as if she were in her mid-twenties, but Rory suspected she was well over fifty.

"The restriction is intended to keep neighborhoods from losing their residential feel," Summer said. "Pearl Island is out of the city limits, though, so a lot of the restrictions won't affect you."

"Oh, good." Allison, who sat on Adrian's other side, leaned forward to smile at Rory. "The more I think about it, the more I like the idea."

Chance finally turned toward them with a concerned look. "You're thinking of starting a B and B *and* a gift shop?"

"Maybe," Rory answered vaguely. His obvious disapproval made her feel dumb.

Chance sighed. "I'd strongly advise against spreading yourself too thin."

She nodded as Adrian and Alli gave him looks of irritation. None of them mentioned they'd also talked about a catering service and a tearoom. The last few days had been filled with talk and dreams, concerns and excitement. Maybe Chance was right about not doing everything at once, but she could see it all so clearly in her mind.

Summer turned off the main road onto a private drive. A short distance later, she stopped before an imposing wrought-iron gate flanked by a tangle of brush. From atop the red stone columns, gargoyles snarled down at them. Not the least intimidated, Summer lowered her window and punched a series of numbers into a keypad mounted on a post. The gate creaked and clanged as it opened.

The minute they drove through the gate and onto the narrow bridge, Rory spotted the house up ahead and caught her breath. She'd never approached it from land like this, had always seen it from the front that faced the cove. But the sight of it had the same powerful effect it always did, as if someone—or perhaps the house itself—were watching and waiting, and drawing her near.

"When I did my preview of the property, I noticed the bridge is in remarkably good shape," Summer said as she drove. She had one hand on the steering wheel as she glanced back at her passengers with the air-conditioning blowing her long fall of silver hair. "So I don't think you'll need to do any repair work there."

"Too bad the LeRoches didn't keep up the rest of the property." Adrian ducked his head to look out the front window.

Reaching the other side of the bridge, they followed the oyster-shell drive through a stand of oak trees that allowed only glimpses of the house. Then suddenly, they came through on the other side, and there it was: three stories of pink granite with a high-pitched, gabled roof, multiple chimneys reaching toward the sky, and a spire over the front turret. Rory stared, transfixed, as Summer pulled to a stop before the chain-link fence.

"Well, here we are," Summer announced, turning off the engine. "What do y'all think?"

The enormity of the moment hit Rory. After a lifetime of imagining the inside of the house, imagining what life had been like within those walls for Marguerite and her daughter, she was finally going to see it. She sat staring at the wide stone steps that led to the veranda. Even in the bright light of mid-day, she felt as if dark shadows and darker secrets waited beyond that imposing door.

Finally, Chance turned to the real estate agent. "I think we should have a look inside."

"You got it." Summer climbed from the Explorer and Chance followed suit, leaving the three of them alone while Summer took care of the padlock and chain at the gate.

Rory glanced sideways and saw her emotions mirrored on Adrian's and Allison's faces. "You feel it, too, don't you?"

They both nodded and then the three of them laughed, each relieved they weren't the only one who felt the house's presence as if it were a living creature.

"Well." Adrian took a deep breath. "Let's go check it out."

Together, they climbed out and headed through the open gate. Summer led the way up the steps and they waited in the cool shade as she opened the lock box and retrieved the key. A shiver of anticipation raced down Rory's spine.

"We haven't had a chance to get a cleaning crew over

here, yet," Summer said. "So I'm afraid the place is covered with about ten years of cobwebs and dust."

"I'm surprised it's not fifty years' worth," Adrian said, since that was how many years had passed since anyone had lived on Pearl Island.

"I was trying not to scare you off." Summer struggled to fit the key in the ornate lock. The lock gave and the door swung open on rusty hinges that screamed in outrage. "Here we go." Summer motioned for the three of them to precede her.

The temperature dropped several degrees within the thick stone walls, and the scent of dust and age filled Rory's nostrils. She blinked against the utter darkness.

"Hang on, I'll get the lights," Summer said. Rory heard her feeling her way through the dark. "The plumbing and electricity were put in back in the twenties, so the wiring is old, but it does work."

A few dim, worn-out bulbs came on overhead, the only ones working in an elaborate chandelier. The weak light revealed a central hall, as wide as a room, with dark wood covering the walls, floor, and ceiling. A massive fireplace filled the space between two doors to the right. At the far end, a stairway swept upward past three tall, stained-glass windows that had been boarded up. To their left, more doors opened into dark mysteries of rooms beyond.

"Wow," Rory whispered, and the sound echoed.

"It's exactly how I pictured it." Allison walked to the center of the room where she turned in a slow circle and laughed. "Well, except I pictured it much cleaner and a little brighter."

Adrian moved to the fireplace and ran his hand over the carved sea serpents that held up the mantel. The theme was repeated in the carved molding near the ceiling, where tall ships rode the backs of serpents beneath the waves. "Marguerite described it well."

"Marguerite?" Chance asked from the doorway.

Rory turned at the sound of his voice and found him

silhouetted in the sunlight. The glare of light shining around him made his image shimmer. For a moment, his shoulders seemed broader, his hair longer, darker, his white shirt became a billowing, long-sleeved affair.

Her breath caught in her throat as she imagined Captain Jack Kingsley swaggering through the door to steal Marguerite's heart. Then Chance stepped toward her, into the dimmer light of the hall, and the illusion vanished. She saw him as he was, tall, a little on the thin side, with his scholarly glasses and dress shirt tucked neatly into suit trousers. He was always so starched and pressed, she wanted to run her fingers through his hair just to muss him up a bit, to see him flushed and fumbling as he'd been in the garden after kissing her.

With a sigh, she looked away and realized Adrian, Allison, and the real estate agent had disappeared into a room to the left of the entry. "Adrian was referring to Marguerite's diary," she explained.

"Marguerite kept a diary?" he asked. "I'll bet the Historical Society would love to get their hands on that!"

"I'm sure they would," Rory answered with a smile, letting him know her family had no intention of indulging Galveston's curiosity. She looked around, all too aware that she and Chance were alone in the cavernous entryway and standing close together. She glanced back and found him watching her.

Their gazes held as awareness grew between them. The moment lengthened, until their breaths came in slow unison. In his eyes, she saw the memory of yesterday's kiss, and the desire to kiss her again.

Yes. Her body leaned toward him. He leaned closer, as well, opened his mouth as if to speak . . . or taste her lips.

"Hey, Rory!" Adrian's voice echoed from one of the rooms, giving her a jolt. "Come check this out."

She jerked back. "I, um . . . have to go."

Chance nodded and turned away.

What on earth had that been about? she wondered as

she went in search of her brother and sister. He said he wasn't interested in her, but the look he'd just given her had her heart racing.

She found Allison peeking under a white dust cover in the center of the room where fingers of light pressed through the storm shutters to stripe the dusty floor.

"Rory, look at this desk," Allison said. "From the style of the carving, I think it might be original to the house." She straightened and glanced about. "This must have been Henri's office."

"Forget the desk, take a look at these shelves." Adrian glanced over his shoulder. "Hey, Rory, do you think these built-ins would be enough to hold my books?"

Rory laughed at him. "There aren't enough shelves in the world to hold all of your books."

"True." Grinning, he turned toward a wall of sliding panels. "How much you want to bet the music room is through there?" He moved to the panels and searched for a handle. Finding it, he slid one panel open, revealing a dark, spacious room beyond. "Bingo."

"Let me see." Allison hurried past him, her voice echoing. "Oh, Rory, come look."

Rory followed and shared her sister's delight at what they found. Enough sunlight seeped in for them to make out a fireplace of rose-colored marble with gilt accents. In the fresco overhead, Rubenesque women cavorted with mermen while winged cupids took aim from peach-and-gold clouds. Allison peeked beneath a dust cover to find a grand piano with lavish gold-leaf accents.

"Do you know if the furniture is for sale?" Allison asked Chance when he joined them. "Although I can't imagine the LeRoche family parting with it."

"Actually, they don't have any say in the matter," Chance answered. "John LeRoche was notified that anything left in the house after last Friday would be forfeited along with the property. Apparently, he didn't take us seriously."

"So the furniture comes with the house?" Allison asked, glancing from Chance to Summer.

"That's up to the bank," Summer said, directing the question back to Chance.

"We'll need to have everything appraised first," Chance answered. "But since we're in the banking business, not the antiques business, I'm sure we'd rather sell everything together."

Excitement lit Allison's blue eyes. "How much furniture is here?"

"There's a dining table big enough to double as an aircraft carrier in the room across the hall," Summer said. "And a few odds and ends in the bedrooms upstairs."

"Really?" Allison said. "Can I see?"

"Follow me," Summer said, and led the way.

In the dining room, King Neptune ruled the ceiling with seahorses pulling his great shell chariot. More seahorses, serpents, and mermaids adorned the backs of each chair. The room was fit for a king's banquet, and Rory could almost see Henri sitting in the thronelike chair at the head of the table with his beautiful wife seated in the smaller throne at the other end.

"This is where Marguerite met Captain Kingsley," Allison said in a hushed voice. "Rory, what did she write about it?" Turning to Chance, Allison explained. "Rory has the most remarkable memory. She might be slow when she reads, but she remembers everything word for word."

"Well, not everything." Rory blushed, wishing her sister hadn't mentioned her slow reading.

Allison smirked at her. "Tell us what Marguerite wrote in her diary."

Rory glanced sideways and found Chance and Summer watching her with interest. Her stomach fluttered at being the center of attention, but her memory was a gift that made her proud. "The night she met Captain Kingsley, Henri was having one of the dinner parties she'd come to hate. Not the lavish sort of parties Galveston was famous for, but the private parties he threw for the coarsest sea-faring men imaginable."

Moving into the room, Rory pictured them, drunken men in their filthy clothes smelling of sweat. She could almost hear their rowdy laughter. "The men were already seated around the table when Marguerite came downstairs. She was wearing a Parisian gown and the jewels Henri insisted she wear whenever he entertained."

Rory turned and faced the door where the others stood, but in her mind she saw the delicate, dark-haired Marguerite, with her skin as pale as pearls and eyes like blue diamonds. Rory summoned the words from her memory. " 'Tonight at dinner there was a man, a man I've not seen before. He was a sea captain, like the others, and yet he wasn't like them at all. I still can picture how he looked in that first moment I saw him. Seated near the head of the table next to Henri, he was leaning back in his chair, holding a goblet of wine. He watched the room with lazy eyes and a half-smile that said he found the other men amusing but beneath him. There was about him an unmistakable arrogance, as if he, not the painted Neptune over his head, commanded the very tides to do his bidding.' "

Rory moved toward the chair where he would have sat. " 'Then his eyes lifted and he saw me. For the barest heartbeat, the detachment vanished and he looked . . . surprised. He rose with the kind of gallantry I once took for granted and now sorely miss. And as his gaze held mine I saw such admiration that some of the numbness in which I've cloaked myself these past years faded. I felt raw, exposed. Like a person again, rather than a porcelain possession with no purpose save that of being displayed. I cannot recall what he said to me by way of a greeting, but the respect in his voice nearly made me weep.

" 'I could almost hate him for that, for making me feel again. Yet a part of me yearns to see him once more. As painful as it was to be in his presence, for a moment this evening I remembered that I am still a woman, I am still alive, and I am still capable of longing for love.' "

Allison let out a sigh. "That's so sad. It breaks my heart every time."

Rory looked up, and found Chance's gaze on her. Emotions shone in his eyes. Admiration. Desire. Her pulse quickened. Was this how Marguerite had felt that night, when her gaze first met that of her future lover?

"Great, Rory," Adrian complained, breaking the moment. "You've got Alli crying like she does at those phone commercials."

"Oh, hush, Adrian." Allison sniffed. "You're a soft touch, too, and you know it. Come on, Rory, let's go see the rest of the house."

Pulling her gaze from Chance, Rory followed, but inside she felt shaken. For the first time she understood that desire can be welcomed yet feared for the uncertainty it brings. Especially when the one desired was off limits.

CHAPTER 8

Chance watched Aurora's excitement build with every room and every new discovery. The parlor was a large room on the same side of the house as the dining room, with an alcove formed by the corner tower.

"Wouldn't this make a great office for checking in guests?" Rory said. "We can have a desk here, in front of the fireplace, and a sitting area there by the windows facing the cove."

"Wouldn't you want the office across the hall?" Allison asked.

"Actually"—Rory considered—"I think that would make a better gift shop, what with all the shelves."

"You think so?" Allison looked thoughtful as she glanced across the hall. "Yes, it would."

"Hey, wait a second, what about my books?" Adrian protested.

"Sorry, brother, you'll have to put your books somewhere else." Allison offered him a sweet smile.

Chance had to smile at how quickly the older sister got caught up in Aurora's enthusiasm. The only one who hadn't lost his head was Adrian—until they made their way through the butler's pantry to the kitchen.

"Wow," Adrian said, moving into the cavernous room. The red-brick walls, plank floor, and beamed ceiling still held a faint hint of wood smoke and spices. "Now *this* is what I call a kitchen! You could fix a meal for two hundred in here."

"On that old stove?" Allison looked with horror at the antiquated appliances.

"Oh, we'll rip all that out and buy brand-new, commercial-grade equipment."

"You realize," Chance said, "you'll probably have to rewire the kitchen to accommodate modern appliances."

"Hell," Adrian said, "I bet we'll have to rewire the whole damned house."

"You're probably right," Chance agreed. "And new plumbing."

"It can be done," Aurora insisted. Her wounded look made him feel like an ogre for pointing out the negative, but if the bank decided to loan them the money for this venture, he didn't want the St. Claires blindly rushing into anything.

Allison wandered into the back hall. "What's down these stairs?" she called to them.

"The servants' quarters," Summer said as they joined Allison in the space behind the main stairs. There was a large food pantry, a laundry room, a door to the outside, and narrow stairs leading to the basement. "Come on, let me show you. I think if you knock out a few walls, you could convert the space into a very nice owner's apartment. That is, if you plan to live on the premises."

"Oh, absolutely," Aurora answered.

"That's *if* we decide to do this," Adrian answered. "And *if* we can qualify for a loan."

Chance watched Aurora worry over those two ifs as they descended the stairs.

The basement was mostly aboveground with the house so close to sea level. At first they saw only a long, dark hall with cobwebs covering the walls and the smell of earth hanging in the air. Even Aurora looked hesitant to go all the way down. Chance couldn't blame her.

"I know it looks unappealing now, but you have to picture the area opened up," Summer insisted as she moved forward opening doors. Dim light seeped into the hall. "Just look at all the windows."

Adrian followed the agent, glancing into each room. "You know, it could work," he said at last.

"You really think so?" Aurora asked, hope rekindling in her eyes.

"We'll practically have to gut the place"—Adrian nodded thoughtfully—"but yeah, I think it has potential."

"Are y'all ready to see the upstairs?" Summer asked, and they eagerly left the musty basement and headed back through the kitchen to the central hall.

At the base of the main stairway, Aurora stopped. "Did you feel that?" she asked in a whisper.

"What?" Allison whispered back as everyone stopped.

"The room just got cold," Rory said and looked down. "Oh, my God, this is where Marguerite died."

Chance found himself looking down with the others. In unison, they all took a step back so that they stood in a circle staring at the floorboards as if expecting to see a body materialize. When they realized what they'd done, they glanced at each other. He and Summer blushed, but the St. Claires burst out laughing.

"Perhaps we'll leave that little detail out of our promotional brochure," Adrian suggested.

"No, people love a good ghost story," Aurora said as they climbed the stairs.

"Okay, then we'll paint a white outline in the shape of a body," he suggested.

"Adrian!" Aurora glanced nervously about, as if looking for the offended spirit. "Have some respect."

"Oh. *Sorry!*" Adrian said to the house at large.

The second floor had another large, central hall with several rooms opening off it. It had also suffered the most renovations. There were five bedrooms in all. The bathrooms that had been installed were woefully inadequate and Chance saw little choice but to tear them out and start over. Although, much to Allison's delight, the largest of the rooms held an odd mix of headboards, chairs, and even an armoire. She found a fainting couch in the sitting room, which was in the tower where sunlight spilled through the storm shutters.

"These must have been Marguerite's rooms," Allison said, and a dreamy look settled on her face. "Here in the tower is where she'd stare past the cove, waiting for Captain Kingsley to return."

"So," Adrian said, joining them. "We have two large suites, two medium-sized bedrooms, and one small room, all with the potential for full baths." He looked at Aurora. "Will that be enough to make a living?"

"I don't know." She looked to Chance.

"We'll have to run some numbers," he answered.

"Actually," Summer smiled, "you could fit more rooms upstairs."

"Oh, that's right." Aurora beamed. "The ballroom."

They found the stairs to the third floor through a door over the back hall and headed up the dark passage. The steps creaked in protest and a chill snaked down Chance's spine. There was an eerie feel to the air that could almost make a person believe the place was haunted.

They reached the top and stood in a close group, held together by the darkness.

"Hang on," Summer said, her voice echoing. "Let me find the light switch." He heard a click, but no light followed. "Darn, it must have burned out. I'll try to open the doors to the balcony."

As they waited, Chance became aware of Aurora standing beside him. He could smell her faint floral scent, hear the soft rhythm of her breathing. He imagined if he reached sideways, his fingers would brush hers. His skin tingled at the thought.

With a pop and a creak, a set of French doors swung open, and sunlight flooded in.

Aurora gasped in wonder. "Oh, Allison, look." She moved into the large open room. Paneling with a faux finish of pink marble surrounded acres of parquet wood flooring. White columns guarded alcoves created by the gabled windows. And overhead the ceiling arched and dipped with a series of frescoes. The scenes depicted French aristocrats frolicking in lavish gardens. Ladies in pastel satin dresses danced with their suitors, waving streamers of flowers. Bewigged gentlemen pushed ladies on swings suspended by floral chains. The style of the paintings, and the fashions depicted, would have been a hundred years outdated by the time the house was built, but Chance marveled at their whimsical beauty. Henri LeRoche had spared no expense in his quest to impress others with his wealth.

"It's just like Marguerite described it," Allison said, joining Aurora in the middle of the room. "Like the inside of a music box." With arms spread wide, she turned about. "Can't you just picture ladies in ball gowns twirling on the arm of gentlemen clad in formal black?"

"What I picture is four good-sized bedrooms," Adrian said.

"Do we have to divide it up?" Aurora asked, clearly charmed by the ceiling as she turned about.

"And what would we do with it if we didn't?"

"Rent it for parties," Allison suggested.

"Actually," Summer said, "that's a good idea. It would also make a good meeting room for day conferences."

"Conferences." Allison scrunched up her face in distaste. "The room is meant for dancing. For letting some divinely handsome man sweep you around the floor and right off your feet."

"May I?" Aurora said in a deep voice and bowed to her sister.

"Why, sir, I'd be honored." Allison batted her eyes playfully. The sight of them waltzing about the room, one petite and dark-haired, the other as tall and golden as a Valkyrie, made Chance smile.

"Rory, that's not how a man dances," Adrian complained. "You're letting Alli lead."

"I have to let her lead. She's older than me." Aurora laughed as they continued to twirl about.

"She might be older but she's only half your size." Adrian intercepted them as they passed by. "Here, silly, like this." He spun Aurora into his arms and whirled through a series of sweeping turns.

"Now isn't this more fun than dividing it up into smaller rooms?" Aurora said. The two moved with fluid grace, and Chance felt a stab of envy that it wasn't his hands guiding her through the waltz.

"You're right." Adrian agreed. "And with all the other work that needs to be done, it certainly wouldn't hurt to leave it as is for now."

"Does that mean you want to do it?" Aurora asked. "You agree the house would make a good bed-and-breakfast?"

"I think it would make a great bed-and-breakfast." He stopped dancing and turned to Allison. "What about you?"

A slow smile came over Allison's face. "I agree."

"Do you mean it?" Aurora looked from one to the other, hope shining in her eyes. "You really want to do it?"

"If we can get the loan," Adrian said. "I say let's go for it."

With a squeal, Aurora leapt against his chest and wrapped her arms about his neck and her legs about his hips. Then, laughing, she bounded to Allison and scooped her sister off the ground in a hug.

"Rory!" Allison squeaked as Aurora twirled her about. "Put me down. We haven't qualified yet, you know."

"I know, but it's going to happen. I can just feel it!" Releasing her sister, she twirled about the room, spinning and spinning with her head thrown back. "We're going to have the best bed-and-breakfast in all Galveston!"

Summer sent Chance a satisfied look before she addressed the St. Claires. "Is there anything else you'd like to see before we discuss your offer?"

"I'd like to see the kitchen again," Adrian said.

"And the music room," Allison added. "Rory?"

"You two go on." Aurora moved toward the French doors. "I'll be down in a minute."

The others headed downstairs, the clatter of their feet and voices fading, while Chance stood absorbing the quiet that followed. A breeze danced in from the open doors, dispelling the mustiness with the scent of sunshine and surf. On the balcony, he saw Aurora arching against the rail with her head back as she breathed the moment in.

Unable to resist, he went to the doors but stopped on the threshold. What a picture she made, a yellow shirt tied at the waist over faded denim cutoffs, her sun-bright hair flying on the breeze, and the azure waters of the cove stretched out before her.

"So, you're really going to go for it?"

She turned with a laugh. "Did you ever think we wouldn't?"

"No. I had a feeling you would."

"Oh, Chance, you can't imagine how happy I am right now."

He wished he could. God, he wished he knew how it felt to be that free and impulsive just once, without worrying about the consequences.

"Do you think she's happy, too?" Aurora asked.

"She?"

"Marguerite? To know her descendants are finally going to win."

"You're a long way from pulling it off, you know."

"Technicalities." She wrinkled her nose at him, and his body responded instantly. Every time she did that, he wanted to pull her into his arms and kiss her freckles.

She hoisted herself up to sit on the rail. With her feet hooked in the stone supports, she leaned back and threw her arms wide. "Hello, Marguerite! We're finally home!"

"Aurora! Be careful!" He leapt forward, grabbed her by the waist, and plucked her off the rail.

"Oh, my." She blinked in surprise as he set her down. Her hands settled on his upper arms as they stood face to face. "You're stronger than you look."

He glanced into her admiring eyes, and his brain clicked off. Just like that. Every thought vanished—except the thought of kissing her, of tasting her sweetness and feeling the soft press of her body. He knew there was a reason he shouldn't, a dozen most likely, but he couldn't seem to remember a single one.

He lowered his mouth to hers, and tumbled into heaven.

She tasted exactly as he remembered—intoxicating, addictive. His arms went around her, as if he could absorb her vibrancy and spirit. Her head fell back as he kissed her cheek, her ear, down one side of her neck then up the other. When he reached her mouth again, the kiss changed so she was kissing him. With her hands buried in his hair, her lips devoured his and her tongue took free rein. The thrilling curves of her body molded to him and desire sank its sharp claws into his groin. His instant response rose strong and hard against her soft belly. Rather than pull away, she increased the pressure of her hips. His hands slipped downward to cup her bottom and hold her tightly to him.

The rush of pleasure made the ground tip sideways. He staggered back, breaking the kiss. They stood staring at each other, his hands on her hips, hers in his hair, their breathing ragged. When the world settled, his eyes widened with shock.

Hers narrowed with anger. "Don't you dare apologize."

"W-what?" he managed. How had he let this happen? Again!

"I can see what you're thinking." She stepped back and lowered her voice to mimic his. " 'This shouldn't have happened. My interest in you is purely platonic. I'm semi-engaged to someone named Paige.' Well, Oliver Chancellor"—she poked her finger into his chest—"if you don't want to kiss me, then stop doing it!"

"I'm sorry—" He cringed at the fire that sparked in her eyes. "I mean, you're right. I shouldn't have done that." His hands shook as he finger-combed his hair. "It was just the moment, or something. You standing there looking so . . . you know." He gestured helplessly toward the rail. "It just caught me off guard, is all."

She studied him while irritation crackled around her. "We seem to have a lot of 'moments' together."

"Yes, I guess we do. But it won't happen again. I swear." He hoped. One more kiss like that, and he'd lose all control.

Her anger shifted to worry. "You will still help us, though, won't you?"

"Of course." He straightened. "I said I'd help, and I will."

She studied him a long time. "But . . . why? Why would you want to help me when there's nothing in it for you? And you're not even interested in me in a personal way."

"I didn't say I wasn't interested. But Paige is out of college now, and it's time we started dating."

Her brow wrinkled. "I don't understand, how can you be engaged to someone you aren't even dating?"

"It's complicated. As for why I want to help you, I have a lot of reasons. One, it's in the bank's best interest to recoup our losses on the LeRoche loan as quickly as possible."

Her eyes lit with interest. "We should get a really good price then, right?"

"The bank is willing to negotiate a *fair* price."

"So what's your other reason?" she asked.

"Envy, I suppose."

"Envy?"

"Not everyone is free to do as they please in life." He shrugged as if settling a weight on his shoulders. "I envy you a bit for your freedom. And your courage. It takes guts to go after something this big. I admire that in you."

Her expression showed confusion. "You admire me?"

"Yes, of course. A great deal."

"Oh." Disbelief joined the confusion. "Well, then," she said. "What next?"

He relaxed as they moved into the familiar realm of action based on logic. "We get started on the business plan. If I make a list of the documents we'll need, can one of you do the running around during the day to get them?"

"Adrian works nights, so he can do it."

"All right, then." He tried to decide where they should meet. Her house would be safer—more people in and out, less time alone—but he'd be more comfortable working on his own computer. "I, um, don't suppose you have any sort of accounting software on your computer?" he asked hopefully.

She laughed. "We don't even have a computer."

He stared, trying to wrap his mind around that concept. "Oh." How did people live without a computer in the house? "Well, then, I guess we'll need to work at my apartment in the evenings. I mean, if you're comfortable with that."

"I am if you are." She shrugged and beamed at him in a way that nearly made him groan.

He didn't think there was a place on the planet where he'd be comfortable alone with Aurora St. Claire. He'd get through it somehow, though. *Without* kissing her again. "My place it is, then."

God help him.

CHAPTER 9

Chance lived in a very strange apartment building, to Rory's way of thinking. It was ten stories tall with a lobby and an elevator. Walking down the hallway on the seventh floor, she felt as if she were in an office tower or hotel. She knew apartments in other parts of the country were built as high-rises, but she'd always thought this building looked out of place in Texas. Here apartment buildings were only two or three stories tall with private entrances to each unit.

Although with the high-rise situated on Seawall Boulevard facing the gulf, she imagined it offered the tenants spectacular views.

Finding the right door, she shifted the paper grocery sack to one arm and rang the bell. When no one answered, she wondered if she had the wrong apartment number. Numbers caused her endless trouble, since she tended to jumble them up unless she sang them like a jingle. What if she'd gotten Chance's apartment number wrong? What if she wasn't even on the right floor?

Just then, the elevator dinged and Chance stepped off.

Relief came first, followed by surprise so great her eyes widened. *Oh, my God.* The man was wearing running shorts and a loose muscle shirt that showed more torso than it covered. Had she really thought of him as skinny? Lean described him much better. Lean with sculpted arms and hard legs. She tried to swallow and nearly lost her tongue.

When he looked up and saw her, he stopped. "Aurora! You're early."

"I am?" She snapped her gaze from his well-defined muscles to his face and hoped he hadn't noticed her drooling. "Darn it, I never can get it right. I'm always early or late. Never on time."

"That's okay," he said as he unlocked the door, an action that sent biceps and triceps rippling. To think a body like that had been hidden beneath button-down shirts and dress slacks! "What's in the bag?"

"Oh." She looked down, grateful she hadn't dropped the thing. "I brought dinner—some of Adrian's killer lasagna, a Caesar salad, and homemade French bread."

"Really?" He smiled. God, he looked good with his hair all wind-blown and a little sweaty at the edges. Behind the lenses of his glasses, she noticed he had incredibly long lashes that were tipped with gold on the ends. "Sounds great."

Not nearly as good as having you for dinner. She gave herself a mental shake and told her thoughts to behave. "We, um, all decided since you were helping us out in such a big way, the least we could do was feed you."

"You certainly won't get any argument from me there. I'm for anything that spares me from my own cooking." He opened the door and swept his arm in a gallant bow. "Welcome to my humble abode."

She stepped inside, curious to see how he lived. The clean lines of Scandinavian furniture blended nicely with the bomber-jacket leather sofa and chair. Recessed lights highlighted a collection of modern art prints but the corners of the room begged for the homey touch of live plants.

Through the sliding glass door to the balcony, she saw she'd been right about the view. The turbulent waves of the gulf tumbled toward shore beneath a sky that showed just a hint of evening color. In another hour, that color would blaze across the horizon.

"Here, I'll take that." He reached for the bag and carried

it into the kitchen. The room was set off from the living and dining area by a pass-through window that doubled as a small bar. Following him, she wondered how anyone could cook in such a tiny space.

"We might want to pop the lasagna in the oven to keep it warm until we're ready to eat," she said, eyeing appliances so new they gleamed. "Unless you want to eat now."

"No, I think I better hit the shower first." He chuckled as he glanced down at his smooth, sweaty chest. Her hands grew damp as she pictured him stripping off the muscle shirt. Setting the bag on the counter, he scowled at the oven as if it were a beast. "I don't suppose you know how to work one of those. The only things in here I can operate are the can opener, the microwave, and the coffeepot."

She laughed. "You go take your shower. Leave the kitchen to me."

"Bless you." He tossed her a quick grin that stirred memories of how that mouth had felt and tasted. Their gazes held and his smile slowly faded as the moment stretched on.

Awareness shimmered between them like heat waves.

Chance wondered how the hell he would ever make it through the next few days without kissing her again. She'd been in his apartment for less than two minutes, and he already wanted to pull her into his arms and lose himself in that luscious mouth of hers. If only she didn't look as if she wanted the same thing, the lure would be easier to resist.

That in itself seemed like a miracle: Aurora St. Claire, the sexiest creature he'd ever known, was attracted to dorky Oliver Chancellor. Was it a fluke? A quirk caused by gratitude because he was helping her? It wasn't greed, he knew that much. He'd met enough gold diggers to recognize the signs and she didn't have any of them. No, she looked at him as if she wanted to run her hands all over him.

It had to be a fluke.

The phone rang and they both jumped. With a nervous laugh, he picked up the receiver mounted to the wall. "Yes, hi, hello."

"Chance? Is that you?"

"Mom!" His gaze darted to Aurora and guilt heated his cheeks, even though he hadn't been doing anything to feel guilty about. Except in his mind. "What is it? I mean, is something wrong?"

"I'm just calling to visit," his mother said. "Am I catching you at a bad time?"

"No, not at all." He was *not* about to tell her he had a woman in his apartment who wasn't Paige Baxter. His private life might be his own in his eyes, but lately his parents seemed to have a difficult time with that concept.

"Well, good. I had lunch with Marcy today. I did tell you the two of us are co-coordinating this year's Buccaneer's Ball, didn't I?"

"I believe you did," he answered, vaguely remembering.

"Well, we came up with a splendid idea."

"Oh?" He cringed, sensing a trap.

"What would you think about announcing your engagement to Paige at the Buccaneer's Ball this fall?"

Across the kitchen, Aurora bent over to work the controls on the front of the stove, and desire pooled in his gut at the sight of her well-shaped bottom. Turning away, he lowered his voice. "I'd rather not discuss this right now."

"Why ever not?"

With a quick glance over his shoulder, he wished he'd installed a cordless phone in the kitchen so he could slip from the room. "For one thing, because I haven't asked Paige to marry me yet."

"Well, the ball is months away. Surely you'll ask her by then."

"Mom"—he took a breath in a bid for patience—"do you think I could handle my relationship with Paige on my own?"

"Actually, no, I'm not sure you can. According to

Marcy, you two haven't even been out on a single date since she returned."

"Exactly." He lowered his voice as much as he could without tipping her off that he wasn't alone. "We've decided to hold off on dating until she feels more settled, so I think planning to announce our engagement is a little premature, don't you?"

"But you and Paige are so perfect for each other. You have the same friends, enjoy each other's company. I don't understand why you're dragging your feet on this."

Maybe because I don't want my mother picking out my wife. He heard the oven door behind him and looked around in time to see Aurora slide a pan in, then close the door. Without looking at him, she moved around the breakfast bar toward the living area. "Hang on," he told his mother, then covered the mouthpiece. "I'm sorry about this." He held up the phone.

"It's okay." She motioned toward the sliding glass door. "I'll just check out the view while you visit."

"I'll try to be quick."

"No, don't worry. You should never rush your time with family."

"Thanks." He smiled in gratitude for her understanding. And she was right. His mother might meddle at times, but he wouldn't trade her for the world. When Aurora had stepped onto the balcony, he brought the phone back to his ear. "Sorry, I was . . . just checking on my dinner."

"You mean you're . . . cooking?"

"Not really." He hedged. "Just heating something up. I'm glad you called, though, because I have a favor to ask."

"Certainly, dear."

"I know you and Marcy have been friends a long time, and you're both eager for Paige and I to get together. However, I think Paige and I would feel more comfortable if we could go about this at our own pace without feeling like everyone is watching over our shoulders."

"I see." Her voice held a twinge of hurt.

"Now, don't do that," he said. "I refuse to feel guilty for wanting some privacy."

"You're right, I suppose." She sighed. "It's just that neither of you are getting any younger. And if you want to start a family, you shouldn't wait too long. Everyone knows women have difficulty conceiving past a certain age. Plus, toddlers are so exhausting, I can't imagine you'd want to be chasing after one in your middle age."

"Mom . . ." he chuckled. "I'm only twenty-eight."

"And growing older every day," she said. "I'm counting on you, Chance, to make me a grandmother."

"I promise to give it my best shot."

"Just be sure you wait until *after* you're married."

"Oh"—he laughed louder—"so now you're putting conditions on it."

"You young people take certain things too casually."

"Not all of us. Look, I really need to let you go."

"Oh, all right!" she groused good-naturedly. "Just promise me you'll think about making the announcement at the ball. It would be so romantic."

"I promise I'll think about it."

"And a winter wedding—black and white, formal but not stuffy," she said. "With red roses, I think."

"Whoa, I'm still thinking about the engagement."

"That's fine, dear. You take care of the engagement. Marcy and I will take care of the rest."

He shook his head in defeat. "Tell Dad I said hi." After hanging up, Chance headed for the balcony. "Thanks for waiting," he said, opening the sliding glass door. The air had cooled a bit with evening, but it was still hot enough to slap his face.

"No problem." She turned her head with a smile, then went back to watching the beach traffic just beyond the seawall. Sunbathers had given way to couples strolling hand in hand. "You have a wonderful view."

"Thanks. Look, can you make yourself at home while

I jump in the shower? There are CDs in the entertainment center and the remote control for the TV is on the coffee table."

"Actually, I think I'll wait here and watch the action on the beach." Along the edge of the surf, a young boy ran with kite in hand and a small dog barking at his heels. The two narrowly missed a collision with an elderly woman combing the sand with a metal detector.

"I'll try to hurry."

"I'll be here." Rory's smile broadened when he ducked back inside. So, it really was true; Chance wasn't even dating this Paige person. Which meant his objection to dating her was all in his head. As far as she could see, there wasn't a reason in the world they couldn't pursue the possibility of a relationship.

Unless he simply wasn't interested.

No. She dismissed that idea. Any man who kissed her the way he had, and looked at her with those hungry eyes was definitely interested.

Maybe he just needed to know his interest was returned.

The idea bubbled up inside her, making her giddy. She wasn't sure where the attraction would lead, but she was more than willing to find out.

True to his word, Chance was in and out of the shower in quick order. He emerged wearing khaki shorts and a dark blue polo shirt that left just enough of his arms and legs exposed to tease her eyes. She had to smile, though, at how perfectly neat his hair was even when wet. There was something about the man that made her fingers positively itch to rumple him up.

"I thought we'd work in here," he said, leading her to a small second bedroom he'd turned into an office. A daybed took up one wall, a computer desk sat against another. "There's not much room to spread out, but we can make do."

He dragged a dining chair in for her, and held it while

she took a seat. Then he slipped into his swivel desk chair and hit the space bar on the keyboard. The monitor sprang to life and greeted them with Clint Eastwood's voice. "Go ahead. Make my day."

Rory laughed. A second later, hot licks from an electric guitar boomed forth followed by Bryan Adams singing about his first real six-string.

"Oops, I forgot I had that in there." He made a motion with the mouse and the music stopped. A CD slipped out of the tower on the floor, as if the computer were sticking out its tongue.

Rory moved her legs to the side when he bent to retrieve the disc. His arm brushed her calf, sending a jolt through her system. He dropped the disc and nearly laid his head in her lap as he retrieved it. He smelled of soap and shampoo, and the enticing scent of male skin. She breathed in slowly to savor it.

"Okay, now to get down to work." Fumbling a bit, he put the disc back away. "Did you bring your financial statements?"

"We weren't sure what all you wanted, so Adrian just wrote down how much we have in savings and checking and such." From the folder she'd brought in the grocery bag, she pulled out a slip of paper.

Taking it, Chance glanced at the list of figures, his eyes bulging when he got to the last one. "Is this right?"

She tipped her head to see. "That's the money from our parents' life insurance. We didn't need it, so we left it in savings."

He stared at her. "Your parents have been gone for years, though, haven't they?"

"Yes, they died when I was two."

"And this has been sitting in a savings account all this time?"

"Aunt Viv took care of us, and she insisted we save it toward retirement or an emergency or something."

"Aurora." He scrubbed his eyes with his thumb and

forefinger, which raised his glasses. "First of all, you should never have this much deposited in any one bank, because it's over the maximum insurable amount. And secondly, this is a lot of money to leave sitting idle like that."

"It isn't idle. It's earning interest."

His hand moved to his temple while he looked at her. "If I'd had my hands on that money, I could have doubled it four or five times by now."

"Really?"

"Really." He shook his head, staring at the figure again with a look of mild shock. "I can't believe you left it in savings."

"Do you think it's enough for us to buy Pearl Island? If we don't get the loan, I mean."

"No!" His eyes flew wide.

"It's not enough?"

"Actually, yes, it's plenty to purchase the property, but not enough to cover the rest."

"But we could use the property as collateral—"

"Good God, no! This money is the bulk of your net worth. You should never risk your life savings on a business venture. If it fails, you'll lose everything."

"But we don't plan to fail."

"No one plans to fail. But it happens. No." He set the paper aside. "You absolutely should not tie this money up in the business. You need to invest it. Here, let me give you the name of my broker." He rummaged through a drawer. "Reinhart also does money management. Follow his advice, and the three of you will retire rich."

She frowned at the card. "We're not interested in being rich. We're interested in having something we can call our own. Something we built together."

"Still, call Reinhart. At least listen to what he has to say."

"I'll discuss it with my brother and sister." She slipped the card into her pocket.

"All right. Fine. In the meantime"—he turned back to the computer—"let's figure out a way to get you the loan, so you don't have to risk your own money."

CHAPTER 10

"So, what'd you bring tonight?" Chance asked eagerly as Rory unpacked their dinner.

"I asked Adrian to keep it simple, so we could eat in front of the computer." She pulled out two long sandwiches wrapped in wax paper and inhaled the tangy fresh scent. "Cajun shrimp po'boys and homemade french fries."

"That's simple?" He laughed. "You know, a man could get seriously spoiled this way."

Grinning, she dove inside a second bag. "I also brought a whole bunch of catalogs from the McMillans for bulk-ordering everything from specialty teas to those little bottles of shampoo and body lotion. And Betsy gave me this list of how many sets of towels and sheets we'll need for each room." Staring at the catalogs, she shook her head. "There are so many decisions to make."

"We can look over all that later. Did you bring the bids from the contractor on rewiring and plumbing?"

"Got it right here." She pulled out a set of papers.

"Great." Chance took it from her. "You bring the sandwiches. I'll take care of this." He left the kitchen reading over the figures from the contractor.

Rory laughed at how quickly he became distracted with paperwork. By the time she joined him in the spare bedroom, he was already fast at work on the computer. The man had a talent for breaking things down into simple steps that made the grandest schemes seem possible.

"You actually enjoy this, don't you?" she said, watching his long fingers play over the keyboard.

"You bet. It's a type of game when you think about it," he answered, without taking his eyes off the screen. "Punching in numbers, manipulating this and that until each bottom line is exactly where we want it."

"Maybe." She set his sandwich and fries on the desk. "Although why you need the computer to add and subtract is beyond me. From what I've seen, your brain works as fast as any machine."

"I'm not *that* fast." He chuckled.

"Well, nearly. Here, you're ignoring your dinner." She nudged the plate closer to the keyboard, then watched as he worked between bites. She loved the way the monitor lit up his face and reflected little squares off his glasses. Sitting beside him made her insides flutter until she could barely taste the sandwich she was trying to eat. Mostly because she couldn't stop wondering when he would kiss her again. They'd been together every evening for nearly a week, yet he barely even made eye contact, much less a move that could remotely be termed a pass.

"That about does it for the report on projected renovation costs." His eyes scanned the screen. "No, wait." He touched the glass with his finger. "I need Adrian to get me the figures from the restaurant supply company for kitchen equipment. Do you know if he has them?"

When he turned to her, she leaned closer in an effort to distract him. Couldn't they ever talk about something other than the business plan? "I think he's too busy drooling over stoves to make up his mind on what he wants."

For a moment, her ploy seemed to work. His gaze held hers for a heartbeat, then slipped to her mouth before it darted away. "I see. Well." He pushed his glasses up his nose. "Tell him he doesn't have to decide right now, but I need something to go on."

Don't we all? she thought as she set aside their empty plates. Could she have been wrong about Chance? Maybe the man wasn't attracted to her. But then how to explain those two searing kisses?

Stretching sideways, he grabbed a notepad and a pen. "Here, why don't you make a list of everything we're missing?"

She stared at the pad as if it were a snake about to strike. "You want me to write something down?"

"Yes, if you would."

Her heart pounded as she pulled her hands up along her thighs, her shoulders curling back, away from the deadly pad and pen. "I'm, um, not very good at making lists. Besides, I don't need to. I have a really good memory."

His expression showed doubt. "Well, you might have a good memory, but I'd feel better if we had a checklist."

Her stomach churned as he picked up a book they'd ordered from the International Association of Innkeepers and he flipped to a bookmarked page. "Here, read down this list, and I'll make a note of anything we're still missing."

Icy sweat coated her skin. Praying her hands wouldn't shake, she took the book and stared at the page filled with words. Being put on the spot always made the letters jumble even more. If she were alone, and had plenty of time, she could sort most of it out. But she'd never do it sitting next to Chance, one of the smartest men she'd ever met, with him waiting for her to read aloud.

For one desperate moment, she thought she might be ill. On impulse, she scooted forward and propped the book on the desk next to the monitor. "Here, why don't I hold it for you and you can compare their list to ours?"

He looked ready to argue, but shrugged and went back to work. Relief came first, a huge dizzying wave of it, followed by fascination as he typed notes in a new document.

The longer she watched, the easier he made it look. Since she was leaning forward, she noticed the words on the lit screen looked different than the ones on a printed page. They were bigger, and the background wasn't stark white, so they didn't float around or have strange ghost shadows.

Even the typing intrigued her, since he watched the screen as the letters appeared. That seemed so much easier than the kind of typing she'd failed at so miserably in junior high, where she'd had to stare at a book and type blind, never knowing how many mistakes she made until she looked at the paper and cringed.

By watching the screen, he knew instantly if he made a mistake. She was stunned to see that Chance actually made quite a few. Even more stunned that the mistakes didn't seem to bother him. Of course, he didn't have to reach for a bottle of correction liquid over and over again until the page turned into one big blob as hers always had. He simply hit the delete key.

Amazing!

"Okay," he said, startling her out of her trance. "I think that gives us a good idea where we stand. Let me print this out so you can take it to Adrian and Allison."

Since she was sitting closer than usual, and watching the screen more carefully, she realized the box that always appeared before he sent a document to the printer had something to do with spelling. It told him he'd misspelled a word, then gave him suggestions for the correct spelling.

Some strange emotion that went beyond excitement, beyond anything she'd ever felt, tingled inside her as he corrected the spelling of three more words with the computer's help. She'd heard people talk about computers and spelling software, but she'd never paid much attention, always assumed she'd never be able to use anything so sophisticated. But Chance made everything look easy.

When he finished checking the spelling, he hit the print command. "All done," he said. "As soon as we tie up these last loose threads, we can start putting the actual business plan in order." As he turned to check the printer's progress, he caught sight of her face. "Aurora? Are you all right?"

A lump rose in her throat, reducing her voice to a whisper. "The computer checked your spelling."

"Yes, of course. I always run a spell check, since I'm a pretty sloppy typist."

She willed herself not to cry. "Can I try it?"

"What, the computer? I thought you didn't like the things."

"I know what I said, but I'd just like to try, if that's okay."

"Sure." He stood and held the chair for her. "Here, let's start a new document." He leaned over her shoulder and hit a few keys.

She started to place her hands on the keyboard, but pulled back. "I don't know what to type."

"How about 'My name is Aurora St. Claire'?" he suggested, standing behind her, watching the screen.

She glanced up and offered a wobbly smile. "Could you please not stand over my shoulder?"

"Oh, sorry." He took the chair she'd just left and watched her face rather than the screen, which only reduced her tension a fraction.

Biting her lip, she tapped her way through the words: "My name is Aurora St. Claire." Since she was reasonably sure she'd spelled all that right, she added the line: "This is my frist time to use a conputor." She read it over, not sure if she'd made any mistakes or not.

"Okay"—she took a deep breath—"how do I tell it to check my spelling?" He leaned forward to show her and she slapped her hands over the screen. "No, don't read it!"

He looked perplexed and a little offended, but he walked her through the steps without looking at the screen. Her breath caught when a box appeared telling her she'd misspelled "first" and giving her the correct spelling. To her surprise, she wasn't mortified. The computer wasn't human, it wouldn't laugh and call her stupid. It simply fixed the problem.

It was so easy. So damn easy! She covered her mouth

with both hands, afraid she'd laugh or cry. Why hadn't she taken a computer class in high school? How could she have gone all these years assuming it would be beyond her ability just because she'd flunked typing? It wasn't beyond her at all.

It was easy!

She'd walked in here tonight, the same old Rory she'd always been, and now everything was different. Without even realizing it, Chance had opened a door to the world for her.

"Hey, hey," he said, and she felt his hand rubbing her shoulder. "What is it? What's wrong?"

"Nothing. Everything," she sobbed. "I'm just happy! And angry! Where was this dang thing ten years ago? Do you know all the things I've missed?" She turned to him, trying in vain to dry her cheeks. "I barely graduated high school. College was out of the question. Not for everyone who has problems, but for me it was. Maybe I'm just too lazy or stupid, I don't know."

"Hey!" His brows snapped together. "You are *not* stupid."

"I feel stupid, though. You don't know how stupid I feel sometimes. I can't even get a decent-paying job, because I can barely read and write. I can't take a phone message without embarrassing myself. Or fill out a check at the grocery store. Do you know how I got the job at Captain Bob's? I took the application home and Allison filled it out for me."

"I don't understand."

She hiccupped. "I have dyslexia."

"Well, why didn't you tell me?"

"Because I didn't want to hear you say it's just an excuse, that I should try harder. I did try when I was in school. You have no idea how hard I tried, but I can't keep up with other people. I'll never be able to keep up. I didn't want you to think of me as lazy."

"I would never think that!"

"And now to discover I can do this. Me! Stupid, lazy Aurora St. Claire can operate a computer! Will you teach me more?" She grabbed his hand. "I want to learn everything. I'll do anything to learn. Please say you'll teach me."

"Of course I will." He cupped her face with his free hand and glared at her. "But only if you promise to never call yourself stupid and lazy again."

Biting her lip, she nodded. "Thank you." The words came out all choked and broken. "Thank you so much." She threw her arms around his neck and clung tight. When his arms went around her, her sniffles turned to sobs. "I'm getting your shirt all wet."

"I don't care. And I meant what I said. You are not stupid or lazy. You're one of the brightest, most take-charge people I have ever met. It's what I admire most about you."

"You really admire me?" She pulled back to blink at him. Even with her vision blurred by tears, she saw his smile. His face hovered bare inches from her. Her heart lurched when his gaze dropped to her lips, and she wondered if he was going to kiss her. Finally. *Please, yes, kiss me.*

"I admire you a great deal," he said, but when he leaned forward, it was her forehead he kissed in a sweet comforting gesture. Which only made her start crying all over again.

"I'm in love," Aurora announced the following week. "I am completely and totally in love. You realize that, don't you?"

She turned away from the computer, and Chance felt the impact of her smile like a punch in the chest. For one wild moment, he wished she were talking about him rather than the machine that had captured her heart. His gaze drifted over her face, so close and glowing with such joy. How easy it would be to bend forward and touch his lips to hers, to close his eyes and breathe her happiness deep into his lungs.

The thought coiled inside him, tying his insides into knots of aching need.

He shook himself free of temptation. One more night. He only had to get through one more night without slipping up—and then his life would be back on its safe, predictable path. Bracing himself, he pointed to the screen. "You just need to add the figures in the bedding and linens category, and we're done with the furnishings report."

"Not a problem." She turned back to the computer and hit the required command. She had a rather imaginative way of using the keyboard, but she was gaining in speed and proficiency. "You know, I never thought I'd say this about paperwork, but I'm actually going to miss this."

"You have a natural ability with the computer. Not everyone picks it up so quickly."

"You think so?" Surprise showed in her clear blue eyes.

"Definitely." He indulged in a moment of admiring her face, the sheer beauty of the sun-kissed skin, the golden-red brows, the expressive lips. All that blended with her quick wit, her humor, and her generous nature was damn near irresistible. Any man who could spend two weeks in her presence and not kiss her should be nominated for sainthood.

"I'd love to learn more," she said. "If you would teach me."

Dangerous thoughts swirled through his head, memories of how well they'd worked together these last two weeks blended with images of their time continuing on into the future. He pulled back to a safe distance, where the exotic floral scent of her hair didn't seep into his senses. "I'd like to, but you'll be way too busy building your business once you get the loan."

He realized suddenly that she wasn't the only thing he'd miss. Somewhere along the way, he'd gotten wrapped up in the excitement of the project. He understood now what drove people to take such risks. It was more than the prospect of a financial payoff—it was the satisfaction of building something from the ground up.

"Do you think we'll get approved?" she asked softly.

He blew out a breath. "It's hard to say. If it were up to me, I'd approve the loan tomorrow. Unfortunately, I don't work in the loan department. I run operations and handle new accounts."

"So, when we get the loan, you'll be our personal banker?" she asked with a quick grin.

"It would be my pleasure," he said, even though he didn't handle many accounts personally anymore. His management duties took up too much time. But handling the St. Claire account would allow him to remain part of the project in a vicarious way. "Are you still planning on tomorrow being the big day when you turn in your application?"

"Yep." When the report finished running, she sent the document to the printer. "Allison has asked the antiques shop for the morning off, and I don't need to be at the pier until noon. So, we'll come down to the bank first thing."

He retrieved the report from the printer. "Let's go through everything one more time and be sure we have it all in order."

Rising, they went to the daybed, where Chance had lined up all the reports and documents in neat piles. Watching him, Rory wanted to groan in frustration. For two weeks, she'd tried every subtle way she could think of to let him know she would welcome an advance. Honestly, she thought, if the man weren't so intelligent, she'd think he was completely dense.

Neither of them was seriously involved with anyone else. She'd only had a couple of friendly-dating relationships in the past year, and she was certain Chance wasn't enthusiastic about going out with Paige. He never called her, and to Rory's knowledge they hadn't had a single date yet.

So, what was the hold-up? They were both available, adult, and attracted to each other. At least she was attracted. Wasn't he curious to see if there was something more interesting between them than compiling business reports?

They stood by the bed with Chance checking off each item as she put them in the large manila envelope. As the envelope grew heavier, and the bed emptier, her desperation mounted. This was their last night together. Unless something happened within the next few minutes, she would lose her excuse to be alone with him like this.

"I guess that about does it," Chance said, staring at the empty bed.

"I guess so." She wanted to cry. Or scream. With the envelope weighing down her hands, she looked up into his eyes. What she saw made her heart jolt. Finally, his guard had dropped, revealing desire that mirrored her own. He wanted her. She could see it so clearly. And she was tired of waiting for him to make the first move.

Now or never, she told herself and pressed her lips to his. She felt him freeze, and she squeezed her eyes shut. *Don't pull away,* she prayed. *Kiss me back. Please kiss me back.*

He swept her hard against him. His clipboard clattered to the floor. The envelope fell at her feet. One of his hands ran up her back, into her hair as his lips took greedy possession.

Yes! she silently shouted as she lifted one leg along the outside of his thigh. His other hand moved downward to cup her bottom.

"Aurora," he rasped as he kissed her neck, her ear. "Aurora."

"Yes," she sighed just before he reclaimed her mouth. This was more than the simple acknowledgment of interest she'd wanted—far more—but his enthusiasm sent a thrill of joy singing through her. All she could think was, *Don't stop, don't stop.*

If he stopped, he'd start thinking, and that logical brain of his would come up with some reason why they shouldn't be touching and kissing. But it felt so right! Couldn't he feel it, too?

With her pulse drumming in her ears, she pressed her body along the full length of his, hoping to show him the answer was yes, yes to whatever he wanted, *yes*! They fit together so well, both of them tall and lean. She felt his erection rise against her belly and she moaned in approval. If just once in his life this man would act without thinking, they might get somewhere. Later, there would be time to think. Right now, she only wanted to feel.

Tugging the golf shirt free of his shorts, she gloried in the tautness of his muscles against her palm. His hands slipped beneath her shirt as well and a moan rumbled deep in his throat. When he kissed her again, with a hunger that left her dizzy, she guided his hand to her breast.

Don't stop, she tried to convey with her lips and her hands, the press of her body.

In answer, he bent and swept her into his arms to carry her. She broke the kiss long enough to gasp in surprise, then pressed her lips back to his. He walked only a short distance, to his bedroom she assumed, before he lowered her and she felt the give of a mattress beneath her.

The smooth cool spread welcomed her weight and she longed for the hardness of his body on top of hers. When it didn't come, she looked at him and saw what she had feared. Doubt had replaced the hunger in his eyes.

No, don't think! she wanted to shout. Hoping to throw him off balance, she took off his glasses and tossed them aside. He started to protest, but she placed both hands on the sides of his head and brought his mouth down to hers.

He responded with gratifying speed as passion exploded. His long fingers attacked the buttons down the front of her shirt, and when he fumbled, she simply pulled the thing off and threw it over her head. His gaze landed on the swell of her breasts above the neon-green bra. She smiled, realizing his brain had finally given up the fight. He trailed kisses down her neck, and she arched to guide him to her satin-covered breasts. He cupped one in his large palm as his mouth moistened the nipple through the bra. Arousal rolled through her like a wave of heat.

Greedy for more, she tugged at his shirt, until they managed to pull it off together. He threw it aside. She ran her hands over his torso, thrilling to the ripple of his muscles. His body was so beautiful, so perfect.

He removed her bra and cool air brought her nipples to aching peaks. Then came the moist heat of his mouth. She all but melted into the bed from the pleasure of it.

Closing her eyes, she let her body sag into the mattress as he delighted her with his soft lips and the bold stroke of his hands. He molded her like putty, nipping her with his teeth, then soothing her with his tongue as he finished undressing her. The tension built deep within as he kissed her stomach. She writhed beneath him. *Oh, yes. Don't stop.*

His hand slipped down over her belly and between her thighs. Her hips shot upward on a gasp of welcome when he touched her. The world started to drop away and she grabbed fistfuls of the bedspread to hang on. She felt him focus all his attention on her as he concentrated on pleasing her. With his lips pressed just below her belly button, he brought her to the edge with those long skillful fingers.

"Oh, God," she panted, and tried to reach for him, needing to feel his body over hers. "Chance, I need you. Now." *Please, now.* But he continued his quest to drive her mad.

With some vague notion of ravishing him, she shoved at his shoulder, forced him onto his back where she attacked the button and zipper on his shorts. With one jerk, she stripped the shorts and briefs down his legs and tossed them away.

Then she turned back and saw him sprawled fully nude on the bed. *Oh, my.* He was the most gorgeous man she'd ever seen. His body sleek and refined, all of him gloriously

proportioned to his long hands and feet, an image of masculine grace rather than raw power.

His eyes drank her in, as well, and dilated with desire.
Reaching up, he pulled her back to him, wrapping her in
his arms as he rolled her onto her back. Every touch of
his hands, every brush of his lips, made her breath come
faster until she felt dazed.

He settled between her thighs, and she gasped in joy at
the first nudge of him against her. A swift thrust and the
gasp turned to wonder at how quickly and deeply he possessed her. *Oh, my!* Gloriously proportioned, indeed. She
laughed with relief to have him finally inside her.

With shared elation, they moved together, rolling across
the mattress, desperate to touch and taste, both of them
laughing now like children, until they suddenly dropped to
the floor.

They landed with her on top, their bodies still linked,
but barely. For a moment, she stared at his equally stunned
face. His cheeks were flushed, his hair tousled, and she
couldn't help but smile. She'd always thought he'd look
good rumpled, and she'd been right.

A devious feeling spread through her as she settled back
over him. He groaned and gripped her hips in his wonderful hands to guide her as she began a slow, steady ride.

The pleasure built, in her heart as well as her loins, until
she dropped her head back, closed her eyes and soared.
The wonder burst around her, inside her, like a flash of
colored light. She felt Chance arch up to join her—and for
an instant, she felt as if his soul touched hers. She clung
to the moment as long as she could. But when it faded, so
did her strength. She collapsed against his chest, and let
his arms enfold her.

For a long moment, Chance simply lay there, staring at
the fuzzy ceiling, wondering what had happened. He remembered standing by the daybed, checking items off his
list. Then he'd glanced up, into Aurora's eyes. Desire had

hit him like lightning. Everything after that was a frantic—fabulous—blur.

He blinked to focus his nearsighted vision, but it didn't help. "Aurora?" he asked.

"Hmm?" she murmured against his chest.

"Are we on the floor?"

"Mmm."

"How'd we wind up on the floor?"

"Hmm-mm."

He turned his head to see her, and got a mouthful of hair. Battling the wild mass, he managed to uncover her face. Her eyes were closed, her cheeks flushed. "Hey, you okay?"

"Mmmm." A smile spread over her face, and he swore he'd never seen anything more breathtaking.

He kissed her forehead, and held her close for a moment, then eased her down to lie beside him. "Wait here. I'll get a washcloth."

First, though, he had to find his glasses. He finally unearthed them on the other side of the bed, beneath a pair of neon-green bikini panties. The memory of how she'd looked in the candy-colored underwear made his blood stir all over again. Smiling, he put on his glasses and padded barefoot to the bathroom where the glare of the light made him cringe.

As he cleaned himself off, he realized he hadn't used a condom, which was completely unlike him. He never behaved so irresponsibly. Cursing himself, he rinsed the washcloth and returned to the bedroom. The sight that greeted him stopped him in his tracks. His normally neat room looked as if a bomb had exploded. His shirt dangled from one corner of the now-crooked picture over the bed and Aurora's green bra hung from his bedpost. In the midst of it all, Aurora lay curled up like a contented cat in the bedspread, which must have fallen to the floor with them.

The reality of what had just happened hit him full force. He, Oliver Chancellor, had made love to Aurora St. Claire.

If one could call that frenzied attack of lust "making love."
Amazing! How in the world had that happened?

And what in the world should he do about it?

Panic tried to gnaw its way into his stomach, but he
whipped it back. He would handle this situation one step
at a time, and the first step was to restore order. Out of
order, a solution would be found.

Carrying the cloth, he knelt beside her, stopping for a
moment to marvel at her satisfied expression. God, she was
so beautiful with that long, tanned body of hers curled up
in his navy blue bedspread. His gaze drifted down the
length of her, and something more profound than desire
warmed him. This gorgeous, vibrant, incredible woman
had shared her body with him.

Trying to disturb her as little as possible, he set aside
the washcloth and gathered her in his arms. She moaned
in sleepy protest as he laid her on the bed beneath the
sheet, then he retrieved the bedspread and settled it over
her. He should probably wake her. But if he did, she might
start talking. The possibilities of what she'd say had the
panic clawing back into his stomach and right up to his
chest.

Would she expect them to have a relationship now?
Something more than him helping her get her business
started? Surely she realized how ill suited they were for
each other—no matter how incredible the last few minutes
had been.

He clung to that hope as he climbed into bed beside
her. Setting his glasses on the nightstand, he promised himself he wouldn't stay there long, but he needed a minute
to collect himself, just a minute or two to think of what
he'd say. Somehow he'd explain that what had just happened was a dream come true for him, but it didn't change
who they were, or the fact that life had set them on different paths. It was all so logical, though, surely she'd see
his point without any messy emotions or hurt feelings getting involved.

With his head on the pillow beside hers, he watched her sleep. God, she was so beautiful! Cautiously, he lifted a hand and pulled a strand of hair away from her eyelashes, then tucked it into the mass of curls that surrounded her face.

In a moment, he'd wake her and they'd talk—but first he wanted to savor the sight of her in his bed a little longer.

CHAPTER 11

Chance swore he'd closed his eyes for only a second, but when he opened them again, the gray light of dawn was seeping around the draperies. For an instant, he wondered if last night had been a dream; then a soft rump bumped into his hip.

"Aurora!" He bolted upright. She lay beside him, curled up in a cocoon of covers. Which explained why he was freezing from the blast of the air-conditioning vent. She'd stolen all the covers during the night.

"Aurora, wake up!" He jostled her shoulder as he fought for enough sheet to cover himself. When that failed, he scrambled from bed and began grabbing up clothes. He had to get her out of his apartment before his neighbors woke, for her sake as well as his own. He had his glasses, his briefs, and his shorts on before she finally stirred.

"Mmm." Purring like a kitten, she sat up and lifted her arms above her head in a glorious stretch. Chance froze, struck by the sight of her body outlined by faint morning light. The bedspread and sheet had fallen away, leaving her naked from the waist up. Slowly, she lowered her arms and turned to smile at him over one bare shoulder. "Good morning."

He managed to untie his tongue. "Good morning."

"What time is it?" she mumbled as she fell back onto her pillow, her breasts laid beautifully before him.

He forced his gaze to the bedside clock and felt a measure of relief at the early hour. "Not quite five A.M."

"In that case"—she held an arm toward him, smiling like a siren—"why don't you come back to bed?"

His body leapt in eager response to the sensual invitation. He even took a step toward her before he caught himself. "No, I can't." Well, maybe just for a minute. No! He turned away and gathered her clothes. "We have to get you out of here before half the town wakes up and sees you leaving my apartment building."

"Oh, that." She sighed as he handed over her clothes.

"Yes, that," he said as he took a seat beside her and combed his fingers through her mass of curls. "As much as I wish I could keep you here all day, we need to run damage control on your reputation."

"All day in bed sounds like more fun." She draped her arms over his shoulders. "Has anyone ever told you, you have a fabulous body?"

"I have a skinny body," he corrected.

"Naw-uh. Fabulous."

Unable to resist, he leaned forward to give her a quick kiss. Then returned for another more leisurely one. Closing his eyes, he gave himself up to a third, hoarding memories of her taste, her feel, the sound of her sighs. Only, why couldn't all this be happening with Paige? Why couldn't *they* have this sort of wild attraction for each other? Or better yet, why couldn't he combine the two women? Take Paige's social polish and reserve, and add it to Aurora's passion for life?

Because the two qualities would mix like oil and water. Which was about how he and Aurora would mix in the long run.

With regret weighing heavy in his chest, he pulled back—a difficult task with her naked breasts rubbing against him. "We really do need to get you out of here. You know how small Galveston can be when it comes to gossip."

"It's not *that* small," she protested.

"It is when your last name is Chancellor."

"True. But when you're one of the Bouchards, you learn not to care what people say."

For a moment, he wondered how it would feel not to care. He'd always cared what people thought, because the bank depended on the confidence of its customers. Scandal was bad for business. And since the St. Claires were about to go into business, it would be bad for them, too.

"Aurora"—he cupped her face with the palm of his hand—"I don't want people to talk about you because of last night. And they will if anyone sees you leaving my apartment at dawn."

"You're right." Taking his hand, she kissed his palm. "And I don't want anything to ruin last night." Her gaze met his. "It was very special."

Alarm bells went off in his head at her last words. The conversation he'd feared last night was barely a breath away. Consequence. Expectations. He stood abruptly and took a quick step back. "I'll, um, just go get the paperwork out of the office while you dress."

He escaped to the office, only to find the papers they'd compiled scattered over the floor. As he gathered them up, he tried not to think about the woman in his bedroom, the woman with whom he'd shared the most incredible sex of his life. She deserved a man who wanted more from her than fulfilling his fantasies. She deserved a man who had marriage on his mind.

He felt like a complete bastard as he tried to stuff the business plan back in the envelope. As for Paige, he refused to let his mind even go there, other than to send up a quick prayer of thanks that they hadn't started dating yet, because then last night wouldn't have been a mere lapse in restraint—it would have been a betrayal.

His frustration mounted when the papers wouldn't fit into the envelope, even though he knew they'd fit last night. Still struggling with the envelope, he headed for the bedroom—only to collide with Aurora in the hall.

Cursing, he grabbed for papers as they fluttered to the

floor. They landed helter-skelter at their feet.

"Sorry." Aurora laughed while he failed to see the humor. This morning, his life seemed as jumbled as the papers lying between them.

"Great," he complained with more resignation than heat as he knelt to gather the papers. "They're completely out of order now."

"Don't worry about it. I'll straighten them out when I get home."

"Yeah, but you'll never get all of them back into that envelope. How did we fit everything in there the first time?"

"It's the box rule," she said blithely, clearly a morning person while he couldn't function on less than two cups of coffee.

"What box rule?" he asked.

"Haven't you ever noticed that when you take something out of a box, it seems to grow? Like when you were a kid and you'd get a new toy. If you took it out of the box only to find out it was broken, you could never get it back in the box to return it to the store." She wrinkled her nose in that sexy way that always scattered his brain cells. "I'm convinced things change shape the minute you take them out of the container they came in."

"You're probably right," he said absently as he handed her the last of the papers.

"Will I see you later? At the bank?" she asked as they stood. Her shirt and shorts covered her decently, but it was a struggle not to picture her standing there in nothing but the neon-green bra and panties.

"Yes, of course." He scrubbed his eyes and prayed for caffeine. "I'll introduce you to Brian Jeffries, the senior VP over personal and commercial loans. He'll assign you a loan officer, who will take care of you from there."

"I still wish we were dealing with you."

"Even if you were, it wouldn't affect the outcome," he explained as he walked her to the front door. "A loan this size has to be approved by a whole panel of people, not just here in Galveston, but at all the bank's branches in the area. Once they've all reviewed the application, they'll set up a teleconference, hash out their thoughts, and vote."

"Oh," she said in a small voice. "Do you think we'll get approved?"

"I don't know." They stopped at the door, and he hated the thought of opening it for her, of watching her walk away. Now that the business plan was finished, they had no reason to see each other again. "We put together a solid proposal. The numbers look good, but your lack of prior business experience will count against you."

"But you'll put in a good word for us, right?" She placed a hand on his arm, her eyes earnest.

"Of course I will." She looked so anxious, he wanted to take her in his arms and tell her everything would be all right.

They stood for a moment staring at each other. Finally, she smiled shyly. "Will you give me a kiss for luck?"

With his heart already cramping at the thought of saying goodbye, he gathered her in his arms and kissed her. He wished the kiss could go on forever, because he knew it would be their last.

His brief time with her had come to an end.

Regret tore at him as he forced himself to break the kiss. Forced himself to smile. "I'll see you at the bank."

She smiled back, in the way only Aurora could smile, as if a light glowed inside her.

"I'll see you then." She kissed her fingers then placed them against his cheek. He closed his eyes to savor the feel of her touch against his skin. When he opened them, she was gone—with only her faint floral scent lingering in the air.

The sun was just coloring the eastern sky as Rory drove home. With the canvas sides of the Jeep off, the chill morning breeze played with her hair as she joined Bonnie

Raitt in singing "Something to Talk About." She couldn't remember the last time her heart had felt so light. The future stretched before her, filled with possibilities: a business to build, a new home, and Chance.

Pulling under the carport behind the cottage, she left the Jeep running while she finished the song. She wasn't sure where she and Chance were headed, but at least they were finally headed somewhere.

" 'How about love, love, lo-o-ve?' " she sang, smiling as the music drew to an end. *Yes, how about love?* she wondered as she killed the engine. That would suit her just fine.

Quiet descended, reminding her of the early hour. She headed down the stone path through the damp grass of the backyard, hoping she could sneak inside and catch half an hour of sleep before Allison's alarm went off.

The back door squeaked, making her cringe, so she turned her back to the room, easing the door shut.

"Rory!" Allison whispered directly behind her.

"Eek!" She nearly jumped out of her skin and landed facing her sister. Sadie let out a yip of welcome, poking Rory's thigh with her front paws while her tail wagged.

"Shh!" Allison glanced toward their brother's room and lowered her voice even more. "Where have you been? No, wait. Let's get out of the kitchen before Adrian wakes up and starts with the twenty questions." She all but dragged Rory into the bedroom they shared. "I've been frantic, trying to think what I'd tell him if he found out you didn't come home last night, and that I didn't know where you were. You know the house rules—always call if you aren't coming home."

Rory shuddered at the thought of sitting through one of Adrian's lectures.

"So," Alli said when they were safely behind their closed door. "Spill it."

"I'll tell you everything . . . later." Rory flopped down on her twin bed by the window, delirious but exhausted.

"Oh, no, you'll tell me now." Alli sat beside her and Sadie followed suit, making the twin bed very crowded. "Do you know how worried I've been? I even called the police station to see if any wrecks had been reported."

"You didn't!" Rory sat up and gaped at her sister as guilt caught her off guard. Of course Allison would call the police—while she was sleeping off euphoria in Chance's bed.

"You were with Oliver Chancellor, weren't you?"

"Well, yeah," she admitted, feeling like the world's worst sister.

"Rory!" Alli scolded, albeit with less heat. "Why didn't you call?"

"I . . . fell asleep."

Alli gave her an exasperated look, then sighed. "So, you and Chance, eh?"

Rory nodded, and tried not to smile, but happiness filled her like a warm balloon.

"I guess I don't have to ask how you feel about him."

"Oh, Alli, he's the most wonderful man in the world." Rory hugged her sister. "He's smart and kind and sweet. I love the way he's always pushing up his glasses. And how he stacks the papers on his desk so neatly. I love his button-down shirts, even though he looks so incredibly sexy in running shorts. And how he's so helpless in the kitchen. And how he makes my head spin when he looks at me. And *oh,* the way he kisses! I especially love that! I just love . . . *him.*" The enormity of it swelled inside her until she thought she would float right through the ceiling. Spreading her arms, she announced, "I love Oliver Chancellor!"

The words landed on Allison like salt on a wound that had never healed. She shouldn't have been surprised, since her baby sister had been glowing for the past two weeks, but the thought of Rory suffering her own fate tore at her heart.

"So," she asked, keeping her voice light. "How does he

feel about you?" What hope she had that she was wrong died as she watched Rory sag.

"I don't know." Lowering her arms, Rory looked momentarily defeated before the glow returned. "But I do know we're good together! We balance each other, Alli. Only, he doesn't seem to see that. Plus, he has it in his head that he's going to marry some debutante named Paige." Rory wrinkled her nose.

"He's engaged to someone else?" Alli tried to stay calm, but her maternal instincts wanted to tear Oliver Chancellor limb from limb.

"No!" Rory hastened to assure her, obviously seeing the murder in her eyes. "They're not even dating. Can you believe that?"

"I think I missed something."

"Actually, I think it's Chance who's missing it. Like I said, he prefers everything lined up and in order. I think, basically, he's got it in that stubborn, overly organized head of his that Paige would be the perfect wife for him. So, when he deems the time is right, he'll start dating her, ask her to marry him, they'll buy a suitable house, and be the perfectly boring couple with two kids, a dog, and a cat."

Allison rose and crossed to the window. The light had gone from rosy to golden, and the sky promised a clear, cloudless day. Perhaps it was wrong to compare Rory's situation to what she had lived through so many years ago, but the parallels were too similar. Except that Rory wasn't sixteen. Oh, but that desperate, foolish expression she saw in her sister's eyes was exactly what she had felt. Before she'd learned how cruel love could be. Defiantly, she lifted her chin. "There's nothing wrong with leading a simple, quiet life."

"Quiet is one thing," Rory said. "Dull is another."

"You are so like Mom." Just as she had been once, so full of life and willingness to love. Resting her forehead against the glass, she tried to block out the painful memories tumbling through her. "Not everyone needs constant excitement to be happy."

"I know that," Rory said quietly. "And if Chance were in love with this Paige person, that would be one thing. But he's not. I think . . . I think he's in love with me. As much as I am with him. Or could be. Except no one wrote 'fall in love with Aurora St. Claire' on his calendar, so he won't relax and let it happen. I wish he would, though, because I can make him so happy. He needs me, Alli. He needs me to show him life doesn't have to be planned down to the nth degree. Sometimes it can just be lived."

"Except"—Alli squeezed her eyes shut—"he's one of *them,* Rory. People of his class live by different rules."

Silence descended. She felt her sister's stunned gaze on her back. "You think he's like Peter, don't you?" The words held a slight edge of hurt. "Alli, he's not. He would never lead me on with lies just so he could . . ."

Rory's words trailed off since the subject had been off limits for the past ten years. The way Peter had lied to her, seduced her, and then bragged about it to the whole football team afterward was not something any of them discussed. Just as they had never discussed Adrian's bloody knuckles and Peter's battered face. Assault charges had been filed against Adrian, she knew, but the whole thing had been swept under the carpet, thanks to her aunt blackmailing Peter's father with the name of the stage actress he'd been seeing in Houston.

While her family's loyalty had helped her cope with the rejection then and now, it still boiled down to the fact that the offspring of the Galveston elite did not marry girls from the wrong families. They might use them for their own amusement, but they did not marry them.

"Allison," Rory said from close behind her. A gentle hand came to rest on her back. "Chance isn't a user. I know he isn't. Can't you give him the benefit of the doubt and be happy for me?"

"For you, I'd do anything." Forcing her fears aside, she

turned and hugged her sister. "Just be careful, Rory. Don't get your heart so set on him that you leave yourself open for hurt. Take it slow, okay?"

"Of course." Rory pulled back with a smile, but Allison could see from the look in her sister's eyes that it was too late. Rory never did anything in half-measures. She'd lost her heart to Oliver Chancellor, and she'd lost it completely.

Rory saw Chance the minute she entered the bank lobby with Adrian and Allison. He stood behind the counter, talking to one of the tellers. She was startled to see him in a suit. After two weeks of seeing him in shorts and golf shirts, she'd almost forgotten how intimidating he looked wearing business clothes.

And how at home he looked within the hallowed walls of the Liberty Union Bank.

Still, her heart swelled at the sight of him. When he looked up, their gazes locked. Her body tingled with memories of his touch. For a moment, he returned her smile, but then his cheeks darkened and he glanced away. Excusing himself from the teller, he came around the counter to greet them.

"Adrian." He shook hands with her brother, than nodded to both her and her sister. She waited for him to smile and notice the care she'd taken getting dressed in khaki slacks and sky-blue shirt. She'd even tamed her hair into a neat ponytail. But he acted as if she weren't even there.

"I'm glad the three of you could make it," he said to Adrian. "Brian always likes to meet all the parties involved when considering a loan. Especially one this size."

"None of us would have missed it," Adrian said. "And we appreciate all your help on this."

"Don't mention it." Chance motioned toward the hall leading to the offices. "Why don't you come on back?"

Adrian fell in step beside Chance, asking if he'd seen the Astros game the evening before. While Chance mumbled something about being too busy helping Aurora with the business plan, Allison gave her a pitying look.

She smiled to assure Alli it was nothing. Chance was just being circumspect. He was not a spoiled, rich jerk like Peter, who thought he could use and discard people at will.

And yet, a little seed of doubt crept into the back of her mind. Was he ashamed of what they'd shared last night? Or of people finding out there was something going on between them? And people would find out if they continued to see each other—which she assumed they'd be doing.

But what if Chance wasn't planning to see her again? Or to only see her in secret? Well, he better not be thinking the latter, or he'd certainly get an earful from her. She wouldn't be anyone's secret lover on the side.

"Here we are," Chance announced as they reached an open door halfway down the hall. "Brian?" he called to the man behind the desk. "The St. Claires are here."

"Ah, yes." A tall, dark-haired man rose, smoothing his conservative striped tie. He had an angular face and dark hair that had gone silver at the temples. "I'm glad to finally meet you." He spoke in the unfamiliar tones of a Northerner, and his formal manner put Rory instantly on guard. When the introductions were done, Chance started to leave.

"Hang on," she said, and stepped back into the hallway with him, just out of earshot of the others. She searched his face, wishing she could read his eyes, but he stared at the floor. "Is something wrong?"

"No, of course not," he said, pushing his glasses up.

A sick feeling settled in her stomach. This morning, he'd held her and kissed her as if he didn't want to let her go. Now he wouldn't even look at her. "Will you call me later?"

He hesitated for a fraction of a second. "It'll take several days for the loan committee to make a decision."

His impersonal tone hit her like a slap in the face. "I

see," she said numbly. "Well, then, I guess I better let you go."

She turned on wooden legs, her insides shaking.

"Aurora?" he called. When she looked back, his gaze met hers. He searched her eyes as if he had more to say than words could express. Then he sighed and offered her a sad smile. "Good luck. I mean that."

"Thank you." She turned and left him standing there, telling herself over and over she was wrong. Chance hadn't just told her goodbye. He'd call her that evening, ask when he could see her again. Everything would be fine.

But her heart ached with doubt.

CHAPTER 12

Chance stood back, watching Aurora scrub down the seats on a pontoon boat docked beside a sign reading: Captain Bob's Big Bay Boat Tours. The green awning over the passenger area shaded her from the afternoon sun, but a fine sheen of perspiration glistened on her tanned back. In deference to the temperature and the wet job, she'd shed her shirt, so only a fluorescent-orange bikini top and blue shorts covered her body.

God, he missed her.

For a solid week he'd thought about calling her every time he saw a phone. He knew he should have called at least once, but he could never figure out what to say. Perhaps silence was better than hurting her more by saying the wrong thing. Even so, he'd had to fight the urge to turn his car toward her house every time he drove down Broadway. Seeing her now—wielding a soapy sponge and singing along to some tune in her head—he wondered how he'd managed it. And how he would manage to walk away once he delivered his news.

"Yo, Rory!" the man Chance recognized as the boat driver called from the metal building that sat on the concrete pier. The tour boat office provided a sharp contrast to the upscale shops and restaurants that stood beyond it. "I just took a reservation for ten people, so I guess we'll be going out one more time today, after all."

She straightened with her back still to Chance. "But I'm almost finished scrubbing down."

"Sorry, beautiful." The man gave her a wink that made Chance's hackles rise. The boat captain had a broad, hairy chest and six-pack abs revealed by the open white shirt. He also looked as disreputable as the building. "Tell you what—I'll clean her when we get back."

"You will not." Aurora laughed at the man. "You'll leave it for me to do in the morning, you lazy bum."

"Hey, watch who you're callin' lazy." The man pulled on the bill of his captain's cap. "And that's Captain Lazy Bum to you."

"I'll watch you, all right." She picked up the bucket at her feet and held it as if preparing to drench him, even though he was too far away. Playing along, the man jumped back inside.

Rory was still laughing when she turned around—and saw Chance standing on the pier. Her smile faded slowly. Had it been only a week or a lifetime since she'd seen him? How could she have forgotten how wonderfully proper he looked in his neat button-down shirt and suit slacks? He'd slung the jacket over one shoulder, but hadn't gone so far as to loosen his tie.

Her heart gave a happy leap that made her so mad, she wanted to dump the bucket of dirty water over his head. How dare he ignore her for a week after they'd made love, then show up out of the blue looking as if nothing had ever passed between them?

He started toward her, and she told herself she wouldn't give him the satisfaction of acting upset.

"Aurora," he said in greeting when he reached the boat. He actually had the nerve to smile—although it was a sad excuse for one. And his eyes . . . dammit! He had no right to look at her in that hungry way that made her insides quiver. The jerk!

"Chance, what a surprise." She smiled right back at him as her hand tightened on the bucket handle. "We don't see too many suits down here on the pier."

"No, I guess not." He looked tired, she realized. "I came

to tell you, the bank made its decision. I asked Brian to let me deliver the news in person, rather than have you find out over the phone."

The bottom of her stomach dropped out. "Oh, my God." She pressed a hand to her throat and waited for him to smile. He didn't. And she knew. "They said no."

"I'm sorry." His eyes filled with empathy. "God, I'm so sorry."

"But—" She glanced around, trying to get her bearings. "Why? We gave them reams of paperwork! Showed them all the figures you came up with! How could they turn us down?"

He loosened his tie and undid the top button of his shirt. "Some of the members of the loan committee were concerned about your lack of business experience. Just as I'd feared."

"Lack of business experience!" She set the bucket down before she dropped it. "Well, how the heck are we supposed to get experience if we don't have a business?"

"That's always the Catch-twenty-two."

"Well, fine!" She scooped up the sponge and started scrubbing down seat cushions with a vengeance. "We'll just go to a different bank. Or go with my first idea and use our savings to buy the house, then use the house as collateral for a loan."

"Aurora, no." He stepped from the pier onto the boat, which sent it rocking. "We discussed that weeks ago. You should never risk your entire life savings on a business venture. If the business fails, you'll lose everything."

"You don't think we can do it, do you?" She whirled on him with sponge in hand, sending drops of dirty water toward him with an angry gesture. "Is that what you told them?"

"Of course not." He jumped back, brushing at his pants. "You know me better than that."

"Actually, I don't think I know you at all." She flung the sponge into the bucket and water sloshed onto his leather shoes. "I certainly never guessed you were a—a user!"

His head jerked up. "I was up front with you from the very beginning. You knew all along that I planned to marry Paige."

"But you aren't even involved with her!"

"Of course I'm involved with her. Our families have been close friends for years."

"But . . ." Her chest tightened. "Not once the whole time I was at your place did the two of you share so much as a phone call."

"What was I supposed to do?" he demanded. "Call Paige and ask her out when I had another woman sitting in my spare bedroom?"

"I wasn't 'another woman.' I was someone you were helping. And maybe if you'd called her a couple of times, or at least talked about her, I wouldn't have gotten the wrong idea."

"What wrong idea?"

"That . . . that you were interested in me."

"God, Aurora." His expression softened. "I—I don't know what to say. I'm attracted to you, yes, but it takes more than that to make a relationship work. And we're totally mismatched."

The horrible thought came to her that Allison was right. Chance wasn't any better than Peter. Except Chance had the grace to face her and, as far as she knew, he wasn't bragging behind her back. Still, the rejection hurt. "You're wrong, you know, about us being mismatched. I think we're perfect for each other."

" 'Perfect for each other'?" He looked at her as if she were insane. "We're complete opposites."

"I know!" She all but stomped her foot.

He pushed his forefinger and thumb up under his glasses and rubbed his eyes. "Christ, I'm never good at this sort of thing. Look, I'm sorry if I gave you the wrong impression. I never meant to hurt you."

She lifted her chin. "I didn't say you hurt me."

He dropped his hand and gave her an irritated look for so blatant a lie. "And I'm sorry about the loan. I know you had your heart set on starting a B and B."

"If you think I'm going to give up just because your bank turned us down, then you don't know me very well."

"Aurora, be reasonable." He started to step toward her, then apparently thought better of it when she retrieved the dripping sponge. He held his hand up as if to ward her off. "You can't *make* something happen just because it's what you want. Determination is fine, but you have to balance it with good sense."

She resumed scrubbing. "You also can't give up at the very first obstacle you reach," she countered. "It takes courage and hard work to make dreams come true, and a willingness to take a few chances. What about you, 'Chance'? Have you ever taken a chance in your entire life? Or are you too afraid to step off the safe path your parents set you on? Of course, considering the path you were born to, I guess you don't have to take chances to get what you want. Well, not everyone has that luxury."

"I see." His back straightened with offense. "Fine, then. If you want to throw your family savings away, that's your business."

"It certainly is." She slung her hand downward to get the excess water out of the sponge and he sidestepped just in time. "Now, if you'll excuse me, I have work to do."

She turned her back and resumed scrubbing. An eternity passed before he stepped ashore, leaving the boat rocking as he stormed away. In a fit of anger, she kicked the water bucket, which knocked it over and nearly broke her toe. Hopping around in pain, she slipped and fell, landing on her backside in the puddle of water.

Since she didn't know whether to curse or cry, she buried her face in her hands and did both. She hated Oliver Chancellor. Hated him with every fiber of her body! Or she would as soon as she stopped praying that he'd turn around and come back. But he didn't come back, and she knew now he never would.

"Of all the stupid, lame-brained, idiotic things to do," Chance muttered under his breath a week later as he paced the sunroom at the back of the Baxters' house. The room overlooked the private boat docks along the canal. Mrs. Baxter had told him that Paige had taken her friend Stacy out on their cabin cruiser, but was expected back any moment.

He prowled the room, trying not to think about Aurora. An impossible task. Mere days after they'd argued on the pier he'd learned the St. Claires had, indeed, purchased Pearl Island. And they'd paid cash! The idiots!

A few days after that, he'd learned through the grapevine that the St. Claires had secured a sizable loan from a rival bank and were going full steam ahead with the renovations. He wanted to wring all their necks. "They're going to lose everything!"

Just then, he saw the Baxters' cabin cruiser turn into the narrow canal that led to their house. In spite of the vessel's size, Paige steered it effortlessly into its covered slip.

Chance waited as she and Stacy Connely gathered up towels and suntan lotion and donned cover-ups over their swimsuits. The two were laughing and flushed from a day on the water as they entered the sunroom.

"Chance!" Paige drew up short. "What are you doing here?"

Her stunned expression took him off guard. "I hadn't seen you in a while, and thought I'd drop by. Hello, Stacy."

"Hey, Chance." Stacy nodded.

"I hope the two of you don't mind," Chance said.

"No, of course not." Paige laughed nervously. "I just wish I'd known so I wouldn't have kept you waiting."

"I don't mind waiting, although I guess I should have

called." The thought of calling hadn't even crossed his mind. Of course, he didn't seem to be able to think of anything lately except Aurora. The woman was driving him insane! "I could come back another time if you're busy."

"Don't be silly." Paige glanced at Stacy, and some secret message seemed to pass between them before she turned back to Chance. "You know you're always welcome here."

"Besides, I was just leaving," Stacy hastened to add. "Oh, wait, Paul was just asking if you'd want to get together with some of the guys for a round of golf."

"Tell him to give me a call," Chance answered.

"Will do." She hugged Paige. "Thanks again for agreeing to be my maid of honor. Paul will be so pleased."

"How could I refuse after you agreed to serve on the Buccaneer's Ball entertainment committee with me?" Paige said, returning the hug.

"True." Stacy laughed. She glanced at Chance then mouthed the words "Call me later" to Paige. With eyes twinkling, she left the two of them alone.

"I'm sorry if I interrupted your time with Stacy."

"Don't be silly." Paige laughed lightly as she came forward and presented her cheek for a kiss. He'd kissed her like that before, many times, but the fact that he now had to bend over so far to reach her cheek was a reminder that the innocent days of their youth were in the past. Why couldn't she be taller? And smell like exotic flowers? And why couldn't heat flare inside him at the mere sight of her?

"I'm glad you stopped by," she said with a polite smile as she set her sunbathing bag on the wicker end table. The bag matched her gold one-piece swimming suit and long white cover-up. "I've barely seen you since moving home."

"Yes, well, I guess we've both been pretty busy."

"Would you like to sit?"

"Yes. Certainly." He sat on a wicker love seat that was too low to the ground for his long legs.

"Can I get you a drink?"

"Please." He tried to make himself more comfortable.

"Crown Royal on the rocks, right?" She crossed to the wet bar flanked by potted palms and got down a cut-crystal tumbler.

"Yes, thank you." While she fixed his drink his mind raced. He had to get past this business with Aurora and get on with his life. A life filled with the friends he'd grown up with, golf on the weekends, holidays with his family, and the obligatory appearance at charity fund-raisers. To him, these were all routines that felt comfort-able—as they would be for Paige. Even if he weren't set on marrying Paige, he couldn't imagine Aurora slipping seamlessly into that world. They were so different. So wrong for each other. Surely any fool could see that.

"Here you are," Paige said, handing him his drink. Join-ing him on the love seat, she tucked her legs beneath her and looked perfectly at ease on the too short, too dainty furniture as she sipped a glass of ice water. "Can I get you anything else?"

"No, actually, I . . . came here to talk."

"Oh? About what?"

He took a deep breath. "Paige, I know we agreed we'd wait a bit before we started seeing each other regularly, so you'd have time to get settled."

"That was several weeks ago. Five to be exact."

He pulled back, startled. "Has it been that long?"

"Umm." She raised one brow in a look that might have been censure. On Paige? No, he shook the notion off.

"Well." He cleared his throat. "I think it's time we start . . . you know, 'seeing' each other."

"I see."

"I mean, if that's agreeable with you." Her manner was so cool, he briefly wondered if she cared one way or the other.

She set her glass aside and looked straight at him. "What did you have in mind?"

"In mind?"

"For a date. I assume 'seeing each other' will involve dating?"

"Yes, of course." Why hadn't he planned something? "Um, how about a movie?"

"I've always preferred books to movies," she said.

"Yes. Of course. I knew that. But I was sort of hoping for something we could do together." His mind drew a blank. "I don't suppose there's anything you'd like to do."

"Actually there is." She brightened some as she extracted a pamphlet from her beach bag. "Stacy and I were just making plans to play tourist this weekend. Maybe you'd like to join us."

"You mean . . . hit the antique shops on The Strand?" He cringed, remembering the hours of boredom his mother had put him through as a youth.

"No, something more adventurous. A flier was mailed to members of the Historical Society advertising a new boat tour."

Chance nearly groaned at the mention of boats. If there was one thing Paige did get passionate about, it was boats. Sailboats, cabin cruisers, pontoons, or catamarans, it didn't matter. If it floated on water, she wanted to try it out. He, on the other hand, barely knew the difference between a schooner and a skiff.

"Not your typical Galveston Bay boat tour," she continued. "This tour stops at Pearl Island for a picnic lunch at the haunted house. The kick-off voyage is this Saturday."

His mind snapped to attention. He hadn't heard of this development. The property was barely in their name, and already they were offering picnic lunches? How could that be?

"So?" Paige asked, looking hopeful. "What do you think?"

He hesitated, entirely too tempted to jump on this excuse to see Aurora, but knowing he should stay as far away from her as possible.

"Come on, Chance," Paige coaxed, handing him the flier. "It'll be fun. And Stacy could even invite Paul to make it a double date."

"Well . . ." He hedged, telling himself he needed to spend time with Paige. If this was what she wanted to do, he should indulge her. His agreeing had nothing to do with Aurora. "I guess we could do that."

"You mean it?" Pleasure brightened her eyes.

"Absolutely." He glanced at the flier, suddenly eager— to please Paige, he told himself, not to see Aurora. "What time do we need to be there?"

CHAPTER 13

"How many reservations do we have?" Rory asked as she bounded into the tour-boat office, short of breath.

"Not many, and you're late," Bobby answered.

"I know. Sorry." She placed a hand over her stomach, hoping to squelch the beginning signs of an anxiety attack. After two weeks of working themselves into the ground, the day had finally arrived for their first haunted-house lunch run—a trial run, really, to see if the idea would even work. She'd been up since dawn helping Adrian and Allison pack pasta salad, fresh fruit, and sandwiches into ice chests. They'd sent out fliers to the Visitors' Center, the Chamber of Commerce, and members of the Historical Society. Now, if only people would show up.

"Maybe no one noticed the request for reservations down at the bottom," she worried. "I knew I should have told the printer to make it bigger. But that doesn't mean people won't come, right? They'll come. Don't you think?"

"Hey, you're not nervous, are you, beautiful?"

"Who, me?" She gave him a wobbly smile, so nervous she'd been nauseous for the past two weeks. "I know it's early to be starting something like this, but we need it to take off. If Adrian's going to be our breakfast cook, he has to be able to quit his night job at Chez Laffite. Pulling two shifts with almost no sleep would be too much. We have to build up this lunch business while we're renovating so everything will be in place when we're ready to open in the fall."

"Just as long as *you* don't quit before then." Bobby stopped restocking the pamphlet display to give her a disgruntled look. "You're the best tour guide I've ever had. I'll never find someone else with your flair for telling a story."

"Thank you, Bobby." She felt so touched, she wanted to cry. But then, her emotions had been running high lately. "That's really sweet."

"Now, don't get mushy on me." He smirked. "Just promise you'll train your replacement."

"I promise." She leaned over the counter and kissed his bristly cheek. "But first, let's get through today. And hope this lunch run doesn't bomb completely."

"It better not, since I could be making two regular runs in the same amount of time." He returned to restocking pamphlets, but stopped when something out the window caught his eye. "Well, look at that."

"What?" She came around the counter and peered over his shoulder. The parking lot closest to them was filling up fast and several people were heading their way. Some of them she recognized as employees of the Visitors' Center, but there were several tourists, as well. "I guess the fliers worked."

"Guess so," Bobby said, a bit stunned. "I hope we have enough room for all these folks."

"I just hope we packed enough food." She laughed even as a fresh wave of nausea stirred in her stomach. Maybe she'd caught the summer flu that was going around.

"Well," Bobby said with a white-toothed grin, "let's get to work."

She hurried out the door to take up her post by the boat. Staying busy calmed her jitters. As long as she concentrated on work, she didn't have time to worry. Or think about Chance.

No, that was a lie. Chance always lingered in the back

of her mind. The memory of how they'd parted made her heart ache until she couldn't sleep. Which made her all the more determined to concentrate on work, and get over the man.

While Bobby sold tickets, she handed out life jackets to the minors. She was laughing through her usual jokes about feeding passengers to the sharks if they didn't obey the safety rules when the last group to board came up behind her.

"Hello, Aurora."

Her whole body went still at the sound of his voice. A thousand thoughts flew through her mind as her heart filled with pleasure, then pain. When she turned, she saw only him. His gaze caressed her face as if he were starved for the sight of her, too. He smiled, but somehow she felt his unhappiness and it gave her hope. Then she saw the couple behind him and the petite blond holding his arm, and her blood turned to ice.

No. Not this. She couldn't handle this on top of everything else she had to deal with today.

Her spine stiffened. "I'm not sure we have room," she said in a flat tone, as the heat of anger melted the shock.

"Oh, but we have tickets," the little blond said. She wasn't a great beauty, but she had pretty eyes and flawless skin.

"Then apparently we oversold." Rory stepped in their way, and felt like an Amazon next to Chance's girlfriend. *So this is Paige,* she thought. No wonder he preferred this dainty debutante to her. Rory hated her on sight.

"I'm sorry," Chance said to Paige, but his gaze remained fixed on Rory. "I guess we're too late."

"You certainly are," Rory said. *Several weeks too late.*

"I don't understand." The other man stepped forward. "Why did you sell us tickets if you don't have room?"

Rory's gaze broadened to take in the whole group. All four of them had the polished sort of looks that pegged them as members of the Galveston elite. It was more than the cost of their clothing and the cut of their hair. It was something in the way people from Old Money stood, the gestures of their smooth hands, the air of relaxed confidence that surrounded them. Seeing Chance with them, so much a part of them, was even worse than seeing him at the bank. She felt foolish for ever thinking she could capture the attention of Oliver Chancellor for more than a fling.

"Yo, Rory!" Bobby said, coming out of the office. "What's the hold-up? Let's get these people aboard and shove off."

"We don't have room." She glared at her boss, hoping he would catch the message in her eyes. No such luck. Captain Bob was too busy smiling at Paige and her friend.

"Of course we do," he said. "We always have room for beautiful women aboard the *Daydreamer*."

"Oh." Paige blushed rather than roll her eyes as Rory would have done. The other woman, an attractive brunette, just laughed.

Brushing Rory out of the way, Bobby stepped aboard and held his hand out to Paige. "Here, let me find you a seat near the captain's wheel. Watch your step, now."

"Why, thank you," she said as she took Bobby's hand and stepped onto the crowded boat in her yellow silk shorts set and white summer sandals. The tennis bracelet that sparkled at her wrist could have bought the *Daydreamer* with diamonds to spare.

"My pleasure. I'm Captain Bob." He tugged on the bill of his cap. "And you would be . . . ?"

"Paige Baxter."

Baxter. Rory might not have recognized the first name, but she definitely recognized the last. Baxter Homes developed neighborhoods throughout east Texas.

As Bobby found seats for Perfect Paige and the other couple, Chance remained by Rory. "I'm sorry," he said quietly. "We shouldn't have come."

"Why ever not?" She forced a smile that quivered a bit

around the edges. "There's no reason we have to avoid each other. And since we apparently have room, after all, grab a seat and we'll be under way."

Chance found space on the bench beside Paige and watched Aurora cast off the mooring lines. Seeing her again had been a mistake. He hadn't realized how much it would tear at his resolve. But then, he hadn't expected her to look so tired and pale. Not pale enough that anyone who didn't know her would notice, but he wondered if she'd had as much trouble sleeping lately as he had.

Then he snorted at the thought. If Aurora couldn't sleep, it was due to the excitement of a new business. Not because she'd been pining away for him. While she'd been upset about him not calling her the day he'd come to the docks, no doubt she'd gotten over it by now. Gotten over him.

Just as he needed to get past his constant brooding over her.

Their lives had crossed paths briefly but were moving in different directions. Still, he wanted them to part as friends so they could both look back on their time together with fond memories. And without this horrible emptiness he felt watching her.

The motor rumbled to life with a coughing belch of smoke, and they pulled slowly away from the pier. Aurora moved to the front of the boat and picked up a mike. "Good morning, everyone. Welcome aboard the *Daydreamer* for our first Haunted House Lunch Cruise. For you visitors to Galveston, I'll be pointing out several historical landmarks on the way. If you have questions just give me a shout."

Taking advantage of the excuse to openly watch her, Chance sat back and drank her in. The wind whipped her white uniform shirt around her body and the sun backlit her hair, turning it to fire. The rest of the world faded as the pontoon boat wove its way around tugs and barges.

Seagulls dove and begged in the wake of an incoming shrimper.

"Right now," she continued, "we're entering the main shipping channel of Galveston Bay, which as you can see carries a lot of commercial traffic. Before the Houston ship channel was dug, Galveston was one of the largest ports in the South. It also has one of the most colorful histories as the home of notorious pirates such as Captain Jean Laffite. In fact, the cove where we'll dock during lunch is one of the possible locations of Laffite's famous missing treasure."

"Mom said we're gonna go right over a shipwreck," a young boy chimed in.

"We certainly are," Aurora responded with suitable enthusiasm. "But I'll wait until we get closer to Pearl Island to tell you the story, since we have a lot of other neat stuff to see on the way, okay?"

"Okay," the boy agreed, smiling at Aurora as if she were the prettiest thing he'd ever seen. Chance felt a tug of sympathy as he remembered his own crush on her in his youth. It had been painful and intense. And he hadn't outgrown it yet. He was beginning to fear he never would.

"So," Captain Bob asked Paige as Aurora resumed her talk on the history of Galveston. "Where are you from?"

"Hmm?" Paige turned to answer the man while Chance continued watching Aurora. "I live here in Galveston."

"Oh, yeah?" The boat driver sounded especially pleased with that. "And where have you been hiding that I've never seen you before?"

"I've been at college the last few years," Paige answered politely. "Even when I'm home, though, I don't get down to the commercial piers very often."

"You don't like boats."

She laughed. "Actually, I *love* boats! My father does, too. Currently, we own a cabin cruiser and a thirty-two-foot sloop. Do you sail?"

"Honey, I used to be king of the Corpus Christi regattas."

"Really?" Paige responded, clearly impressed.

"Oh, no." Stacy laughed from her seat across from them. "I think we just lost Paige for the day."

"Fine with me." Paul smiled at his fiancée. "Now you'll pay more attention to me."

Chance glanced at Paige to be sure the overly friendly captain wasn't bothering her. She'd turned fully toward the man, so he couldn't see her face, but he heard the excitement in her voice as she and the captain fell into a discussion on sailing. Deciding she didn't need rescuing, he turned his attention back to Aurora.

Half an hour later, they pulled into the cove at Pearl Island and he got his first glimpse of the house. So much had been done in such a short time, he could hardly believe it. Where storm shutters and boards had been, now glass gleamed in the mid-day sun. They'd also torn down the chain-link fence and laid sod on the slope down to the private beach, creating a blanket of emerald-green grass. A path of white oyster shells lined with crape myrtles and azaleas led from the beach to the house. The shrubs were small now, but would form an eye-catching trail as the plants matured.

It seemed odd that they would have landscaped so quickly, but he supposed they'd needed to do the outside first for the lunch run.

Aurora had just finished her story about Marguerite and Captain Kingsley when the boat bumped up to the dock. "And now for lunch." She turned off the mike and leapt out to secure the lines. "Everyone, watch your step," she cautioned as she helped passengers disembark.

"Oh, isn't it lovely?" Paige said as they rose and waited for their turn to step onto the dock. Her eyes sparkled as she linked her arm through his. "I've anchored in this cove before, and have always wanted to see the house up close."

"Do you think it's really haunted?" Stacy asked in a hushed tone.

"Don't worry," Paul said, pulling her snugly against him. "I'll protect you . . . from everything but me." Stacy giggled as Paul kissed her neck. The giggles increased at something he whispered in her ear.

Paige cast them an envious look, then turned away. "The new owners appear to have fixed the house up quite a bit."

"Yes, they certainly have," Chance muttered, surprised by a twinge of resentment. After all the work he'd put into helping the St. Claires with their business plan, it didn't seem right that he should be left out of the execution.

When they stepped onto the dock, he hesitated long enough to catch Aurora's eye. "Have you decided what color you'll paint the trim?"

"Actually, we haven't," she answered without looking at him. To the passengers at large she called, "Just follow the path on up to the house. Lunch will be served on the veranda."

The brush-off wasn't unexpected, but it rankled nonetheless. He brooded over it as he and Paige started up the path.

Rory let out a sigh of relief as she watched them go. Thank goodness Chance and his friends hadn't been the last passengers off the boat. She wasn't sure she could have handled walking right behind them all the way to the house. Her stomach hadn't stopped churning since she'd turned around and found him standing on the pier.

Now that they'd landed, she didn't have the microphone to hide behind. The jittery current in her gut climbed into her chest, making every breath a struggle. She tried to ignore it as she and Bobby followed the passengers up the trail.

"Welcome to Pearl Island!" Adrian greeted the visitors from the top of the stairs. He presented a dashing sight in the big-sleeved shirt and wide leather belt that Allison had talked him into wearing. Rory wished Alli could have been there to see him, but the antique shop had refused to let her off on a Saturday.

"Come. Have a seat," Adrian invited with a sweep of his arm. The actor in him couldn't help but play the part of pirate host. "Let us serve you our sumptuous island delights."

The female guests either sighed or giggled as they made their way to the tables. Rory was glad to see Adrian had managed to get everything set up in time, from the white tablecloths to the candles and fresh flowers. The hanging baskets they'd found on sale added just the right finishing touch to the setting. More than one guest remarked on the beautiful view of the cove as they took their seats. The breeze couldn't have been more perfect, soft on the skin and scented with salt water, the kind of breeze that invited people to sit back and enjoy the day.

When everyone was settled, she joined Adrian by the ice chests to load small bowls of fresh fruit onto the serving trays.

"Good grief," Adrian whispered. "How many tickets did you sell?"

"A bunch," she answered, sharing his excitement in spite of her nerves.

"Although I'm surprised to see Chance here," Adrian said. "I figured he'd lose interest in us since his bank turned us down."

Rory managed a casual shrug. "Maybe he's just curious."

"Maybe so." Adrian lifted a tray to his shoulder. "Well, let's get these people fed."

She took a deep breath and lifted her own tray, planning to ignore Chance and his friends the best she could.

Adrian's laugh boomed forth as he played his role to the hilt. She envied him his ease. She enjoyed people as much as he did, and was just as good at making them feel welcome, so why did she have to be cursed with this horrible, irrational anxiety at times?

Except it wasn't really people that made her panic. It was the fear of making a mistake, of appearing stupid, that caused her nerves to go haywire.

She was down to a handful of bowls on her tray when she realized Chance's table hadn't been served. And that Adrian's tray was empty. She tried to send her brother a pleading look, but he was headed for the iced-tea pitchers to make a round of refills.

Okay, I can handle this, she told herself as she neared Chance's table. She approached them quietly from Chance's back, hoping she could set their fruit bowls down and slip away without him realizing she was the one serving them.

"I hate to bring up a bad subject on such a pretty day," Paige was saying to her friend, "but do you know if we're any closer to finding a location for the Buccaneer's Ball?"

"Unfortunately, no," the brunette said. "Ashton Villa and the Menard Home are both taken that weekend."

"Wait a second," the brunette's boyfriend said. "I thought you were using the ballroom at the Hotel Galvez this year."

"We were," the brunette explained as Rory lifted a fruit bowl and bent her knees to slip it between Chance and Paige. "But they had some pipes break and it caused water damage throughout the whole lower floor. So now we have to find a new location, and on such short notice."

As Rory's hand moved past Chance's shoulder, he started and jerked around, bumping her arm. The bowl tipped sideways, and the fruit headed straight for Paige's lap.

In agonizing slow motion, Rory tried to stop it, only to lose her balance on the tray. It slipped and fell in the other direction. Fruit bowls and the serving tray hit the stone floor of the veranda with a resounding crash that went on and on as the objects spun slowly to a halt.

When the noise finally ended, Rory looked up to see everyone staring at her. Except Paige, who stared at the glop of fruit in the lap of her yellow silk shorts. Chance's horrified gaze bounced between Paige and Rory. Someone at a far table whistled, and then others began to applaud. It was the expected response when a waiter dropped a tray. She should have laughed it off, taken a bow, then cleaned up the mess.

Instead, her chest constricted like a vise around her lungs. She couldn't breathe.

Couldn't . . . breathe.

With the heel of one hand pressed to her breastbone, she ran blindly toward the front door. It banged behind her as she dashed inside, needing somewhere to hide.

"Aurora!" Chance called and ran after her, past a startled Adrian. Adrian started to follow, but Chance waved him back. Once inside, he closed the door, then came to a halt. Rather than the dark musty hall he'd seen before, sunlight filtered in through the doors to the outer rooms. The stained-glass windows across from him bathed the hall and stairs in colored light. The place had a long way to go, but at least the cobwebs and dust were gone. "Aurora?"

Her name echoed into silence. He stood, listening. The thick stone walls blocked the sounds from outside. He strained to hear any noise that would tell him which way she'd gone.

From somewhere overhead came the faint sound of weeping. The eerie echo of it prickled the hair on his arms. Following the sound, he climbed the stairs toward the second floor. The step next to the top creaked—and the weeping stopped. The prickly feeling moved to the back of his neck.

"Aurora?" he called, listening. He heard her then. Not crying at all, but sucking in huge gulps of air. He found her in Marguerite's sitting room in the tower. She sat on the fainting couch, her head between her knees, her hands shielding her face. Her whole body heaved in the rhythm of her heavy gasps.

Alarmed, he rushed forward and dropped to his knees. "Aurora!" A shaft of sunlight came through the windows, nearly blinding him with its stark light. He touched her hair, her shoulder, needing to see her face. "What's wrong?"

"Nothing." She gasped. "I just . . . can't breathe."

"Can I help you? Tell me what to do. Should I call an ambulance?"

"No!" To his surprise, she laughed as she sat up on an in-drawn breath. "No ambulance. It's just . . . a panic . . . attack."

"A panic attack?"

"It'll stop . . . as soon as . . . I relax."

"Okay. All right." He felt a bit panicked himself as he wondered what to do. "Here, lie down." He pressed her back onto the fainting couch. Sunlight gleamed off the dust cover, making her skin look nearly white.

"Oh, God," she groaned, draping an arm over her eyes. "I made . . . a total . . . fool of myself."

"No you didn't." He swung her legs onto the cushion then knelt at the foot of the couch and removed her canvas deck shoes. "You dropped a tray. So what? People drop trays all the time. Besides, it was as much my fault as yours, since I bumped your arm."

"I wanted . . . today to be . . . perfect. And I ruined it!"

"You didn't ruin anything." With his thumbs on the soles of her feet, he began to massage. "Deep breaths. Relax." He watched her carefully as her chest rose and fell. Gradually the deep gasps slowed and steadied. "That's it," he said softly, concentrating on his task. Her long, slender feet fit perfectly in his hands, soft clean skin over fine bones. The nails were neatly trimmed but free of polish.

He moved his hands to her ankles and continued massaging. As her ankles relaxed, he moved up the calves, feeling the muscles dissolve beneath his fingers. Her breathing settled to match his own. He closed his eyes halfway, attuning himself to her body. He thought if he listened carefully enough, he'd hear the beating of her heart.

His own pulse deepened at the feel of her supple skin against his palms. He tried to ignore the stirring of arousal as he smoothed his hands up her shins, curled his fingers around her calves, and drew his hands slowly back to her ankles.

"That feels good," she whispered.

Bowing his head, he continued the long sensuous strokes over muscle and bone. Up the shins, down the calves. Blood pooled in his groin, an ache of wanting he knew he couldn't fulfill. He ran his hands up, then moved his fingers around to press the sensitive pulse points at the backs of her knees. A hum of pleasure reverberated in her throat as he drew his hands downward to massage her ankles. She moaned again and the rush of his desire became harder to ignore.

"I think you need to stop," she murmured in a husky voice.

His hands stilled on the tops of her feet. Opening his eyes, he let his gaze travel up the length of her bare legs, over her flat stomach and full breasts, to her face. She looked back with eyes that mirrored his need.

"Yeah, I guess you're right." He offered a lopsided smile, then kissed the tip of one toe before rising. She sat up, swinging her legs to the side, and he took a seat beside her.

"Feel better?" he asked.

"Yes and no."

Her humorless laugh perfectly expressed his own frustration. He was sitting alone with Aurora, his body aroused, while the woman he intended to marry sat right outside. Not one of his prouder moments, even knowing he wouldn't give in to temptation.

"I should get back downstairs," she said. "And clean up the mess I made."

"Not yet." He placed his hand over hers. "Give yourself a minute."

She started to argue, then relaxed and nodded.

"So, um . . ." He searched for a neutral topic. "How go the renovations?"

"We approved the plans from the contractor yesterday." Her expression turned sad as she looked about. "I guess next week they'll start tearing the place up."

"You knew they would, though. When you decided to convert the house to an inn."

"I should have, yes. But I guess I saw it more as restoring what once had been." She shook her head. "You can never recapture the past, though, can you?"

"No, I guess not." Their eyes met for a moment. "So"—he cleared his throat—"how are you doing with the bookkeeping? Did you get the software I told you about?"

She groaned. "I haven't even gotten a computer yet."

"Then how are you keeping track of everything?"

"By sticking all the receipts in a shoe box." She offered a sheepish grin.

"Aurora—"

"No, don't even start." She stood and moved away, to gaze out toward the cove. "We'll manage on our own. We aren't helpless, and how we do things is no longer your business."

"I see." He frowned over that for a minute. "I wish it were, though."

"Were what?" Irritation edged into her voice.

"I wish it were my business." Surprise came first at how much he wanted it, followed by excitement. "I mean that. Literally."

She gave him a wary look. "I'm not sure I understand."

"Aurora . . ." He spoke carefully as figures, data, potential, and risks clicked through his brain at lightning speed. In the end, none of the numbers mattered, only the sense

of exhilaration singing in his veins. He lifted his gaze to
hers. "Would the three of you consider taking on a partner?"

"A partner?" She drew her head back.

"I'm serious. I can put up an amount equal to whatever
portion of the business you're willing to sell. And I'd be
an asset. I could handle the books, be involved as much
or as little as you want, as long as it doesn't interfere with
my duties at the bank, of course."

"But . . . why would you want to?"

The answer came with startling ease. "Remember the
day you came by my office and said how nice it must have
been to grow up knowing what I'd do with my life?"

"Did I say that?"

"Something to that effect. The point is, I never picked
my future. It was just handed to me, and I never questioned
it. Banking is what the Chancellor men have done for a
hundred and fifty years. I'm a Chancellor, so I became a
banker."

"Are you saying you don't like being a banker?"

"I—" He hesitated, searching within. "I thought I did.
But maybe I should at least try something else before I
settle down."

"Before you settle down," Rory echoed. As in, before
he committed himself to married life with Perfect Paige.
Is that what she had been to him? An experiment to see
what else was out there before he settled down to marriage? Well, apparently he'd decided his little debutante
was the right one, after all. "How do you think Paige will
feel about your going into business with me?"

Some of the enthusiasm dimmed from his eyes. "I—I
don't know." He rose to pace as he thought aloud. "I don't
see how it would matter. I'd be going into business with
all three of you—not just you. So there'd be no reason for
her to be jealous."

"Maybe not of me, but what about the inn?" At his look

of confusion, she continued. "Do you have any idea how many hours the three of us are putting into this every week? We have no time for personal lives. We have our regular jobs and this. Are you willing to give up all your evenings and weekends?"

"You're right, I'll need to juggle my schedule a bit so Paige won't feel ignored. But it can be done." *So much for playing golf with the guys on the weekends, though.*

"Chance"—she stared at him—"won't you feel awkward working with me? After we . . . after what happened?"

His gaze held hers. "Would it be so hard for us to be friends?"

"I . . . don't know." She turned away, needing some distance to think all this through. "I'll have to talk to Adrian and Allison."

"Yes, of course. Will you call me as soon as you decide? We'll need to have papers drawn up, with everything spelled out so all of us are comfortable."

She nodded. "I better get back to work."

"I'll go with you." He fell into step beside her. "You know, I wonder why I didn't think of this while we were working on the business plan. We'd have had better luck getting the loan from Liberty Union if they'd known I was willing to put up capital."

She stared at him, wondering how he could be so happy when she was so miserable. But then, why wouldn't he be? He had the woman he wanted waiting outside, a job at the bank, and the possibility of a business on the side. Just as long as he didn't plan to have her on the side, as well.

If he so much as suggested that, she'd give him a knee right to his vitals.

Halfway down the steps, he stopped and looked around. "Aurora?"

"Yes?"

"Right before I found you, were you crying?"

She snorted. "I was too busy trying to breathe to waste time crying. Why do you ask?"

"No reason." He shook his head and they continued down the steps.

The thought of facing the tourists outside had her stomach churning again, but it couldn't be helped. She just hoped she made it through the afternoon without getting ill. One humiliation a day was all she could handle.

CHAPTER 14

By the time Rory got off work, the nausea had grown so intense, she was sure she'd caught the flu. *What a perfect end to a perfectly rotten day,* she thought. The last thing she needed was to be laid up with a stomach virus while there was so much work to do.

Of course, there was one other possibility. A possibility that didn't even bear thinking about. She tried to count the days since her last period, but couldn't remember.

Deciding to rule out the unthinkable, she stopped at a pharmacy on the way home to pick up something for her stomach and an early pregnancy test. Thankfully, the person working the cash register wasn't anyone she knew, so she didn't have to suffer any questioning looks or raised eyebrows.

When she reached the cottage she heard Allison and Adrian in the kitchen, but headed straight for the bathroom. Five minutes later, she lost what little food she'd managed to eat that day. Cold sweat coated her brow by the time she joined her brother and sister.

"Hey, Rory." Allison turned from the stove with a smile. "Adrian was just telling me about your great day."

"Great day?" Rory collapsed at the kitchen table, too shaken to even give Sadie an absentminded pet.

"We filled nearly every seat." Adrian retrieved a fresh tomato to add to the cucumber on the chopping block. "Which means no leftovers for us tonight." Grinning broadly, he twirled a knife and started chopping. Rory looked away from all sight of food as her stomach rolled. "If the lunch runs are going to be this popular, we may need to add another day—if Bobby is willing."

"How'd we do money-wise?" Allison asked.

"I'm not sure." Rory dropped her forehead to her arms on the table and concentrated on taking slow steady breaths. "I'll figure it out with Bobby tomorrow."

"Are you okay?" Allison put the lid on the soup, and joined Rory at the table. Taking the chair next to her, she ran a motherly hand over her hair.

"Oh, I'm dandy." She laughed without humor. "Why wouldn't I be on the most miserable day of my life? After the disastrous lunch, I had to do two more regular tours."

"But Adrian said the lunch run went great."

"Did he tell you Chance was there?" She lifted her head and pushed her hair off her clammy forehead.

"No, he did not." Allison spared their brother an irritated look.

"And he brought a date," Rory added.

"He what?" Allison's flare of anger dissolved quickly to sympathy. "Rory, that's awful. How'd you handle it?"

Rory groaned. "I dropped a bowl of fruit in her lap."

"You didn't!"

"Well, not on purpose," she insisted, then covered her face. "I was such a dork, I ran inside to hide, and Chance ran after me, which just made everything that much more embarrassing."

"Rory, it wasn't that bad," Adrian said from the chopping block. "People probably assumed the two of you were going to get towels or something."

"And when we didn't come back?"

"They were too busy having orgasms over my Caribbean pasta salad to notice how long you were gone," Adrian said. "But what's the big deal about Chance bringing a date? It's not like you're interested in him."

Rory stared at her brother, wondering how he could be so dense when she'd done nothing to hide her attraction to Chance. "Actually, I was very interested."

Adrian's eyes widened. "In Oliver Chancellor?"

"Yes, Oliver Chancellor, who happens to be one of the smartest and sexiest men I've ever known."

Adrian laughed. "So *that's* why you two were gone so long?"

"No, it's not." Rory looked away, trying to decide how much to tell them and where to begin. "Chance asked if we'd consider taking him on as a partner."

"Well, that's sort of out of the blue, don't you think?" Adrian finished the tomato and started on some carrots.

"Not really," Rory said. "Considering how much time he spent helping us with the business plan."

Adrian shrugged. "I figured he was just hoping to score with you. And when he realized you weren't interested, or at least I thought you weren't interested, he gave up."

"That's not exactly how it happened." Rory plucked at the hem of her shorts.

"What do you mean?" Adrian scraped the vegetables into the salad bowl.

Rory exchanged a look with her sister before she forced herself to admit the truth. "Chance is the one who isn't interested. At least, not now. Not after . . . not after he got what he wanted."

Adrian halted with the knife still in hand. "What are you saying?"

Tears welled up in Rory's eyes. "I'm pregnant."

Adrian's heart stopped as he stared at his little sister. "Oliver Chancellor got you pregnant?"

"Apparently." She nodded and tears spilled past her lashes. "I thought it was the flu, but I just took a drugstore test, and . . . I don't believe it. It doesn't seem real!"

Allison looked stricken while Adrian cussed under his breath. In all his years of raising Rory, he'd never seen her look so frightened and hurt. A cold fist of anger tightened around his gut. "I'll kill him."

"Why?" Rory swiped at her cheeks. "This isn't Chance's fault. It's mine."

"It takes two to make a baby, sis." He plunged the tip of the knife into the cutting board. "You didn't do this on your own."

"It was my fault." She looked away as if ashamed. "I threw myself at him."

Adrian looked from Rory to Alli. Alli looked back with wide blue eyes as if waiting for him to fix everything. How the hell was he supposed to fix this! "Dammit, Rory, how did this happen? I mean, I know how it happened but— Jesus, you know about birth control. And if you tell me you did it without a condom, I'll strangle you." He rubbed his face in an effort to compose himself. When Rory had turned sixteen, he'd given her a box condoms and a very frank lecture about safe sex, and told her when she felt old enough to have sex to use protection. Did she think he was joking? How could he keep his sisters safe if they wouldn't listen to him?

Rory sniffed softly. "I'm sorry."

Trying to control his temper toward himself, toward Chance, toward the whole situation, he took a seat on the other side of Rory from Allison. "So, what happened?"

"I don't know," Rory said through her tears. "I guess I wasn't thinking."

"Neither was he, apparently." Adrian rubbed his forehead as memories intruded. A man shouldn't have to face this sort of thing twice in one lifetime. At least Rory was in her twenties, not sixteen as Alli had been. He'd handled that badly, as he remembered. Very badly. And he didn't want to repeat the mistakes of the past.

"Does Chance know?" Allison asked quietly. Always the gentle one. The peacemaker and healer. How painful this must be for her.

Rory shook her head.

"Are you going to tell him?" Allison stroked her sister's hand.

"I don't know." Rory took a shuddering breath. "I guess I'll have to eventually. It's not an easy thing to hide."

"How do you think he'll react?" Allison asked.

"I don't know," Rory answered in a small voice, her eyes and nose red against her pale skin. "He's very big on doing things the right way. I'm scared he'll feel obligated to marry me, which is a terrible solution."

"Then you don't want to marry him?" Adrian asked.

"Not if he feels obligated," Rory said.

"Well, dammit, he should feel obligated," Adrian insisted. "It's his baby, too. And you need to tell him, Rory. A man has the right to know. Even if he is a stupid, irresponsible jerk."

"Chance is none of those things!" Anger lit behind Rory's tears. "I'm the one who's stupid and irresponsible."

"Irresponsible maybe, but you are not stupid!" he shouted back.

She looked ready to argue, but subsided. "I'll tell Chance, okay? Just not right away."

"Why not right away?" Adrian demanded. "If I'd fathered a child, I'd damn well want to know. And I'd want to be a part of any decisions about doctors and such. This baby is just as much his as it is yours."

"Adrian," Allison scolded gently. Her gaze met his, asking him to calm down. "We're not talking about you. We're talking about Oliver Chancellor. Aside from the fact that he's helped us a lot lately, or tried to, none of us knows him all that well. What if . . ." Allison's eyes clouded with old pain. "What if he asks her to have an abortion?"

"Then I really will kill him." Adrian reached out and squeezed Allison's hand. They'd never told Rory about Allison's pregnancy, or Peter's demands that she abort it. Rory had only been fourteen, and Allison had been too distraught to confide in anyone but him at first. He'd finally talked her into telling their aunt. Alli had refused any thought of abortion, wanting desperately to keep her baby even though she'd been scared half to death. Two weeks later, she'd miscarried. And Adrian had taken his anger out on Peter's face for everything he put Allison through.

But that was Peter, and this was Chance. Adrian had gone to school with both of them, and the men couldn't be more different, even if they did both come from money. "There's no need for her to even consider abortion. If Chance doesn't want to claim responsibility, fine, the three of us will raise the kid together. It's not like I've never changed diapers."

"Oh, Adrian." Fresh tears welled up in Rory's eyes. "Thank you. That means so much, even though I know you must be disappointed in me."

"Don't say that! Don't even *think* it!" He gathered her into a fierce hug and she buried her head under his chin. He stroked his hands over her back in soothing circles as he'd done a hundred times while she was growing up. It had been a long time, though, since he'd comforted her through a crying jag. "You could never disappoint me. Neither one of you could." He smiled at Allison, who'd stopped fighting the silent tears that slipped down her cheeks.

"What am I going to do?" Rory sniffed against his neck. "This is all so scary."

He looked to Allison, pleading for help.

Allison took a breath and dried her cheeks. "First we're going to get you an appointment with a doctor to be sure you and the baby are doing fine."

"Do I have to do that right away?" Rory sat up enough to look at both of them. "I'm not even a month along. It seems so soon to see a doctor."

"It's never too soon for that," Alli insisted, rubbing her sister's back. "As for when and how you tell Chance, that's your business, and we'll support you in whatever decision you make."

Adrian started to object but closed his mouth when Allison gave him a warning look.

"In the meantime"—Allison straightened Rory's hair—"what do you want us to tell Chance about being a partner?"

"I don't know." Rory sat back with a groan. With effort she reined in her runaway emotions enough to talk in a steady voice. "A part of me wants to tell him yes, because he really would be a help, and because I can't stop thinking—hoping—that if we spend more time together, he'll come to his senses and realize how good we are for each other. But another part of me wants to tell him no, because I'm so mad and hurt and I want to hurt him back, even though I know it's childish. But I can't help it, and I swear, if he brings Perfect Paige near me again, I may toss her into the bay."

"I don't blame you for feeling any of that. But Rory"—Alli folded her hands on the table—"that's something you need to think about. If we take Chance on as a partner, you'll probably see a lot of Paige."

"You're right." She blew out a breath and thought it over a moment. "I guess I'll just have to handle it."

"What if you spend time with him, and he marries Paige anyway? What will you do then?"

Die, she thought. How had he become so important to her in so short a time? Somewhere along the way, he'd become as important to her as Pearl Island. If only she could feel as confident about winning his love as she did about making the inn a success.

With him, though, the future was so uncertain. Was that how he felt, too? The reason he'd backed off after they'd made love? In a way she couldn't blame him, because the emotions he stirred inside her were frightening.

His words came back to her from that day when they'd argued on the pier: *You can't make something happen just because it's what you want. Determination is fine, but you have to balance it with good sense.*

He was right. Even if she managed to win his love, she had no guarantees it would work out for them. Maybe they were too different. But how could she live with herself if she didn't even try?

She looked at her brother and sister. "If he spends time with me, then marries Paige anyway, I'll find a way to live with it. I'll have to."

"So, you want us to take him on as a partner?" Allison asked.

"From a business standpoint, it makes good sense," she answered. "Regardless of what happens between us personally, I want Pearl Island to be a success. And"—she took a deep shuddering breath—"if it becomes too awkward, we'll buy him out."

"I agree," Adrian said. "He would be an asset. Alli?"

Allison nodded, hesitantly.

"Very well." He turned back to Rory. "I think I should handle the negotiations, though."

"I'm not a coward, Adrian," Rory insisted.

"I know, but you're too emotionally involved to be objective on this one. For the sake of the business, let me deal with Chance on the partnership agreement."

"All right." Rory nodded, suddenly too overwhelmed with exhaustion to argue.

Chance wasn't quite sure what had possessed him to become business partners with the St. Claires—or why they'd agreed. None of them seemed particularly thrilled with the arrangement. The day they'd met at the lawyer's office, Adrian and Allison had been cordial, but cool. As for Aurora, she'd acted so nervous, he'd half expected her to call the whole thing off. But she hadn't. They'd signed the papers, he'd handed them a substantial check, and the deal was done.

Crossing the bridge to the island Saturday morning, he tried to sort it all out. He had no idea where he stood with Aurora. He wanted the friendship they'd shared while they'd been working on the business plan, minus the attraction. The friendship had been fun, exciting—and a large reason why he'd just invested a considerable amount of money in a risky venture.

Apart from that, or perhaps added to it, he wanted to be involved with a project for once, not just hear about the ups and downs through his accounts at the bank. Building a business from scratch was new to him. A challenge. He hadn't had enough challenges in his life.

When the house came into view, his pulse quickened. If he wanted a challenge, he'd picked a big one.

He found a place to park amid the pickup trucks that crowded the area behind the house, where they wouldn't be visible from the dock. Being Saturday, there would be another lunch run at noon, and none of them wanted the guests to see a construction site parking lot when they arrived.

Lifting the box he'd brought from the passenger seat, he made his way to the front of the house. There was a back entrance, of course, but he preferred the full impact of entering through the front. They'd finished painting the trim, a deep burgundy that provided a pleasing accent to the pink stone. The outside was nearly finished. The inside was another matter entirely.

A table saw buzzed in the central hall, producing a steady stream of boards that were carried off in every direction. Hammers pounded out an offbeat rhythm, the sound attacking Chance's ears as he made his way to the back of the house. He found Adrian in the kitchen helping one of the men install a commercial-grade vent.

"Did they deliver the restaurant equipment already?" Chance asked.

"Not yet," Adrian said, straining to hold the massive copper hood in place while the construction worker bolted it to the red-brick walls.

"Here, let me help." Setting the box down, Chance grabbed one end of the vent.

"Thanks." Adrian spared him a puzzled look, as if surprised by the amount of weight he took. "I heard the steakhouse over on Market was going out of business, and couldn't resist this baby." When the hood was secure, Adrian stepped back, dusting off his hands. "Isn't she a beauty?"

"That depends. How much did she cost?" Chance cringed, waiting.

Adrian laughed. "You don't want to know."

"You're probably right. I'll just close my eyes when I enter the expense."

"So what's in the box?" Adrian asked.

"A surprise for Aurora." Chance could hardly wait to see her face when he gave it to her. "I assume she'll be here to serve lunch?"

"Actually, she and Alli are down in the basement going over the floor plan for our apartment."

"I thought they both worked Saturdays."

Adrian shrugged. "Alli threatened to quit if she couldn't get off every other weekend. And Rory talked Bobby into giving her some time off."

"Oh? I'm surprised he agreed."

"He didn't have much choice," Adrian said. "Rory hasn't been feeling well, and the motion of the boat makes her sick. It's bad for business to have your tour guide puking over the rail."

"She's sick? What's wrong? Is it serious?" He remembered how pale and tired she'd looked at the lawyer's office.

"She's claiming it's just a touch of the flu."

"Then what's she doing here? She should be home in bed."

"Feel free to tell her that. She and Alli are right downstairs."

With box in hand, Chance made his way down the narrow back stairs. He heard the sisters before he reached the bottom.

"I'm sorry, Rory, I just don't see how we're going to get a fourth bedroom in here," Allison was saying.

"Well, it won't be a big room. Here, I'll show you."

He reached the last step and halted in surprise. The area had been transformed from a dark hall and cramped rooms to a vast open space with nothing left but the concrete floor and thick beams supporting the floor overhead. Sunlight poured through the high windows, lighting motes of sawdust. The sisters were bending over a blueprint that was spread on a plywood frame that looked like the beginnings of a kitchen counter. He couldn't help but appreciate the view of Aurora's shapely backside, and long legs left bare by a pair of shorts.

"See"—she took up a pencil and wrote as she talked— "if we shift the bathroom you and I will share, and move my room forward just a bit, we'll have room in this back corner for a nur—" Her words cut off abruptly when she turned and saw him. "Chance!"

Allison whirled around.

"Good morning," he greeted, wondering why they looked so startled. He'd told them he'd be coming by today to help. "Are those the blueprints for the rooms down here?"

"Uh . . . yes," Aurora answered, and to his relief, she didn't look pale at all. In fact, her cheeks had a healthy flush of pink.

"Can I see?" He stepped off the last stair and headed toward them.

"No! I mean . . ." Aurora rolled them up and held them to her chest. "You can't because . . ." She glanced at her sister.

"They aren't finished," Allison said.

"Right." Aurora nodded. "They aren't finished. Yet."

"Oh," he said, disappointed at this further evidence that he wasn't entirely welcomed as a partner. "I saw Adrian upstairs. He said you aren't feeling well."

"My stomach's been a bit iffy, is all." She looked away. "I'm fine as long as I stay off boats."

"I hope you get to feeling better."

"Thanks."

Feeling awkward, he glanced about. "Wow, they really did a number on this place."

Aurora turned away, fidgeting with the blueprint. He hated the strain that had fallen between them since they'd slept together. If only he could think of the right words to make things comfortable again.

Allison glanced between the two of them, then answered, "Other than the support beams, there wasn't much worth saving. So we decided to start from scratch."

"Probably a good idea," he said absently. Should he apologize to Aurora for giving in to temptation? If he did, it would be an empty apology since he wasn't sorry. He wouldn't trade the experience for anything. Except maybe for her to be comfortable around him again. And happy. She seemed so sad and tense lately.

"What's in the box?" Allison asked.

He looked down. "I brought a surprise for Aurora."

Aurora turned, curiosity lifting her brows, but she made no move to come toward him.

"Well," Allison said. "If you'll excuse me, I'll go see if Adrian needs any help getting ready for lunch. The boat should be here in less than an hour."

"Wait," Aurora called, and thrust the blueprint at her sister. "Will you take these with you?"

"Certainly." Allison headed upstairs.

When the footsteps faded, Chance realized they were alone. He shifted his eyes from the stairs to Aurora as a world of possibilities played in his mind, memories of her body moving beneath him, over him. The wild rush of passion that had stolen all logical thought.

Color rose in her cheeks and he wondered if she'd read his mind. "So"—she gestured toward the box—"what do you have?"

"An office." He smiled.

"A what?"

"Since everything is so unsettled right now, I knew we

couldn't set up a real office yet, so . . ." He moved to a board that lay across two sawhorses. Setting the box down, he reached inside and pulled out the laptop. "I brought you a portable one."

"Oh, Chance." Her whole face softened.

"This way you'll be able to work wherever you want." He lifted the top.

"I thought you were doing the bookkeeping," she said, but excitement filled her eyes as she watched the screen come to life.

"You can do more on a computer than that. You can design fliers, write letters, search the Internet."

"Really? I can design our fliers without having to rely on the guy at the print shop?"

"Supposedly." He used the tap pad to open some software. "In fact, I went ahead and bought the graphic-design software the salesperson recommended."

"Can you show me how to use it?"

"I wish!" He laughed. "I'm afraid I'm clueless when it comes to anything creative. However, since I know how you feel about reading books . . ." He reached in the box and pulled out a plastic jewel case. "I bought this along with the software."

"What is it?"

"A CD Rom tutorial." He slipped the disc into the computer. A movie began to play, complete with a soundtrack of upbeat jazz. The narrator welcomed them to the world of page layout made simple with their cutting-edge software.

He watched Aurora's face as she gazed at the screen. He could almost see the wheels of her mind turning as she took it all in.

"Oh, my goodness," she breathed. "This looks really easy."

"For you, maybe." He smiled at her. "Personally, I'll stick with balancing spreadsheets."

"You can have them," she laughed.

"We all have our strengths in life. And this"—he pointed to the screen—"is not one of mine."

"Which is why we make a good team, don't you think?"

She smiled at him with all the happiness he'd longed to see shining in her eyes once again. Those beautiful blue eyes that reached inside his chest and made everything feel tight and achy. His gaze slipped to her lips and her smile faded as temptation pulled at him, urging him to lean toward her.

If he could kiss her just one more time, maybe the ache would go away. Maybe then he'd stop wanting her.

Just one more kiss . . .

"Chance?" a feminine voice called. "Are you down here?"

He straightened in surprise as footsteps sounded on the stairs. He turned and stared. "Paige!"

CHAPTER 15

Rory battled both resentment and guilt at the sight of Paige looking so fresh, elegant, and perfectly coordinated. The woman wore a navy blue cover-up over a white one-piece swimsuit that looked outrageously expensive. She even had matching deck shoes, navy with little gold anchors embroidered on the tops. Her blond hair was held back with a big white ruffle clip.

"I know we weren't planning to get together until this evening," Paige said in a soft voice. "But Daddy and I were out boating and I wanted to drop by and see how everything was going. I hope you don't mind."

"No, of course not," Chance assured her. "Your father's here?"

"He's upstairs visiting with the contractor about some development he's thinking of building." Crossing the room to Chance, Paige lifted her cheek for a kiss and sunlight sparkled off enormous diamond stud earrings. Rory turned her head, but still saw Chance bend down to oblige.

"Aurora," he said, after kissing the debutante's cheek, "do you have room for Paige and her father to have lunch?"

"I'll have to ask Adrian," Rory managed to say in a neutral voice even as she called herself ten times a fool. Why had she thought she could handle seeing Chance and Paige together?

"That would be great," Paige said. "Last week's lunch

was excellent." She turned to Rory. "We haven't met officially, I'm Paige Baxter."

"I'm sorry about the fruit." Rory felt sick with embarrassment and envy as they shook hands. "I hope it didn't stain your outfit. I'll be happy to pay to replace it or have it dry-cleaned."

"Don't be silly." Paige waved a manicured hand. "My mother is such a fiend for shopping, I have lots of clothes I only wear once."

Rory stared, unable to grasp such wealth—or such waste!

"I would like to talk to you about the inn, though," Paige continued. "Do you think you'll be open for business by October?"

"Why do you ask?" Rory said.

"Because"—Paige smiled slowly—"I'd like to propose your inn as the location for this year's Buccaneer's Ball."

Rory's heart skipped a beat. To have an event of that magnitude at the inn would be a major coup. "Yes! We can be open by then. Absolutely."

"Aurora." Chance frowned at her. "Our business plan projected November as the completion date."

"So we step it up a month. We can do it." She saw doubt in his eyes. "We can," she repeated.

"Oh, good," Paige said. "I'll need to look at your facilities to be sure the inn will work, then have the site approved by the rest of the planning committee, but since Chance's mother is one of the coordinators, I don't think we'll have a problem." She smiled at Chance. "I'm sure she'll want to support her son's new venture."

"Yes, of course." Rory beat back her jealousy. As much as she'd like to tell Paige to take a hike, the inn was too important for her to throw away this opportunity. "Do you want a tour now? I mean, everything's all torn up, but you'll get a feel for how it will look."

"I'd love a tour," Paige said.

"Well, then, follow me." Rory headed for the stairs,

unable to believe their good fortune. The Buccaneer's Ball would give them a chance to show off Adrian's catering skills. Not to mention the instant income from renting the inn for such a huge party. "As you can see," she said when they reached the top of the stairs, "our kitchen facilities will be extensive."

Adrian glanced up from the pasta salad he was taking out of the ice chests. He appeared puzzled to see her acting so friendly to Paige.

"This is my brother, Adrian, who's also our chef. He has years of experience catering parties and weddings. He'll be happy to discuss menu options with you. Adrian, Paige is with the Buccaneer's Ball planning committee. They're thinking of renting the inn for this year's event."

"Oh?" His puzzled frown was transformed into a look of stunned delight. "Oh! Well, yes indeed. I'd be very happy to talk menus with you."

"Aurora," Chance whispered in her ear, standing so close behind her, her skin tingled. "Are you sure about this?"

"What's not to be sure about?" she whispered back.

"Whether or not the inn will be ready in time."

"We'll be ready," she insisted.

"When is the ball again?" her brother asked.

"The first weekend of October," Paige answered.

"October?" Adrian's eyes widened. He looked at Rory, silently asking if she was nuts. "But we won't be open for business until November."

"No," Rory said very calmly. "We're opening in October. In fact, the ball can be our grand opening celebration."

Allison swept into the room with an empty tray tucked under one arm. "Okay, I've got the tables set. What next?" She came up short at the sight of Rory's beaming smile.

"Paige," Rory said. "I'd like you to meet my sister Allison."

"Yes, we met when I was on my way in." Paige nodded.

"Alli"—Rory took the tray from her—"come tell Paige your plans for decorating the first floor. The Historical Society is thinking of renting the inn for the Buccaneer's Ball."

Allison frowned. "Isn't that in October?"

"Yes, it is," Rory answered blithely as she set the tray aside and led the way through the butler's pantry to the main part of the house.

Chance followed, feeling as if he'd just been bowled over. Did Aurora even know the word "impossible"? Did schedules mean nothing to her? In order to open in time for the ball, they'd have to be ready in six weeks.

He trailed the women through a maze of construction workers while Allison explained her vision for the first floor over the noise of hammers and saws.

"The central hall will be a lobby of sorts, with Victorian sofas and chairs set in conversational groupings so guests can enjoy the fireplace. In here"—Allison stepped into the music room, where wall panels had been removed to replace the wiring—"we'll have a tearoom. We also plan to rent it for small parties. And the front room will be a gift shop. Of course I can't possibly have enough inventory to open as early as October."

"No," Rory agreed. "But we can have the rooms put back together and furnished by then."

"Coming through," one of the construction workers called. They all moved out of his way as he passed with an extension cord and drill.

"Oh, would you look at that ceiling?" Paige said, stepping gingerly over debris to get a better view. "To be able to decorate such a house. I envy you." When she lowered her gaze, a longing Chance had never seen shone in her eyes. "I don't suppose you'd want help? I studied interior design at UT and I'd offer my services free. It's the least I can do, since I'm asking you to open early just for the ball."

"You studied interior design?" Allison asked, clearly intrigued.

As Allison and Paige fell into a conversation about furniture styles, Chance pulled Aurora aside. "You can't be serious about this. You have to be reasonable."

"I am being reasonable," she answered. "I'm not saying we have to be ready to rent rooms by October, just have the place put back together and decorated by then."

He glanced around at the mess. "Even if we manage that, do you know how big an event we're talking about here? Hundreds of people from all over the state attend this ball. They have live entertainment, extravagant food, open bar."

"Adrian has cooked for events every bit as lavish, and he has lots of friends we can hire as wait staff. Oh, and we can have it on the lawn overlooking the cove. The weather's perfect in early October!"

"And if it rains?"

"It won't." When he started to object, she raised her hand. "We'll watch the extended forecast, and if it looks like there's a chance of rain, we'll use the ballroom."

He shook his head. This couldn't possibly work . . . could it? "I don't know. It's a lot to do in a very brief period of time. You can't just make things happen because you want them to."

"You know what? You're right. Wanting alone isn't enough. It takes hard work, commitment, and faith. If you want something badly enough, you have to earn it." She laid her hand on his arm. "Trust me, Chance, we can do this."

He looked into her eyes, and saw more than hope. He saw conviction. His breath let out in a rush. "Maybe so."

"See"—she smiled—"that didn't hurt a bit, now did it? Right now, however, we have lunch to serve. Wanna help?"

He laughed, wondering what he'd gotten himself into.
"I might as well."

Leaving Allison to finish up with Paige, he followed
Aurora back to the kitchen, where he received his first
lesson in how to balance a serving tray.

CHAPTER 16

"Chance actually waited on tables?" his mother asked Paige the following day. He and Paige had joined his parents for a Sunday lunch of his mother's lemon chicken and rice pilaf served in the informal breakfast room. Chance had always liked the relaxed feel of the room, with its green and white striped wallpaper. The white curtains stirred with the fresh gulf breeze coming through the open windows. An occasional golf cart whizzed by, since the course was always busy on the weekends.

"It was quite a sight," Paige said, her eyes bright with laughter as she smiled at him.

"I'm trying to picture it." His mother stared off into space. "Nope, I'm sorry, I just can't."

"Hey, I wasn't that bad," Chance said with mock offense, enjoying the teasing mood. Even though he had a million things to do out at Pearl Island, he was glad he and Paige had accepted his mother's invitation. "I just need a little practice."

"Is *that* how you plan to spend your weekends?" his father asked, his voice tight with disapproval. "Waiting tables?"

Chance glanced at him, surprised. He hadn't expected his father to be thrilled about his venture with the St. Claires, but he hadn't expected the objection to be this strong. "I do what needs to be done."

Paige shifted in her chair across from him. A confused frown dimpled her brow before she turned back to his mother. "Have you been out to see the house yet?"

"Not yet." His mother smiled, ignoring her husband's dark mood. "I'm waiting for an invitation."

"You're welcome anytime," Chance said. "Although the place looks like a demolition site right now."

"No it doesn't," Paige countered. "It's just the usual mess that comes with construction. Oh, but Mrs. Chancellor, it's going to be beautiful. Allison gave me a tour yesterday, and I can just picture how it will look when it's finished. In fact . . ." She let her voice trail off as excitement built in her eyes. "That's why I'm so glad you invited us for lunch. I wanted to talk to you about my idea."

"Oh?" his mother asked.

"Yes." Paige folded her hands on the edge of the table. "You know what trouble we've been having, trying to find a new location for the Buccaneer's Ball. So, what would you think of renting Pearl Island? They haven't finished installing the landscaping, but the grounds will be as lovely as anything Galveston has to offer."

"Pearl Island?" His mother turned thoughtful. "Now there's an idea. I've never been inside the house, though. Do they have adequate space?"

"Oh, yes," Paige said. "And we wouldn't even need to scramble for a separate caterer since they have catering facilities at the inn. In fact, Adrian St. Claire is a chef at Chez Laffite, and you know how wonderful their food is."

Ellen glanced at her son. "I didn't know you were going to offer catering."

"We might as well." He shrugged. "The place has a huge kitchen, and Adrian is a phenomenal chef."

His father snorted. "And we all know the failure rate for catering companies."

Chance took a slow breath and ignored his father's barb. Later, they would talk in private, where they could each be as frank as they wanted.

After an uncomfortable look at him, Paige turned back to his mother. "There's another reason I'd like to have the ball at Pearl Island. And that's their deepwater cove."

"Oh," Ellen prompted.

"Yes." Paige seemed to brace herself for objection. "Yesterday while Chance was serving lunch, I visited with Captain Bob. He's the owner of the tour-boat business down at Pier Nineteen. When I told him of my idea to have the ball there on the lawn, overlooking the cove, he said all we needed to complete the picture was a pirate ship."

"A pirate ship?" Ellen sat back, her expression intrigued. Chance felt more surprised than intrigued, since this was the first he'd heard of the idea. "You mean like the *Elissa*?" his mother asked, referring to the fully restored tall ship docked by the Texas Seaport Museum on Pier Twenty-one.

"No, not the *Elissa*." Paige shook her head. "She's a fine ship, don't get me wrong, but everyone in Galveston has already seen her. Besides, she's too big since she's built for hauling cargo across the Atlantic. What we need is the smaller, faster type of vessel a pirate would have used, like a wooden-hulled Baltimore clipper."

His mother laughed. One couldn't live on Galveston Island without knowing a little bit about old sailing vessels. For years, the Historical Society had been wanting to buy a Baltimore clipper, the type of ship most likely used by the pirate Jean Laffite during the time when he'd lived on the island. But they were outrageously expensive and extremely rare.

"And where would we get one?" Ellen asked.

"Corpus Christi." Paige's smile broadened. "Captain Bob has a friend who owns one that's available for charter. A real one, not a replica. She's even named the *Pirate's Pleasure*. Oh, wouldn't it be perfect? To have the Buccaneer's Ball on Pearl Island, a place rumored to have been frequented by pirates, with a pirate ship docked in the cove?"

"Paige, my dear, you are a true romantic." Ellen chuckled. "And yes, it's a splendid plan—*if* you can pull it off on such short notice."

"You mean it?" Paige's face lit up.

"Absolutely." Ellen turned to Chance. "What do you think?"

"It's a great idea," he said, knowing Aurora was going to love it since it would have people talking about the event and the inn all over the state for years to come.

"Very well," his mother said to Paige. "Put a proposal together and present it to the committee. As long as you don't go over budget, you have my vote."

"Oh, thank you, Mrs. Chancellor." Paige squeezed her hand. "I just knew you'd agree."

"Oh, yes, by all means, let's turn the event into a real spectacle." Chance's father pushed his plate away with a look of disgust. "What better way to keep people talking about this sordid business with John LeRoche?"

The women's enthusiasm dimmed instantly. Chance turned to his father, knowing he should let the comment lie, but he'd had enough. "Is that why you're so against my going into partnership with the St. Claires? Because of the LeRoche foreclosure? Which is a dead issue at this point."

"It should be dead, yes, since I let Brian Jeffries have his way. Then you come along and start adding grist to the mill." His father faced him head-on. "Or don't you realize how it looks for you to be part owner of a house we foreclosed on? It makes the bank look as if we had ulterior motives in calling in the loan."

"That's ridiculous," Chance shot back. "First of all, I don't own any part of the house. I only bought into the business. And secondly, even if I did own part of the house, bank employees can purchase foreclosed property any time they want, as long as they don't take advantage of prior knowledge to make early bids. And that's all I am, an employee of the bank. An employee who had nothing to do with the decision to call in John LeRoche's loan."

"No"—his father leaned forward—"you're the son of the bank president who used to own that bank. Whether your behavior is legal or ethical doesn't matter, what you've done looks suspect. And it looks even worse for you to be involved in a business that doesn't even bank with us."

Anger tightened Chance's shoulders. "The St. Claires wouldn't be banking with a competitor if we hadn't turned them down."

"As much as I hate to agree with Brian Jeffries, if we turned them down, it was with good reason." His father stabbed the table with his index finger to punctuate his words. "For you to turn around and go into business with them makes people wonder whose judgment is faulty, the bank's or yours. Either way, you're undermining people's faith in the bank."

Chance dropped his fork on his plate with a clatter. "So I'm supposed to pull out of my investment because it might shed a bad light on the bank? The bank doesn't own me, Dad. I have a right to spend my personal time as I choose."

The fury that flashed in his father's eyes startled him. "I did not devote my entire *life* to that bank so my son could thumb his nose at it!"

Silence fell.

Chance glanced around. Both his mother and Paige sat uneasily toying with their food. Hoping to end the conversation, Chance turned back to his father and spoke as calmly as possible. "Dad, I appreciate how you feel, but the fact is, we don't own the bank anymore."

The fury shifted to hurt. An emotion far more uncomfortable to witness. "Do you hold that against me?"

"No, of course not!" Chance assured him, his chest aching. "You made the decision that was best for everyone concerned. I have no problem with it. You're the one who's having trouble letting it go."

"Because nothing changes the fact that Chancellors built

that bank. Chancellors made it what it is today, saw it and this town through boom times and through recessions. No matter who owns it now, the people of this community will always associate it with the Chancellor name. How can you think to sully that name just to play innkeeper on the weekends?"

"I'm not playing at this," Chance shot back in frustration. "All right, yes, I'm enjoying myself. So what? Why shouldn't I enjoy being part of a new business and watching it grow?"

"Is it worth jeopardizing your career?"

"I don't think I am."

His father snorted. "If you think that, you're living in a dream world, son. You're a grown man now. It's time you pulled your head out of the clouds, settled down, and started thinking about your obligations to the Chancellor name."

"Isn't that what I've been doing my whole life?" Chance sat back, stunned. How could his father think of him as an irresponsible dreamer when everyone else saw him as a "chip off the old block"? Another dependable, dedicated, upstanding, *boring* Chancellor. Shaking his head, Chance laughed at the absurdity of his father's comment. "I wonder what the first Chancellors who came to Galveston would think of us."

His father straightened in surprise. "What's that supposed to mean?"

"At least they had the courage to travel to a frontier town, risk their lives, as well as every dime they could scrape together, to do something adventurous. Something daring. When's the last time anyone in this family had the guts to risk anything?"

"It's easy to take risks when you have nothing to lose. Our forefathers came to this island with little more than the clothes on their backs."

"And the balls in their pants, apparently," Chance snorted.

"You'll watch your mouth when you're sitting at my table in mixed company." His father pointed his finger at Chance's face.

Chance clenched his fists against the urge to slap the finger away, to tell his father he wasn't a child, and he damn well wouldn't be disciplined like one, especially not in front of his date. But the lifetime of rules that had been drummed into his head, to respect his elders and behave properly at all times, could not be slapped away in an instant. He forced his hands to uncurl. "My apologies, Paige, Mom, if I offended either of you."

Paige let out a nervous laugh. "You forget I grew up with Harry Baxter as a father. It takes a lot more than that to offend these ears."

Dropping his napkin onto the table, Norman Chancellor thanked his wife for lunch, then rose and left the room with the excuse of seeing to his coin collection. The mutual release of tension was like an audible sigh.

After a moment, Ellen rose to clear the table.

"Here, let me help," Paige said, and gathered her own plate and silverware.

Chance sat a moment, feeling his muscles relax one by one. The women moved around the counter that divided the breakfast room and kitchen. Their soft voices and the sound of running water soothed his frayed nerves.

"So," his mother asked Paige, "what do you two have planned for this afternoon?"

"Well, I don't know about Chance," Paige answered, "but I promised Mom I'd go into Houston with her. Nordstrom's is having a shoe sale."

"Shopping in Houston? On such a pretty day?" His mother made a face of disbelief. "I can see that for Marcy, but not you. You and Chance should spend the day together. Go out on the boat, take in a round of golf, or rent some horses and ride along the beach."

Chance felt his mother's gaze and looked up. Her pointed look silently said, "Ask the girl out, you goof."

"I can't," he said, checking his watch. "I have to get out to Pearl Island to help the others."

"Will I see you this evening?" Paige asked him as she came back to the table for more dishes. "We don't have to do anything special. We can just go over the plans for the ball if you like."

"Actually, that's a good idea." Setting his napkin down, he rose and gathered his own plate. He carried it to the kitchen, then stood back, out of the women's way. "I know Aurora's completely confident we can pull this off, but I'd like to get a firm handle on what needs to be done when in order to be ready."

"Aurora?" his mother asked. "Isn't she the youngest of the St. Claires?"

"The youngest, maybe, but the unofficial leader on this project," Chance answered. Leaning against a counter, he smiled. "She's really something. In fact, the whole idea of buying the house was hers. I was skeptical at first. More than skeptical." He laughed. "I thought she was insane, but she pulled it off. I'm beginning to think she can pull this off, too."

"Pull what off?" his mother asked, rinsing dishes to put in the dishwasher.

"Having the inn ready in time for the ball," he answered.

His mother raised a brow. "Is there a question about that?"

"Actually"—he cocked his head, thinking of Aurora—"I don't think there is. We'll be ready on time, even if Aurora has to pull the place together by the skin of her teeth. She's incredible. And a very demanding taskmaster. Or -mistress." He laughed.

His mother stared at him, an unreadable expression settling over her face. Then she turned to Paige. "Paige, if you and Marcy are going to Houston, you should probably get moving. You know how your mother is if you make her late to a shoe sale."

"Do I ever," Paige agreed, rolling her eyes. "Just let me finish helping with the dishes and I'll be on my way."

"No, no." His mother shooed her away. "Chance can help me finish." When he and Paige both looked at her, startled, she sighed. "If he can pull kitchen duty at Pearl Island, he can pull it here."

"Very well," Paige said, doubt lining her brow.

"I'll, um, walk you to the door," Chance offered, wondering why his mother wanted to speak with him alone. He escorted Paige through the family room to the more formal part of the house. In the white marble entry a stairway curved upward, around a crystal chandelier. "I'll come over this evening after I finish whatever chores Aurora has planned for me today."

"Yes, that will be fine." She seemed suddenly nervous standing alone with him.

He realized she was waiting for him to kiss her. Not the buss on the cheek they usually exchanged—but a touching of lips more appropriate to their new status as a dating couple. He chastised himself for forgetting the altered state of their relationship. After years of being friends who knew someday they'd be more, the time had arrived for that "something more."

He leaned down and fitted his mouth lightly over hers. She stiffened briefly, then relaxed. One of her hands came to rest against his chest but their bodies didn't touch. He thought of deepening the kiss, but it didn't seem right with his parents so near. Still, the exchange was pleasant, not nearly as awkward as their first real kiss that night by the footbridge.

When he straightened, she gave him a timid smile. "I'll see you this evening."

When she was gone, he headed back toward the kitchen. "Well?" he said. "You wanted to speak with me?"

"Whatever gave you that idea?" his mother asked with a poor attempt at innocence. "I just wanted you to help clear the table so Paige could be on her way." He raised a brow, and she sighed in defeat. "Oh, very well. I did want to talk to you." She took a breath. "Chance, I'm concerned about you and Paige."

"Mom . . ." He sighed.

"I know." She held up a hand. "I promised not to pry. It's just . . . you two seem so . . . *formal* together."

"We're just going through a period of adjustment," he assured her. "It's hard to go from thinking of her as a friend to thinking of her in . . . other ways. Which is why I asked you to let Paige and me handle this at our own pace. The last thing we need is our parents pressuring us to get on with things."

"I agree, and I'm not pressuring. Truly. In fact . . . I'm doing just the opposite."

"Excuse me?" He stared at her.

"Chance . . ." She closed the dishwasher. "Your interest in Paige—it isn't solely based on the fact that us old folks want you to get together, is it?"

"What old folks?" he teased her.

"Stop that." She blushed. "You know perfectly well I'm old enough to be a grandmother."

"Yes, I know." He sobered.

"I just . . . I just don't want to push you into something you don't want."

"You're not pushing me. I simply want to take things slowly. Marriage is serious business."

"Yes, it is." She leaned her hip against the counter. "But sometimes I fear you take it *too* seriously."

"Pardon me?"

"Chance, don't you ever want to say to heck with what's right and proper and just have fun?"

"Fun?" He rocked back.

"Yes, fun," she said. "Falling in love is like making mud pies. It's not any fun unless you're willing to get dirty."

"I'm not sure I understand."

"No, I don't suppose you do." She got that indulgent

look in her eyes she always did when she told him he was just like his father.

Fun. He let the concept roll around in his head, but failed to fit it with something as serious as deciding who to spend the rest of his life with. "Is that how it was for you and Dad?"

A humorless laugh escaped her. "We're not talking about your father and me."

"I'd still like to know. The two of you are so well suited, so comfortable together. But how did you know it would work?"

"We didn't. And . . ." She looked away. "I'm not always sure it does."

Her words were quietly spoken, yet they rocked the very foundation beneath his feet. "But . . . you get along so well."

"We've learned to make do. Your father has the bank, and billiards, and his coin collection. And I have"—she trailed a hand through the air—"my clubs and things."

He couldn't believe the words he was hearing. They refused to stick in his brain, to make sense. "Are you saying you don't love him?"

"Oh, no." A soft smile settled over her face, but sadness crept into her eyes. "I love your father more than anything, including my pride, apparently. Like I said, love is messy business."

"I still don't understand."

"Just as well." Her smile became a bit too bright to be real. "I'm just feeling my age. Promise me one thing, though." She closed the space between them and took his hand in hers. "If you aren't in love with Paige, in love to the point you don't care what others think, or what sacrifices you have to make to be with her, to the point that everything else in life fades in comparison, don't marry her."

"But . . . I thought you *wanted* me to marry Paige."

"I want you to be happy." She squeezed his fingers.

"Both of you. And I care about that girl too much to bear the thought of her living her life knowing her husband only married her because she was the 'right choice.' " Her gaze met his. "No woman should have to settle for that. Far better to be the worst choice in the world, but still the one that's taken."

An image of Aurora flashed through his mind, sending his world even more off kilter. She was the worst choice he could imagine for his wife, no matter how desperately he wanted her back in his bed. Marriage was a decision that should be based on logic, not runaway hormones. Still . . . a lifetime with Aurora? Vibrant, passionate, unpredictable Aurora? The idea was so at odds with everything he'd ever pictured for his future, he couldn't get his mind around it.

"Well," his mother said, "I've held you up long enough. You have work to do out at your new inn, if you're going to be ready in time for the ball."

"Hmm? Oh, yes. Yes, of course." He pulled his wits together enough to kiss his mother's cheek and thank her for lunch.

"Just promise you'll think about what I said."

"Don't worry, I will." He laughed, doubting he'd be able to think of anything else for the rest of the day.

And he was right. When he reached Pearl Island and was caught up in the whirlwind of hard work, enthusiasm, and chaos that always surrounded Aurora, his mother's words hovered at the edge of his thoughts. Being with Aurora excited him on every level, but to spend the rest of his life with her? Surely they were too different in background and temperament to make a long-term relationship work. And how would she feel about fulfilling the social obligations that would come with marrying a future bank president? The thought of a friendly tea party nearly gave her a panic attack, and he knew the society matrons she'd have to deal with as his wife would not be nearly as accepting as the McMillans.

And yet . . . he enjoyed her company.

The thought remained with him that evening as he sat with Paige in the Baxters' quiet sunroom.

He glanced across at the woman he intended to marry. She sat on a white wicker love seat, her head bent over a notepad, her blond hair pulled into a neat ponytail. Her manicured hands guided a silver pen over the paper, making orderly notations.

She was everything he'd ever wanted in a wife: calm, cultured, comfortable. They shared the same friends, the same political views, and even a few of the same interests. She would also assume the role of hostess with a minimum amount of fuss. Surely his mother couldn't have been thinking straight to suggest he not marry Paige because they were *too* right for each other.

Although, lately, he'd felt decidedly *un*comfortable around her. Why was that?

It was his damned attraction to Aurora, he realized with a silent curse. His lust for her was out of control and wreaking havoc on his life. He had to master it. And he would, he vowed. He would!

CHAPTER 17

By the end of that week, the Buccaneer's Ball Planning Committee had voted to hold the ball at Pearl Island. The next day, Rory quit her job with Captain Bob. While her motion sickness no longer gave her problems, school was back in session so the tourist season had waned. Plus, they all agreed that one of them would be needed at the house full-time if they were going to meet the new schedule. Rory was the logical choice.

Adrian and Allison spent every spare minute they had at the house. As did Chance and Paige: Chance in the official capacity of partner, Paige in the unofficial role of interior design consultant.

The other bed-and-breakfast owners pitched in, as well, with valuable advice that sped up their progress. To celebrate, the St. Claires invited the other innkeepers to hold their September meeting at Pearl Island, in the newly finished music room.

"I guess that does it for this month's business," Sam Kinnaird, the association's president, said. He stood by the fireplace, with the members seated in chairs from the veranda. "Before we adjourn, does anyone have any announcements?"

Rory raised her hand and stood when he nodded to her. "I just want to thank everyone for helping so much over the last month." She looked at all the new friends she'd made. "Without y'all's advice, I know we couldn't have come this far, this fast. And I want everyone to know how much we appreciate your help."

"That's what we're here for," Betsy McMillan said. "Isn't that right, Ron?"

Her husband, Ron, who'd been unbelievably generous over the last weeks, blushed. "Just remember which of us helped the most when your inn is booked solid and you have to refer potential guests somewhere else."

"Don't worry." Rory laughed as she took her seat.

"Aurora, wait," Chance called from where he and Adrian stood across the room. He'd come in late, straight from work, and had missed the first part of the meeting. "Did you tell them about the Web site?"

"Oh, yeah." She stood back up. "Thanks to Steven, our Web site is finally up, and . . . we got our first inquiry yesterday."

"That's great!" Everyone applauded.

"We haven't booked a room yet," Rory said. "But at least we got a call."

"Congratulations." The president nodded his approval. "Anyone else have an announcement?"

No one raised their hand.

"Adjourn, already," Daphne groused. "So we can get on with the tour."

"Meeting adjourned."

Conversation instantly filled the room as everyone stood. Rory found herself the center of attention as other innkeepers gathered around to ask about the progress of the renovations, and the upcoming ball.

"Sorry I'm late." Chance's voice came from right behind her. "I had some things to do at the bank, and couldn't get away."

"That's okay." Trying to look as relaxed as possible, she turned and smiled. Beneath her calm façade, though, her pulse hummed at the sight of him. His presence always affected her more on days like this, when he didn't have Paige in tow. "Will you help me lead the tour while Adrian sets up coffee and dessert in the dining room?"

"I'd love to." He smiled back at her, making her heart beat faster. "If everyone will follow Aurora, we'll show you the rooms upstairs."

"Remember, though," Rory said, "we're a long way from finishing with the decorating. Alli and I are going shopping in Houston tomorrow."

"Speaking of Allison, where is she?" Steven asked as he joined her on the stairs.

"She couldn't get off work, but she might make it here before everyone leaves." They reached the top of the stairs, and she opened the door to the smallest of the rooms. "We decided to go with a shipping theme for the room names, so this room here will be the Crow's Nest. It needs draperies and bedspread, obviously. And some art for the walls, but I like the antiques Alli found."

Rory stepped out of the way so everyone could see inside, then led them into the wide upper hall. A sideboard filled one wall, while a love seat and two chairs created an inviting place for guests to linger. "Betsy, we're going to follow your example and have tea and coffee service up here."

"And what a perfect area for it." Betsy nodded in approval.

"Thanks." Rory indicated the four remaining doorways. "The two medium-sized rooms are the Captain and the First Mate. The tower suite will be the Pearl, named after our resident ghost. And the other big suite across the hall will be the Baron, since 'shipping baron' was the kindest term we could think of for Henri LeRoche."

Everyone wandered through the rooms, voicing approval for the combination of paisley and striped wallpaper they'd selected in varying shades of burgundy, blue, and green. Several of the B and B owners suggested ways to make the rooms more guest-friendly. Rory was still taking mental notes as they headed downstairs.

In the dining room, Adrian had set up the silver coffee and tea service on the sideboard, along with some sinfully rich brownies and cheesecake. Betsy rolled her eyes in pleasure as she sampled some of each. "Well, if there's one thing you don't need advice on, it's your food."

"Adrian's always been very talented in the kitchen." Rory smiled at her brother as he rearranged the desserts for better presentation.

"I bet that's not the only room he's good in." Daphne gave him a blatant once-over from head to toe, clearly approving the fit of his faded blue jeans and tight red T-shirt.

"Daphne, behave," Betsy scolded mildly. "You'll embarrass the boy."

"I doubt that." Daphne moved closer to Adrian as she helped herself to another brownie. Her age showed beneath the heavy coat of makeup and in the inch of white roots at the base of her orange hair. Still, she smiled up at Adrian like a flirtatious schoolgirl and licked rich, gooey crumbs from her fingers. "If chocolate really is an aphrodisiac, I bet these brownies could keep a man up all night."

"Daphne!" Betsy gasped, but Adrian boomed with laughter.

He slipped an arm around the woman's thick waist, making her cheeks turn pink beneath the circles of apricot blusher. "Some men don't need chocolate. Just the right woman."

"Honey, I'll be happy to test that theory—if you think you can handle the challenge."

"I can handle *anything*," Adrian answered suggestively.

While the others laughed, Steven headed for the silver service for more coffee. "Hey, Rory," he said, lifting the lid and glancing inside. "I think we need another pot."

"Oh, sorry. I'll get it." She grabbed the ornate silver urn. When she turned, she found Chance watching her, as he so often did—with desire barely showing beneath his carefully guarded expression. "I don't suppose you'd care to help?"

He hesitated slightly, since they'd be alone in the kitchen, then set his cup of coffee aside and followed her through the butler's pantry. The voices and laughter became muffled when the door swung closed behind him. "Do you think it's wise to leave Adrian in there with Daphne, unprotected?" he asked.

"Oh, Adrian can hold his own." As they passed into the kitchen, she lowered her voice to a whisper. "Personally, I think he gets a kick out of turning the old girl on."

"Obviously." He chuckled. "But do you think it's healthy at her age, to have heart palpitations like that?"

"I say more power to her." She set the urn on the counter and retrieved the canister of coffee beans. "What's wrong with her having a few fantasies about what she'd like to do with my brother's body if he'd let her?"

"Aurora, please." Chance shuddered as he leaned against the counter next to her. "There are some things I just don't want to picture."

Scooping beans into the grinder, she cast him a sideways glance. "You don't think people should have fantasies?"

His guard slipped a notch as his gaze held hers.

She leaned closer, hoping to push him just a bit into admitting he still wanted her—had never stopped wanting her. "Personally," she said, "I've always thought fantasies were normal. We all have things we like to think about, things we'd like to do. Don't you ever have wicked thoughts?"

"I have a few," he confessed in a low voice. "There's a difference, though, in having wicked thoughts and acting on them."

"True. But life would be boring if we never gave in to temptation. Don't you think?"

His gaze dropped to her mouth, and her lips tingled. *Yes*, she wanted to say. *Kiss me*.

"Am I too late?" Allison came through the back door.

They sprang apart, Rory knocking over the grinder and scattering coffee beans. She swore silently as she scooped them up. "No, you're not too late at all." *You're too early!*

Sadie gave a happy bark and trotted straight for Chance, who made himself busy petting her. Alli raised a brow and glanced from Rory to Chance, then back to Rory's warm face. "Anything wrong?"

"Not a thing." *Except your timing.* Rory forced a smile.

"I saw cars, so I assume some people are still here."

"They're in the dining room," Rory said. "Chance and I were just getting a second pot of coffee."

"Do you need help?" Allison asked, a layer of frost just beneath the surface of her words.

"No, we can manage." Rory wondered about her sister's disapproval. It wasn't the first time she'd felt it.

"All right, then. Come on, Sadie," Allison called and left them alone.

When Rory turned back to Chance, she saw his guard was back up, and he was ready to act as if nothing had happened. Or almost happened.

"I'll get some more cream for the pitcher," he said, moving to the refrigerator.

Cursing under her breath, she ground the beans . . . a bit longer than necessary. The sound of the grinder matched her mood. Would Chance ever realize—much less admit— they belonged together?

They rejoined the others, and a few minutes later, Chance excused himself to go pick up Paige. Apparently, they had a double date with Stacy and Paul. Rory's heart sank. It all seemed so hopeless. Maybe Chance *didn't* return her feelings.

The fear made her all the more sensitive to her sister's chilly attitude as they cleaned up in the kitchen. They had the house to themselves since Adrian had left for work. Finally, Rory couldn't take it anymore. "Alli, if you have something to tell me, I wish you'd just say it, and get it over with."

Alli looked up from the serving plate she was drying. "What are you talking about?"

"I'm talking about the way you're acting, like you're mad at me or something."

"I'm not," Alli insisted, then hesitated. "I guess I'm just . . . uncomfortable. It's awkward, seeing you and Chance making eyes at each other, knowing he's practically engaged to Paige. Especially since I've met her. I happen to like Paige."

"I know." Rory sighed. Even though she didn't want to, she liked Paige, too. How could anyone *not* like Paige? She was quiet, sweet, thoughtful . . . and so much like Allison it was spooky sometimes. "I know how you feel. It's uncomfortable for me, too. But I hope you know I would never go after him if they were actually engaged. I'm not like that."

"I know, but it's still uncomfortable."

"What did you expect me to do, stand silently by, pining away and praying Chance would come to his senses all on his own?" Rory searched her sister's face, needing reassurance. "If I did that, he and Paige would be married and miserable before he realized he'd made a mistake."

"But . . ." Alli gripped the plate. "How do you know it would be a mistake? Paige seems so perfect for Chance. Okay"—she held up her hand—"I know you love Chance, but can you honestly say you want to be Mrs. Oliver Chancellor for the rest of your life?"

"What do you mean? Of course I want to marry him!"

"Rory, think about what you're saying!" Alli pleaded. "Families like the Chancellors are the closest thing we have to gentry in this country. That kind of status comes with a lot of responsibility and expectation. Are you up to playing the role of society wife?"

She felt her spine stiffen, because she'd tried so hard not to think of Chance like that. To think of him only how he was when they were alone. But she couldn't forget how commanding and refined he looked wearing a suit, how at ease he always seemed no matter the situation. That kind of confidence came from more than genes, it came from training.

She turned away. "I still say I'd make him a better wife than Paige would, because I love him, Alli. I make him happy!"

"And she doesn't?"

"Not the way I do." Her heart ached with doubt even as she said the words. "Okay, I admit, I was so eaten up with jealousy when Paige first started coming over here, it took me a while to see it, but Chance and Paige would be a disaster together. They have a bond, but they act like some old couple who've been married for forty years and gotten so complacent, all the fire has gone out of their relationship."

Allison finished drying the plate and put it in the cabinet. "There's more to life than passion. There's . . . trust and companionship." She turned back. "You can't tell me Chance and Paige don't have that. They *like* each other. They get along. And as for their supposed lack of passion, how do you know they don't have any? You don't know what they're like when they're alone."

The words were like an arrow, straight to the heart of all Rory's doubt. Because she didn't know. And she didn't want to imagine it. To picture Chance and Paige locked in a lover's embrace made her ill. She placed a hand over her stomach, to still a sudden swell of queasiness.

"You're out of your depth, Rory." Her sister placed a comforting hand on her arm as if to lessen the sting of her words. "And you're playing with people's lives. Yes, it's obvious you and Chance are extremely attracted to each other. It's . . . embarrassing sometimes, because it's happening right in front of Paige, and she seems so oblivious. Plus, I keep thinking about the fact that you're carrying his baby, but neither one of them knows."

The baby.

Rory continued to caress her stomach, no longer out of nausea, but out of a need to protect her child. What would happen when Chance found out? Would he want the baby as much as she had come to want it?

"Rory, you need to tell him."

She glanced up, wounded. "I thought you were on my side. That you agreed I should wait until I was ready."

"I didn't think you'd take this long to build up the courage."

"It's not a matter of courage. It's a matter of protecting my future with Chance . . . *if* I have one." She struggled for a way to explain. "I can't tell him until he realizes that what he feels for me is lasting and real in spite of our differences. That what we could have together will bring him so much more joy than what he has now. If he finds out I'm pregnant, and breaks up with Paige to marry me because it's 'the right thing to do,' neither of us will ever know for sure if he feels anything more than obligation—which could easily turn to resentment."

Alli grew still, her voice hushed. "How do you know he'll break up with Paige to marry you when he finds out?"

Rory pulled back, surprised. "Because he'll want to do the right thing."

"Rory," Allison sighed, "for men like Chance, the right thing might be nothing more than making some legal settlement to provide for you and the baby. I know that possibility hurts, but you have to face reality. He's Oliver Chancellor, for heaven's sake. One of *the* Chancellors."

"You think he'll toss some money at me, then go ahead and marry Perfect Paige just because she's a Baxter?"

"Possibly. If she'll still have him. Which she might. If they have a strong relationship, they could work this out, and go on to have a good marriage."

"*If* they have a strong relationship—which I don't think they do."

"Rory . . ." Alli started to argue, then shook her head.

"Okay, maybe you're right. Maybe they are wrong for each other. Maybe you and Chance can find some common ground. I just . . . I don't want you to get hurt."

"It's too late for that." Rory fought back tears. "I'm already hurting."

"I know. I'm sorry." Alli's face filled with empathy as she opened her arms and pulled Rory into a motherly hug.

Rory went eagerly into the embrace, holding on tight. "I'll be okay. This will work out, somehow. You'll see."

"Always the sunshine girl." Allison pulled back with a sad smile and straightened Rory's bangs. "Just one last thing . . . do you still want to go tomorrow?" Allison said, referring to the shopping trip they had been planning for days. A shopping trip that included Paige.

Rory nodded. "I can handle it."

"Are you sure?"

Rory's eyes narrowed. "If anyone is going to be left out of tomorrow's shopping trip, it's Paige, not me. She might be helping us out, but she isn't family, and I refuse to step aside and let her have free rein to decorate our inn."

"Okay." Allison raised her hands in surrender, recognizing the stubborn set of Rory's jaw. "We'll all go shopping together."

CHAPTER 18

She must have been insane, Rory decided the following day. It was the only reason she could think of for why she'd insisted on going to Houston with Allison and Paige for their shopping trip.

She sat in the back seat of her aunt's luxury sedan, where the blazing heat of September made her so light-headed all she wanted to do was lie down and rest her cheek on the cool leather. Would the first "Blue Northern" to end summer never come? To make matters worse, the farther they drove from the breeze off the gulf, the heavier the air felt. Even the air conditioner blowing full blast couldn't compensate for the scorching rays of sunshine beating in through the windows.

In the front seat, Allison and Paige mapped out their shopping trip like a SWAT team planning a raid. Rory marveled that anyone could stare at a street map and read discount coupons in a moving car without getting sick. The mere thought of it made her stomach churn.

Finally, Paige lifted her head, triumph in her eyes. "We have our route. And our mission, ladies, should we choose to accept it, is to find linens, pillows, bedspreads, shams, throw rugs, and Lord willin', some decorative art and knickknacks at prices that wouldn't send Chance through the roof."

"Is that possible?" Allison asked. "From what I can tell, no one is as tight-fisted as Chance."

"Chance isn't tight-fisted," Paige protested before Rory

could. "Quite the opposite. He has an eye for quality and appreciates the best. Which means, if we left the decorating up to him, he'd blow the whole budget on a few items with the plan to add more as money allowed."

"Oh, now that would give the inn a real cozy atmosphere," Allison said.

Rory frowned at the back of Paige's blond head. She had suspected the same thing about Chance, but hadn't known for sure. Because she was still getting to know him, while Paige had known him most of her life. Which did *not* mean Paige would make him a better wife!

"Just one word of warning." Paige turned in her seat so she could speak to both of them. "Don't tell him we went to discount stores, factory outlets, and dare I say"—she pressed a hand to her cheek—"thrift stores to get everything we needed without busting the budget he gave us. Chance hates shopping under the best of conditions, but he thinks discount stores are disorganized, dirty, and totally lacking in service."

"Uh, Paige," Allison interjected, "they are."

"I know." Paige's eyes twinkled. "But he thinks that means they have inferior merchandise. He doesn't understand that *(a)* it's the same merchandise you find in department stores, but at a fraction of the price. And *(b)* it's exhilarating to search through all that disorganized mess, like you're digging for buried treasure. It takes knowledge, experience, and nerves of steel to find the gold and snatch it away from the other treasure hunters."

Allison took her eyes off the road long enough to give Paige a look of admiration. "Are you sure we're not twins separated at birth?"

"Soul sisters, maybe." Paige laughed, making Rory feel like a third wheel. She almost wished she hadn't come. The soul sisters in the front seat didn't need her, and being near Paige was just making her sick with guilt and self-doubt.

She watched as the woman folded the map and stuffed

the discount coupons back into the envelope she'd brought. She found it ironic that Paige kept discount coupons in a cream-colored envelope with her monogram embossed on the flap. And that she dressed in diamonds and designer clothes to shop at thrift stores.

"You know," Paige said after a while, "there's something I've always been curious about."

"What's that?" Allison asked while Rory rested her head on the seat back and closed her eyes. With luck she'd drift to sleep.

"The legend of the Pearl," Paige said, her voice blending with the sound of the tires on the highway. "I know the Pearl is Marguerite herself, and not an actual pearl, but how can a person be a good-luck charm?"

"It has to do with her birth," Allison answered. "Marguerite was the daughter of a French prostitute in New Orleans, and was born in a brothel. The Creole woman who delivered her practiced voodoo. She knew Marguerite's mother planned to send the baby to an orphanage, but the thought broke her heart because she knew how horrible those places could be. So, when the baby was born, she held her up above her head and named her Marguerite, which means 'pearl,' then cast a charm that included the words 'Whoever keeps this pearl shall be blessed with good fortune.' It's a shame she didn't say 'takes good care of' instead of just 'keeps,' but once the words were spoken, the magic was cast."

"A voodoo charm?" Paige asked, sounding intrigued. "Do you think such things work?"

Allison thought a moment. "I'm not sure what I believe. But Marguerite's mother was very superstitious—and greedy. She kept her baby simply to see if the blessing would come true. Sure enough, a few months later, a wealthy gentleman became wildly infatuated with her and set her up as his mistress in a fancy town house. His own finances drastically improved after that, and the mother told him it was due to Marguerite, which effectively discouraged him from ever dismissing her as his mistress."

"I'll bet." Paige laughed.

"The man doted on Marguerite," Alli said. "Perhaps out of genuine affection, perhaps out of greed. Mostly, though, he indulged her love of music by taking her to the opera whenever he took her mother.

"When she was old enough, she joined the stage as a singer. The theater where she started wasn't one of the best, but it quickly grew in popularity, making the owner very rich. He heard the story of Marguerite's birth, and treated her like a queen to keep her from ever leaving. Word of Marguerite's power as a good-luck charm spread, and eventually Henri LeRoche heard the tale."

"He was already living in Galveston, wasn't he?" Paige asked.

Allison nodded. "He was older than her and not that good-looking, but according to Marguerite's diary he 'wore his power like a cloak of danger that enticed even as it frightened.' "

"You have her diary?"

"Several of them. Both the originals, which I can sorta-kinda read since I took a lot of French, and the English translations my great-grandmother did.

"Anyway, when he first came to see her backstage, he swore he'd fallen in love with her at first sight. She'd heard all that before, though, and tried to gently send him on his way. But Henri was not the kind of man to take no for an answer. He courted her without mercy, showering her with flowers and jewels, offering her anything she desired if she would be his. But Marguerite was a wealthy woman in her own right by that time, and was not about to become any man's kept mistress. Her price was marriage. After months of trying to seduce her, Henri finally gave in and proposed."

"How romantic."

"Not exactly," Alli said. "As soon as they were married, the 'courtship' ended very abruptly. He beat her on their

wedding night to prove that she was his property now, for
him to do with as he pleased."

"That's horrible!" Paige gasped.

"Yeah, it is," Allison agreed quietly.

Sitting in the back seat with her eyes still closed, Rory
wished her sister hadn't begun the tale. It was too easy to
picture it all, to almost feel Marguerite's terror and despair.

"The wedding night was only the beginning," Allison
continued. "Even though he abused her, Henri's fortune
grew dramatically once he brought her to Galveston and
the house he built for her. After one particularly brutal
beating, Marguerite tried to escape, which was when he
quit letting her leave Pearl Island. The house that was supposed to be her wedding gift became her prison."

"That's so awful," Paige said. "But if she was kept so
secluded, how did she meet Captain Kingsley? Much less
find enough time alone with him to fall in love?"

"You forget," Allison said. "Captain Kingsley was a
smuggler before the Civil War, and a very cunning one at
that. He was used to slipping beneath people's guard to
accomplish his goal. From the moment he saw Marguerite,
she was his obsession. She tried to discourage him at first,
out of fear of Henri, and because she was married, after
all. She might have hated her husband, but she was Cath-
olic to the bone and believed devoutly in keeping her
vows. But Captain Kingsley was impossible for her to resist. Swaggering, confident, larger than life, gorgeous to
look at, and willing to do anything to win her, even die
trying to save her."

"Can you imagine?" Paige sighed. "I don't envy her the
rest of her life, but to have a man like Captain Jack Kingsley sweep you off your feet . . ."

"It is exciting to think about . . . but in the end, all it
did was get her killed," Allison said. "And yet . . . it's nice
to know that after all the people who used her during her
life, at least she found someone who truly loved her in the
end."

"What a sad story."

"Sadder still is one of the last entries she made in her dairy."

"Oh?"

"I can't remember it word for word, but basically she says it took her her whole life to realize there are many kinds of false love—love based on lust, greed, desperation, and even obligation. Those kinds of love are false because they only touch the surface and require very little to maintain the illusion. True love takes courage, because you have to offer yourself, everything you are, weaknesses and all. And that is the greatest fear of all because rejection of self from someone you love would be a pain beyond enduring."

"Yes," Paige said quietly, "that is the greatest fear."

Her voice sounded so defeated, Rory opened her eyes. She found Paige gazing out the side window. Marguerite's story had a way of making anyone feel sad, but there was something different about Paige's response, as if the tale had hit her too close to the heart. Puzzled, Rory caught her sister's eye in the rear-view mirror. Allison shrugged, apparently having no clue what had caused Paige's withdrawal.

"I talked to Captain Bob the other day, about the ship for the ball," Paige said, effectively changing the subject. "He says the *Pirate's Pleasure* needs some repairs before she can leave her slip, but the captain is hiring on extra hands to get it done in time."

Following Paige's lead, Allison turned the talk to the preparations for the ball. Rory let her eyes drift closed again, but she couldn't shake a nagging sense of curiosity stirred by Paige's response. Had the story made Paige think of her relationship with Chance?

Rory thought of Marguerite's words, that true love took courage and a willingness to share oneself. Was that what was wrong between Chance and Paige? Had they been raised with such a strict sense of what was proper that they didn't know how to express something as messy as emotions?

And if that was true of Chance, how would Rory ever get him to admit he loved her—if he even did?

Six grueling hours later, the three women were flushed from the thrill of victory. So far, no blood had been shed, but it had been a near thing at Saversmart when Paige had spotted a Laura Ashley bedspread the same instant as another shopper. After that skirmish had been settled in Paige's favor, they realized they'd saved enough to squeeze in some silk plants from a wholesaler where Mr. Baxter's construction company had an account.

Then onto their final stop, the thrift store. Allison and Paige barely contained their inner excitement when they discovered a truck had just delivered the leftovers from an estate sale. The two of them set about filling cardboard boxes with porcelain figurines, ruby glass bud vases, brass candlesticks, and hand-tatted doilies while Rory wandered deeper into the shop.

There in the back, she discovered another room . . . filled with baby furniture and clothes. Her heart clutched as she stood on the threshold. Bassinets, cribs, and brightly colored toys beckoned her inside. She glanced over her shoulder, wondering what she'd say if Paige saw her shopping for baby things.

She shouldn't risk it. She knew she shouldn't. But the lure was too great to resist.

She moved toward a display of clothes for newborns, and marveled at outfits so tiny they looked like doll's clothes. Oh, and a christening gown! With miles of white lace and pink ribbon. A shelf of shoes nearly made her weep as she pictured a child stumbling through those first steps.

She turned and found a playpen filled with stuffed animals. She'd loved stuffed animals when she was a girl, and still had all of her favorites put away in the top of her closet. Although one could never have too many stuffed animals, she decided as she started lifting one after the other out of the pen.

A pink pig made her smile, while a green frog with a floppy yellow crown brought outright laughter. Then she spied the cutest rag doll angel she'd ever seen. Picking it up, she admired the sweet round face with hand-painted blue eyes. Braided yarn served for hair and gold lamé stuffed with cotton formed the wings. She straightened the shiny tinsel halo, and felt her heart melt.

"I'm going to have an angel," she whispered to the doll. The trusting blue eyes smiled back at her. *And I can't wait to hold her. Or him. But I hope it's a her, with pretty blond hair just like yours.*

"Rory?" Allison's voice came from the other room.

She turned in time to see her sister appear in the doorway. With a jolt, she looked for Paige, and sighed in relief when she didn't see her.

"What are you doing?" Alli remained in the doorway, staring at the room as if it held all the demons from hell.

"Sorry"—Rory offered a weak smile—"I couldn't help myself."

Alli nodded and averted her eyes. "We're um . . . ready to check out."

"I'll be right there." Rory started to put the angel back in the playpen, but the doll was gazing up at her with that sweet face, and she just couldn't do it. Pulling it to her chest, she headed for the front of the store.

"Rory, you can't buy that," Alli said in a frantic whisper. "What will Paige think?"

Just ahead, Rory could see Paige at the register helping the volunteer worker sort out all the items in the cardboard boxes. "I'll tell her it's a gift for a friend."

Alli started to object, but by then they were within earshot of Paige, so she subsided. Fortunately Paige accepted Rory's "for a friend" story without batting an eye.

"Well," Paige said once they'd loaded everything into

the car. "I don't know about y'all, but I'm starved. How about if we stop for something to eat on the way home?"

Alli and Paige decided on a popular Mexican restaurant that was on the road back to Galveston. By the time they arrived, the place was hopping with the happy hour crowd. They placed their orders at the counter, then managed to find a table in a reasonably quiet corner.

"I can't wait to tell Chance about our good luck today," Paige said as they settled in their chairs.

"I'm sure he'll be thrilled about how much money you saved us," Allison said.

"Oh, it isn't just the money," Paige said. "It's the whole project. I haven't seen him enjoy himself this much since he got his first Monopoly board." Paige's eyes twinkled with laughter. "Whenever we played with the other kids in the neighborhood, he always insisted on being the banker."

Rory folded her arms, thinking if she had to listen to many more of Paige's stories about Chance, she'd scream.

Their order number came over the loudspeaker. "I'll get it," Allison offered. "Who wants salsa?"

Paige said she did and Allison took off to weave her way through the crowd.

Alone with Paige, Rory shifted with discomfort. She should have offered to go get the food. Although this was a good opportunity to get the answers to some of the doubts that had plagued her since her talk with Alli yesterday. She had to know once and for all if winning Chance's heart was a lost cause.

But how to start?

"Um, you and Chance, you've known each other a long time," Rory said.

"Forever, it seems," Paige answered offhandedly.

Rory tapped her fingertips on the tabletop. She wanted to ask if their relationship was as dispassionate as it seemed. Or if they were wild for each other when they were alone. But how to ease into that? "I was just wondering . . . what was he like, you know, as a boy?"

Paige thought for a while. "Serious," she finally said. "Quiet, but not shy. He was always very self-sufficient, and perfectly happy with his own company, even though he's always had plenty of friends."

Yes, but when did you two become more than just friends? Glancing toward the counter, Rory tried to judge how much time she had alone with Paige. Her sister had picked up their order but the line at the salsa bar would take a while to get through.

She racked her brain for a subtle way to ask what she needed to know. Only there didn't seem to be a subtle approach, so she steeled herself and jumped right in. "I know you and Chance aren't officially engaged, but there seems to be an understanding, and well . . . I just wanted to know how you felt about that."

Paige sighed. "Like I said, Chance and I have known each other a long time. It's always been assumed that we'd marry someday."

"Yes, but . . ." She leaned forward, desperation making her heart pound. "Do you *want* to marry him?"

Paige sat back, her face going pale. "Well, yes, of course." Her eyes darted from side to side. "I mean, I guess I do."

"You *guess* you do?" Rory repeated in stunned disbelief. If Chance wanted to marry her, there'd be no guessing how she'd feel. She'd be brimming over with so much joy she wouldn't be able to contain it all. "What do you mean, you 'guess' you do?"

"I mean—of course I want to marry Chance." Paige fumbled with her napkin. "Why wouldn't I? I'd be a fool if I didn't. Besides, I don't have a choice. My mother's already planning the wedding, and Daddy is practically handing out cigars and birth announcements for his first grandchild. It's too late to back out now."

"Paige—" Rory fought the urge to shake her. Chance deserved more than a wife who would join him at the altar only because her parents were pushing her there. He deserved someone who loved him beyond reason, someone who would do anything to be with him, someone who could barely face the thought of life without him. He deserved . . . *her,* dammit! She sat back, seething. "It's never too late to break off an engagement."

"But it is!" Paige's eyes filled with tears. "You don't understand. Chance and I *have* to get married. We don't have a choice!"

The words slammed into Rory with the force of a physical blow. Paige was pregnant. With Chance's child. The son of a bitch! Chance hadn't just gotten her pregnant. He'd gotten Paige pregnant, too.

She wanted to murder the man, cut off his vitals and the hands that had touched another woman after he had touched her. Or maybe even before. It didn't matter that he and Paige were dating, that Paige had more claim to him than she had. Logic had nothing to do with the sense of betrayal burning through her veins. As soon as they returned to Galveston, she'd hunt Chance down and kill him.

CHAPTER 19

Chance realized he was in trouble. After showering, he fixed himself a drink and took it out on the balcony hoping to ease the tension in his shoulders. They'd all planned on taking the evening off since Adrian had to work and the women didn't know how long they'd be in Houston. But then the construction foreman had called to say the desk they'd ordered for the office had been delivered.

Allison had searched through an ungodly number of furniture catalogs before she'd found a desk that would work, one with the look of an antique but the functionality of a computer desk. He couldn't resist setting it up as a surprise for Aurora, so he'd headed out to the inn as soon as he'd gotten off work.

The crew had gone by the time he arrived, so he had the place to himself. It was the first time he'd ever been alone in the house, he'd realized as he settled in the parlor-turned-office. With only the creaks and pops of an old house to keep him company, his mind had had too much time to wander. He'd been sitting cross-legged on the floor, attaching two panels when a strange sense of aloneness came over him—like an odd hush in the air.

He'd looked around, trying to pinpoint the source of his uneasiness. Even with evening sunlight pouring through the tall slender windows of the tower, the house had felt like a vast cave lacking the life that normally pulsed in the air. It lacked life because Aurora wasn't there. Of all the people who usually filled the house, she was the only one he missed.

Fast on the heels of that unsettling thought had come the knowledge that she was the real reason he'd become involved with the inn. There was still the thrill of a challenge to start a new business, but that paled when compared to his need to simply be near Aurora.

Rattled, he'd redoubled his efforts to finish the desk and think about Paige, the woman he should have been missing. He'd managed to get the massive L-shaped piece of furniture together and standing before the fireplace, then he'd gone about setting up the computer system. When he'd finished, he'd stepped back to consider the placement of the keyboard and monitor. An image of Aurora sitting there, working away, had risen clearly in his mind. He'd pictured her glancing up, smiling at him, and something warm and thrilling yet frightening in its strength had filled him so swiftly, he'd nearly staggered backward.

And that's when he'd finally accepted that he was in trouble. Serious trouble. The woman was taking over his brain. It was the only explanation for why he couldn't stop thinking about her. No matter what he did, his desperate need to be near her kept growing, pushing everything else out of the way, until he feared soon there would be nothing left but the ache of wanting to be with her.

He'd quickly finished setting up the office, and had headed straight home for a shower and a break from the inn. But even now, standing on the balcony, he couldn't shake the nerves that made his hands tremble. To escape his thoughts, he concentrated on the sounds of traffic seven stories below. On the other side of the busy seawall, sunbathers and surfers were packing up their ice chests and beach bags.

How long had it been since he'd whiled away a day on the beach with friends? Years, he realized with disgust. Lately he hadn't even had time to go jogging on the seawall, dodging bicyclists and camera-toting tourists. He spent his weekdays rushing through work so he could spend his evenings and weekends working at Pearl Island. With Aurora.

His thoughts went instantly back to her.

God help him, he was in trouble. And he didn't know what to do about it. He couldn't look at her or even hear her voice without wanting to touch her, to feel her body pressed against his, to taste her lips and go on tasting them until she filled his senses. Resisting her was becoming more of a torture, not less of one, as he had hoped.

In the midst of his whirling thoughts came the echo of her voice: ". . . life would be boring if we never gave in to temptation. Don't you think?"

Reckless thoughts followed. Memories and fantasies blended to form an image of life with Aurora at his side. It would be a far cry from the order he preferred. But the chaos would be balanced by the contentment of waking up each morning with her beside him. Of seeing her smile before he even had his first cup of coffee. Of walking into the inn every evening when he finished at the bank, and having her take him into her arms and kiss him with all that passion she had for life.

Staggered, he leaned forward and braced his hands against the rail. How easy it would be to give in to temptation and let himself fall in love with her. For a second, he thought he *was* falling, literally, off the balcony to the hard pavement below.

He jerked back from the rail just as the doorbell rang. Taking a breath, he tried to calm the racing of his heart. The last thing he wanted was company, but at the moment, he'd welcome any distraction. Returning to the coolness of his air-conditioned apartment, he set his glass aside as he moved toward the door. The bell rang again, several times in a row.

"Goddammit, Oliver Chancellor." A fist pounded on the panel. "Open this door!"

"Aurora?" His pulse quickened as he rushed forward,

alarmed. "What is it? What's wrong?" He opened the door and had only a moment to absorb the shock of seeing her angry face before she threw herself against his chest with her fists clenched.

"You son of a bitch!"

"Aurora! What's happened?"

"I hate you!" She hit his chest with the side of her fist.

"Ouch! That hurt!"

"Good! I hope it did." Tears welled up in her eyes, making her voice wobble. "Because you hurt me!"

"What are you talking about?"

"I just found out." She swiped angrily at her cheeks. "Paige told me!"

"Paige told you what?"

"That she's—that you—that she's pregnant!"

"What!" Another punch from her fist couldn't have knocked him back as far. "Paige is pregnant!"

"As if you didn't know, you son of a bitch!" She hit him again, but the gesture had lost its heat. "I just want to know, were you already sleeping with her when you went to bed with me?"

"Whoa, wait. Back up." He ran his hands through his hair. "Who told you Paige is pregnant?"

"She did! Barely an hour ago."

He pressed a hand to his forehead, trying to take it all in. *Paige pregnant?* Her parents would kill her. "Did she tell you who the father is?"

Aurora stared for half a second, then erupted. "What do you mean? *You're* the father, you jerk!"

"Me!" He froze, confused, then a burst of stunned laughter escaped him. "I'm afraid that's impossible. Unless it was immaculate conception."

"What?" She went still, frowning.

"Aurora." He smiled as the world settled back into place. "Paige can't possibly be pregnant. She and I have never been together, and I doubt she's seeing someone else."

"But she said—" Her brow dimpled. "At least I thought she said . . ."

"Why don't you come have a seat and tell me exactly what she did say?"

Looking a bit lost, she let him lead her to the sofa. "Now"—he sat beside her—"tell me what happened."

"I went shopping with Alli and Paige today."

"Yes, I know that."

"When we were done, we stopped to eat. Paige and I started talking about things. Well, you mostly. And she said the two of you *had* to get married. That's exactly what she said, that you *had* to. Everyone knows when a couple says that, there's a baby on the way."

Chance shook his head. "Not in this case."

"I don't understand." Her eyes searched his for answers.

He took a breath and let it out in a noisy rush. How to explain something that had always just been? "Paige and I were close growing up. At first because our mothers were such good friends, so I spent a lot of time over at her house, and she spent a lot at mine. As we grew older, we started doing things on our own because we enjoyed each other's company. You know, movies, school dances. At some point, one of our mothers said, 'Wouldn't it be great if Chance and Paige got married? Then we wouldn't just be friends, we'd be family.' Somewhere along the way it quit being a question and turned into an assumption."

She frowned at him. "You and Paige are going to marry because your mothers think it would be neat to be related?"

"No, of course not. There's more to it than that." *Isn't there?* The thought stopped him cold. A realization that had hovered on the edges of his mind moved full blown into the light. Marrying Paige had never been his idea. She'd always been more his friend than his girlfriend. Which was why kissing her felt so wrong—like kissing a sister.

The knowledge brought relief that swamped him like a tidal wave. He shook his head to clear it and nearly laughed. "You know what? It doesn't matter. Not anymore."

"What do you mean?" She frowned as if he'd gone mad.

He looked at her and felt as if he were back up on a precipice, but this time he knew nothing would pull him back. He was ready to take the final step over the edge. "Aurora, I'm not going to marry Paige."

"What?" she whispered as her expression filled with hope.

"I can't. I can't do that to her. Or me. I'm not in love with her, and I realize now I never will be. I think I know what love feels like, and it has nothing to do with the comfortable, easy things I feel for Paige. In fact, it feels more like having the flu—you know, dizziness, nausea, cold sweats—not something I particularly like, but it's there, and I can't stop feeling it."

The look of hope shifted to confusion. "What are you saying?"

"I'm saying"—he smiled gently and cupped her cheek with his palm—"you ruined everything. I had my whole life carefully planned out. What I'd do for the next five years, ten years, even what I'd do when I retired. Then you came along and changed it all. Because you changed me. I don't know anything about the future anymore or if this has a chance in hell of working out. I only know I love you."

His heart pounded as he waited for her eyes to go soft. Waited for her to sigh and say she cared for him too. Love was too much to ask for so soon, but he suspected— hoped—she cared.

Instead, she kept staring at him as if she couldn't believe what he'd just said. He could hardly believe it himself. Dizzy with emotion, he tipped his head and started to lower his lips toward hers.

"Hold on." She braced a hand in the center of his chest. When he pulled back, he realized her eyes were narrowed with something that looked like anger. "Let me get this straight. You're in love with me—a fact that makes you nauseous—and because of this unpleasant, and unwanted emotion, I've ruined your life. Is that about it? Or did I miss something?"

"Only the part about me not wanting to marry Paige because I want to be free to spend time with you."

"Well, now, isn't that just too bad. Since I suddenly have no desire to be with you."

"Excuse me?" He pulled back in disbelief as she stood and stalked toward the door.

"Don't bother to show me out. I know the way." She reached the door and turned to him. "I'd tell you to have a nice life, but I guess it's too late for that, since I've already ruined it, so I'll simply say goodbye."

"The hell you will." Before he knew how, he was across the room with one hand on the door to keep her from opening it. "I tell you I love you and you walk out on me?"

"You also said that being in love with me made you sick at your stomach."

"Dammit, Aurora!" He struggled to find the right words. "I'm no good at this, all right? I don't know how to explain what I feel because you terrify me to the point I can't think straight. The only thing that scares me more than the thought of being with you is the thought of being without you."

"I frighten you?" she asked in a small voice.

"I said 'terrify.' 'Frighten' is too mild a word, trust me."

"But . . . why?"

"Because you could hurt me so easily. Because I can't imagine you ever feeling something this huge for me." He cupped her face in his trembling hands and stared into her eyes, willing her to understand, because he couldn't handle it if she walked out that door. "I want you so much. I'll take whatever you'll give, if you'll just let me be part of your life."

"You idiot." Tears welled in her eyes. "You really don't know, do you?"

"Know what?"

"How much I do love you." She clutched the front of his shirt as if she wanted to shake him, but clung instead. "I love you so much, it's eating me up inside. I've been dying of love for you for weeks. Do you know what it's been like, feeling this way, wanting you so desperately, and having to watch you with Paige?"

The words and the tears were like knives to his heart. "Oh God, Aurora . . ." He gathered her in his arms, cradling her head on his shoulder. "I didn't know."

"How could you *not* know?" She sniffed. "I love you so much, I hate you. Every day you've hurt me more than anyone has ever hurt me."

"I'm so sorry, baby. Don't cry. I'm so sorry." He kissed her forehead, her cheek. "Forgive me. Please. Hate me all you want, but please, don't stop loving me."

His mouth settled over hers and he poured everything he could into the kiss, praying for forgiveness, praying she still loved him. To learn he'd had her love all along only to lose it now would kill him. He pulled back enough to cradle her face in his hands. "I'm sorry I hurt you." He kissed her cheek. "I'm so sorry. I didn't know." He kissed her forehead. "Forgive me." His lips touched each corner of her mouth. "Let me love you."

"Yes." She sighed and kissed him back. "Yes, yes. Love me, Chance. Make the hurting go away."

"I will. I promise I will." With trembling arms, he scooped her up to carry her into the bedroom, kissing her all the way, even as he laid her on the bed. Greater than the need to join his body to hers was the need to soothe her hurt. His fingers fumbled with the buttons on her blouse. She tried to help, but he brushed her hands away.

"No, let me," he whispered, his voice hoarse with emotion. "Let me love you."

She relaxed into the pillows, her eyes still bright with

tears as she watched him. The longing he saw made his heart ache. He kissed her cheeks, her eyelids, tasting the saltiness of her sorrow, then he moved to her chin, her neck, where her pulse beat against his lips. As the shirt opened, he trailed kisses downward, between her breasts, over the warm skin of her stomach. He felt her muscles quiver, and desire rushed through him, but he pushed his own need away to concentrate on her.

He removed her clothes and his own so they could lie together, skin to skin. His hands shook as he ran them over her sides, down her legs, then back up in long soothing strokes. He kept his kisses light, a swirl of tongue around her navel, a slow lick up toward her breasts. Her nipples rose to hard tempting peaks, begging his attention. When he took one into his mouth, she arched beneath him, calling his name.

"Shh, I'm here, I'm here," he cooed as he moved to the other breast.

She barely heard his words over the frantic beating of her pulse. His gentle touches eased the pain in her heart, but not the ache of desire. Every caress made her crave more. Her breasts were so sensitive from the baby they'd created, she needed him to suckle them harder, even as she feared it would be too much. She buried her hands in his hair, trying to guide him without words. He cupped one breast, sucking the nipple into his mouth. She cried out as pleasure knifed through her.

"Did I hurt you?"

"Yes. No. I don't know. Just love me, Chance. Love me."

"I will. I do." He moved upward and gave her one of his deep drugging kisses that had every nerve ending in her body tingling as he moved a hand over her stomach. She shivered in anticipation as his fingers slipped between her legs. She opened her thighs eagerly, desperate for release, but he teased her with feather-light touches. Grabbing his head, she kissed him with abandon, twisting and moving her body against him.

He broke the kiss and slipped lower, over her collarbone, her breast. His tongue forged a maddening trail down her stomach.

"Chance, please," she begged as her hips lifted and fell, seeking relief. She reached for his shoulders, trying to pull him back up so he would end the torture of anticipation.

"Shh," he soothed. "Let me."

She fell back, afraid she'd drown from the pleasure rushing through her veins.

He settled between her legs and his breath tickled her curls. Then, his mouth reached its goal, and she came undone. With his hands cupping her bottom, he held her to him, pleasuring her through wave after wave until she fell limp and gasping for air.

She didn't even feel him move, but suddenly, he was over her again, his weight braced on his arms as he watched her. When her vision cleared, he smiled. "Better?" he asked.

"Yes," she breathed, and nearly laughed from the giddiness that had invaded her limbs. Though she felt almost too weak to move, she lifted her hands and ran them down his firmly muscled chest to his taut stomach. Air hissed through his teeth as he sucked in a breath, and she realized the trembling wasn't all hers. His whole body quivered at her slightest caress.

Warm satisfaction filled her as she watched his face. She reached lower to take him in her hand and gently squeezed. His stomach muscles jumped and he swore as a bead of moisture escaped his control. He pulsed with life as she moved her hand up and down, reveling in the feel of him.

"I've wanted you so much," she whispered. "Ever since the first time, I've thought about being with you again every day."

"I've wanted you too. More than I can possibly say." His face lined with strain.

"Then show me."

"I will." He kissed her briefly, but to her surprise, he pulled away. When he glanced toward his nightstand, she understood. A condom, she realized, and shook her head. "No, don't. You don't need anything."

He looked torn, but she guided him to her, lifting her hips. His eyes closed as he slipped inside that first little bit. She moved her hands to cup his bottom, felt his muscles flex as he filled her slowly with small thrusts, going deeper each time until they were fully joined.

She sighed at the sweet bliss of having him inside her, for the link went beyond a physical joining. He lowered his chest and slipped his arms beneath her so they were heart to heart.

Closing her eyes, she held him tight as he moved over her. *Yes,* she thought, letting the joy heal all the pain and longing of the past weeks. Tears rose up, filling her throat, but she swallowed them back and clung to him. He cradled her head, kissing her mouth as if starved for her taste as his thrusts increased in strength and speed.

They were both gasping for air and straining together as the pleasure built. It crashed over them in a hot, sweet burst of light. They clung to each other, holding on to the moment until the surge of passion faded to leave them trembling in each other's arms.

He sagged so heavily against her, at first she wondered if he'd passed out, but the effort of asking was beyond her. She lay as limply as he, her heart hammering against her ribs. Or was that his heart pounding?

"Am I crushing you?" he mumbled into the pillow.

"I don't think so," she murmured back, her body so sated she wasn't sure how she felt.

"Good." A delayed tremor moved through him and he groaned. "I don't think I can move just yet."

"Me, either." She smiled, wanting to lie there and hold

him forever. Somehow, she managed to tighten her arms and legs about him.

He moaned as the motion pulled him deeper inside her and she realized he was still semi-hard. The feel of him renewed her strength a bit, enough to nudge him with her hips. He groaned and, apparently able to move after all, lifted his weight onto his forearms. He kissed her deeply as he lengthened inside her, not as hard as he'd been before, but definitely not slipping away.

Lifting his head, he gazed down at her and flexed his hips, not a thrust, just a small movement that pressed him deeper.

As if nothing at all were going on below the waist, he smoothed the hair back from her face. "Stay with me," he said softly.

She glanced toward the window to see the sun wasn't even down. "We have all evening."

"No." He kissed her cheek, nuzzled her ear. His hips flexed again and he lengthened a bit more. "All night."

She tried to think. "I'll need to . . . call Allison. Let her know . . . where I am."

"Later." His hips moved and her vision went dim. He shifted lazily to her other ear. "Are you sore?"

She skimmed her hands down his back and lifted her hips. "Ask me in an hour."

"If I live that long." His body shook with laughter. "God, if you knew how badly I've been wanting you . . . and all the things I've fantasized about doing."

"So, you do have wicked thoughts."

"Oh, yeah."

His words and his expression sent a shiver of excitement through her as a few of her own fantasies came to mind. "Like what?"

He hesitated a moment, searching her eyes. What he saw was an eager desire that matched his own. Smiling, he moved onto his knees so her bottom was cradled between his thighs. She moaned and arched to keep the link from being broken. He lifted her feet onto his chest and leaned forward, bracing his hand on the backs of her thighs, delighting in her limber, well-toned body.

Slowly, he pressed forward, going even deeper than he had before. *Oh, God.* He closed his eyes against pleasure so intense it sank into his gut like claws. After a few breaths, he opened his eyes and saw her expression of greedy wonder. With a little sound, almost a pout, she wiggled her bottom, wanting more.

That was all it took for the beast to break free. He gave himself over to it, no longer trying to hold back, moving strong and hard. The climax ripped the air from his lungs. He heard her cry of welcome, realized she was right there with him, her neck arched back, her eyes closed in ecstasy. Satisfaction wrung the last drop of strength from his bones.

He collapsed beside her, rather than on top. A good thing, since he really wouldn't be able to move this time. Not until his heart and lungs stopped convulsing.

"Good God!" he breathed, staring at the ceiling. Turning his head, he gazed at her in awe. She was lying on her back just like him, with arms and legs sprawled, chest heaving with every breath. "Are you all right?"

She turned and dazzled him with a grin. "I think I died for a second there."

"Me, too." He smiled. "About five times in a row."

"Sorry." She laughed. "I'll try to be more gentle with you next time."

"Come here." He reached for her and helped her roll toward him until she was cradled against his side with her head resting on his shoulder. Love swelled inside him. "I think I deserve a medal."

"You were pretty spectacular."

"Not for that!" He gave her bottom a light swat. "For *not* doing that." He moved his head against the pillow until he could see her face. "Do you have any idea how hard it's been to resist you these past weeks?"

Her expression sobered as she propped her chin on his chest. "You didn't have to resist."

But he had needed to. He wasn't a man who switched tracks easily. He'd needed these weeks to examine the situation from every angle, to be sure he was making the right choice—especially a choice this life-changing. Letting his gaze roam over her face, a sense of peace filled him. He'd made the right choice, and he was glad he'd given himself the time to do it slowly so there would never be any regrets. Consequences, yes, but no regrets. What he felt for Aurora went beyond anything he'd ever imagined. She completed him.

She trailed a finger across his lower lip. "That's some smile you've got there. Wanna tell me what you're thinking?"

"How much I love you. And yet how little I really know about you."

"What do you mean?" A frown puckered her brow. "We've seen each other nearly every day for a whole summer."

"True, but it isn't enough. I want to know everything about you from the day you were born until the day you accosted me on Pearl Island."

"I didn't accost you." She rose up in mock offense.

"You knocked me down and beat me with that foreclosure sign."

"You fell down, and the wind blew the sign against you."

"If you insist." He rolled her onto her back and gave her a thorough kiss using every ounce of skill he possessed. When he raised his head, her eyes looked dazed. "Are you hungry?"

"W-what?" She blinked up at him.

"Hungry. Food. Eat." She just stared at him so he kissed the tip of her nose. "Well, I'm starved. How about we order a pizza? We can eat right here in bed while you tell me your life story. Then we can try out a few more fantasies. Whadaya say?"

She gave him a "get real" look.

"Okay, if you insist, we'll skip the talking and go straight back to making out. But first I need food."

They stayed up half the night, eating, talking, loving. She told him about growing up with her aunt and siblings, and a little about her parents' life on the road with the theater troupe, even though she'd been too young to remember it. He told her about growing up as an only child, the Chancellor heir, the friends he'd made in college and some of the pranks they'd pulled. Yet, somehow, it sounded a little lonely to her, in spite of the privilege of wealth. He'd loved his parents and had lots of friends, but he really was the loner Paige had described.

Paige. The name brought a twinge of guilt. She pushed it away to concentrate on the sleepy rumble of Chance's voice. She snuggled deeper in his arms, inhaling the scent of his warm skin. Her last thought before drifting to sleep was a wish that morning would never come. With morning would come reality. A reality that included Paige and a child she hadn't yet told him about.

CHAPTER 20

The radio alarm clicked on, spilling out the morning news. Vaguely aware that it had done so a few times already, Chance hit the snooze button and started to go back to sleep but stopped when he saw the time. Okay, so he'd already hit the snooze *several* times. He was also freezing from lack of covers.

Cursing the air-conditioning vent over the bed, he rolled toward Aurora, hoping to warm himself with her body heat before he braved getting up. She'd created a cocoon with the covers, so he had to peel away the bedspread and sheet before he even found her. He revealed her mass of reddish-gold hair, then her face. A few more tugs, and her peaceful expression turned to a pout.

"Come on, Aurora, I'm freezing." He managed to wiggle his way inside her cocoon and up against her blazing hot body. He tucked his hands between their chests and wedged his feet between her calves.

"Cold feet," she protested sleepily and tried to move away.

"Oh, no you don't." He wrapped his arms around her and hauled her on top of him where he could rub his hands on her back, and his thighs against hers, trying to create as much friction as possible.

"Chance," she grumbled, batting her hair away from her face. "What are you doing?"

"Trying to get warm. You stole all the covers."

"Oh." She looked down at him, her eyes sleepy. "Sorry."

He marveled that any woman could look so good upon first waking. "You're forgiven. As long as you warm me up."

A lazy smile spread over her face. "I think I can handle that." She lowered her mouth to his for a slow good-morning kiss. Using just her lips, she molded her mouth to his for a series of teasing touches. She tilted her head to a different angle, tasted his bottom lip, the corners of his mouth. He hardened against her belly and she purred in approval.

Rolling her onto her back, he took over the kiss but kept it all tantalizing lips that sent tingles racing through his system. She arranged the covers around them, until they were lost in a dark cave of warm pleasure. He slipped inside her so naturally, almost as if the link had never been broken, and he absorbed her moan as she absorbed his body. They moved together, slowly, languidly, the kiss deepening apace with the beat of their hearts. He cradled her head, kissing her endlessly.

A rush of love spread through him, and he closed his eyes as he gave himself over to the pleasure. When she peaked, he followed a heartbeat behind, never breaking the kiss. The last shudder finally subsided. He lifted his head and smiled down at her. God, he loved her so much, he wondered that he didn't die from it.

Her expression was both glowing and mischievous. "Did that warm you up?"

"Oh, yeah." He laughed and gave her one more quick kiss. "Too bad we can't try it again now that we're both fully awake." At her puzzled look, he said, "I have to get to work."

She frowned and looked away. "So, I guess I need to get out of here so you can dress."

"No need to rush." Easing their bodies apart, he settled beside her where he could smooth the hair from her face.

"I need to take a shower, but do you want to duck into the bathroom first?"

She nodded, not quite meeting his eyes. "Do you have something I can wear?"

"There should be a robe hanging from the hook on the bathroom door." He wondered at the awkwardness that had suddenly fallen over her as she slipped from the bed. But the sight of her tall, beautifully nude body erased that thought and all others as she padded toward the bathroom.

She emerged moments later, wearing his terry-cloth robe, her hair combed but still a tumble of curls hanging to her waist. She hesitated, as if unsure if she should come back to bed, or dress and leave. "Do you want me to fix coffee while you shower?"

God love the woman, he thought as his heart melted a bit more. "That would be great. The grounds are in the cabinet over the coffee maker."

Rory nodded and headed for the kitchen, desperately needing to get her bearings. Last night had been magical, but she wondered what came next as she found the grounds and filters. He'd said he loved her, and that he wasn't going to marry Paige. But he'd also said he had doubts about their future together. Maybe Alli was right, that the thought of marrying her might not even occur to Chance because she was so far outside his social circle. Passion was fine when choosing a bed partner, but outside the bedroom, he needed someone with polish and poise.

Would the love he felt for her be enough to make up for her social shortcomings? Her heart said yes, that she could make him happy. But doubt remained, tormenting her.

It was simply too soon, she told herself. They'd only admitted how they felt about each other less than twelve hours ago. Knowing Chance, he probably needed time to adjust to such a big change in his master plan for life. Only she didn't have time! She was two and a half months pregnant and would start showing within a few weeks. Her plan to hide her expanding waistline would hardly work if they were getting naked in bed together.

And—social differences aside—what guarantee did she have that Chance was even considering marriage? Men didn't always think along the logical lines of falling-in-love-equals-getting-married. From listening to Adrian and his friends over the years, she knew men actually thought that admitting they even had emotions was such a huge accomplishment it should be enough. They seemed perplexed, and even angry at times, that women expected something more—like commitment. Which had led her to the conclusion that if women didn't press the issue, marriage wouldn't even exist.

Although she needed to be careful, take things slowly and keep it light. Pushing Chance too soon might scare him off. So, with the coffeepot gurgling and filling the kitchen with aromatic steam, she turned her thoughts toward fixing breakfast.

"Is the coffee ready?" Chance asked a few minutes later as he strode into the kitchen.

She turned from the freezer and her heart skipped a beat. Good heavens, the man looked good wearing gray slacks, a crisp white shirt, and knotting a tie with his exquisitely long, very talented fingers.

He moved toward the pot as it let out a final groan, signaling that the brew was done. "Oh, bless you, baby. Bless you."

As he poured them each a cup, her eyes roamed over his back, and renewed longing blossomed inside her. This man, this wonderful man who was everything she desired and admired, had said he loved her. Her. Aurora St. Claire.

She smiled to herself as a mischievous imp took hold. "You know, Chance, we really need to have a serious talk," she said in her gravest voice.

He went still, as she knew he would. "About what?"

"About"—she was tempted to make him squirm a bit, but took mercy—"your refrigerator."

"What?" A comical blend of relief and concern spread over his face. "Is it broken?"

"No. It's practically empty." She gestured to the open doors of the refrigerator/freezer. One side held a few soft drinks and some unidentifiable leftovers in take-out cartons. The other side held a smattering of cardboard boxes. "Chance, you can't live on frozen preservatives zapped in the microwave."

"Sure you can." He sipped his coffee. "I've been doing it since I left home for college."

"Well, you're not a college kid anymore." Closing the door, she headed for the toaster with the frozen waffles she'd found. "You need food. Real food."

"I tell you what." He slipped his arm about her waist and pulled her against him. "Make out a shopping list and I'll buy anything you want—as long as you promise to cook it."

"Why can't we shop and cook together?"

"We can shop together all you want." He settled her more comfortably against him with his arms looped about her. "But trust me when I say you don't want to eat my cooking."

"I bet I could teach you." Grinning, she ran a fingertip along his jaw to his chin.

"Hmm, tempting." He gave her a leisurely kiss that made her heart pound.

The toaster dinged, popping up four golden waffles. Breathless, she pulled away. "Our breakfast is ready."

"Too bad," he sighed, and let his arms drop to his sides.

She had to take a deep breath to clear her head before she placed two waffles on a plate and handed it to him. "Go eat and behave yourself."

Taking up her own plate along with the syrup she'd found, she joined him at the dining table. It felt oddly natural to be sharing his morning.

"I'll need to leave as soon as I finish these," he said. "But you can stay as long as you like. There's shampoo in the shower, and I left a clean towel for you on the counter."

"Can I use your razor?"

He cringed. "I guess. But put razors on the grocery list." He took a sip of coffee. "Do you have anything special planned for today?"

"Not really," she said. "Although they're supposed to deliver the silk plants we bought yesterday."

"Oh, yes, your shopping trip." His brow wrinkled and she knew he was thinking about Paige.

"Chance?" She pushed a piece of waffle about her plate. "What will you tell her?"

He heaved a sigh. "I don't know."

"She's planning to come to the inn as soon as Alli gets off work. They're both eager to see how everything looks."

He nodded in understanding, but didn't look at her. "I'll try to catch her before that. I don't want to . . . talk to her at the inn. It would be too awkward. For everyone."

Rory's stomach ached with empathy. "She's going to be hurt."

"Yeah. I know. I'm sorry for that."

"Me, too."

After a moment of silence, he checked his watch. "I need to go."

She rose when he did and walked with him to the door, wishing things could be different, that she and Chance could be together without hurting Paige.

"I'll see you this evening," he said and gave her a kiss. She leaned into him, almost afraid to let him go. He gathered her against him, deepening the kiss until they were both trembling with renewed desire. "Oh, man." He exhaled a breath and a small laugh. "Hold that thought." He gave her one more quick peck, then stepped out the door, leaving her with a strange blend of euphoria and guilt.

CHAPTER 21

By mid-day, Chance was beginning to think the hardest part of breaking up with Paige was going to be finding her. He'd called her parents' house twice, but Mrs. Baxter didn't have a clue where her daughter had gone. He tried Paige's mobile phone, but she was either out of the service area or didn't have it turned on. By late afternoon, desperation had set in. He tried her friend Stacy, to see if the two of them were out shopping for bridesmaids' dresses.

Stacy didn't know where Paige was, but she did fill Chance in on all the wedding plans and how thrilled she was that Paige would be her maid of honor. He nearly groaned when she said she couldn't wait to return the favor—someday soon, she hoped.

After hanging up, he took off his glasses and rubbed his eyes. Standing before a firing squad appealed to him more than humiliating Paige in front of their friends, but he didn't see any way around it.

As a last-ditch effort, he took off work early and drove out to the country club since Paige occasionally docked in one of their day slips when she went boating. As he pulled into the parking lot, a pickup truck was pulling out—and he swore the man driving looked like Captain Bob. He dismissed his curiosity, though, since he had far more important things on his mind.

Dread dogged his heels as he walked through the breezeway between the office and the pro shop toward the docks. Why couldn't he have realized years ago that what he felt for Paige wasn't love? Why had he let himself get backed into this corner where the only way out was to hurt a lifelong friend?

He spotted the Baxters' boat instantly, thirty-two feet of sheer luxury. Paige was lounging in the cockpit, her back against the cabin. She wore a black one-piece that accentuated her slight curves. Her eyes were closed behind sunglasses, and a dreamy smile softened her pink lips. He wondered about her sublime expression until he noticed the romance novel resting at her side.

Paige, he thought with a pang of fondness, always dreaming of romantic adventure, of being swept off her feet by some dashing hero. He wondered suddenly what she'd ever seen in him, a tall skinny banker. Most people probably saw him as straitlaced. Except Aurora. When she looked at him, he felt like the most dashing hero who had ever lived.

"Chance?" Paige woke looking sleepy and confused. "What are you doing here? Is it after five already?"

"No, I took off work early." He thrust his hands in his pockets while she reached for a swimsuit cover-up. Stalling for time, he nodded toward the clubhouse. "You know, I thought I saw Captain Bob leaving just now."

"Captain Bob? Oh, yes," she said. "He came by to catch me up on the progress with the *Pirate's Pleasure.*"

"Progress? Is there a problem?"

"Nothing to be alarmed about," she assured him. "The ship needs some minor repairs before it can leave dock. Since tourist season has slacked off some, Bobby's decided to go down to Corpus to help out."

"Do the St. Claires know about this?" A problem with the ship would have a serious impact on the ball.

"Yes, I filled Allison in yesterday when we were shopping." She smiled up at him, the sunlight bright on her hair. "I can't wait to show you everything we found. We really hit the jackpot. Do you want to head over to the inn now so you can see?"

"Uh, no." The weight of dread grew as heavy as the humidity. A trickle of sweat snaked down his back even though he'd removed his jacket and tie. "I came early so we could talk. Can I come aboard?"

"Of course." A slight frown dimpled her brow. "Come on into the cabin, I'll get you something cold to drink."

He followed her down the steep steps into the plush interior done in beige, black, and white. She headed for the chrome and teakwood galley with smoky glass cabinet doors.

"Do you want a soft drink, or something stronger?"

"I'll take a whiskey, if you have it." He could use something to settle his nerves. Rolling up his sleeves, he sat on the U-shaped sofa in the bow and waited for her to join him. A half-eaten wedge of brie cheese, some crackers, and the leafy remains of strawberries littered a serving tray on the coffee table. An empty bottle of Pouilly Fuissé had been thrust neck first into an ice bucket.

"Are you hungry?" She nodded toward the leftovers as she handed him his drink.

"No. Just curious." He wondered what all had gone on during Captain Bob's visit. Although the fact that he felt more protective than jealous confirmed that he'd made the right decision. "Looks like you were having a party." *Or an illicit rendezvous.*

"Don't be silly." She sipped ice water from a cut-crystal glass. "Bobby and I just got to talking about ships and sailing, so I pulled a few things out of the fridge."

He studied her face, but saw no sign of guile or guilt. Besides, the image of Paige and Captain Bob having an affair refused to gel in his mind. She'd be drawn to someone cultured and debonair, not a man who wore wrinkled shirts open to the navel to expose a hairy chest. And Captain Bob might have shown signs of interest in Paige, but the man wasn't stupid. He had to know Paige Baxter outclassed him in every way imaginable.

"So," she asked, tucking her legs up beside her on the

cushion. "What did you want to talk about?"

His stomach tightened. God, if only he could turn the clock ahead and have this be over. "Paige, I . . ." He leaned forward, bracing his forearms on his knees and stared at the coffee table rather than her. If he looked at her, he'd never get the words out. "I want to tell you how much your friendship has meant to me over the years. Still means to me. I don't want anything to take away from that. We've known each other forever, and I hope you'll continue to . . . value the times we've shared, because I know I will."

"Of course I will." Her voice wavered between confusion and amusement.

"Paige . . ." He forced himself to look up, to meet her gaze. "I don't want to hurt you. Please believe that."

She looked back at him a moment before understanding dawned in her eyes. "Oh, my God." She nearly dropped her glass of ice water as she set it on the coffee table. "Are you breaking up with me?"

Regret tore at his heart. "I'm sorry, Paige. I'm so sorry."

He started to reach for her, but she stood and scrambled backward, staring at him in horror. "Chance, you can't. My parents will die. You can't do this to me. To them. You just can't!"

Her *parents* would die? What about her? He shook his head. "I'm sorry, Paige. I care for you a great deal, so I thought we'd make a perfect match. But I've come to realize caring and friendship aren't enough. The thing is"— he took a deep breath—"I'm not in love with you."

"But *why*? What did I do wrong?" She dropped to her knees at his feet as tears welled in her eyes. "Just tell me. I'll change."

Startled, he sat back. "You didn't do anything wrong. I just . . . I don't love you the way a man should love the woman he marries. It would be crueler for me to marry you now that I've realized that." He took her hands and squeezed them. "You deserve someone who will love you, Paige."

"Daddy's going to kill me." She dropped her forehead to their joined hands. "And my mom! She'll die. She'll just die!"

He stared at the top of her head, stunned by her reaction. He'd expected tears and hurt, but not this. "What about you, Paige? Doesn't this affect you?"

"Of course it does." Her head came up, her eyes pleading. "Chance, please don't do this. It's going to hurt so many people. Not just my parents, but yours, too."

"Paige . . ." He struggled for the right words. "Doesn't this hurt *you*?" She started to answer, but he stopped her. "No, let me rephrase that. Sit up here and let me ask you something." He helped her back onto the sofa. "Paige, do you love me?"

Her whole face softened. "Of course I love you. I've always loved you."

"As a lover? Or as a friend?"

She opened her mouth to answer, but no words came.

"It's okay," he assured her. "I won't take offense because I feel the same way. I do love you. I think I have since we were kids. But I'm not 'in love' with you, if that makes sense."

She nodded, looking miserable.

"As for our parents, I'll take full blame and let them know the whole misunderstanding was my fault. I led you to believe we'd get married, and I'm the one breaking things off. Unless you'd rather tell them you broke things off with me?"

"No!" She looked horrified at the thought. "Then Daddy really would kill me. He'd want to know what was wrong with me, and badger me to get back together with you."

"All right then, we'll tell them the truth. That we like each other a lot, but not enough to get married."

"But you don't understand what this means to them!" She buried her face in her hands. "How could you when your family has everything?"

"That's ridiculous." He frowned at her. "There's very little difference in our families' net worth."

"Net worth!" She snorted loudly, an unladylike sound that shocked him. "Life isn't just about money. Can't you understand there are things money can't buy? Things that you can't earn, or borrow, or even steal." She glared at him through a sheen of tears. "No, of course not. You wouldn't know about wanting those things because you've had all of them since birth."

He sat back. "I don't think I'm following you."

"You have all the things my parents want. Daddy is rich, as rich as Midas, but the money is barely two generations old. His family was still considered New Money when they came to Galveston."

"Maybe so, but he married Old Money when he married your mom."

"This isn't about money!"

"Okay," he said slowly, wondering where sweet, gentle Paige had gone and who this passionate woman was. "Why don't you explain it?"

"It's about two hundred years of missing the boat," she said angrily. "Neither side of my family immigrated to America before the Revolution. Neither Mom nor Dad have ancestors who fought for the South during the Civil War. Daddy's family moved to Texas one year after Statehood. One year! And even though my mom was born on Galveston Island, her family didn't move here until *after* the Nineteen Hundred Storm."

"Oh." Understanding came with a bitter taste. The Baxters wanted him for his pedigree. People he'd known all his life, who'd been like a second set of parents to him—and all they wanted was a damn pedigree!

"Don't you see?" Paige pleaded.

"Actually, yes, I think I do."

"No amount of money can buy one's way into certain circles," she continued unmercifully. "No matter how rich Daddy gets, he can't be a member of Sons of the Republic or Sons of the Confederacy. No matter how active Mom is in the Heritage Society, she can never have a Daughters of the Revolution plaque on her grave, or be a member of First Families of Virginia like your mom. And nothing they do will ever allow them to swap stories about what their grandparents endured and lost during the Great Storm."

Unable to bear it, he rose and moved away. "God, I'm sick of it! As proud as I am of who I am and what I come from, lately I'm sick of it." He turned to face her. "What difference does it make? We are what we make of ourselves no matter what our ancestors did."

"To Mom and Dad it makes a lot of difference. And it was the one thing I'd hoped to give them. I knew I wasn't smart enough to be valedictorian or pretty enough to be homecoming queen, but if I married you, I could give them grandchildren who were Chancellors."

His shoulders sagged. "Is that all I am to you? All I ever was?"

"No! Of course not." She rushed to him and took his hands in hers. "You're one of my closest friends. All my life, you were always there for me. And I'd promised myself I'd make you the best wife I could."

"I don't want a wife who is loyal out of obligation!" He jerked his hands away. Surprise flashed in her eyes, but he didn't care. To think he'd worried about *him* hurting *her*. Christ! He turned to stare out a porthole. He wanted a wife who loved him for who he was. Someone who saw him as a man, not just another link in the Chancellor chain. A desirable man with more to offer than his brains and his brokerage account. He wanted Aurora—and the way she made him feel.

When he had his anger under control, he looked at Paige over his shoulder. "Tell me how you want to handle this. Do you tell your father, or do I?"

"I don't know. I need time to think." Her face lined with dread, then suddenly cleared. "Oh, no! The ball!"

"What?" He frowned.

"We can't tell anyone before the ball."

"Paige . . ." He closed his eyes in a bid for patience.

"No, hear me out. You know how Mom can be when she's angry."

The words "catty" and "petty" came to mind, but he kept them to himself. Marcy Baxter had her good points, but when she was mad she had the judgment of a spoiled teenager.

"When Mom finds out we're breaking up she's going to be furious. She'll probably give me the silent treatment, but you . . ." Paige looked at him with pity. "Chance, she'll want to get back at you. The fastest way to do that is to mess up the ball so your inn looks bad."

"How can she do that?" He shrugged the objection away.

"Through the power of gossip," Paige answered. "If she boycotts the ball and tells everyone she's doing it because you and your partners are completely incompetent and impossible to work with, it could hurt your catering business for years to come."

"And when people come to the ball and see that we're perfectly competent?"

"They'll look at everything more critically and spend the whole evening talking about why my mother isn't there. Which will lead to talk about you and me." She wrung her hands. "Oh, Chance, we can't tell anyone now. Everyone will know eventually, but if they find out before the ball, they'll spend the whole evening talking about us. I just can't stand it."

"What do you suggest we do?" He snorted. "Pretend we're still dating until after the ball?"

"Would it be so hard?" she pleaded. "It's only two weeks away, and you said you wanted us to still be friends. I could continue to help at the inn. Then, when the ball is over, I'll find a way to tell Mom and Dad."

He turned away, disgusted to realize she was right. The

circles in which they moved loved gossip and he couldn't have picked a worse time to break up with her. "As much sense as your plan makes, it won't work."

"Why not?" she asked.

"Because . . . it would be awkward for you to continue helping at the inn." He glanced back at her. "I'm . . . seeing Aurora."

Paige's face went blank for an instant before fury replaced shock. "You've been seeing Rory behind my back?"

"No!" He struggled for a way to explain. "It's not like that. I haven't been seeing her all this time."

"Are you saying you two became an item overnight?"

"I'll admit, the attraction's been there for some time, but I didn't act on it while I was seeing you. I wasn't two-timing you, Paige. I would never do that to you, or her."

Her brow dimpled. "Does Allison know?"

He nodded, wondering what that had to do with anything, but Allison had to know, since Aurora had called home last night to tell her sister where she was staying.

"Nooo!" Paige stomped over to the sofa and dropped to the cushions. "Why did you have to take that away, too?"

"Take what away?"

"My friendship with Allison and helping with the inn!" She grabbed a throw pillow, punched it a few times, then hugged it to her chest. "For the first time in my life, I felt useful."

His heart melted a little in understanding since he felt the same way toward the inn. Being part of it, watching it take form, fulfilled him in ways nothing else had. He went to sit beside her. Thought about taking her hand, but decided not to. "I'm sorry."

"You should be," she said testily. "You realize that your seeing Rory makes everything worse, don't you? Now people really will talk. And you can forget about Stacy hiring Adrian to cater her wedding, she's going to be livid." Paige glared at him. "If it weren't for how all this will affect Allison, I'd almost be glad. You deserve it."

"Maybe I do," he sighed. *But Aurora doesn't.* "And I wish we could wait until after the ball to tell anyone, but I don't see how. I won't lie."

"Well, there is one way," she said, sounding reluctant now to help him.

"What?"

"I could go to Corpus Christi to help get the *Pirate's Pleasure* ready. If I'm not here, no one will question why we're not seeing each other."

"You mean, *work* on a ship with a bunch of men?"

She looked irritated. "Men aren't the only ones who love working on old sailing vessels. I'm perfectly capable of pulling my weight as a crew hand. Besides, the captain of the *Pirate's Pleasure* is a woman, so I won't be the only female on board."

His gaze ran over her, taking in the sleek hair, diamond earrings, and delicate bones.

"You don't think I can do it, do you?" Her eyes narrowed.

"I didn't say that. It's just . . . all right, I know you're good with boats, but crewing on a Baltimore clipper?"

"I've trained aboard the *Elissa* here in Galveston. I know my way around the rigging."

"Maybe so, but won't your mother and the rest of the planning committee be upset if you take off two weeks before the ball?"

Paige thought that over. "I'll tell everyone I'm going to Corpus to be sure the ship arrives here on time. Since it's our big attraction, no one will argue. All you have to do is keep quiet about us while I'm gone."

Which meant he'd have to be discreet about his relationship with Aurora. The thought didn't sit well on his stomach.

"It's only for two weeks," Paige said. "And it will make things a lot easier for all of us."

He tried to think of another way, but couldn't. "You'll

tell your parents as soon as the ball is over?"

She nodded, reluctantly. "I know I can't put it off for-ever."

"Okay, then," he agreed. He would wait—for the sake of Aurora and the inn, as well as for Paige. "I won't tell anyone."

"Thank you," she said in a sad voice. "For that at least."

They looked at each other a moment, then as if by mu-tual consent, leaned forward and embraced.

"I really am sorry," he said, closing his eyes and breathing in the innocent scent of baby oil.

"Me, too." She pulled back and gave him a watery smile.

Moved by the sorrow in her eyes, he bent down and pressed a kiss to her lips. "Take care of yourself."

"I will." Fresh tears welled in her eyes.

His chest felt tight with empathy as he left.

Driving to the inn, he tried to relax. He hadn't lied the day before when he'd told Aurora he'd had his whole life planned out. Now everything was a mass of uncertainty, his emotions bouncing from the happiness he'd shared with Aurora to the gut-wrenching sorrow of the scene he'd just left. And through it all was the underlying fear that asked if he was doing the right thing. Or was he throwing everything away on a relationship that wouldn't last and a venture that would fail?

He knew what he felt for Aurora was more than lust. This turbulent blend of adoration, respect, and longing had to be love. But where was it headed?

He tried to picture her fitting into his life long-term. The older he got and the higher up he moved at the bank, the more expectations there would be from the community. He knew if he asked Aurora to host parties, join clubs, and help organize fund-raisers, she'd do it. She was brave enough and determined enough to do anything.

Unfortunately, the only way she'd fit in with the other wives was if she learned to talk, dress, and act just like them. If he asked her to do that, wouldn't he be stifling the very spirit that had drawn him to her? And what right did he have to ask her to change? She'd be miserable, and she'd come to resent him for causing that misery.

All those thoughts were still tumbling through his mind when he arrived at Pearl Island.

CHAPTER 22

The inn seemed oddly empty when Chance walked in the front door, almost like a church with the sunlight streaming in through the tall, stained-glass windows of the stairwell to gleam quietly off the polished wood of the central hall. He took a moment to admire how much they'd done. How much he'd done. A good amount of his time and sweat had gone into transforming a neglected old mansion into a B and B on the verge of its grand opening.

Victorian settees and high-backed armchairs sat in conversational groupings around richly colored Oriental rugs. Silk plants in brass pots had been added that day, giving the room its final finishing touch.

In Henri's old office, Allison had managed to set up the beginnings of a gift shop. A sampling of figurines, books, dolls, and porcelain tea sets filled the built-in bookshelves. She needed more display cases and merchandise, but the room already invited shoppers to browse.

The inn was going to be so much more than he'd imagined in the beginning. Not just a place for guests to stay while visiting Galveston, but a small resort with elegant meals, a private beach, meeting facilities, and their own gift shop. He'd even heard Aurora mention ideas such as bungalows to increase their guest capacity and a hike-and-bike trail. Heaven only knew what else she'd dream up in that amazing mind of hers.

A noise to his right drew his attention. He smiled, realizing she was in the office. He wished he'd been there to see her face when she discovered his surprise. Stepping toward the doorway, he pictured her seated at the desk working at the computer.

It was not the image that greeted his eyes.

He stopped short at the sight of Aurora bending over the desk, her bottom toward him, her shorts rising high on her long shapely thighs. The position conjured thoughts that sent desire surging through him.

"Is this how you plan to greet our guests?" he asked.

With a shriek, she turned around. "Chance! You startled me." She laughed, holding one hand to her chest. "When did you get here?"

"Just now. Didn't you hear me come in?"

She waved a hand in dismissal. "The construction crew has been coming and going so much today, I've learned to block it out."

"Please tell me you haven't been giving them such a spectacular view."

"Hmm?" Her honest confusion made him want to laugh.

"Never mind. I take it the crew is gone since your Jeep is the only vehicle I saw."

"Oh, yeah, I guess so." She glanced around as if noticing the quiet for the first time. "Which means, other than the final walk-through tomorrow, they're done."

"Oh, really?" he said, his mind veering back to her body. "So, we're alone?"

The realization sparked in her eyes, too, and her smile turned devious. "Completely. Adrian's already left for work, and Allison won't be here for at least an hour."

"You don't say." He moved closer. "In that case, why don't you kiss me?"

"Gladly."

When she slipped her arms about his neck, he lowered his head, fitting his mouth to hers as need pulsed to life. Both their hearts were pounding before the kiss ended.

"God, I missed you today." He rested his forehead against hers. The hum in his blood urged him to turn her around and bend her over the desk, to take her in a hard, fast rush. That image contrasted nicely with the simple pleasure of holding her in his arms. He lifted his head and brushed the hair back from her face.

Questions flickered in her eyes: had he talked to Paige? Should she ask?

Later, he told her silently, grateful when understanding registered in her eyes.

"So," he said, stepping back, "what do you think of the desk?"

"I love it! It's perfect." She turned to admire it. "The desk, everything. I was just trying to get the scanner to work, but that can wait. First let me show you what I did today." She bent forward to retrieve something. He couldn't say what, since his attention swept down her back to the mesmerizing curves she presented.

"See?" she said, straightening. "What do you think of something like this for our brochure?"

Since she hadn't turned to face him, he had to look over her shoulder. His mind took a second to clear of lust before admiration set in. What she held was a mock-up for a trifold pamphlet with a description of the house on the front and a brief mention of the legend.

She opened it as she explained her idea. "On the inside we'll list all the rooms with pictures and the rental rates for each. Contact information will go on the back."

"Good grief!" he said, admiring the professional quality of the typesetting. "You did all this today? But how?"

"It's easy. You just sit down and start playing." She looked at him over her shoulder. "And you know how much I like to play."

"Play?" He ran a fingertip down her bare arm and felt her shiver.

"Of course, I need to figure out the scanner so I can insert the pictures once we have some. I was wondering if you would . . ." She bit her lip.

"Yes?" He trailed his hands up her arm, lifting her hair

out of the way so he could nuzzle her neck.

"If you would . . . mmm, that feels good . . . read the instruction book and tell me . . . how to do it?" She leaned back against him, all supple and warm and tempting.

"You don't know how to do it?" he teased as he tugged the tank top from her shorts and slipped his hands to the smooth skin of her stomach. "If I remember correctly, you slide flap A into slot B."

"Not that!" She laughed. "The scanner."

"You mean there isn't a flap A involved in this operation?" He fit his hips more snugly to her bottom, letting her feel the ridge of his erection.

"Mmm," she purred. "Maybe I'm wrong. There could be a flap A."

"I think this bears further investigation." He slid his hands up to cup her breasts. "If you think we have time."

"We have nearly an hour," she assured him as she rested her head against his shoulder.

His pulse leapt as he weighed the fullness of her breasts in his palms. Touching them wasn't enough, though, he wanted to see and taste as well as feel. When the want became need, he pulled off her tank top, tossing it aside. Her bra quickly followed. She started to turn, but he held her in place until she settled back against him.

With afternoon sunlight filling the room, he gave in to months' worth of desire. His hands roamed freely over her, teasing her rosy nipples to hard peaks. The little sounds she made had his body straining to possess, to take her quickly and keep on taking her until she was a part of him.

She rubbed against him and he bit back the driving urge to plunge quick and fast. His fingers fumbled as he undid the snap and zipper of her shorts. After he'd removed them, she turned and attacked the buttons of his shirt. Catching her urgency, he kicked out of his shoes and took care of his pants. In seconds, they were both naked.

"God, what you do to me," he rasped before he kissed her. His hands fisted in her hair as desperation surged through him, frightening in its strength. No matter how hard he loved her, no matter how often, it would never be enough. He'd die of this wanting before he ever had enough.

"Chance," she managed to gasp between greedy kisses. Her hands ran over his body, her eyes glowing with admiration, making his breath hiss in through his teeth. "I want you so much."

She started to climb on the desk, but he stopped her and turned her around, gripping her hips. "Lean forward," he said against her ear, nipping her earlobe before she did as he asked. He nudged her feet apart until she stood with her hips thrust toward him, her legs braced. He closed his eyes to savor the sensation as he pressed into her warm softness and held. It would never be enough, he thought and gritted his teeth against the demands of his body.

She pressed backward, taking him deeper. Her gasp of wonder nearly broke his restraint. But he held his control as firmly as he held her hips and pleasured her slowly, thoroughly. His nostrils flared with the scent of her excitement. When he felt the tension coiling inside her, straining to break free, he bent over her, slipping one hand to where their bodies were joined. His other arm held her close as he let himself go.

They climaxed together in a flare of passion that left them both shaken and gasping for breath.

Somehow Rory managed to get her underwear on, Chance his briefs and trousers, before they collapsed on the settee. "We should finish getting dressed before Allison shows up," Rory murmured against his shoulder. She sat on the sofa with her legs draped across his lap. He was sprawled out, half reclining with his head resting on the wooden edge above the velvet upholstery.

Neither of them moved. His hand continued to stroke her back. A full minute passed.

"Well," she sighed, "I guess one of us has to be strong

and make the first move." She managed to lift her head.

"Wait." He slipped his hand around her arm. She turned back, and waited as he sat up straighter. "I need to talk to you about Paige."

She went perfectly still. "Yes?"

He didn't pull away physically, but somehow the space between them seemed to widen. "I told her about my decision, that marriage would be a mistake. She was . . . upset, naturally."

"I know. I'm sorry," she said, empathetic to what he must have been through.

"Yeah, well, the thing is, it didn't go exactly as I expected."

"What do you mean?"

He hesitated. "I didn't understand *why* she wanted to marry me. And how much it meant to her."

"Oh?" A tremor of alarm moved through her belly. Had Chance changed his mind about breaking up with Paige? No, he wouldn't have made love to her just now if that were true.

"It doesn't matter." He shook his head. "What does matter is that Paige felt, and I agreed, that we should wait until after the ball to let anyone know we've split up."

"What do you mean, wait?"

"I know it sounds awkward, but it'll be better for all of us if Paige's parents don't find out until after the ball, especially with Marcy Baxter on the planning committee."

"Are you saying that you and Paige will pretend to keep dating for the next two weeks?"

"No, I won't outright lie about this. We just won't tell anyone. Paige has even decided to go out of town until the ball. She's going to Corpus Christi to help get the ship ready. Everyone will just assume our relationship is status quo."

"And what does that mean for you and me?" Her stomach tightened. "That we can't see each other?"

"No, we can see each other. We'll just have to be discreet."

"Discreet," she echoed numbly. Like a married man seeing his mistress.

"I don't like it, either." He rubbed her arm. "But it really is best for you as well as Paige. And for the inn. If the news gets around before the ball, it will overshadow the whole event."

She would have scoffed if her nerves weren't in knots. "Do you really think that many people will care?"

"Oh, yes. I grew up around these people. I know how they can gossip and how much damage it can do."

"I suppose. It's just . . ." She couldn't help wondering if he was leaving a back door open. If things didn't work out for them, he could always get back together with Paige when she returned and no one would be the wiser. Or maybe he was embarrassed for his family and friends to know about her.

"What?" he asked.

She searched his eyes, her heart racing. "You are certain about this, aren't you?"

"About what?"

"Us. I mean, if you're having second thoughts, tell me now. I can take it, I swear. I can take anything as long as you're honest with me."

"Honestly?" He studied her, and her fear mounted with every second. Then his face softened with a sad smile. "I am sure of how I feel. I love you and I want to be with you. I hope . . . you feel the same."

"Of course I do." She waited for him to say something about the future. Anything. He caressed her cheek. "Stay with me tonight."

"I thought we had to be discreet."

"I didn't say run naked through the street with me." He gave her a teasing smile. "As long as you aren't seen leaving my apartment during morning rush hour, I don't see any reason we can't be together these next two weeks."

"I don't know." She felt torn between fear and hope.

"Stay with me." He cupped her jaw and kissed her lightly on the lips. "It's not enough seeing you here. I want to be with you as much as I can. We have a lot of time to make up for."

She should tell him no, that they would wait until they could be together openly. But in two weeks, her pregnancy would be that much closer to showing—and she could be that much closer to losing him. Right or wrong, she wanted this brief time with him. Come what may.

"All right." She nodded, and closed her eyes as he kissed her again.

CHAPTER 23

The day after Paige left for Corpus Christi, a tropical depression moved into the gulf and set itself down for a nice long stay. The resulting rain drenched the coast from Mexico to Florida for days on end. As if that weren't enough to dampen the mood at the inn, Paige's absence meant they all had to deal directly with the Buccaneer's Ball planning committee.

Rory nearly had heart failure the first time she met Chance's mother, but Ellen Chancellor proved to be gracious, kind, and practical in all things.

Marcy Baxter, on the other hand, would test the patience of the pope.

Sitting at a worktable in the kitchen, Rory battled a mild sense of guilt since Adrian was currently trapped in the dining room with Ellen and Marcy going over the menu. Still, she and Allison had their hands full altering the costumes the committee wanted them to wear, so Adrian would just have to handle Marcy on his own.

Thunder rumbled, adding an ominous feel to an already dreary day. While Sadie hid beneath the table and whined, Rory stared out at the rain that ran in rivulets through their newly planted landscape. "Do you think it'll ever stop raining?"

"Only if the cool front the weathermen keep promising shows up," Allison answered as she plied a needle and thread to a bit of satin and lace. "Otherwise, we'll have a nice steamy sauna for the ball."

"I don't suppose there's such a thing as a stop-the-rain dance."

"Not that I know of." Allison chuckled. "Besides, even if it doesn't stop, we can move everything to the ballroom upstairs."

"I know." Rory sighed and returned to her own sewing. "But it won't be the same. After all the plans we made, I want it to be perfect."

"It will be," Allison insisted. "We have a whole week to go. The rain is just getting itself out of the way now, so the night of the ball will be cool and clear."

Rory looked up, surprised by her sister's confidence. When had the two of them switched their roles of optimist and devil's advocate?

"There. Finished," Alli announced. Shaking the dress out, she stood and held it to her shoulders. It was one of many costumes they'd rented from the opera house. They'd lucked into peasant dresses and pirate crew garb for the servers they'd hired, and two elaborate sea captain outfits for Adrian and Chance. Alli's ice-blue gown with black lace had needed some repair while Rory's peach and cream affair had needed the hem let out as far as it would go.

"What do you think?" Alli asked as she twirled about, flaring the wide skirt.

An image flashed through Rory's mind of how Marguerite must have looked, the elusive Pearl of New Orleans—gossiped about for her scandalous past, but held in awe for her enchanting beauty. "I think you'll make a perfect pirate's mistress."

Alli grinned. "Only if I let some handsome pirate make a dishonest woman out of me."

Rory laughed, but her sister's words left her feeling hollow inside. A dishonest woman was exactly what she felt like after the past week of sneaking in and out of Chance's apartment. Every day she told herself she should quit spending the night with him until they could be together

openly, but the attraction between them was like a ravenous hunger that came upon them whenever they were
alone—wherever that might be. They were like children
who'd been set loose in a candy store, giddy with abandon.
Even now, just thinking of him, she felt her thighs quiver
with anticipation. But how long could this insatiable need
for each other last? And where was it going?

As a child, when she'd thought of falling in love, she'd
imagined it as something safe and warm that would add
stability to her life, make her feel secure. Instead, she'd
never felt more vulnerable and uncertain. She placed a
hand over her stomach, frightened of what the future held
for her and her baby. Would she ever be more to Chance
than a weakness he couldn't resist?

"I'm going to murder that woman!" Adrian announced
as he burst into the kitchen.

Rory looked up with a start and noticed the frustration
coming off her brother in waves. "By 'that woman,' I assume you mean Marcy Baxter?"

"Who else would I mean?" Adrian asked rhetorically.
"Do you know what she wants now?"

"I haven't a clue," Rory said.

"A champagne fountain out on the lawn."

Allison burst out laughing. "You're joking!"

"No, I'm not." Crossing to the counter nearest them, he
started digging through a pile of catalogs and cookbooks.
"The ice sculpture for the dessert table, that I agreed with
because it will be inside in the dining room. And at least
she went for the mermaid instead of those ridiculously formal swans she wanted. But a champagne fountain on the
lawn? Give me a break!" He moved to a pile of papers.
"This is supposed to be a pirate camp cookout, not a frig-
gin' wedding reception."

"What are you looking for?" Rory asked.

"The catalog from the rental company that shows the
portable bar we picked out so she can see how stupid a

three-tiered silver fountain would be next to a bar that looks like a bamboo hut with a grass roof."

"I think I know where it is," Allison said, setting aside her costume to help him look.

"Rory," Adrian said over his shoulder, "will you do me a favor?"

"Depends on what it is," she answered with a grin.

He gave her an exasperated look. "Take Ms. Chancellor and Ms. Baxter some of those macadamia nut cookies I baked yesterday to placate them while Alli and I look for the catalog."

Rory almost groaned at the thought of braving the lion's den, but she gathered a plate of cookies and the iced-tea pitcher from the massive stainless steel refrigerator. She was passing through the butler's pantry when she heard Ellen say, "Marcy, I've never seen you be this indecisive when planning a party. I know you always worry over details, but not like this. Is there something wrong that you're not telling me?"

"Nothing's wrong," Marcy said as Rory entered the dining room. The women sat near the head of the table with menus and notes spread before them. "I just want the event to be special. You know how important this night is."

As unobtrusively as possible, Rory slid the plate of cookies between the women, then moved quietly to refill Ellen's glass. Marcy behaved as if she weren't there, but Chance's mother glanced up and smiled. "Thank you, Aurora. You always have the best tea here."

Rory smiled back, amused at how Ellen used her full name, just like her son did. "The secret is to keep it refrigerated, rather than let it sit at room temperature."

"I'll have to remember that." Ellen sipped and nodded with approval.

"The thing is," Marcy continued as Rory moved to refill her glass, "it's not just another Buccaneer's Ball. It's the grand opening of your son's new business."

Rory scowled at the top of the woman's head. The inn

wasn't "Chance's business." It was a joint effort between all of them. She caught Ellen watching her, and quickly smoothed her features into a blank mask. Amusement flickered in Ellen's eyes.

"What's more," Marcy said, "it's the night Chance and Paige will announce their engagement."

Rory jerked, knocking over Marcy's glass. Ice and tea splashed across the table, soaking papers. Both women gasped and leapt to their feet as tea ran off the sides of the table onto the floor.

"Oh! I'm sorry!" Rory reached for the papers, trying to rescue them but it was too late. They sagged like wet rags in her hands, stained and dripping. "Did I get you wet?"

"No, I'm fine," Ellen assured her.

"Oh, of all the—" Marcy stared down at her silk blouse and linen pants, drenched from the waist to the knees.

"Oh, no. Hang on. I'll get a towel." Rory raced into the pantry and dug through a drawer for kitchen towels. Hurrying back, she offered one to Marcy, then started sopping up the mess. "I'm so sorry," she said, her heart pounding.

Marcy's words about Chance and Paige rang in her ears even though they couldn't be true. They couldn't! But why did the woman think they were? Did Chance know about this? She dabbed frantically at the soggy papers, her hands shaking.

"Aurora," Ellen said softly and placed a hand over hers. Rory glanced up into the woman's kind eyes. "It's all right. Accidents happen."

Her throat constricted. The word "accident" reminded her that she and Chance had created one of the biggest accidents of all: a baby. "I—I'll get more towels."

She fled to the pantry, then dropped back against the wall, closing her eyes to control the shaking. How many people were going to be hurt when the truth came out? Would Ellen, who'd treated her with a kindness that bordered on motherly affection, look at her in disdain when she found out about the baby?

"All right, Marcy." Ellen's voice was muffled by the closed door. "Before Aurora comes back, tell me what you heard. Chance hasn't breathed a word to me, the little rat. If he's proposed to Paige, I want to know."

"Well, that at least makes me feel a little better," Marcy said.

"What?"

"That Chance is being as closemouthed with you as Paige is being with me. My guess is they want it to be a surprise, since they know how long we've waited for this."

"So how did you find out?"

Rory strained to hear, her heart aching with each hushed word.

"I overheard Paige talking to her friend Stacy before she left town. She said she wanted 'it' to be a secret until the ball. And since we both suggested to them that the ball would be a perfect time to announce their engagement, what else could 'it' be?"

"A lot of things," Ellen pointed out.

"True. But I have a feeling it's the announcement we've been waiting for."

"Well, just to be on the safe side, why don't we keep this particular 'feeling' to ourselves?" There was a pause before Ellen let out a heavy sigh. "Marcy, I know that guilty look. Please tell me you haven't already talked to someone about this."

"Only Stacy's mother," Marcy groused. "I wanted to know if Stacy had told her anything. Unfortunately, the woman was clueless."

"You told Winney Connely?" Ellen asked in rising tones. "Marcy! You might as well have made a public service announcement to the entire town."

"Don't worry. I asked her to keep it to herself."

"Asking Winney to keep a secret is like asking Niagara Falls to hold back the water."

Adrian came up behind Rory. "What are you doing?"

She shrieked and turned, her face flaming at being

caught eavesdropping. "I—I need to call Chance. Here."
She grabbed some towels and thrust them into Adrian's
hand.

"Hey, wait. Is something wrong?" he called after her.

Ignoring him, she dashed back into the kitchen, past a
startled Allison, and down the stairs to their private quarters. They had yet to make a full move from the cottage,
but they'd bought some furniture at least.

She grabbed the cordless phone from the table near the
stairs and paced as she punched in the number for the
bank. When she asked for Chance, she got Doris instead,
the woman she'd come to think of as the guardian of the
offices. She asked again to speak with Chance, but the
executive assistant insisted he was in a meeting and
couldn't be disturbed. Rory asked Doris to have him call
her as soon as he was free, but the woman informed her
that the younger Mr. Chancellor was very busy and might
not be able to get back to her until the following day.

After disconnecting, Rory stared at the phone in disbelief. Doris was always a bit snooty, but she'd never
blown Rory off completely.

Well, Chance might be busy, but this was something
that couldn't wait. Snatching up her purse and the keys to
the Jeep, she headed back upstairs. If she couldn't talk to
him over the phone, she'd go to the bank and talk to him
in person.

Chance stormed from the boardroom, numb with shock.
He vaguely registered Doris coming to her feet as he
headed past her desk, his only goal to get to his office
where he could absorb the emotional blow he'd just been
dealt.

"Oliver," Doris said, all but blocking his path. "There's
a young lady—"

"Not now, Doris," he said, brushing past her. His anger
mounted as he registered the alarm in her expression. She

knew! Goddammit, she already knew what had happened in the boardroom. Maybe her knowledge came only by intuition, but if Doris knew, how long would it be before everyone in the bank figured it out, then everyone in Galveston?

He stormed into his office and slammed the door.

A female shriek brought him up short.

"Aurora!" The sight of her standing before the window caught him off guard. "What are you doing here?"

"I have to talk to you." She stepped forward. "Marcy Baxter was at the inn today, to go over the plans for the ball."

"Not now." He pressed a hand to his forehead, determined not to take his anger out on her. "Please. The last thing I want to think about is Marcy Baxter."

"But you don't understand," she insisted in a panicked voice, and he realized she was pale and half soaked from the rain. "Marcy thinks you and Paige are going to announce your engagement at the ball. She's told Stacy Conneley's mother, so half of Galveston must know. What are we going to do?"

"Aurora," he said, his patience threatening to snap. "I said not now."

She frowned at him. "Chance, what is it? Is something wrong?"

"I just need a second to think."

"What do you mean?" She came toward him, concern lining her face as corkscrew curls of wet hair hung past her shoulders. "You look upset. What's happened?"

He fell back against the door as a wave of weariness overtook him. "They fired my father."

"What!" She drew up short. "They can't do that."

A bitter laugh escaped him. "Actually, they can. It was all quite civilized, of course. The chairmen of the board came down from the home office on the pretext of a routine visit. Then he called my father into the boardroom and politely requested he take early retirement."

"Oh, Chance." She stroked his arm. "How did he take it?"

"I don't know. I haven't even talked to him. We were called into the boardroom separately. My dad was leaving the bank just as I went in to hear the news." He rubbed his forehead, trying to ease the sharp pain behind his eyes. "Aurora, I need to go."

"Yes. Of course." She stepped back, giving him room to open the door.

He was halfway into the hall when he turned back to her. "We'll talk about Marcy later, all right?"

"Fine. Just go."

He nodded, and left. The drive to his parents' house went by in a blur. He found his father in the game room. The room was dark, the draperies drawn. His father was standing at the wet bar, his hands braced on the counter, his head sagging forward. A highball glass with half-melted ice sat next to an open bottle of Crown Royal.

"Dad?"

His father drew in a deep breath as he straightened. "I guess they told you?"

"Yeah." Chance closed his eyes, remembering the pity on Doris's face as he'd left. The rumors were probably already spreading through the staff. As soon as Norman bowed to their "request," an official announcement would be made, followed by a retirement party. People would wish Norman good luck to his face, then shake their heads and say "What a shame" behind his back.

"Forty-two years," his father said, pulling a second highball glass down from the lighted shelf and filling it with ice. "Forty-two goddamn years, and they ask me to leave. As if they have the right!"

Chance hated the fact that they did have the right. His father had sold it to them.

"Do you know, I still remember the first day I walked into that bank as an employee rather than just the owner's son." He poured amber liquor into both glasses. "I was seventeen, getting my feet wet while I made some spending money for college. I worked as a teller the first few summers, then a loan officer."

Chance managed a smile as he moved closer. "And Granddad worked you twice as hard as he did everyone else. The same way you worked me."

His father nodded. "And I loved every minute of it. Saw it as my rite of passage." Turning, he handed a drink to his son. "My trial by fire."

"Same here." Chance raised his glass in a salute.

As if he'd aged twenty years in the last hour, Norman moved to one of two leather chairs that bracketed a small table. He sat, staring across the room, his eyes lost. "Did they tell you who they plan to promote to fill my place?"

"Brian Jeffries." Chance took a seat in the other chair and braced his forearms on his thighs.

"A goddamn outsider." His father snorted. "That'll go over well with the locals. If they were smart, they'd have offered the position to you."

"They think I'm too young. Although they made it clear they want me to stay on. They plan to move me into Brian's job as VP of loans as part of my grooming to be a president in the future."

"Like you need grooming to run a bank you grew up in." Norman took a deep drink. "So, what did you tell them?"

"Nothing yet."

"Oh?"

"I'm not sure I want to stay at the bank under the circumstances."

"Now don't go throwing your career away because of this. I hate to say it, but they were right about one thing. I'm a stubborn, old-fashioned goat who's too used to running the whole show. You're younger, more adaptable, which makes you better suited for the job of a branch president than I ever was."

"It's more than what they did to you, although that's

enough to make me want to walk out." He swished the Crown Royal around in his glass. "They want me to sever my partnership with the St. Claires."

He waited for his father to say "I told you so." When he said nothing, Chance looked up.

"What did you tell them?" his father asked.

Chance gave a scoffing laugh. "I'm tempted to tell them to fuck off."

A slow smile rearranged the wrinkles on his father's face, and Chance realized he'd had more than one drink in the short time he'd been home. "You know, at the moment, I think I'd like to see you do that."

The smile faded as Norman rested his head back against the chair. "It's odd. They say when you're drowning, your whole life flashes before your eyes. Well, I guess I must be drowning, because ever since I stepped into that boardroom, bits of my life have been passing through my mind. Mostly all the things I gave up to follow in the Chancellor footsteps. I keep wondering what would have happened if I'd gone the other way."

"The other way?" Chance asked.

"There was a time, the year after I graduated from UT, when the world seemed young and filled with possibilities." He held his glass up to study the light as it glowed within the amber liquor. "Like most young men, I thought my parents were hopelessly ignorant and terminally boring. I, on the other hand, knew everything. Especially how it felt to fall in love. God"—he took a swallow, then let his head fall back, his eyes close—"what a summer. She was the most intoxicating creature I have ever known. I was so wild for her, I think I would have done anything to lay the world at her feet."

"I didn't realize it was like that for you and Mom."

"Don't be absurd. This was before I came to my senses, let her go, and married your mother."

The words blindsided Chance, left him staring at his father in shock.

"It turned out to be for the best. For her as well as me." Rising, Norman went back to the bar to refill his glass. "She'd started making noises about giving up her chance for a real career to stay in Galveston and be my wife. It was one of those foolish dreams we have when we're young, filled with talk of children—raised in poverty, of course, since your grandfather was threatening to disown me." He held the bottle out to Chance, but Chance shook his head.

"The problem was," his father continued as he came back to his chair, "sacrifice didn't become either one of us. We fought, I can't even remember over what. Isn't that odd? I remember how livid I was, and exactly how she looked while she was ordering me out of that tiny house she'd grown up in—she had a remarkable temper—but I can't remember what we fought about." He rubbed his forehead. "Well, no matter. That was all years ago. Although I find it incredibly ironic that you've become a business partner with her nephew and two nieces."

The air left Chance's lungs. "Vivian Young? You were in love with the Incomparable Vivian?"

"Still am, I suppose."

"You son of a bitch," Chance muttered so low, his father didn't hear. Standing, he crossed to the window and pulled back the drapes enough to see outside. The rain had stopped, but water still clung to the glass, distorting the world beyond. "Are you telling me you don't love Mom?"

His father took a long time to answer. "There are many kinds of love."

He glanced over his shoulder and remembered the words his mother had spoken the day he and Paige had come for lunch. She'd told him no woman should have to settle for being the right choice. Far better to be the worst choice, but still the one that's taken.

"You realize she knows, don't you?" Chance said. "Mom knows she was your second choice."

"Don't be ridiculous." His father took another swallow

of his drink. "I've never given your mother any reason to doubt my feelings for her."

"I didn't say she doubted them." He dropped the curtain, plunging the room back into darkness. "I said she knows what those feelings are. And for reasons I'm having trouble understanding, she accepts that. I suspect because she does love you. More than I think you deserve at the moment."

His father flinched. "You're right. She doesn't deserve a man who can't even run his own bank."

"I'm not talking about the bank! I'm talking about my mother, one of the most remarkable women I know. A woman who deserves better than what you did to her. Because, when you settled for your second choice, you condemned her to life with a man who could never love her the way she deserves to be loved. If you hadn't married her, she'd have been free to find a man who would put her first. So, maybe instead of sitting here wallowing in self-pity, you should think about the ego blows Mom has endured over the years."

The stunned look on his father's face reminded him that he'd come here to console, not judge. Afraid of what he'd say next, he excused himself and left.

CHAPTER 24

Chance felt as if the world as he knew it were falling apart as he drove from his parents' house to his apartment. Everything he'd expected out of life, everything he'd assumed to be true, was changing and shifting.

For years, he'd thought he was in love with Paige, but what he felt for her was no more than brotherly affection. He'd expected to spend his life working at the bank, but in the last months the job had become hollow and meaningless to him. He'd assumed his parents had the perfect marriage, because they seemed so comfortable together, but was that comfort simply a lack of passion? An acceptance on both their parts for something less than what they really wanted?

Pulling into the parking lot of his apartment building, he looked for Aurora's Jeep. He didn't even realize he was looking until he didn't find it. Had she gone back to the inn? Why wasn't she here? He needed her here. It was as simple as that, he needed her.

He sat for a moment, debating what to do. He wanted to go find Aurora and bring her back. He wanted someone to talk to, someone to help him make sense of what was happening to his life, and what was happening to him. Some days he didn't even feel like the same person he'd been three months ago.

Before he saw Aurora, though, he needed to change out of his suit and wait for his hands to stop shaking. He climbed out of the car, and started for the entrance to the building, but the thought of going inside to an empty apartment left him feeling edgy. On impulse, he turned, waited for a break in traffic and jogged across Seawall Boulevard. The recent rain dampened the pavement and scented the air. Cars swished by, their tires kicking up small sprays of water and sand.

He descended a set of concrete steps to the deserted beach. The damp sand was hard packed, so he left his shoes on and started walking. Overhead, clouds still brooded. The pulse of the gulf beat against the long stretch of land, the rush and retreat of it never ceasing. That at least was one thing that never changed. But the rhythm didn't soothe him as it usually did. Bits of his life played out in his head, the illusion of expectation shattered by the reality of fact. He felt as though he were riding a train that had been switched to the wrong track and was careening into the unknown.

But was it the wrong track? Or one he'd chosen on his own without even realizing it.

He walked out onto one of the massive rock fingers that stretched into the gulf to break up the waves before they reached shore. They'd been built to protect the island from the fury of hurricanes, but Chance felt a wild urge to go to the edge of that protection, to dare fate to make his life any more chaotic than it already was.

The wind grew stronger as he moved away from the beach. His shirt whipped against his arms and back in stinging slaps. Waves crashed against the rocks near his feet with a force that reverberated up his legs. The warm, salty spray erupted around him, splattering his clothes and face.

He walked to the end, until he could go no farther without stepping off into the gulf itself. There he stood with the wind buffeting his body, the clouds rolling overhead, and the water brewing beneath him.

This is it, he told himself. End of the line. Time to make a decision. When he turned and walked back to the safety of the beach, he could either work to get his life back to where it was, or he could sever his ties to all his old plans.

He almost laughed when he realized there wasn't any choice at all. He'd already made his choice, had been making it in a hundred small steps over the summer. He'd chosen the inn over the bank, Aurora over Paige, himself over a hundred and fifty years of Chancellor tradition.

To hell with what others expected. He'd chosen himself.

His spirits lifted suddenly as nature continued to rage all around. He'd chosen the life he could have with Aurora. She would never fit into his old life. But he could fit perfectly into her life . . . if she'd let him.

If she'd let him.

That thought brought him back to earth. She'd said she loved him, but what assurance was there in that? He'd said he loved her before he'd known if it would go further. Loving someone didn't mean you wanted to spend the rest of your life with that person. What would he do if he committed himself to this new direction, severed his old ties, only to learn she didn't want him?

Would that make a difference in his decision about the bank?

No. Even if she didn't want him, he no longer wanted his old life. It didn't fulfill him anymore. He wanted to build a new life and he hoped it would include Aurora at his side.

Her words came back to him from the day on the pier when he'd told her to accept the bank's decision, to accept defeat. She'd asked if he'd ever taken a chance on anything.

He hadn't. But the time had come for him to live up to his name. He turned, determination squaring his shoulders. It was time to take the biggest chance of his life.

Rory stood at a window in the office staring out toward the cove. Her mind couldn't seem to settle on one thought, but shifted from Chance and his father, the scene at the bank, to Paige's mother, the ball, her own family, the inn. Everything was a jumble that somehow seemed connected. Every action she'd taken over the past three months seemed like a stone being thrown into a pond, the ripples spreading outward, affecting everyone and everything.

She'd talked her family into risking their entire savings to start an inn, with no thought to the possibility for failure. She'd tumbled into bed with Chance with no thought to the consequences. Because of those two actions, her life and the lives of everyone around her were forever changed.

"Rory?" her sister said from behind her. "Did you hear me?"

"Hmm?" She turned her head.

Seated at the desk, Allison gave her a worried look. "Are you all right? You've seemed so on edge since you got back from the bank."

"I know. I'm sorry." How could she explain that the world suddenly felt too big and frightening? Was it the pregnancy that had her emotions running so out of control? "I guess I'm a bit distracted. What were you saying?"

"I was going over the To Do list for next Friday." Allison looked over the pad in her hand, her expression a mix of dismay and determination. "There's so much that has to be done, and all of it in one day. Adrian will be tied up with the cooking, and I have a ton of running-around-town stuff to do, so you'll need to be here all day to accept the deliveries. The flowers won't be here until Saturday morning, but the rental company will be here Friday afternoon with everything else. Except the bar. That was taken for a party Friday night so they won't be able to bring it until Saturday morning. As for the liquor delivery . . ."

Allison's voice faded into the background as Rory turned back to the window. Where was Chance? Was he still with his father? Absently, she rested a hand over her stomach, a reaction to the strange flutter of nerves. Then the flutter came again, and she realized what it was. Not nerves at all.

"Oh, my . . ." she breathed, looking down in awe.

"What is it?" Alli asked. "What's wrong?"

She stared at her sister. "The baby just moved."

"Are you sure?" Alli stared back, looking equally stunned.

She just stood there, unable to answer as the reality of the life inside her crashed over her. No longer was the baby some vague concept off in the future. It was here, now, miraculously alive. A baby. Her baby. Alive and tucked safely inside her.

Tears welled up in her eyes, joy, terror, amazement. "My baby moved," she choked out.

Allison hurried over and enfolded her in her arms. "It's okay. You're all right." Cooing softly, her sister guided her to sit on the settee. "Don't cry, Rory. Everything will be all right. Adrian and I are here to help you, no matter what happens."

"No, it's not that. It's—" She sniffed and smiled through her tears. "It's just so wonderful. And frightening!"

"I know." Allison smoothed her hair. "I know."

The sound of the front door opening and closing made both of them stiffen. Rory wiped frantically at her cheeks, but knew the gesture was useless.

"Hello?" Chance called a moment before he appeared in the office doorway.

Rory looked up, feeling exposed—and knew the minute he saw her tears.

"Aurora?" He rushed over to kneel before her. "What's happened?"

"Nothing. I—" She glanced at her sister, a silent plea for help.

Tell him? her sister begged with her eyes.

But fear still held her back. *I can't!* she wanted to wail. *Not yet.*

"Aurora?" Chance said softly, his face lined with concern.

Allison squeezed her hand. "I'll go see if Adrian needs help in the kitchen."

When Allison left, Chance moved into the space she'd vacated. "Aurora, what is it?"

She stared at him feeling more vulnerable than she ever had in her life. She hadn't expected love to make her feel that way. She'd expected it to make her feel cherished and safe. But it didn't feel that way at all!

If only she knew the right thing to do. The thing that would hurt the least number of people.

"Nothing's wrong," she said, taking the coward's way out. But she needed time. Just a little bit more time to decide when and how to tell him.

"What do you mean, nothing?" His brow wrinkled. "I find you here crying, and you say nothing's wrong? Is it that business with Marcy? If so, it'll be okay. Paige will handle her mom when she gets back."

"It's not just Marcy Baxter. It's . . . everything! The ball, the inn. We've all been working so hard, and what if we fail?"

"Hey, what's this?" He gathered her into his arms. "What's this talk of failing? And what did you do with Aurora St. Claire? The Aurora I know would never talk of failing. She's much too brave for that."

She almost laughed—almost told him she wasn't brave at all. She was frightened and foolish and she had no idea what to do about the mess she was in. "You're right," she said instead. "It's just that I'm so worried. I keep thinking maybe I should have listened to you about the money. If the inn fails, we'll lose everything, and it will be all my fault, because I'm the one who talked everyone into this." She buried her face in her hands. "What was I thinking?"

"Aurora . . ." He pulled her hands away, his eyes full of understanding and support. "First of all, your enthusiasm is very persuasive, but you didn't arm-twist anyone into anything. To be honest, I'm glad you didn't listen to me, or none of this would be happening." He cupped her jaw and stared at her as if willing her to stay confident. "We're all in this together, and we are not going to fail. Do you hear me? We've already started getting calls, and once the ball is over, word of mouth will start spreading. I'm proud to be a part of this, and you should be, too. We'll be fine, Aurora. We'll be fine."

"You really think so?" She sniffed, hating her own doubt.

"Yes, I do. So stop worrying. That's my job." He dried her cheek with his thumb. "Your job is to dream big dreams. Mine is to find ways to make them happen. Together I think we make a pretty good team. Don't you?"

She wanted to say yes, but how deep was his commitment to making her dreams come true? Did he even know those dreams had shifted to include a lifetime with him? Somehow he'd become everything to her. How could she have given him so much power over her happiness, her heart, her life? What would she do if he didn't share the same depth of emotion she felt for him?

She straightened and dried her face. "You're right. We make a very good team. I'm just tired, is all."

"You have a right to be tired. You've been working way too hard. So why don't we take the evening off and go back to my place? I could use some downtime after the day I've had."

She remembered now. The scene at the bank. "Did you find your father?"

"Yeah." He started to tell her everything, his conversation with his dad, his revelation on the beach, his decision to quit his job at the bank rather than give up the inn. All of it welled up inside him, including the desire to ask her to marry him. He wanted to blurt it all out, but it lodged in his throat.

His heart started pounding, making it hard to breathe.

In a rush, he stood, forcing air into his lungs.

"Chance?" she asked, still seated. "Are you okay?"

No, he wasn't okay! He was on the verge of throwing his entire world at her feet and terrified she'd reject it. Reject him.

"I'm fine," he managed. "Like I said, it's been a rough day."

He started to pace and she stared at his legs. "Why are your pants legs all wet?"

"Hmm?" He looked down. "Oh, I went walking on the beach." He paced a bit more. "Look, why don't we get something to eat, then go to the apartment where we can . . . talk?"

"Okay," she sighed, sounding incredibly tired. "I guess it won't hurt to take one night off. Just give me a minute to tell Alli and Adrian we're leaving."

He nodded. The minute she left the room, he dropped forward and braced his hands against his knees as he gulped in air. What a narrow escape that had been from a really stupid move. He couldn't just blurt out a proposal of marriage. He needed to plan what to say and how to say it.

First, tonight, they'd talk. He'd tell her about his decision to leave the bank. Then, depending on her reaction to that, he'd figure out the right time and way to propose. The last thing he wanted to do was make an ass of himself while he asked her to spend the rest of her life with him.

Except, they didn't talk that night. Or the next day. At least not about anything more important than getting ready for the ball, which was now only a few days away.

Chance decided not to turn in his resignation until after his father's last day. He didn't want it to look as if he were walking out in protest, or people would know rather than merely suspect that his father wasn't leaving of his own free will. Besides, it would make his father's last days at the bank and the retirement party less stressful for everyone.

As for proposing to Aurora, he was definitely putting

that on hold until after the ball. Every day, she seemed more emotional and on edge. The last thing she needed was for him to put her on the spot and ask her to make a decision that would affect the rest of their lives.

Yes, waiting was best. Definitely best. Besides, it gave him time to order a ring.

CHAPTER 25

Chance was going to break up with her. Rory just knew it. Every day, he grew more distant. He acted nervous and distracted. Several times, he'd seemed on the verge of telling her something—something big—but then he'd stop himself. If she asked what was wrong, he'd make some vague comment like "Let's get through this weekend, then we'll talk."

Talk about ending their relationship, she assumed.

Would that mean ending his involvement with the inn as well? How in the world would they deal with that? He'd been a godsend with his knowledge of business, taking care of so many things they never would have thought to do.

Well, they would deal with it, somehow. The inn would survive. Even if her heart didn't.

By Friday afternoon, she was an emotional wreck, but doing her best to hide it. Chance had taken off the whole day to help them get ready. They were working together outside, helping two men from the rental company unload the truck. In addition to the tables on the veranda and lawn, they would set up tables on the deck of the ship—whenever it arrived.

With one hand shading her eyes, she glanced toward the cove, wondering when the *Pirate's Pleasure* would appear. The last thing they needed was some huge catastrophe, like the ship not showing up on time.

Although with the ship would come Paige. The thought tied up her insides even more.

Rory searched the horizon for some sign of the ship, but all she saw was blue water and cloudless sky. At least the weather had cooperated. A cool front had blown through mid-week, ending the rain and leaving them with clear sunny days.

Adrian and two of his friends, Rusty and Jeff, were down on the beach arranging large driftwood logs to serve as benches near the pit where the Hawaiian *kalua* pigs had been roasting since yesterday. In the morning, they would add the *lau lau,* another Hawaiian dish, this one made of pork hash wrapped in *ti* leaves. Once the food was removed from the pit tomorrow afternoon, they planned to light a big fire. The buffet line would be set up nearby on the lower yard, well lit by dozens of tiki lamps. The dance floor and entertainers would be on the ship, and the dessert buffet would be inside the house, in the dining room, to entice people closer to the silent auction that would be set up in the music room.

"Aurora," Chance called, emerging from the truck with his arms loaded. "Where do you want the tray stands for the buffet line?"

She turned back to the task at hand, trying to act normal, as if she didn't know Chance's feelings for her had changed. "Go ahead and take them to the kitchen. We won't set up the tables until the morning."

He started to pass her on his way to the house, but something behind her must have caught his attention. She turned to see what it was . . . and her eyes widened with surprise. There, clearing the line of palm trees, was the *Pirate's Pleasure* coming in under full sail. "Oh, wow," she breathed, temporarily forgetting all her worries at such a spectacular sight. Even though Bobby had shown them pictures, nothing could compare to the real thing—a beautiful Baltimore clipper flying over the water with billowing white sails.

"I take it that's the ship we've been waiting for," Chance said.

"I'd say so," she answered.

The men on the beach stopped to stare, as did the two from the rental company. The sound of a high-pitched maritime whistle came across the water, like an echo from bygone days. As the ship neared the mouth of the cove, Rory could see the crew scurrying up into the ratlines. The sails came down, like a great bird folding its wings, and the ship slowed. A dinghy was lowered over the side and four crew members climbed in. When the outboard motor roared to life, the dinghy headed for the pier.

"Do you think they need help docking?" Chance asked.

"I don't know," Rory answered.

"Well, either way, let's go have a closer look." He set the tray stands aside and headed down the path to the pier.

Conflicting emotions played tug-of-war in her stomach as she followed: her apprehension over Paige pulling her back, her eagerness to see the boat pulling her forward. Adrian and his friends were already on the pier when she got there. He turned with a broad grin. "Not exactly something you see every day, eh, sis?"

"Not exactly," she agreed.

The dinghy bumped up to the dock long enough for two of the four crew members to hop out, then it raced back in a wide arc toward the *Pirate's Pleasure*.

"Ahoy," one of the crew called, his voice thick with the sound of the Caribbean or Jamaica, Rory wasn't sure. His tall, dark-skinned body rippled with muscles and his teeth flashed white in the sunlight.

"Hey, you need help?" Chance asked.

"No, we got it. Just stand clear."

Taking that as a request to stay out of the way, they all backed up a few steps. The docking maneuver was quite a sight to behold, with the dinghy serving as a tugboat to guide the larger vessel in. As it drew near, Rory marveled at its lavish beauty, a black-hulled vessel with red and gold accents on the railing. The mermaid that adorned the bow had golden hair that trailed backward as if tossed by the wind.

Bobby and Paige stood at the rail, Bobby in the bow, Paige midship. There was another woman on the quarter-deck handling the wheel and calling out orders. Bobby and Paige tossed lines to the crew on the pier, and within minutes the vessel was secured, an actual Baltimore clipper tied *right there* to their pier!

"Man, that's what I call a ship," Adrian's friend Rusty said.

A set of wooden steps, complete with handrail, was hoisted over the side and lowered to the dock.

"Hey, beautiful!" Bobby called to Rory as he sauntered down the steps. "Couldn't wait to see me, eh?"

She laughed, shaking her head. "I came to see the ship and you know it."

"She's something, isn't she?" He turned to admire the vessel.

Rory nodded, but her eyes shifted back to the steps as Paige started down. Although, if she hadn't known it was Paige, she would have had a hard time recognizing this disheveled, windblown woman dressed in gym shorts and a T-shirt that looked as if they'd come from Academy Surplus rather than a designer boutique.

Chance went to greet her, holding out his hand to help her down the last few steps. "So, how did you enjoy sailing your first pirate ship?"

"It was fun," Paige answered, but her smile was sad.

Rory watched as the two of them moved toward the end of the pier, out of earshot. They stood close together, almost touching as they talked.

"Hey," Bobby said, "I guess I should introduce everyone." The black man with the island accent was the first mate. The other crewmembers ranged in age and background from a college student to an old dockhand with skin as weathered as driftwood.

"Welcome to the Pearl Island Inn," Adrian said. "We're glad y'all made it."

While Adrian and his friends visited with the crew, Bobby followed Rory's gaze. "You know, for a little rich girl," Bobby said, "that Paige is one heck of a sailor. Pulled her weight and didn't complain once on the whole trip up here. Although maybe she was too terrified to complain."

"Terrified?" Rory asked. "Of what?"

"Not what. Who."

Just then a figure appeared at the top of the steps, a white ball cap shading the face. "You laggards have this ship secure?"

"Aye, aye, Captain!" the first mate called back.

"Well, then, get back up here and grab your gear so we can go ashore."

All the crew but Bobby and Paige scrambled back on board. After giving a few more orders, the captain came down the steps, pulling a shirt on over her swimsuit top and tying it at the waist. Then she freed a long, mahogany-colored braid from the shirt so it hung down her back. She wasn't a tall woman, but she had incredibly long, lean legs beneath a pair of very short, very frayed cutoffs.

"Rory, Adrian," Bobby said as the captain stepped onto the pier. "Meet Captain Jackie, owner of the *Pirate's Pleasure*."

The woman lifted her head, revealing a face that was more interesting than attractive, with strong cheeks, a square jaw, and a wide mouth. "Pleased to meet you," she said in a low, husky voice. "So, this is Pearl Island?" She gazed about at the house and cove, her expression difficult to read. "One of the possible resting places of Jean Laffite's treasure."

"You're familiar with our local lore," Adrian said.

Jackie tipped her head back to see him better from beneath the brim of her cap and Rory revised her first impression. The woman wasn't beautiful but there was something there to attract a man's eye. A fact her brother seemed to home in on right away. "My father was a treasure hunter and I was raised on tales of the pirates. He was especially enamored of your blockade runner, Captain Jack Kingsley, which is why he named me Jackie."

"Really?" Adrian cocked his head and gave her one of his lazy smiles that could seduce at twenty paces. At point-blank range, it was downright lethal. Amazingly, this woman didn't seem to notice.

Bobby stared at the captain. "You never told me you were named after Jack Kingsley."

Jackie merely shrugged as if it weren't important. "So, which one of you wants to fill me in on this shindig tomorrow night?"

"I'll be happy to go over everything with you," Adrian volunteered. "Would you like a tour of the house and grounds?"

"Sure," Jackie said. "But first, I need to arrange a ride into town for my crew. They'll need a rental car and a hotel while we're here."

Adrian assigned that task to his friends, then turned back to Jackie. "But what about you? Have you made plans on where to stay? If not, we could get one of our rooms ready, even though we're not officially opened."

Rory wanted to kick him, since they wanted guests at the ball to roam freely through the house.

"That's okay, I'll stay on my ship," Jackie said, saving Rory from having to inflict bodily harm on her brother.

"No, really," Adrian insisted. "It wouldn't be any trouble. And I'm sure you'd be more comfortable."

"And I assure you," she said in a slow, succinct voice, "I'll be perfectly comfortable on board my ship. The *Pirate's Pleasure* is where I live."

"Where you live?" Adrian frowned. "As in full-time?"

Jackie gave him a challenging look. "Do you have a problem with that?"

"No, not at all," he insisted. "Why don't you follow me up to the house, so I can show you around while your men gather their gear?"

Adrian turned to lead the way.

"Aurora?" Chance said, as he and Paige joined them. "If you and Adrian can handle things here, I'm going to drive Paige home. Bobby, I'll be happy to give you a lift, as well."

"Sure," Bobby answered. "I'll just grab my things."

Rory watched him and Paige head back on board. Her heart sank at the thought of Paige and Chance being together, even though someone had to take Paige home.

"Hey, you okay?" Chance asked.

She nodded. "Will you be back tonight?"

"Of course I'll be back." He chided her with a laugh. "With everything we have left to do? I wouldn't be much of a partner if I bailed out tonight of all nights."

Paige and Bobby came back down the steps, each carrying a duffel bag. Paige greeted Rory but didn't quite meet her eyes.

"Are you ready?" Chance asked Paige.

"I suppose so," Paige sighed as she glanced down at her rumpled, dirty clothes. "Although I'm not looking forward to having Mom see me like this."

"Maybe you can sneak in and get cleaned up before she catches you," Chance teased.

"And maybe her mother should quit trying to run her life," Bobby piped in, surprising all of them. "Well, it's true," he insisted when Chance glared at him. "Paige is a grown woman, perfectly capable of deciding how she wants to dress and what she wants to do." He turned to Paige, whose cheeks had gone beet-red. "And your parents will never stop bullying you as long as you let them get away with it."

Chance straightened to his full height. "I fail to see how

Paige's relationship with her parents is any of your concern, since you barely know her, and don't know them at all."

Bobby spread his hands. "Just stating my opinion."

"Chance," Paige said when he looked ready to argue more. "It's okay."

After a tense moment, Chance nodded. "Very well. If y'all are ready, let's go."

Rory stood watching as they headed up the path, wondering if Chance regretted breaking up with Paige.

Chance had his first inkling that something was wrong between Rory and him that night when she told him she wanted to stay at the inn rather than go to his apartment. Okay, logically her decision made sense. With everything that needed to be done, of course she'd want to stay there and get an early start in the morning.

But it was the first time she'd ever spent the night at the inn.

Adrian and Allison had moved there gradually over the last few days. Since his breakup with Paige, though, Aurora always came home with him. It was a situation everyone seemed comfortable with. Adrian and Allison might send him minor looks of disapproval, but no one had said anything outright. He truly didn't think they were pressuring Aurora to not sleep with him.

So why tonight of all nights did she want to stay at the inn? Was it just the ball, or was it something more as his gut kept telling him? As he drove home he went over their parting conversation: her assuring him she was just tired and wanted to go straight to bed, and him insisting she could do that at his place. It wasn't like they had to make love every night, even though they'd been basically insatiable so far.

What had him the most worried, though, was the way she hadn't looked at him when she'd said she didn't want to go home with him. Was he imagining that there was something wrong? Or was she getting ready to ditch him?

And what would he do if the latter was true?

Fight like hell, was his gut reaction, even though it went against all his training as a dignified Chancellor. If Aurora tried to leave him, would he do anything it took to keep her? Or would he accept her decision with a stiff upper lip and his pride intact?

He hoped he never had to find out.

CHAPTER 26

Rory woke feeling disoriented, at first wondering why Chance wasn't snuggled up beside her. When she reached out for him, her hand found the edge of the mattress and she wondered how the bed had shrunk. Then she remembered. She wasn't in Chance's bed. She was in the twin bed they'd moved from the cottage to her room at the inn.

Lifting her head, she looked around. The room was spare, with little more than the narrow bed she'd slept in most of her life, a chest of drawers, and a single chair. The rag doll angel she'd found in Houston sat on the nightstand, watching her.

Picking it up, she ran a hand over its braided yarn hair. *At least my room has furniture,* she thought.

The nursery beyond the connecting door stood empty. She remembered the white wicker bassinet she'd seen in the thrift shop, and felt a physical yearning deep in her chest. She wanted to drive to the nearest baby store and buy drawers full of tiny outfits and minuscule booties and diapers. Of course, she couldn't do any of that without telling Chance about the baby. Until then, there'd be no baby showers thrown by friends or even anyone outside the family asking her how she was feeling and when she was due.

Dropping her head back on the pillow she hugged the angel as she realized how badly she wanted those things. She wanted to share her news with the world. She wanted to share it with Chance.

But fear of his reaction held her back. Especially now that he was acting so weird. How would she handle losing him? Her eyes squeezed tight against the pain.

Enough! she told herself.

Today was the big day they'd all been working toward. It was not the day to lie in bed and bawl over things she couldn't change or control. Besides, she doubted the breakup would happen today. Her best course of action was to put all of her angst on hold until tomorrow.

With that in mind, she rose and dressed, ready to meet whatever challenges the day would bring.

Controlled chaos, that's what Chance found when he arrived that morning. Aurora stood on the lawn with clipboard in hand directing a motley crew of workers on where to set up the buffet line, how many tables to take to the ship, how many sets of silverware to roll into linen napkins, and who should be down on the beach stacking the wood for the bonfire.

Dismissing the presence of their temporary staff, he crept up behind Rory, slipped an arm about her waist, and pulled her back against him.

She let out a shriek and dropped the clipboard. "Chance!" She whirled to face him with a hand over her heart. "Don't scare me like that."

"Sorry." He laughed at her expression. "I didn't mean to startle you that badly." They both bent to retrieve the clipboard, bumping heads. When they straightened, he handed the board to her.

"Thanks," she said, rubbing her head. "I guess I'm a bit stressed today over everything that needs to be done."

"Well, if you need help relieving your stress, let me know." He wiggled his brows. "I'm sure I could come up with something."

"I'm sure you could." Her laughter helped to ease some of the doubts that had kept him up half the night. Leaning forward, he pressed his lips to hers, needing the reassurance of her kiss. "God, I missed you last night," he said and leaned in again, but she pulled away.

"You shouldn't do that." She glanced nervously toward the house. "Marcy Baxter is here."

"So early?" He wanted to say "So what?" but knew better. *One more day,* he told himself, and then it wouldn't matter who knew that he was in love with Aurora St. Claire.

Aurora made a face. "Marcy and Paige are in the music room arguing over how to set up the silent auction. Allison was going to help, but the last I saw she'd retreated to the kitchen to help Adrian."

"I can't blame her. I've seen Marcy in one of her obsessive moods, where she can't make a decision about anything and changes her mind every five seconds."

"I don't suppose you could put a leash on her and keep her out of our way?"

"Not likely." He chuckled. "So what would you like me to do instead?"

She handed him a sheet off her clipboard. "Take this diagram down to the ship and be sure Jackie and her crew set the tables up right. We don't want anything in the way of the performers and dance floor."

And so the day progressed, with each of them running roughshod over a different area. The workers moved in a constant stream, lining the pathway, buffet area, and lawn with two hundred tiki lamps. Floodlights were secured high in the trees to provide a discreet amount of more modern lighting. The tables were covered with brightly colored cloths, and tray stands were carried down to the food line. The florist arrived just past noon with an arrangement of tropical flowers for each table, and thick candles protected by hurricane shades.

He realized it would take the entire staff half an hour just to light all the lamps and candles when the signal was given. But what a spectacular display it would make.

The performers arrived mid-afternoon to set up on the

quarterdeck of the ship. Many of them had been in the opera house's production of *The Pirates of Penzance* two years ago. They planned to re-create some of those numbers and mix them with old sailing ditties in between sets of dance music. The quarterdeck provided a convenient stage where they'd be visible even to the guests on the veranda. The leader of the troupe decided that swinging down to the main deck on ropes would add dramatic flare, so Jackie and her crew set about rigging up the rope they used for just such a feat.

As Chance watched, he heard someone call his name from the pier. Going to the rail, he found Adrian shielding his eyes against the sun.

"Have you seen Bobby?" Adrian asked.

"I didn't even know he was here," Chance answered.

"He came by earlier to see if he could help. And now that I actually need him, no one can find him."

"Why did you need him?"

"To drive into Houston and pick up the ice sculpture."

"I thought we were having that delivered."

"We were," Adrian said in disgust. "But the company just called and said their truck is broken down. Rusty said we can borrow his van, but I need him here to set up the bar."

The mention of going to Houston caught Chance's attention. The engagement ring he'd ordered had been ready since Thursday, but he hadn't had a spare minute to go get it. "Where in Houston is this place?" he asked. When Adrian gave him the address, he couldn't believe his good luck. The jeweler was practically on the way. "I'll go get it."

"No, you're too busy helping set up," Adrian said.

"Actually, Jackie can take over for me here, and I'll be back before you know it."

Adrian hesitated only a second. "Okay, you got it. Come on up to the house and get the keys."

When Chance turned to give his list of instructions to

Jackie, he found that her crew had finished rigging the fake halyard and she was showing the performers how the "Errol Flynn" maneuver was done. As nimble as a gymnast mounting a balance beam, she leapt onto the rail of the quarterdeck. The first mate tossed her the rope and she grabbed it with both hands, then jumped up and back for a bigger swing. With legs lifted before her, she let the line carry her straight toward the mast at an alarming speed. He realized quickly that most people would smash their faces if they tried such a thing. But she landed with her feet against the mast, pushed off, then let go of the line to drop lightly on her feet.

Everyone applauded as she took her bow. "And that, my friends, is how you swing from a halyard, Hollywood style."

When she finished bowing, he called her over so he could give her the diagram and list of things to do. She told him no sweat and sent him on his way.

He headed for the house, his mind racing with plans now that the ring would be on hand. He'd had days to think about how he wanted to propose, and he had nearly every detail worked out. The plan was romantic enough to appeal to Aurora, but private and dignified, which appealed to him. He was nervous enough about proposing without allowing room for public humiliation if she said no.

Somehow, miraculously, everything got done on time. Just before twilight, Rory stepped onto the veranda, the skirt of her gown swishing as she moved to the rail and surveyed the lawn one last time. They'd woven their enchantment well, she decided, creating a fanciful setting for grown-ups to play pretend.

Dressed in their costumes, the serving wenches moved about lighting the lamps, and each new blaze added to the whimsy. The men, dressed as pirate crew, were putting the finishing touches on the food table near the beach where the bonfire was just beginning to blaze. Adrian strode among them in his tall jackboots and flamboyant red coat, supervising every detail. What a striking pirate he would have made.

On board the *Pirate's Pleasure,* Jackie and her crew wore the costumes they'd brought: the big-sleeved white shirts and tight black pants they dressed in whenever they chartered the ship for special parties.

"Ah, so here you are."

She turned at the sound of Chance's voice, and found him standing in the doorway. First came relief that he'd made it back from Houston in time, then a thrill of admiration as he came toward her. Where Adrian's jacket was a cocky red, Chance's was a royal-blue, the gallant captain rather than the roguish pirate. White lace spilled from his throat and cuffs, and a dress sword hung at his side.

"Oh, my." She laughed as heat swept through her. "You look"—*sexy enough to ravish*—"very handsome."

"Thank you, madam." He swept a courtly bow. "You flatter me when it is I who should be praising you, for you are absolutely stunning in that gown." He took her hand and kissed the back, his eyes gazing deeply into hers. "I'll have to keep a close watch on you, lest some presumptuous knave try to steal you away."

His words made her laugh as her heart filled with hope. Surely he wouldn't say such things if he intended to break up with her.

His gaze dropped to her breasts, which swelled to dangerous proportions above the low, straight neckline. Ecru lace continued around her arms to form off-the-shoulder sleeves. The peach-colored bodice hugged her to the waist, where the skirt flared out over the petticoats.

"I'm beginning to wish the night was already over," he said, the intent in his eyes making her pulse flutter.

"And I'm beginning to wish we dressed up more often." She flashed him a coquettish look through lowered lashes. "If this is how it affects you."

"I'd much rather get *un*dressed." He pulled her closer and slipped an arm about her waist to dip her backward.

"Chance!" she gasped, gripping his shoulders for balance as he nuzzled her neck.

"I've been wanting you all day," he whispered in her ear.

"Chance, let me up." She was laughing and flustered by the time he complied. Her gaze swept the grounds to see who was watching. Fortunately, everyone looked busy. "Behave yourself."

"But it's so much more fun to misbehave," he said. Car doors sounded in the distance, signaling the arrival of their first guests. "Damn, I guess I'll have to behave after all. Should we greet guests here at the top of the steps, or go down to the lawn?"

"I don't know," she said as nerves sprang to life in her stomach. "Allison will be inside to show people around, and Adrian will be covering the ship and the beach." She looked toward the end of the tiki lamp trail that would guide people from the parking lot to the front of the house. "The lawn, I suppose."

"Very well." As they descended the steps, he linked her hand through the crook of his arm. She clung tightly, hoping she didn't trip on her skirt or say something stupid. "You're not nervous, are you?" he asked.

"Petrified," she admitted, exhaling loudly.

"Well, don't be." He placed his hand over hers and squeezed. "You should be proud. People are going to rave about the inn, and you deserve to soak up every word. None of this would have happened without you."

"Thank you," she whispered just as the first group of guests came around the corner. They came in a steady stream after that, exclaiming over the lawn and the house and the costumes. With each couple that arrived, Rory began to relax and enjoy herself a bit more. She became caught up in the enchantment of the evening, the role she played as mistress of the manor welcoming people into her pirate lover's home.

Later, as she strolled about the lawn making sure everyone had enough to eat and drink, inviting them to go inside and tour the house, she glanced up toward the veranda and felt her heart swell with happiness and pride. The scene before her was what she had imagined that day when she'd stood in this very spot asking Chance what it would take to buy the house. The chain-link fence was gone and lush grass covered the ground beneath her feet. People sat on the veranda laughing and visiting. The house itself glowed with welcoming light from within.

She could see it this way for years to come, sheltering guests, providing a home and income for her and Adrian and Allison.

Then she saw Chance leaning against one of the stone columns, and her questions and fears stirred back to life. Was he part of the permanent picture, or was he simply passing through this phase of her life? He looked so at ease, visiting with the guests, as if he were a guest himself, not one of the staff. But then this was the first time he'd ever attended the Buccaneer's Ball as something other than a guest. The people she waited on were his peers, while the staff doing the serving were hers.

Trying to push the thought aside, she continued her way through the tables, asking if anyone needed anything, picking up dirty plates and empty glasses. Conversation buzzed around her, blending with the sound of the performers down on the ship as they belted out the bawdy lyrics of a sailing song. The ship was ablaze with candlelight and every table was filled.

"The St. Claires have really done a great job restoring the house," a woman said from behind her, making her smile as she set her tray on a table and began loading it with dirty dishes.

"With the help of Oliver Chancellor, don't forget," another woman added.

"Well, I wouldn't expect that to last long."

Rory glanced over her shoulder and saw three women seated at a table with their backs to her so they could watch the stage while they talked. They were as sleek and sophisticated as the rest of the guests, wearing dresses that probably cost even more than the price of a ticket to the ball, and jewels that sparkled in the torchlight.

"What do you mean?" one of them asked.

"You haven't heard?" The older woman's tone said she had a juicy bit of gossip to share. "The bank is threatening to fire him over his partnership with the St. Claires."

Rory turned away, her heart pounding.

"No!" one of them gasped. "Surely they wouldn't fire one of the Chancellors."

"They fired Mr. Chancellor, didn't they?"

"They did not. He took early retirement."

"He was *asked* to take early retirement. Trust me, my nail tech has a client who works in the loan department. According to what she's heard, the bank gave Norman the old heave-ho, then told Oliver to end his business relationship with the St. Claires or he'd be out the door, too."

"That's terrible. I guess he'll be giving up his interest in the inn, then."

"Not necessarily." The third one snickered. "Since business isn't the only relationship he has with them." The voice lowered to a titillating stage whisper. "I heard he's sleeping with the youngest sister."

"You're joking!" The older woman laughed. "Oh, that's rich. Still, even if he is cheating on Paige, I can't believe Oliver Chancellor would be stupid enough to throw away his career at the bank over an affair with Aurora St. Claire. Lord, she can't be that good."

Rory turned slowly and faced the three women. Carried away with laughter, one of them fell against her friend. As she straightened, she caught sight of Rory and paled. "Uh-oh."

"What?" The other two turned in unison. "Oh, dear."

On wooden legs, Rory moved past them, picking up speed with each stride. Every fear she'd tried to hold at bay broke free. Why hadn't she listened to Alli? And what had she done to Chance? Because of her, he was being forced to choose between the inn and the bank, which was no choice at all. Of course the bank would win. That was a part of his real life. The inn was just play for him.

He didn't belong in her world any more than she belonged in his. She'd never fit in with people like those three women, people who attended events like this—not that she wanted to if that was how they behaved. She'd been foolish to think she and Chance could ever be together long-term. She'd been so very, very foolish!

With no goal but escape she continued down the hill, her breath turning ragged. When she reached the beach, she turned away from the pier and hurried past the people gathered around the bonfire.

"Rory?" her brother called.

Fighting back tears, she lifted her skirts and ran, fleeing the words that pursued her. Not the ones she'd just heard, but Chance's words from the day on the pier when he'd told her he didn't want a relationship with her, that all he felt for her was physical attraction. He'd tried to tell her then that they were mismatched. Why hadn't she listened!

And later, when he'd admitted the attraction had turned to love, he'd said she'd ruined his life. And he was right.

There had to be a way to fix the damage she'd done. There had to be!

Chance frowned in concern when he saw Aurora take off down the lawn. Excusing himself from his conversation with Frank and Carol Adams, he followed her at a slower pace, smiling and nodding to people as he passed them. The last thing he wanted to do was create a stir by chasing her at a dead run.

When he reached the beach, Adrian waved him over.

"What's wrong with Rory?" her brother asked, low enough so that no one else would hear.

"I don't know," Chance answered. "Did you see where she went?"

"Not exactly. She just ran down the beach, that way. I hope she's not having one of her weird panic attacks."

"Me, too." His concern mounted as he remembered her last one. "I better find her."

Adrian nodded and Chance headed down the beach, leaving the lights and noise of the party behind. His steps slowed as darkness closed about him. The water lapping against the shore became more pronounced.

"Aurora?" he called, squinting into the tangle of trees and undergrowth. The moon washed the island in soft blue light, but the shadows of the trees were too black to penetrate.

Where could she have gone? His concern turned to fear the farther he walked. Could she have stumbled and hurt herself while running in the dark?

"Aurora?" he called again, louder this time. He listened intently, but all he heard was the lapping of the water and the chirping of night bugs. Finally, his eyes adjusted enough to the dark to see a trail of footprints in the sand. He followed them until they veered away from the beach into the dark shadow of the trees.

He found her in a clearing washed in moonlight. She sat on a driftwood log, her hands covering her mouth as silver tears coursed down her cheeks.

"Aurora! What is it? What's wrong?" As he hurried toward her, she rose and flung herself into his arms.

"Oh, Chance, I'm so sorry," she wept as she clung to his neck.

"For what?" He tried to pull away enough to see her face.

"For everything. For getting you involved with the inn. For causing trouble between you and Paige. You would have been better off staying with her."

"Whoa, wait—"

"It's just that I love you so much." She lifted her head and his heart twisted at the sight of her anguish. "I know it was wrong to seduce you that first time, but I didn't know then how it would turn out. I should have listened when you said we were mismatched."

"We are not mismatched! And I'm glad—"

"But how can you ever forgive me for ruining your life?" she rushed on.

"Would you stop? You didn't ruin—"

"It's just that I love you so much, and—"

He kissed her, more as a way to make her stop talking than anything else. But the moment his mouth touched hers, she seemed to ignite in his arms. She returned the kiss with a desperation that knocked him back a step.

He braced himself as her arms tightened about his neck. He tried to pull his mouth from hers long enough to speak, but she followed, pressing her body against him. Blood surged to his groin when her hips molded to his. Jesus, he'd been half hard all evening with visions of getting her out of that dress. Or taking her while she was still in it. Not that it ever took much to get him aroused when she was around.

Unable to resist, he decided to kiss her back just for a minute, then he'd find out what was wrong. He slanted his head to mate his mouth more fully with hers and let his tongue slip inside. She tasted so good, so unbearably good, he couldn't pull away. He needed more. Just a little more.

His hands moved to cup her breasts. She moaned as she came up on tiptoes, her pelvis rubbing his erection. Her arms lowered and her hands slipped inside his jacket to caress his stomach, his sides, and up his back.

Somehow the dress slipped lower and he was holding her naked breast, her nipples teasing his palms, begging to be tasted. He broke away from her mouth and trailed a line of kisses down her neck.

"Yes, oh yes," she rasped, arching her back and offering

her breasts up to him. With one arm around the small of her back to support her, he lavished attention on each breast in turn, before sucking one nipple into his mouth.

A choked sob escaped her, a sound filled with more pain than pleasure. Startled, he lifted his head and found her still crying. "Aurora, what is it? Did I hurt you?"

"No, I just—I want you so much it hurts." She burrowed her face against his chest, crying softly. "I know it's wrong, but I want you. Just one more time and then I'll do the right thing." She kissed his neck, his jaw, the underside of his chin. "Love me one more time, Chance. Please love me."

He tried to make sense of her words as she tugged his shirt from the waistband of his trousers, but his pulse was roaring in his ears. Her hands found his bare skin, making him flinch. He was so hot, he probably scorched her fingers. She found his mouth and kissed him with such desperate longing, he gave up on rational thought.

Later, he decided, he'd find out what had upset her. Later. Right now he had to touch her, taste her. Without breaking the kiss, he looked about the clearing. Twigs and leaves littered the ground. God, what he wouldn't give for a blanket!

A stout oak stood just behind her, offering at least some support. He walked her back a couple of steps. When she felt the trunk, she leaned against it while her hands tugged at his belt. He undid the buckle and the sword fell to the ground. He shed his jacket and flung it away while she unfastened his trousers. Kissing her, he lifted the yards upon yards of skirt and petticoats until he found the warm smooth skin of her thighs.

Her underwear was quickly dispensed with. When his hand slipped between her thighs, her head dropped back against the tree. A look of pleasure softened her face even as tears continued to course down her cheeks.

Longing to take the tears away, he kissed her cheeks as he stroked her gently with his fingers. But the feel of her so hot and wet had his body aching with a different need, one to bury himself deep inside her.

"I love the way you touch me," she whispered, her eyes closed.

His groin clenched at her husky words. He freed himself and braced his feet wide apart, his thighs forcing hers to open. "Aurora," he rasped. "Hold on to my neck and wrap you legs around me."

Her legs went eagerly around him. Cupping her bottom, he poised her, then plunged with near brutal force. She gasped and stiffened in his arms.

"Aurora," he rasped as she clamped her legs around him, pulling him deeper, and his control snapped. She moved with him, calling his name, telling him she needed him, loved him. Then she stiffened against him, her head flung back. Her expression of rapture sent him over the edge.

His climax hit him like a physical blow, leaving his limbs weak. His knees nearly buckled before he managed to lock them. He collapsed forward, supporting her more with the pressure of his body than his arms, which had turned to rubber.

They remained that way a long time, their harsh breathing drowning out the sounds of the night. Her head had fallen forward onto his shoulder. When he felt he could move, he pressed a kiss into her hair.

"You okay?" he asked in a surprisingly steady voice.

"Yes." Her own voice sounded small and unsure.

"Calmer now?"

She nodded, her cheek moving against his shoulder.

"Then do you think you can tell me what's going on?"

She lifted her head and nodded but didn't meet his eye.

He eased her feet to the ground and helped her straighten her clothes. Then he gathered his jacket and sword. When they were seated side by side on the driftwood log he waited for her to begin.

"Well?" he prompted.

She plucked at the folds of her skirt. "I overheard some women talking. They said your job at the bank was in jeopardy because of your partnership with us."

"That's *it*?" He sagged with relief. "God, Aurora, never scare me like that again. I thought something serious had happened. And the way you were babbling a minute ago, I thought you were trying to break up with me."

Her head snapped up and fire shone in her eyes. "What do you mean, 'That's it?' You're about to lose your job because of me, and you don't think that's serious?"

"I'm not about to lose my job because of you—"

"Are you saying the bank didn't give you an ultimatum?"

"Yes, they did. And I'm sorry, now, I didn't talk to you about it sooner. But I thought you had enough to deal with this week without finding out that I'd decided to leave the bank."

"No!" Her face paled. "You can't. I won't let you."

"Aurora, it's okay." He tried to reassure her. "If you're worried about the money, don't be. I make enough off my investments to live reasonably well. And once the inn takes off, we'll have income from that."

"It's not the money, it's your life. I really have ruined it. First your relationship with Paige, now your career. No, Chance, I won't let you throw everything away like this. You belong at the bank, not running an inn. The three of us will buy you out."

"The hell you will!"

"If only I could put everything back the way it was."

"I don't want it put back."

"But I can't do that." She shook her head, clearly not listening to him. "Oh, Chance, it's even worse than you realize. I'm so sorry for what I've done to you, but I can't change it now. And I know it's selfish, but a part of me is glad, because even though I can't have you, I can have—"

"What?" he asked, his thoughts reeling.

She looked at him, her eyes shining with tears in the moonlight. "I can't have you, but at least I can have your baby."

The world stopped dead on its axis. He tried to speak, but his lungs didn't work.

Tears spilled down her cheeks. "I'm pregnant, Chance. I'm going to have your baby."

"B-baby?" he managed. She was pregnant and he'd just taken her against a tree with all the gentleness of a battering ram? "Why didn't you tell me?"

"I know I should have. But I was so afraid you'd feel obligated to marry me. I wanted you to want me without knowing, but now I realize how stupid I've been to think you'd ever marry me."

A baby! His mind worked past the immediate fear of having hurt her just now to the wonder of what she was saying. Aurora was going to have his baby! The concept was too huge to take in all at once.

"You have every right to be mad that I didn't tell you sooner," she said. At least he thought that's what she said. He stared at her mouth as other words tumbled out. Something about it happening the first time they'd made love. She'd been pregnant all this time and he hadn't had a clue. He felt a bit cheated over that, but the emotion didn't stand a chance against the others that were crashing through him. As soon as the world started turning again, he was going to shout at the moon. Aurora was going to have his baby!

He tried to concentrate on her words, but she was talking so fast, and crying again. She assured him he'd have as much access to the child as he wanted. But he mustn't feel guilty if he didn't want to be an active father because Allison and Adrian would be there to help her. And through her whole jumbled revelation, she kept insisting that he mustn't feel obligated to marry her.

"What do you mean?" he finally managed to say. "Of course we're getting married."

"No! Haven't you been listening to me? I don't want a

marriage based on obligation. The baby and I will be fine."

"The hell you're not going to marry me!" She was pregnant with his child but refused to marry him? "We'll go to the courthouse first thing Monday and get a license."

"See, I knew you'd react like this!" She rose in a rush. "But I won't let you. I love you too much to let you throw your life away. You have a career at the bank, and family and friends who will never accept someone like me. Nothing changes who we are or how differently we were raised. We belong to different worlds! And there's no point even discussing this any more, because I won't let you throw your life away over this." She turned and fled from the clearing.

He tried to stand and go after her, but his legs weren't working yet. He sat there, staring into the dark, trying to sort out what had just happened.

He'd asked Aurora to marry him, and she'd said no. Even knowing she was having his baby, she'd still turned him down. She'd said they belonged in different worlds, which sounded like she didn't want him in hers.

The thought brought a sense of devastation so great he felt numb.

He fumbled in the jacket pocket for the ring. He'd kept it on him, since he didn't feel safe leaving it at the house with so many people coming in and out. The diamond winked at him in the moonlight, almost as if laughing at him.

She'd turned him down.

What the hell did he do now?

CHAPTER 27

Realizing he couldn't just sit in the clearing for the rest of the night, Chance headed back to the house. How he would face people when he had a huge hole in his chest he didn't know. He'd get through it somehow, though. And tomorrow he and Aurora would talk. He'd ask her if she'd meant what she'd said—that she didn't want him to be part of her life . . . or even the inn.

The whole idea seemed ludicrous. Did she really think that cutting him off from everything he cared about would be saving him from ruin? If so, he needed to set her straight . . . And yet, he knew how stubborn she could be. If she thought pushing him away was the right thing to do, he might never talk her out of it.

And what if all that talk was just her way of sparing his feelings? Maybe she simply didn't love him. But she'd said she did. Dammit, none of it made sense!

When he reached the bonfire, he looked for Adrian. He wanted to know where Aurora had gone so he could avoid her for a while at least. He didn't feel capable of dealing with her until he'd had time to think things through logically. As if logic and Aurora would ever go together!

Adrian, however, wasn't on the beach. Chance started to ask one of the servers where he was, but a commotion on the deck of the ship drew his attention. Glancing that way, he saw Jackie and Mr. Baxter involved in a shouting match. From Harry's aggressive stance, he thought the man was about to hit her. Alarmed, he raced to the pier.

By the time he reached the main deck of the ship, Adrian was standing between the arguing pair with Mrs. Baxter wringing her hands while she watched.

"What the hell is going on!" Chance demanded.

"Chance, thank God you're here." Marcy grabbed his arm. "You have to help us find Paige."

"What do you mean?" he asked.

Harry turned to him, his face flushed with rage. "Paige has been missing most of the evening. When Marcy asked if anyone had seen her, Frank Adams said he'd spotted her earlier struggling with one of the men from this ship. She broke away, but the man chased after her. Since her car is still here, I think she's been abducted."

"Abducted!" Chance shook his head, trying to think. Kidnapping wasn't out of the question, considering the Baxters' wealth, but he found it hard to believe. And why had Frank waited so long to tell Marcy, unless the scene with Paige wasn't as bad as Harry was making it sound. *Think,* he told himself. *Think!* He looked to Jackie. "Are any of your men missing?"

"No," she answered stiffly. "And no, I haven't seen the little princess. And yes, I'm sure she is not aboard this ship because I just came from below deck, and she's not there."

"I say we search the ship anyway," Harry said.

The first mate stepped forward, a solid wall of muscle ready to block Harry's way while guests stood by watching in horrified fascination.

"Mr. Baxter." Chance moved toward him. "There are other places Paige could be, and I don't see any reason to believe Jackie is lying. Rather than waste time arguing, why don't we search the grounds and house?"

Harry looked torn, but nodded.

"Fine." Chance turned to Adrian. "Will you lead the search of the grounds?" Adrian agreed and Chance looked over the crowd of guests, picking out the ones he knew to be the most levelheaded. "Paul, Eric, Jeremy, you three help him. I'll go with Mr. Baxter to search the house."

Without waiting, Harry headed down the steps to the dock.

Adrian let his breath out in a loud rush. "Be sure he doesn't tear the place apart, will ya?"

"I'll try." Chance started to leave, but stopped long enough to ask, "Have you seen Aurora?"

"She's in Jackie's cabin crying her eyes out, which is why Jackie didn't want the man charging down there. And as soon as we find Paige, I want to know what the hell is going on between you two that has my sister so upset."

"I wish I could tell you," Chance said, feeling hollow. Before Adrian could question him further, he headed after the Baxters, meeting up with them right before they reached the house. His parents joined them on the veranda.

"Harry, what is it?" his father asked.

While Harry explained, Chance noticed that word was rapidly spreading through the crowd. The moment they entered the house, Harry started calling his daughter's name, which drew stares from everyone on the first floor. Allison came out of the music room, clearly startled.

"Mr. Baxter." Chance said, alarmed at how quickly the situation could get out of control. "Let's try to do this calmly. As of yet, we don't even know there is a problem."

Harry turned on him. "Considering it's your fiancée who's missing, I can't believe you'd suggest I stay calm."

Chance opened his mouth to explain that he and Paige weren't even dating, but stopped himself. Now was not the time. Besides, if Aurora were the one missing, he'd be just as frantic as Harry.

Harry charged up the stairs, mounting them two at a time. Chance and his father followed with Marcy and Ellen trying to keep up. The minute Harry reached the top of the stairs, he looked about then turned to the only closed door. The door to the Crow's Nest.

"Paige!" he bellowed, and ran to the door only to find it locked. "Paige!" He took a step back and raised his foot.

"Wait!" Chance shouted as Harry kicked the door in. He

heard Paige scream just before he reached the door. Frightened by the sound, he pushed his way inside, past Harry who had come to a stop. He stopped as well, stunned.

There in the bed, a naked Paige and Captain Bob grabbed at the sheet to cover themselves.

"Daddy!" Paige gasped, her eyes huge.

Harry's eyes went from his daughter to the man in bed beside her. "You son of a bitch!"

"Daddy, no!" Paige screamed as Harry lunged.

Chance and his father grabbed Harry's arms while Bobby grabbed Paige by the waist and hauled her from the bed, sheet and all, so they stood against the far wall.

"I'll kill you for touching her!" Harry bellowed. "Do you hear me?"

"Daddy, please!" Paige clung to Bobby's neck as he tried to push her behind him and keep them both covered with the sheet. "Don't hurt him! Please, don't hurt him!"

Marcy reached the door, took in the scene, and started shrieking. Chance thanked God his mother was there to grab her friend, hug her tight and shut her up. Harry stopped struggling and stared at his daughter as if he'd never seen her before. "Paige, how could you take up with this—this low-life dock bum!"

She stared back at all of them with frightened eyes.

"Sweetheart," Bobby said softly, "if you're ever gonna stand up to your parents, I'd say now would be a good time to start."

Paige loosened her death grip around Bobby's neck enough to look up at him. She was so delicate and pale against his dark, muscle-bound body that even seeing them together, Chance couldn't believe it. Which made her expression of adoration that much more startling to behold. "You're right," she whispered. Her face looked serene when she turned back to the doorway. "Mom, Dad, I'm in love with Bobby, and I've agreed to marry him."

Marcy made a strange, breathy sound and Chance turned just in time to see her collapse to the floor in a dead faint. His mother knelt quickly to see to her friend. Behind them stood a crowd of guests. Their faces mirrored his own shock at the scene playing out before them. Paige Baxter and Captain Bob?

"Paige, you can't be serious," Harry said, clearly rattled. "You can't marry *him*. You're engaged to Chance."

"Um, actually," Chance put in, "Paige and I split up before she left for Corpus Christi."

Harry looked at him as if he'd lost his mind. "Now, son, there's no need to do anything rash. Women act strangely sometimes. There's no reason for you to break things off with Paige over one foolish indiscretion."

Chance started to explain, but became aware again of the crowd gathered behind him, hanging on every word. "Mr. Baxter, I think the best course of action is for you to take your wife to one of the rooms until she recovers. Bobby and Paige can join you when they've had a chance to dress. Then all of you can discuss this calmly."

Harry noticed his passed-out wife for the first time. "Marcy!" He knelt, grabbing her hand. Then his eyes lifted, filled with panic. "Someone call an ambulance!"

"Harry, she'll be fine," Chance's mother said. "Let's just get her somewhere comfortable." Ellen looked up at Chance.

"Marguerite's room," he said. "It has a bed where Marcy can recover and a sitting room where they can talk in private once Paige and Bobby join them."

Nodding, his mother turned and shooed the onlookers away. "Go downstairs, folks. Peep show's over."

Once they were gone, Harry carried his wife toward the tower suite with Ellen following to see to her friend. Chance spared Paige a look of empathy before he closed the door the best he could against the splintered doorjamb, leaving himself and his father alone in the upper hall.

"What a mess," his father said. Then he looked at Chance. "I'm sorry, son, this must be difficult for you, having Paige behave so outlandishly."

"Actually, it isn't. At least not the way you mean. I realized two weeks ago that things weren't working out for us, but Paige wanted to wait until after the ball to tell her parents we'd split up." He shook his head at the irony. "She didn't want people gossiping about us during the ball."

His father gave a snort. "Well, thank God we'll all be spared that."

Chance tried not to laugh, but it was hard.

"I am sorry, though, that things didn't work out." His father placed a comforting hand on his shoulder. "A breakup is never an easy thing to deal with, even though I'm sure you handled it with the same good sense you always use."

The devastation Chance had felt earlier at Aurora's rejection washed back over him. No, a breakup wasn't easy to deal with.

"You know," his father said, "I've never understood why people have to make such fools of themselves when it comes to this business of falling in love. Much better to approach it calmly and rationally."

Chance stared at him, seeing far too much of himself—his old self—in his father's words. How boring his life had been before he'd fallen in love with Aurora. And how filled with joy it had been since. There was nothing calm or rational about what he felt for her.

Suddenly, it all came together, like pieces of a puzzle, and he realized where he'd gone wrong. He'd tried to apply logic to falling in love!

He laughed at the absurdity. "Don't you see, Dad? The things in life that make us foolish are the very things that make life worth living. And you know what they say, there's no greater fool than a fool in love."

He slipped his hand into his pocket and curled his fingers around the jeweler's box. He'd wondered several times over the last week what he'd be willing to do to win Aurora, and now he knew. Anything. He'd do anything.

"Where are you going?" his father called when he headed down the stairs.

At the landing, he turned and smiled. "To make a fool of myself. Where else?"

Rory realized that hiding in Jackie's cabin was the coward's way out. Although she was grateful her brother had stopped her mad dash for the house. When he'd seen how upset she was, he'd hustled her below deck with very few people seeing her since the guests had been watching the performers. If she'd continued toward the house, she'd have created quite a stir.

Still, it wasn't fair to Adrian and Allison to abandon her duties. The ball would be over soon, and it was time she pulled herself together and went back out there—even if it meant possibly running into Chance. As she ducked into a tiny lavatory in the captain's cabin, she wondered where he was. The memory of his stunned expression when she'd told him about the baby, and the anger that had followed tore at her heart. Adrian was right, she should have told him weeks ago.

Determined not to think about it right then, she splashed water on her face. She needed to get through the night, first. Tomorrow she'd call Chance and they'd talk things out somehow. Drying her face, she looked in the medicine-cabinet mirror. Her eyes were puffy and her nose was red, but only noticeable if someone looked closely.

She left the cabin, which was tucked beneath the quarterdeck, and wound her way past the crew's quarters, the galley, then up through the center hatch to the main deck. It was far more crowded than she'd expected for so late in the evening. Surely the guests would start heading home soon, leaving the staff with the chore of cleaning up.

But no one looked the least interested in leaving. They stood in groups along the railing, gesturing toward the house and talking in scandalized tones while the band played on the quarterdeck.

"Are you saying it wasn't Chance?"

"No, it was that guy who runs the tour-boat business, Captain Bob."

"Poor Chance. How humiliating."

"Actually, Chance said he and Paige weren't even dating anymore, but that could just be him saving face."

Rory headed to where Jackie was directing her crew to clear dishes off some of the tables. "What's going on?"

Jackie turned to her, looking uncomfortable. "You okay?"

She nodded, embarrassed to remember that Jackie had led the way down to the cabin earlier and seen her blubbering like an idiot. "I'm better. Thanks."

"Well, you missed all the excitement," Jackie told her, sounding none too pleased. "That jerk, Mr. Baxter, got some harebrained idea that Paige had been kidnapped and he had the balls to accuse my crew. Chance convinced him to get off my ship before I threw him overboard. So he charged up to the house to look for her there. Apparently he kicked in one of your doors and found his precious baby with Bobby."

"With Bobby? As in *with* Bobby?"

"Well, *ye-ah,*" Jackie said as if any fool would expect as much. "They've only been all over each other for the past two weeks."

"Paige and Bobby?" Rory looked around, trying to get her bearings. "Where are Adrian and Allison?"

"Up at the house, I suppose."

Rory nodded and headed across the deck toward the steps.

"Aurora St. Claire!" a deep voice boomed over the crowd.

She turned, as did everyone else, to find Chance standing on the quarterdeck, bracing his hands on the rail. He looked every inch the dangerous sea captain with the determined look on his face.

"I have a few things to say to you."

"Chance . . ." She looked nervously about. He'd certainly gained everyone's attention, talking loud enough for even the people on the pier to hear. "What are you doing?"

"Setting you straight," he told her, clearly not the least concerned about their audience. "First of all, I don't know where you got the idea that you've ruined my life, because nothing could be further from the truth. You saved me from a fate worse than death—and that's a boring life. So how dare you say I don't belong here at the inn? That I don't belong with you? You're the best thing that ever happened to me, and I'm not going to give you up just because you want to be noble and force me back into a life I don't even want. I want a life with you, woman. You got that?"

She stared at him, afraid to believe her ears. Then she nodded, numbly.

"In fact," he went on, "the only thing you ruined tonight was my proposal."

"Your proposal?" she said, her heart starting to flutter.

"Yes, my proposal. I had it all planned out. I was going to have Carmen fix a dinner for us and leave it at my apartment. Then I was going to tell you it was a thank-you for all the meals you've fixed for me lately, so you wouldn't suspect what was coming. You see, for dessert, I was going to have Carmen make this chocolate thing she does that's hollow." As he spoke, he reached into his pocket and pulled out a small black box. "And when you broke open your dessert, this was going to be inside."

He opened the box and she gasped as an enormous diamond sparkled to life. "Oh, my God. Is that a ring?"

"An engagement ring, to be exact."

"For me?"

"No, it's for me." He gave her a look of exasperation. "Of course it's for you."

She kept staring at it, wondering how it had magically appeared in his pocket. "But how did you get it?"

"I ordered it from a jeweler in Houston several days ago."

"Several days ago?" She thought back over the last week and how strangely he'd been acting. "All this time you've been planning to propose? Why didn't you say something? You've been acting so weird, I thought you were planning to break up with me."

"Is *that* why you wouldn't go home with me last night?" He looked incredulous.

She nodded as relief and joy had her eyes welling again.

"Aurora." He sighed. "Why would I break up with you when you make my life complete? The only thing that's missing is for you to say yes."

She stared at him through a blur of tears, not sure that this was real. He was offering her exactly what she wanted, a life with him here at the inn. He was willing to give up his old life to make a new one with her. It seemed too wonderful to be true. "Can I . . ." She sniffed. "Can I see the ring?"

Understanding softened his face. He turned toward the steps that led down from the quarterdeck but found them crowded with onlookers. They were all smiling broadly, although some of them looked on the verge of laughing. Well, he decided, as long as he was giving everyone a show, he might as well make it a good one.

Spying the rope the crew had rigged up for the performers, he dropped the ring back into his pocket. He grabbed the rope, climbed onto the rail, and nearly lost his balance.

"Chance! Be careful," Aurora called.

Yeah, no kidding, he thought, looking down. The rail was higher than he'd thought, and suddenly this didn't seem like such a great idea. *Well, no guts, no glory,* he told himself, and jumped.

The world flew by in a blur as he headed straight for the mast. He heard Aurora shriek and managed to lift his legs in time to save his face from hitting first. He tried to push off and land on his feet, the way Jackie had done it, but he let go too soon and landed on his butt right at Aurora's feet.

How appropriate, he thought, shaking the stars from his eyes.

"Chance!" Her skirts bellowed about her as she dropped to her knees. "Are you hurt?"

"Only my dignity," he said, wincing. "But then, who needs dignity?" He smiled up at her. "All I need is you."

"Oh, Chance," she sighed, cupping his face with her hands. "Don't scare me like that. I need you too badly."

"Does that mean the answer is yes?" he asked as he pushed his glasses back into place.

She grinned at him. "You haven't actually asked anything yet."

"I haven't?" He thought back over everything he'd just said and realized she was right. "Oh, well, give me a minute, will ya? This isn't as easy as it looks." He sat up, grimacing at the pain in his back, then dug the black velvet box out of his pocket. He opened it and stared at the ring, a five-carat marquise-cut diamond solitaire with perfect clarity. Everything hinged on her accepting this ring, accepting him.

With a deep breath for courage, he turned the box toward her. She stared at it with a look of wonder as it winked and sparkled. "Aurora," he said softly. "Will you marry me?"

She lifted tear-filled eyes and smiled. "Yes, Chance. Oh, definitely yes." She flung herself into his arms. He held her tight, closing his eyes to savor the moment as everyone cheered.

Up on the veranda, Ellen leaned against her husband's shoulder, smiling at the scene on the ship. "Remind me not to be on the planning committee next year."

"Why is that, dear?" Norman asked, looking suitably rattled by the whole evening.

"Because"—she slipped an arm about his waist—"nothing could ever top this year's Buccaneer's Ball."

EPILOGUE

"Dearly beloved, we are gathered today to reaffirm the vows between this man and this woman, spoken once before the laws of man, spoken today in the eyes of God."

Rory hadn't expected the day to be so emotional. After all, she and Chance had technically been married a year. Mere days after he'd proposed, he'd hauled her before a judge, insisting they'd do it legally for the baby's sake, and again later for their own sake. She'd tried to tell him that one ceremony was enough. She'd had her brother and sister there, he'd had his parents, and they'd had each other. What more did they need?

Now, standing in a clearing near the house at first light, she was glad he'd insisted. They'd created the clearing for just this occasion, but it was so perfect she knew they'd host other weddings for years to come. The giant oaks spread their limbs overhead like the rafters of a chapel. Potted flowers offered blossoms even in the shade while newly planted ivy climbed up the arbor where she and Chance stood with the minister.

Behind them were the people who'd come to mean the world to her: her brother and sister of course; but also Chance's parents, with his mother holding six-month-old Lauren; Aunt Vivian, who'd flown in from New York; and Bobby and Paige.

Tears of joy misted her eyes when the minister asked her and Chance to face each other and join hands. Chance looked so handsome in his pearl-gray suit, the first suit she'd seen him wear in nearly a year. She wore her grand-mother's dress, a tea-length gown of cream silk covered in white lace. A circlet of white roses and baby's breath adorned her hair. From the expression Chance had worn since she'd walked into the clearing on her brother's arm, he liked what he saw.

"Do you, Oliver Chancellor, take this woman, Aurora Chancellor, to be your wife, not merely in the eyes of man, but in the eyes of God? In sickness and in health? To love, honor, and cherish her as the other half of yourself until death do you part?"

He smiled and spoke with surety. "I do."

As the minister turned and repeated the words she and Chance had decided on, the present blurred behind months of memories. Memories of Chance's excitement the day they'd checked in their first guests, and how that excite-ment had grown for both of them as the inn grew in pop-ularity. Memories of the house he'd built for them a short walk down a tree-lined path behind the inn. His pride as he'd watched her stomach swell with his child. The way he'd slept at night with his hand on her tummy so he could feel the baby move.

And the awe on his face when the doctor had laid their screaming daughter, Lauren, in his arms.

"Miss?" the minister whispered.

"Hmm?" she said, coming out of her daydream.

"You're supposed to say, 'I do.' Unless you don't."

"Oh." She blushed. "I do. I definitely do."

"Then, by the powers vested in me by God and the state of Texas, I now pronounce you husband and wife."

Chance kissed her as their families sighed with ap-proval.

They turned to accept congratulations and hugs from the small gathering. Adrian and Allison came first, then Chance's mother, who had tears in her eyes. She held Rory close and whispered, "You're so good for him."

"Thank you." Still misty-eyed herself, Rory reached for

Lauren, who was happily snuggled in her grandmother's arms. How in the world would she leave her baby for even a brief honeymoon? Already her heart ached.

"Oh, must you take her so soon?" Ellen protested.

"Come on, Gran'ma," Norman teased. "Give the baby back to her mother. You'll have her for three whole days while they're in New Orleans."

"It's not three whole days." Ellen pouted even as she relinquished her grandchild. "It's one whole day and two half days. Hardly a proper honeymoon at all."

"We promise to take some longer trips when Lauren is weaned," Chance said, beaming at his daughter. He was such a good father, Rory turned to mush every time she watched them together.

Realizing she was the center of attention, Lauren kicked her feet and let out a gurgling coo that had everyone laughing.

"I need to talk to her about that." Aunt Vivian, who looked every bit the stylish Broadway actress in her linen suit and flame-bright hair, leaned forward to stroke the baby's cheek. "No overacting, young lady. And no upstaging your mother on her special day."

"How about we move this inside?" Adrian suggested. "I have a champagne breakfast waiting in the dining room."

Crossing the lawn, Rory smiled at the house that filled her life with such joy. Because of the wedding, they hadn't booked any guests this weekend. The place seemed oddly empty without people on the veranda, children playing in the yard, or sunbathers on the beach.

"Can I hold her?" Paige asked, coming up beside Rory.

Rory gave her an arch look. "You're not practicing, are you?"

"Heavens, no." Paige blushed and looked at her husband. She and Bobby had married months ago in an enormous society wedding. That had been their one concession to the Baxters' wealth. The couple now lived on the houseboat they'd bought and ran the tour business as a team. The lunch run to Pearl Island had become so popular, they'd recently added a dinner run on the weekends. "Bobby and I are happy with just the two of us for now."

Aurora settled Lauren on Paige's shoulder, and watched Bobby soften at the sight of his wife holding an infant.

Chance slipped his arm about her waist as they mounted the steps. "How long do you think they'll wait?"

She laughed and shook her head. "Who knows what the future holds? It's filled with too many surprises to guess."

"Or to plan," he added.

Once inside, champagne glasses were passed around. Toasts were made, some serious, some in jest to the newly wed—or rather re-wed—couple, and to the one-year anniversary of the Pearl Island Inn. The only person who seemed melancholy was Allison, but then, the last year hadn't been as kind to her. Quiet, sensible Alli had stunned them all by having a flaming affair with one of their guests. An affair that had ended badly, if indeed it really had ended.

Finally the time came for Rory and Chance to leave for the airport. While Rory went to change, Chance saw his father standing out on the veranda with Vivian. He forced himself to wait until the woman went back inside before he joined his father.

"Care to tell me what that was about?" Chance asked.

His father smiled at the accusing tone. "It was about letting go." Norm turned and leaned a shoulder against one of the stone columns. Even though summer had passed, the ceiling fans offered a cooling relief from the Texas heat. Ferns grew in hanging baskets and in the distance the blue waters of the cove lapped against the white beach. "I have to admit, I was a bit nervous at first when I heard Viv would be here. But now I'm glad she came."

"Apparently."

"I'm glad because it confirmed something I've been coming to realize during the last year. Now that I'm not working at the bank, your mother and I have a lot of time together. It took a little while for her to get used to having me underfoot. Took me a while to realize she didn't need me to be president of the household."

Chance smothered a smile at that, picturing all too well the "conversations" in which his mother informed her husband she'd been running the house for several years now, and didn't need his "help."

Norm glanced through a window into the house and a smile settled over his face. He suddenly looked more relaxed than he had in years. "You know, I'm thinking, when you and Aurora get back from your trip, I may take your mother to Europe for a month or so. Sort of an extended second honeymoon."

Chance relaxed at that. "I think that's a great idea."

"Well, I'm ready," Aurora announced, coming through the front door surrounded by family and friends.

Chance took the small overnight case from her. The rest of their luggage was already in the trunk of the limousine his father had hired. Kissing her cheek, he whispered, "You got anything sexy in here?"

"Maybe." Her eyes twinkled.

The family lined up along the path with birdseed in hand while he and Aurora fussed over Lauren, saying goodbye and promising to be back soon. Bobby rushed to the lawn with the camera. "Okay, you two, make a run for it."

"Hang on." Aurora glanced at her sister, wanting so much to share her own happiness. With a smile, she drew back her bouquet. "Are you ready?"

"Rory, no, don't!" Allison protested too late. The flowers arched toward her with ribbons fluttering. They landed neatly in her arms as Bobby clicked the camera.

Joining hands, Chance and Aurora dashed toward the limousine, ducking the hail of birdseed. In the safety of the car, they waved out the back window as they drove away.

"Chance, look!" Aurora pointed toward the third-floor balcony. "Do you see that?"

He glanced up, and blinked in surprise. Perhaps it was the angle of the sun, but it looked as if the gargoyles were smiling.

"Do you think she's happy?" Aurora asked.

"Who?"

"Marguerite."

"I don't know, but I am." He cupped her cheek and smiled into her eyes. He thought of all the careful plans he'd once made, and none of them had included this wonderfully vibrant, unpredictable woman. "Thank you."

"For what?"

"For ruining my life."

"Anytime." Leaning forward, she touched her lips to his.

READ ON FOR A PREVIEW OF
JULIE ORTOLON'S NEXT BOOK

Lead Me On

Coming soon from St. Martin's Paperbacks

Scott figured if a guy couldn't get lucky on Galveston Island during tourist season he had to be a loser. And luck was exactly what he needed right now—in more ways than one.

The thought made him tighten his grip on the steering wheel as he pulled the black Jaguar to a halt before the Pearl Island Inn. The inn sat on a private island on the bay side of Galveston Island. He hadn't been to Galveston in years, and hadn't particularly wanted to come back now. But his situation had grown so desperate he was willing to try anything. "Take a break," his agent had told him. "Go somewhere and relax. Get laid if that's what it takes. But for God's sake do something to get your old charm back before your career goes down the toilet."

Get your old charm back. The words had brought the mansion on Pearl Island instantly to mind. Setting the brake, he looked up at the three-story gothic structure with its gargoyles and gables, surprised at how much the place had changed since the last time he'd seen it. It seemed odd, seeing the old monstrosity with clean windows, fresh paint, and baskets of ferns hanging on the stone veranda.

Staring up at it, he wondered if he was nuts for coming here, nuts to believe in old legends about good-luck charms, and even more nuts to think a vacation fling would cure his recent bout of writer's block. If he had any sense left in his brain, he'd turn the car around and head straight back to his townhouse in New Orleans and force himself to write. Discipline was what he needed—not luck.

He reached for the gearshift—ready to call the whole plan off—but stopped when a movement on the veranda caught his eye. There in the shadows he swore he saw the figure of a woman. Her pale, gauzy dress gave her an ethereal quality that brought to mind every ghost story he'd ever heard about the "Pearl." Then the figure faded deeper into the shadows, making him wonder if he'd imagined her.

Stepping out of the air-conditioned car, he lowered his sunglasses and squinted against the glare of afternoon light. The salty breeze off the nearby cove ruffled his shirt and hair, relieving the humid heat along the Texas gulf coast.

The figure appeared again, this time stepping fully into the light. Definitely not a ghost, but a flesh-and-blood woman with the face of an angel and hair as black as French lace. The ghostly attire was actually a white cotton sundress that left her arms bare as she raised a pitcher to water one of the hanging baskets.

As she lowered her arms, she spotted him and smiled. "Hello," she called. "Are you Mr. Scott?"

Hello yourself, he thought as he gave one curt nod. Maybe his agent didn't have such a crazy idea after all. A little quality time relaxing on a beach with a beautiful woman might be just what he needed to clear the cobwebs from his brain.

Grabbing his laptop from the passenger seat, he headed up the oyster-shell path to the wide sweep of stone steps. "Yes, I'm Scott," he said as he mounted the steps to stand before her. Her face tipped upward, since she barely came to his shoulder, and he saw her eyes were a pale shade of blue, almost gray. "Although it's not Mr. It's just Scott."

"Oh, sorry." A blush tinted her cheeks. "My sister Rory

took the reservation, so I wasn't sure. I'm Allison St. Claire." She held out her hand. "Welcome to the Pearl Island Inn."

Oh, God, she even had one of those soft, Southern-lady accents that always turned him on. In contrast, her handshake had a firmness that surprised him. Friendly but impersonal. An innkeeper welcoming a guest.

"Come on inside, and I'll get you checked into your room." She took a moment to carry the pitcher to a shadowy alcove on the veranda, then led the way to the ornate front door. Her walk was graceful, yet somehow as straightforward as her handshake, nothing sultry about it. Even so, he tipped his sunglasses down again to better see the feminine sway of hips beneath her loose-fitting dress.

"Do you want to bring your bags now?" she asked over her shoulder. "Or get them later?"

"Later."

As they stepped inside the wide, central hall, the temperature dropped several degrees. He noticed the vast space had been converted into a lobby with Victorian sofas and chairs set before the fireplace. Rather than cobwebs and dust covering every surface, sunlight poured in through the doorways of the outer rooms, adding a soft, welcoming glow.

The stillness of the place seemed almost reverent, especially with the three tall, stained-glass windows that lit the stairway at the far end of the hall. The room to the left, the old library, had been turned into a gift shop.

"We have you booked into the Baron," Allison said as she led him into the parlor to their right. She took a seat at an ornate desk before a rose-marble fireplace. "It's one of our larger rooms, and the only one with a desk, which Rory says you requested." She glanced at the computer screen. "You'll be staying through the end of March?"

"Correct." *A month*, he thought, remembering his agent's advice and hoping that would do it. Although he never should have confessed to Hugh Ashton how long he'd been without a woman. Two years was an embarrassingly long time for a healthy man to stay celibate. Well, that was about to end. Hopefully.

The thought must have added a glint to his eyes since Allison St. Claire glanced up and froze. For a moment she stared back at him as awareness warmed the air between them. She was everything he liked in a woman: attractive face, slender but shapely, and well-spoken. The last was a must in his opinion, even for a temporary liaison. As he'd matured, he'd decided that sexual partners should be as stimulating out of bed as in—which probably had something to do with his long bout of abstinence.

Holding her gaze, he allowed an inviting smile to lift one corner of his mouth. Color flooded her cheeks and her eyes widened. She looked away, fumbling at the keyboard. "Yes, well, if you'll give me just a minute, I'll, um, have you checked in and can show you to your room."

Okay, so she wasn't interested, he thought, trying not to flinch from the direct hit to his ego. Or maybe he was so out of practice at smiling that he'd snarled at her instead. He knew his expressions could be intimidating at times, but the dark scowls were supposed to scare off blood-sucking leeches, not potential lovers.

Although, watching Allison St. Claire, he became almost relieved. The woman had an aura of basic goodness that pegged her as the marrying kind. Which was *not* what he was looking for. Too bad. He would have enjoyed discovering the body beneath that dress.

"I, um . . ." A frown puckered her brow. "I see you reserved the room with a credit card, but some information's missing. Do you have the card on you?"

"Certainly." He knew exactly what information was missing—his last name. He'd intentionally rattled the person who took his reservation so he wouldn't have to give it. A last-minute impulse to pay for the whole trip with cash made him hesitate slightly before reaching for his wallet. For once in his life, he wanted to be Scott Nobody, just to see how it felt.

Resigned, he laid the card on the desk . . . and knew the moment she read the name.

"Scott Lawrence?" Her gaze shot up and awe filled her eyes. "*The* Scott Lawrence?"

He nodded curtly, disappointed at how quickly her chilly rejection melted away.

"Oh my." A brilliant smile lit her face. The smile made her positively breath-taking, dammit. Why couldn't she have given him that smile before she knew his name? "I love your books!" she said. "All suspense novels really—the more hair-raising the better—but your books are some of my favorites! I know, you probably hear that all the time, but I really mean it. I can't tell you how often you've kept me up all night biting my nails." She leaned forward, her face glowing. "I especially like how you throw ordinary people into so much danger, and have them win over such impossible odds. It's positively riveting!"

"Thank you." He frowned, surprised that someone so innocent-looking would actually have read his somewhat-gritty books.

"Oh goodness." Still smiling, she entered his name into the computer. "This is so exciting. Our first national celebrity. I can't wait to tell Adrian, that's my brother, and another big fan of yours. He's going to be so jealous that I met you first."

A weary sigh escaped Scott as he took back his credit card. He could already hear it coming, all the predictable questions people asked when they met a writer.

"So"—her gaze flickered to the computer case—"are you going to write a book while you're staying here?"

"Not a book. Just a proposal." A seriously past-due proposal. And if he could manage to even start one, he'd be grateful to the writing gods.

She lowered her voice. "You know, I've always wondered, where do writers get their ideas?"

He nearly laughed, not just because that was the biggie—the number-one most-frequently-asked question—but because at that moment he desperately wished he knew the answer. Instead he gave her his best deadpan look. "Personally, I order mine online from BookIdeas.com."

She covered her mouth as laughter danced in her eyes. "Sorry. I guess that was a silly question."

"Yeah, pretty much." He gave her a lopsided smile.

She retrieved a sheet from the printer and laid it before him. "Here, if you'll just sign this, we'll be done."

Setting the computer case down, he leaned over the desk to review the room charges. Alli had barely a moment to study him unobserved. Though the smile was gone, its effect lingered, for it had transformed the aloof expression of his absurdly handsome face into something that bordered on . . . mischief. Not boyish mischief, though. It was too carnal for that.

And the look in his eyes as his gaze held hers had sent flutters of alarm rioting through her system. For just a second, she'd thought he was flirting with her. Except men never flirted with her. They flirted with her sister, Aurora, all the time—not that Rory ever noticed—but Allison they treated with utmost respect or sisterly affection.

Then she'd seen his name, realized who he was, and knew she was being foolish. Someone like Scott Lawrence, an internationally famous author, would hardly notice a background fixture like her. He was just being kind when he smiled. What a relief. And what a thrill to actually meet him. In the flesh!

As he signed the form with swift, bold strokes, her gaze skimmed over his short, dark hair and closely trimmed beard. The short-sleeved black shirt and tan slacks accentuated his broad shoulders, narrow hips . . .

He straightened abruptly, and his whiskey-colored eyes caught her in mid-gawk. That sardonic brow of his lifted and she realized the beard did nothing to soften the razor-sharp edges of his face.

Her cheeks heated as she took the printout and set it aside. "Well then, I'll um . . . just show you to your room." Her hands trembled slightly as she retrieved a key ring from a drawer and came around the desk to hand it to him. Oh my, he was taller than she'd first realized. Not as tall as Adrian, who was well over six feet, but he definitely towered over her less-than-impressive height. "My brother and I live on-premise. Right downstairs. In the basement. Well, in an apartment in the basement. What I mean is, if you need anything, there's always someone here." Was she babbling? Surely not. She never babbled. Taking a deep breath, she composed herself. "We lock up at night, so you'll need the gold key to get in the front door after dark. The silver key is to your room."

"Got it." He gave her another lopsided grin and butterflies danced in her stomach. God, he was so gorgeous when he did that, like a movie star who would play nothing but villains and still have every woman in the audience swooning.

Trying to look casual, she led the way back into the hall, describing the inn's policies. He nodded absently, seeming more interested in looking about than in what she was saying. "You've really fixed up the place," he said as they started up the stairs. "I never would have imagined it could be this . . . inviting."

Startled, she paused on the landing, where the stained-glass windows bathed them in colored light. "You've been here before?"

He shrugged. "My family vacationed in Galveston a lot while I was growing up. It was a common enough dare for kids to sneak out here and see if they could stay all night without running scared from the ghost. My sister and I took it a step farther and broke into the house with sleeping bags and séance candles." As if realizing he'd just admitted to breaking and entering, he quickly added, "This was, of course, long before your family owned the place."

"*Ghost Island*," she breathed in awe. "Your first book."

"My first *published* book," he clarified.

"It was about three boys who broke into a haunted house on a dare, and wound up discovering a storeroom for international art thieves." She looked about, seeing the house through different eyes. "You based that house on this one?"

"Pretty much."

"Can we tell people that? I mean, would you mind?"

He shrugged. "Doesn't matter to me."

"Oh, this is great. I think guests will be fascinated." Excitement washed through her. "So, did you make it the whole night?"

"Barely." He chuckled. The sound was even more appealing than his lopsided grins. "Although once the sun was up, I'm not sure if we were relieved or disappointed that Marguerite never put in an appearance."

She laughed nervously, suddenly aware of how closely they stood together—so close she caught the faint scent of soap and his freshly laundered shirt.

"So, what about you?" he asked, tipping his head to study her.

"What about me, what?"

"Did you ever sneak out here as a kid to see if Marguerite would reveal herself?"

"No, um, actually . . . none of us, Adrian, Rory, or I, ever did." To gain some distance, she started up the stairs again. "That probably sounds odd, since Marguerite is our ancestor. I guess it was just too much of a sore spot for all of us."

"What do you mean?"

"The house wasn't ours by right of inheritance, as it should have been. We still wouldn't own it if it hadn't come up for sale on a bank foreclosure a year ago. Marguerite's husband, Henri LeRoche, left the island and all his wealth to his nephew rather than his daughter, Nicole."

"Except Nicole Bouchard wasn't Henri LeRoche's daughter. Otherwise, why would she have taken her mother's maiden name?"

A flare of anger stopped Alli at the top of the stairs. "I see you did spend a lot of time in Galveston to have heard that bit of old slander."

He shrugged, not looking the least contrite. "We writers are a curious lot, which is probably the answer to your question about where ideas come from."

"Well, you can let your curiosity rest on that subject. The rumors are nothing more than vicious lies against Marguerite, invented by the LeRoche family to justify keeping Nicole's inheritance."

"It can't all be lies. After all, Marguerite *was* trying to run off with her pirate lover the night she and her husband fought on these very stairs"—he gestured downward, to the grand sweep of stairs—"and she fell, breaking her neck."

"First of all"—Alli straightened, ignoring a sudden rush of dizziness—"Marguerite didn't fall. Henri pushed her down these stairs. And secondly, her lover, Captain Jack Kingsley, was a Confederate blockade runner, not a pirate or a spy preying on both sides."

"But he was her lover."

"That hardly means Nicole Bouchard was illegitimate. She was born years before Marguerite even met Captain Kingsley."

Scott started to argue the point further, amused to see the kitten had claws when her fur was rubbed the wrong way. Instead, he glanced about the upper hall, his attention drawn by the scent of lemon polish and fresh flowers. He found the open area had been turned into a sitting room with comfortable chairs and a sideboard for serving coffee and hot tea. "Impressive."

"Thank you," she said in a crisp voice that made him hide a smile. What a shame Allison St. Claire was too sweet for him to even think about seducing, since she apparently had a spark of passion beneath the surface.

Turning, she headed across the sitting area, her back rigid.

"So, have you ever seen her?" he asked as they reached the door to his room.

She shook her head. "Marguerite never actually shows herself. She makes her presence felt in other ways."

"How so?"

Allison looked up in the process of unlocking the door. "I'm surprised you don't know, since you seem so well-versed in the legend."

"Amuse me." He leaned against the door jamb, which brought him closer to her eye level.

"Marguerite is considered to be a good-luck charm, because of a blessing from the voodoo midwife who birthed her."

"Well, I knew that. I was hoping you could offer some

proof that the charm really works. Or at least tell me if it works for anyone staying in the house, or only the owners."

Curiosity replaced the anger in her eyes. "Is that why you're here? To borrow some of Marguerite's good luck?"

"Maybe." He shrugged as if the matter were of little importance.

Her gaze flickered over his face. "I'm surprised a man with your talent would feel the need for magic."

He studied his fingernails to keep her from seeing any hint of desperation in his eyes. "In addition to being curious, writers are notoriously superstitious. If I thought it would get me a number-one slot on the *New York Times* Best-seller list, I'd write naked in the middle of Times Square."

"You've already done that."

"What? Write naked in Times Square?" He grinned at her.

"No!" A breathy laugh escaped her. "I mean you've made number one on the best-seller list. Many times."

"Hey, it never hurts to hedge your bets." The vivid pink in her cheeks intrigued him, and he wondered what it would take to make her cheeks go all the way to red. "And who's to say the success of *Ghost Island* wasn't due in part to Marguerite? I did get the idea while staying here."

"Does that mean you're setting another book here?"

"I haven't decided," he said evasively.

"Oh. Well, whatever you decide, I've always thought the power of a charm comes more from believing in it than anything supernatural."

"If it works, it works."

"True." With a jiggle of keys, she opened the door and headed for a bedside table, where she clicked on a lamp.

Scott took in the paisley wallpaper, heavy four-poster

bed, and other furniture that gave the room a masculine feel. Whoever had decorated the inn had a taste for quality antiques.

She flung open three sets of heavy draperies, revealing a wall of windows that faced the cove. Sunlight poured in as she rattled off the routine for laundry and room cleaning. She opened another set of draperies, revealing a door to the second-floor balcony. He knew a larger balcony, off the ballroom on the third floor, loomed directly above. It was from that balcony Henri had fired a cannon on Jack Kingsley's ship, killing his wife's lover. The remains of the ship and Kingsley's ghost were said to still be at the bottom of the cove . . . with the two ghosts, Marguerite and Jack, forever looking for a way to reunite.

"You'll want to keep this door locked, since you share the balcony with the Pearl."

"The ghost?"

"No." Allison laughed lightly. "The Pearl is what we call Marguerite's old suite, since she was heralded as 'the Pearl of New Orleans' during her days as an opera singer. Just as we call this suite the Baron, since 'shipping baron' was the nicest term we could think of to describe Henri."

"Makes sense." Scott nodded.

"I think that covers everything." She folded her hands before her, looking perfectly composed except for the color that still glowed in her cheeks. "Do you have any questions?"

"Just one." He stepped back to see under the desk. "Where's the modem hookup?"

"Oh, we don't have phones in the rooms. So many people carry mobile phones, we decided it wasn't necessary."

He stared at her a moment. "No phones in the rooms?"

"I'm afraid not." Worry flickered across her brow. "Is that a problem?"

"Actually"—he smoothed his beard to hide a smile—"that's the best news I've had in weeks."

"Oh." The comment obviously confused her. "Well then, I'll leave you to settle in."

He nodded as she made her way back through the bedroom area.

At the door, she turned to him. "If you need anything at all, please let us know."

"I'll do that."

The moment she left, he glanced about. "Hear that, Marguerite? If I need anything at all, I'm supposed to let you know. Well, right now, I could use a damn good idea for my next book." Taking a seat at the desk, he booted up the computer, then stared at the blank screen. His mind remained equally blank. After several minutes he let his gaze drift back to the door. "Although, as long as I'm asking for 'anything,' how about you make your great-great-great-granddaughter a little bit less of a 'nice girl'?"

Jim Lincoln

Most authors say they grew up reading. But not Julie Ortolon. Born with dyslexia, she didn't even learn to read until her early twenties when she discovered that romance novels were worth the struggle. It was only with the additional discovery of computers with spell-check that she was able to turn her favorite hobby—daydreaming romantic stories—into a career. Having her first two novels hit the *USA Today* bestseller list is a dream come true.

Julie lives on the shore of Lake Travis near Austin, Texas, with her journalist husband, exuberant Australian Shepherd, and spoiled tabby cat.

You can learn more about Julie by visiting her web site at www.ortolon.com, or write to her at JulieOrtolon@aol.com. She loves to hear from readers.

WHAT HAPPENS WHEN MR. SLOW AND STEADY...

The forecast is smooth sailing for Oliver Chancellor, scion of Galveston's premier financier. Destined to take his place in the hallowed marble corridors of his family's bank, Chance is content with the future that's been mapped out for him, right down to his upcoming engagement to a prim debutante enthusiastically approved by his socialite mother.

FINDS HIMSELF ON A COLLISION COURSE...

But when beautiful Rory St. Claire crosses his path, Chance recklessly plunges into uncharted territory with nothing but his heart to guide him—and a beautiful woman to tempt him...

WITH MS. FULL-SPEED-AHEAD?

Propelled by a lifelong goal to buy the island home reportedly haunted by her colorful ancestors, Rory desperately needs Chance's help in securing a business loan, and she won't take no for an answer. In the midst of convincing the hesitant blueblood to take a chance on her dream, Rory unexpectedly lands in Chance's arms, stunned by his red-blooded passion—and her own awakened desire. Now, the mismatched pair can't keep their hands off one another, and something tells Rory she's headed for trouble—trouble in the name of love...

"Julie Ortolon takes her wonderfully colorful and appealing characters on an unexpected journey of discovery. Be prepared to laugh."—Christina Skye, author of *2000 Kisses*, on DEAR CUPID

ISBN 0-312-97872-3

97872

U.S. $6.50
CAN. $8.50